Clara Louise Burnham

The Mistress of Beech Knoll

A novel

Clara Louise Burnham

The Mistress of Beech Knoll
A novel

ISBN/EAN: 9783337027339

Printed in Europe, USA, Canada, Australia, Japan

Cover: Foto ©Andreas Hilbeck / pixelio.de

More available books at **www.hansebooks.com**

THE MISTRESS OF BEECH KNOLL

A NOVEL

BY

CLARA LOUISE BURNHAM

"Love can love but once a life."
TENNYSON.

BOSTON AND NEW YORK
HOUGHTON, MIFFLIN AND COMPANY
The Riverside Press, Cambridge

The Riverside Press, Cambridge, Mass., U. S A.
Electrotyped and Printed by H. O. Houghton & Co.

CONTENTS.

iv CONTENTS.

THE MISTRESS OF BEECH KNOLL.

CHAPTER I.

BEECH KNOLL.

" I SHOULD think the whole town had lost its wits! " observed Roxana Sherritt scornfully.

She was sitting by the dining-table in Dr. Joy's house, polishing the roses on a silver coffee-pot. Whatever Roxana did, she did with her might, and she concentrated her attention now on the antique silver with the same care which she bestowed habitually on all the doctor's belongings, including his niece Phyllis, who sat near by, rubbing silver forks with a piece of chamois skin, and laughing softly at the housekeeper's intolerant remarks.

" You must remember that nothing ever happened before, in Snowdon," replied the girl.

" Humph! Where human bein's live, you can be pretty sure there 's plenty happens," remarked Roxana.

" Well, nothing ever happened to me before," said Phyllis, lifting her brilliant face to her companion. Her cheeks had a soft brunette coloring, her dark eyes held in them two flashing stars; her black, fine hair, worn short, had a gloss as though each hair were separately polished, and it waved in such thickness that a parting refused to divide it, much to Mrs. Sherritt's sorrow. Indeed, the worthy woman considered this her only failure in bringing Phyllis up. She had never been able to conquer the boyish, curly crop, whose appropriateness to the pretty oval face she was not able to see.

That it was a pretty face, Roxana knew well enough, and she was struck afresh by the gleaming smile with which the girl now regarded her.

" What 's the matter, you rogue? " she asked, with a reluctant answering smile. " Why do you consider that anything has happened to *you?* Beech Knoll bein' sold has n't brought any cash into your pocket."

" Cash! " The thin scarlet lip curled scornfully. " What do I care for cash? "

" It 's a convenient thing to have around," remarked Roxana, continuing her vigorous rubbing, " and I hope you 'll never know the want of it. Next to health, it 's the most important thing in " —

" Well, then," interrupted Phyllis, " the sale of Beech Knoll has brought health to a great many persons."

" What on earth are you talkin' about? "

" Why, it has developed a taste for walking in every woman in town. Even the feeblest is able to take a walk along the road to Beech Knoll since it has come out that the purchaser wishes to be anonymous. Uncle Doctor says his business is completely ruined;" and Phyllis laughed again, in enjoyment of the expression upon Roxana's face.

"The amusing part of it is that each couple of strollers look with such suspicion and disfavor upon each other couple of strollers, as though questioning their right to saunter along that particular highway. Jealous already, you see."

Mrs. Sherritt tossed her head. "There are more different sorts o' simpletons in this town than I ever had the least idea of."

"I, for one, am very much obliged to the promenaders for their fine detective work," declared Phyllis demurely. "There is an immense deal to be discovered up at the old place, and I am intensely curious; yet my bringing up cuts me off from hanging about the fences and picking up stray bits of wall paper that have floated out of the windows, or watching the loads of furniture go in. Oh, Roxana," she added, in a different tone, "he must be awfully rich."

"Well, yes, Miss Jones yesterday insisted on tellin' me all she knew, and she has found out more than any one else could in the same space o' time, and there must be a pile o' money bein' spent on the place."

"Yes," returned the girl eagerly, "it will be utterly changed. Roxana," she added mysteriously, "don't you think he must be a misanthrope to be willing to make such a beautiful, secluded home in this sleepy little town?"

Mrs. Sherritt looked up sharply. "If it's a 'he' at all, he prob'ly has a whole drove o' children, and is comin' out into the country to turn 'em loose."

"Roxana!" Phyllis regarded her reproachfully, yet pityingly. Poor Roxana! She could not be expected to care for a romance.

"What I keep thinkin' of is Miss Redmond," continued the housekeeper. "What would Miss Rebecca say to all these fine doin's, decorations, and the dear knows what? Spiders were the only decorators known at Beech Knoll in her day, and small peace she left 'em with her broom. She was a tidy little body and a good woman, if one ever lived."

"I remember Miss Redmond," said Phyllis reflectively. "The last time I saw her she gave me a large scalloped cookie with caraway seeds in it."

"She made 'em better than any one in town," said Roxana reminiscently. "Oh, what a time she did have of it, one way and another; and yet you sit up there and say nothin' ever happened in Snowdon."

"Oh, I don't mean such uninteresting things as sickness and death," said Phyllis explanatorily. "Of course I remember her sister-in-law, Mrs. Richard Redmond, who was an invalid and always wore a little black shawl; and I remember when she died, and when old Mr. Redmond died,

— that is n't the sort of thing I mean; I mean something happy and — and romantic, or romantic anyway, even without the happiness."

"Oh, well," responded Roxana curtly, "if you 're willin' to take romance dry so, without any sugar, there was a romance happened right there at Beech Knoll, where you 're settin' up a hero to suit yourself. There have been heroes enough there, to my way o' thinkin'."

Phyllis looked up with parted lips. "Did Miss Redmond have a lover — that white-haired old lady?"

"She was n't born white-haired, you little goose, and she ain't old if she 's alive to-day. Her hair turned white along of a trouble she had. A cousin o' hers brought a college friend to make a visit at Beech Knoll, and Miss Rebecca fell desperately in love with the young man, and he fell just as deep in love with her."

"Then why" — exclaimed Phyllis eagerly.

"Because he was engaged already," returned Roxana shortly. "Don't ask me why nor where-fore, 'cause I don't know. Some boy and girl af-fair, I suppose. Anyway, the young man found out he 'd made a mistake; but it was too late. His sweetheart was frail, and he thought 't would kill her if he should try to break off, so he pre-ferred to go on makin' mistakes, and went away from Beech Knoll and got married to her."

"It did not turn out well, then?" asked Phyllis with interest.

"I don't know one thing about it," said Roxana firmly, "except on general principles I s'pose it did n't." Mrs. Sherritt always waxed pessimistic on the subject of marriage, her own having been an unmitigated failure. "I should never have known anythin' about Miss Rebecca's love affair except for goin' to help nurse Mrs. Richard Redmond in her last days; and she, about worshipin' her sister-in-law, always wanted to talk about her, so she told me this story. She did n't tell me the man's name, and I should n't have remembered it if she had," added Roxana hastily, forestalling the question she saw hovering on Phyllis's lips.

"Poor Miss Redmond! How she must have suffered!"

"Oh, she had enough trouble one way and another," said the housekeeper, nodding her head, and rubbing a silver cream pitcher until it shone again. "Her father did n't make provision for her in his will — that's the way with men, it never seems to occur to 'em that their daughters would enjoy independence as well as their sons — and the first thing Miss Rebecca knew, one fine day her brother sold the old home right over her head without consultin' her a word. That was a mighty mean trick, and Miss Redmond felt it. Her brother was a man o' business in the city, and had n't any use for the old place himself, now his wife was dead, and he just wrote a note to his sister that he'd do anythin' she liked in the way o' findin' a boardin' place for her and payin' her

expenses, but she'd have to move out o' Beech
Knoll and not even take a stick o' the furniture
with her. Miss Redmond was a quiet, gentle sort
o' person, but that treatment provoked her. She
refused his help and went away, and that's all we
know about her."

"What a shameful kind of a brother!" exclaimed Phyllis indignantly, "after all the kindness Miss Redmond had shown to his poor sick
wife."

"Yes," remarked Roxana, with a grim smile.
"Men ain't any great, but Mr. Richard Redmond
was rather below the average. Why, about a
year before his wife died, he brought a fifteen-year-
old girl home there to Beech Knoll to spend her
school vacation, and the way he cavorted with that
girl, rowin', drivin', fishin', walkin', runnin', and
rompin' generally, for four weeks, was a performance to see, considerin' his wife was such an invalid she couldn't leave the house, and he'd never
been able before to spare more than two or three
days at a time from business to visit her. It was
enough to make that poor, sick wife miserable to
see the goin's on, tho' he was callin' Elise, that
was the girl's name, nothin' but a child, all the
time. He couldn't get out o' bringin' her, he said,
because her father was his friend, and as he lived
way out in California he had asked Mr. Redmond
to let the girl spend part of her vacation with him
and his wife. That experience was a trial to Miss
Redmond. She told me right out she was afraid

it made her sister sad to see so much life and
health about, when she did n't have any herself ;
but she spoke kind o' the girl. 'Elise is a well-
behaved, good child,' she said to me, 'a very innocent, happy child.' Richard Redmond was a
mass o' selfishness," finished Roxana rather inco-
herently. "He was never " —

The speaker was suddenly interrupted by a clash
of silver, as Phyllis, dropping a handful of forks
upon the table, started up and ran to the window.

"Well, well, what are you up to now?" demanded Roxana tartly. It hurt her in a sensitive
place to have solid silver thus recklessly handled.

"It is the dépôt carriage," said Phyllis breath-
lessly, as the sound of wheels became louder.
"There *is* somebody inside to-day. Oh, why can't
I see! "

Roxana was human, and, after all, she had
not wholly escaped the prevailing epidemic. She
pushed her chair back and hastened to look over
the girl's shoulder in an effort to distinguish the
passenger. At the same time she spoke excitedly.

"Phyllis Flower, it will be a disgrace if you
let Jake Harvey see you cranin' your neck after
his carriage. *Forever!* " she ejaculated, with a
start, while Phyllis gave a low ripple of laughter.
"Phyllis, that ne'er-do-well, good-for-nothin' Jake
Harvey winked at us. I saw him as plain as I see
you this minute."

"Don't mind, Roxana," said Phyllis, still laughing. "Jake did n't mean any harm. He sym-

pathizes with us all. He knows what pangs we suffer. I only wish I understood what his wink meant. Was n't there some one in the carriage?"

"There must have been," replied the house-keeper, still smarting, "for there was a satchel on the front seat."

"Then I think I had better go out for a walk," said the girl mischievously.

"No, you won't go for a walk," replied Mrs. Sherritt hotly. "No one can say that you 've done any o' the gallivantin' that 's been done in this town this spring, nor you won't begin now."

Phyllis laid a coaxing hand on her shoulder.

"Just see how unreasonable you are, Roxana; you won't let me have a look at the place now it is done," she said. "Why, they say the turf already looks lovely, the hedges are trimmed, and where it all used to be so ragged and unkempt, now one would think the very stones of the house had been washed. Come, you ought to see it. Come with me, there 's a dear. After the hero, or the misanthrope, or whatever he is, arrives, you won't want to seem to hover around" —

"Fiddlesticks! Phyllis Flower, look at me. Do I look like a person in the habit o' hoverin' around other folks's grounds?"

"No. I *say* you do not. Come, Roxana, let us take a walk up there for once. Have n't we as much right there as any one else?"

Roxana gathered up the shining silver with determined hands. "I know my faults," she observed, "and I ain't afraid to say that curiosity ain't one of 'em. Them new people can come to Beech Knoll and live there for six months, and if I don't lay eyes on 'em the whole time, I shall sleep and eat precisely as well as if I was visitin' 'em every day."

"What is the matter?" asked a masculine voice, and Dr. Joy came into the room. He was a stout, genial-looking man, whose face looked florid in contrast to his short, white side whiskers. "What is the excitement, Phyllis?"

"We are saying," returned the girl, the stars in her dark eyes twinkling, "that Roxana is not in the least curious, but that, to gratify my curiosity, and to show a proper interest in the Redmond family, she ought to walk up to Beech Knoll with me this afternoon."

"That's Phyllis's story," said Mrs. Sherritt rather sulkily. "For my part, I think there's enough folks to oversee the improvements up there without us."

"Uncle Doctor, I have not seen it since you drove me there in the buggy a month ago, and now everything is finished and the grounds are in order, and I want to go this very afternoon. May I not?"

"Why, yes, certainly. I would take you myself but that I must go in the other direction now. There is one old man in town whose rheumatism has kept him at home through all the excitement, and so he deserves double sympathy. I have been glad to have you kept out of the committee of investigation so far; but I think it is all right now, Roxana, for the child to have a view of the place before it is inhabited."

"Very well," responded Mrs. Sherritt stiffly, " if she goes, I go too."

" Have n't I invited you?" said Phyllis gayly, skipping across the room and hugging the doctor *en route.* " Uncle Doctor, you 're a dear! "

" Oh, yes, that 's all right," grumbled Roxana, " but it 's a mighty good thing that I 'm in this house for a balance wheel. Get your hat on. I 'll be ready as soon as you are."

CHAPTER II.

As the two set forth in the cool, fresh air, it did not take long for Phyllis to talk her companion into good humor. Secretly, Roxana thought she would enjoy seeing Beech Knoll reclaimed from its old familiar shabbiness, and making the excursion as it were, under protest, suited her very well. She contented herself by austere nods to the few friends who passed them on the road, as though to warn them against confounding her motives with theirs for traversing the well-trodden path.

They had completed about half the distance when an acquaintance, whom Mrs. Sherritt particularly disapproved, was discerned coming swiftly toward them, and waving them back with both hands.

" What's the matter with Miss Jones ? " muttered Roxana.

" He's come, he's come ! " exclaimed the spinster, rushing up to them breathlessly. " Jake Harvey has just gone in at the driveway with a trunk and satchel. There was no one inside the carriage, and he nodded to me in a knowing way and said, ' The gentleman preferred to walk.' I 'm going to get a look at him or know the reason why," and the speaker was off before Roxana could pronounce a repudiatory speech.

"There," she said to Phyllis, with exasperation, "you see what we've got into now. Do you think I want you mixed up with that kind of a vulgar performance?"

Phyllis tried to repress her laughter. "We will do anything you say, Roxana," she said meekly; "but," with sudden and irrepressible interest, "I would *love* to see him. Would n't you?"

"The cat's foot and the kitten's elbow! What should I want to see him for? Phyllis Flower, we are goin' home."

Phyllis stopped a moment, half minded to mutiny. She had been brought up with old-fashioned, strict ideas of obedience, and it never occurred to her that she had grown too old for the housekeeper's jurisdiction; but this afternoon she had her uncle's promise, and his was a higher court of appeal than Roxana's.

The latter looked at her, surprised at her hesitation.

"I want to see Beech Knoll," said Phyllis obstinately.

"But you don't want to be seen gapin' at his property by the new man, do you? You don't want to feel about as small as a pint o' cider half drank up, do you?"

After meditating a moment, Phyllis seemed to decide that she did not. At any rate, she turned about and walked on by the housekeeper's side,

secretly supported by the hope that the new proprietor was an accomplished pedestrian, and that
they might meet him before reaching their own
door.

Her silence smote upon Mrs. Sherritt. "Your
uncle shall drive you around by Beech Knoll," she
said consolingly. "It ain't goin' to run away;
and if the new people are such as he can visit in a
social way, you 'll have the satisfaction o' knowin'
that you have n't gone snoopin' around like the
most o' folks. Phyllis, who is that walkin' kind
o' slow up the street?"

The girl raised her eyes eagerly, but the light
went out of them as she saw approaching only a
slight, small woman in a black dress.

"I don't know," she replied.

"That walk" — pursued Roxana, hurrying a little. "It can't be — It must be — Why, I *know*
it is! It is Miss Redmond. Miss Rebecca, Miss
Rebecca!" she exclaimed, almost running forward
to meet the white-haired lady, whose hands she
grasped and shook with joyful energy. "You
have come back at last, Miss Rebecca, at last!"

"I have come back," said Miss Redmond, returning the pressure of the honest hands, much
pleased at this unhoped-for welcome; "greatly to
my surprise, too, Roxana, for I never expected
to see Snowdon again. Who is this?" she continued, as Phyllis advanced. "Not little Phyllis,
— surely not Phyllis?"

"Phyllis herself," responded Mrs. Sherritt,

striving to keep her loving pride out of her voice. "Isn't she grown a great girl?"

"A great girl," said the newcomer musingly, taking her hand. "I had just been asking myself if I were not a ghost revisiting its old haunts, and this grown-up child makes me realize more than ever that ten years is a long time."

"Yes," replied Phyllis, looking with interest into the calm gray eyes, where a suspicious moisture had crept, "you were much larger when I was nine."

Miss Redmond shook her head and smiled. "I have to look up to you, now, — but it is worth the trouble."

The girl colored a little. "That is the prettiest compliment I shall ever receive, I am sure," she replied.

"The sight of your face is good, Roxana," said Miss Redmond, looking back. "I have feared to find many changes here. At least you are the same. How are all the friends? How is my dear old minister?"

Roxana shook her head. "Mr. Dunham is dead and gone, Miss Rebecca, but such is life, you know. Ten years is a long time, and, considerin', I think you'll find things have stood pretty still in Snowdon. Why am I keepin' you standin' in the street all day! I hope you was on your way to our house. The doctor will be amazin'ly glad to see you, and he'll take it very kind that you came out to see us. I don't know any one else in town who has a claim before ours."

"Thank you, Roxana, not just yet. I must go up to the old home first."

Mrs. Sherritt nodded her head sympathetically. "Very natural you should want to, Miss Rebecca, but you'll find changes there."

Miss Redmond's lips tightened, and a shadow of pain flitted across her face.

"Does it look so very different?" she asked wistfully.

"It has been sold again," explained Mrs. Sherritt, "to somebody with more money than he rightly knows what to do with, I guess; and from what I hear, the old house is rigged out complete. Truth to tell, I have n't been near it myself. Most o' the women in town have put off their house cleanin' to oversee the improvements, and I thought I could be spared."

"They will not let you in, Miss Redmond," added Phyllis gently, "not even inside the grounds, I have heard people say; and would n't that be — be hard for you?"

Miss Redmond smiled faintly and looked at the speaker a moment in silence.

"You are a kind child," she said; then, after a pause, she went on: "I do not understand how all this has been done so quietly, but evidently you do not know what has brought me here. I have come back to live at Beech Knoll. It is to be my home again."

Roxana and Phyllis remained a moment in speechless amazement; then, "Good, good, good!"

burst from Roxana. She shook Miss Redmond's hands violently in her excitement. "If that ain't like a fairy story come true, I would n't say so."

"It does sound so," said Miss Redmond, "but I can give you my little history since I left Snowdon in a very few words, and then you will understand. The first few years I will skip. They were hard ones for me. Then I received word that my brother had married Miss Beckwith, a California heiress. You remember, Roxana, the young girl who visited us that summer, during the first Mrs. Richard's lifetime? Well, that was the girl. Her father died suddenly, she was recalled from school to his funeral, and in her loneliness and unhappiness she married my brother. They went to Europe, and in a few months I was sent for, as he was ill. I arrived to find him dead, and as Mrs. Redmond wished me to remain with her, I did so. We traveled for three years abroad; then we returned to San Francisco, where we have lived until now. My sister-in-law always remembered Beech Knoll affectionately, and one day she bought it, and then nearly took my breath away by informing me of it. It has been prepared for our home, and I preceded her here by one day because — because " —

The speaker's eyes filled with tears. Phyllis took her hand with shy sympathy, and her own heart swelled. She even forgot that the situation was not far from being romantic, in her spontaneous appreciation of Miss Rebecca's feelings.

"Is there anybody up there to get your tea?" inquired Roxana practically. "To go into that big house alone is kind o' forlorn."

"There are servants already there, thank you, Roxana. I shall be very comfortable, and to-morrow I shall be ready to welcome Mrs. Redmond, who spends to-night in Boston. I fear she has done a foolish thing to choose to live in Snowdon, when she is used to so much life and stir. You must come and see her, Phyllis. She is nothing but a girl herself, poor child! Well, I am glad to have met you both. I am sorry you had to give me the news of Mr. Dunham's death."

"We've got a new man we like first rate," replied Roxana. "He's a jewel, now, don't you worry," for Miss Rebecca was shaking her head dejectedly.

Phyllis laughed. "If Roxana says so, you must believe her. There are two classes of men for her in this world. Uncle Doctor and Mr. Terriss form one, the rest of mankind form the other; and the less said about the latter class the better."

"Good-by, good-by," said Miss Redmond hastily. "It is pleasant to know that we shall meet again soon," and, giving a parting nod, she walked away with the erect, prim air which all the soft breezes of the Riviera had been powerless to ameliorate.

Phyllis pouted a little and raised her eyebrows. Her bubble had burst strangely. There was to be no more excitement, no more long-drawn-out wonder and speculation.

"After all," she said, as she and her companion moved on their way, "it only means two more women added to the nunnery."

"Phyllis," said Roxana, her plain face beaming, "you have n't built one castle in the air that was near as good as the truth. Miss Rebecca in calico, or Miss Rebecca in silk, is just the person we want in Snowdon; and now you won't have any more cause to complain that you can't see as much o' Beech Knoll as you want to. After all, you 've got the first invitation there of anybody in town. I wonder," she added, with a humorous recollection of the acquaintance who had fallen a victim to Jake Harvey's joke, "I wonder if Miss Jones will get to Boston before she stops."

CHAPTER III.

REBECCA REDMOND hastened along her road with a new agitation at her heart. This meeting with old friends had stirred her more deeply than she liked. All the way out from Boston in the train, she had been preaching herself an edifying little sermon. The subject was unselfishness. "Elise meant well in buying Beech Knoll," so Miss Redmond reasoned with her rebellious heart. "Now, let me not disturb her happiness by any nonsense or vapors. I am through with emotions by this time, I should hope. It is absurd to nurse old associations in a way to annoy other people. There is no one left with whom I can share those old associations. Let them drop, Rebecca, bury them. Take care of Elise. Make her happy. What if you are going to see the river, and the old bridge, and the willow-tree, you absurd little woman? You can never suffer again as you suffered on the old bridge that summer evening, and I hope you don't want to, do you? You're glad it is all over, aren't you? Then, for pity's sake, don't think any more about it."

Thus, over and over, and with variations, Miss Redmond talked herself into what she felt to be a wholesome frame of mind. It lasted, scarcely disturbed, until the fresh lips of the young girl pronounced the name Rebecca shrank to-day from hearing.

"Terriss, Terriss!" The name echoed in her ears as she hurried along, instinctively trying to flee from it. "Done with, a lifetime ago," she murmured; and then the walls of her old home broke upon her view.

"Dear old place. Well, well, how smart it looks, I declare," she thought, hurrying on toward the gateway.

A gardener was spading earth in a border. At sight of her he came forward and touched his hat respectfully.

"Mrs. Redmond, ma'am?"

"Miss Redmond," she answered, a little tremble in her voice.

"I hope you find the place looking well, ma'am?"

"Extremely well," she answered, with a smile, passing on toward the house.

She glanced askance at the piazzas as she ascended the steps, with an odd fancy that the house was aware of its finery and rather enjoyed it.

She rang the bell, and a trim maid appeared, who looked at her expectantly.

"I am Miss Redmond," she said pleasantly. "I presume my baggage has arrived."

"Yes, ma'am, it is upstairs."

"Very well. You may leave me to myself. I will sit down awhile before going up."

When she was left alone, she passed into the broad old parlor. Nothing here to remind her of bygone days; everything dainty and luxurious! She sat down in one of the deep chairs and looked about her. The room, despite its freshness, had not the comfortless appearance of never having been lived in.

The piano was open. A tall lamp stood near it, as though its light might, on the previous evening, have illumined the open sheet of music that lay on the rack.

She continued to look about her like one in a dream; but the utter transformation of the rooms strengthened her courage.

"Elise is a Monte Cristo on a small scale," she said to herself, "and I might be in England so far as any familiarity goes. This is not hard to bear."

She rose and went back into the hall and up the thickly-carpeted stairs. From one room to another she went: first to her father's, then to Mary's, then to the once shabby spare chamber, then to her own old bedroom. Everywhere the luxury was so complete — walls, ceilings, wood-work, so changed — that she looked on each object with a dazed sort of wonder. As Miss Jones had assured Roxana, the many-paned sashes had been removed from the windows, and sheets of plate glass substituted.

"One can see the river better," thought Rebecca, wondering if it were really here that she used to stand and observe the comical distortions into which the landscape was twisted in spots by the imperfections of the glass.

But looking out of the window was dangerous to that calm which Miss Redmond was priding herself upon preserving. She went into the corridor, and her glance fell upon the sole-leather trunk which Elise had given her.

"Which is my room?" she mused. "It is plain to see which is Elise's." She cast a look toward the front of the house, where a door stood open into what had been used by her father for a writing-room. She wondered what would be his sensations could he see its present fittings of pale green, white, and silver.

She moved to the stairs that led into the attic. "Perhaps there is a billiard-room up there," she thought. "At any rate, I might as well see the whole."

She went up, and paused at the top to accustom her eyes to the half light. She perceived at once that there was a mass of furniture crowded together under the eaves. She came nearer, and all at once her heart, which had been so agreeably calm, gave a great start. Color flew into her delicate cheeks. Here, huddled in the silence and the twilight, stood the old, familiar objects. Here was the narrow mirror that had reflected her bright eyes while she thought of Philip Terriss, and below it the bureau drawers that had held her girlish finery. There was her father's writing-table, the old sofa that had so often supported Mary's frail body, and the faded rocker which always used to stand in the warm corner by the stove. To her, each piece of the worthless lumber had all the pathos of a forgotten exile. Instantly, came a severe reaction from her strained cheerfulness. An agony of homesickness and compassionate longing swept through her. She fell into her father's rusty, rubbed old leathern armchair, clasped her arms about its unyielding back, and burst into the saddest tears she had ever shed.

"Dear old friends," she sobbed, "I have come back. Oh, do you know me? Don't you care a little — a *little?*"

For a long time she wept in the silence, and the pathos of her solitariness became lessened in this companionship. She laid her cheek lovingly against the worn spot where her father's head had rested for so many years, and patted the unresponsive arm. "We are old, old," she murmured. "New times, new people, new fashions."

She lay musing in the chair for some time longer; then, inspired by a sudden idea, she rose and moved to an unpainted door, which she opened. It led into a plastered room which had been finished long ago, when guests had not been a rarity at Beech Knoll, and an extra chamber had been in demand.

Into this room she drew several of the old chairs and the sofa. Next came the tall, narrow bureau. She looked in vain for a bedstead. Evidently the old bedsteads had been too cumbrous to carry up the steep attic stairs, and had been disposed of.

She sighed. " Well, if it cannot be a bedroom it shall be a sitting-room. Up here I will have a little bit of the old life."

The twilight deepened. Miss Redmond bethought herself that she might already have given cause for comment to the servants, and gently shutting the door of her treasure-chamber, she hastened downstairs, meeting in the hallway the white-capped maid, who, she imagined, looked at her curiously.

" I came up because I heard strange sounds in the garret, Miss Redmond. I did not know you were up there. The cook wished me to say that dinner is ready."

" I will be down directly. I must wash my hands first," said Rebecca. She hesitated a moment; then, from the necessity of making a choice, entered the smallest of the bedrooms on that floor. It was the one that had been Mary's. The maid followed with the satchel, which had been resting on the trunk, and then went noiselessly away.

Rebecca bathed her face and hands, and smiled a little, as she smoothed her hair before the broad, beveled mirror of the perfectly-appointed dressing-case. She was thinking tenderly of the meagre and worn old objects shut away upstairs in what seemed like another world, and she smiled for enjoyment of a possession which she was sure no one would dispute with her.

"It was a very good plan for the foolish little woman to come out here alone and get over the first tears and sighs," she thought, as she sat at her solitary meal. The exquisite linen and delicate table service did not strike her as novel. Rebecca had grown accustomed to luxurious living in the few years past. It had seemed very wonderful, at first, to leave the life of hard work and scanty pay, and to commence an utterly new existence; but her young sister needed her and wanted her, and she found that Richard had left to herself the little he had, enough to give her a feeling of independence; so she did not scruple to follow Elise's fortunes, indeed, she could not conscientiously leave the young widow; and now the latter's vagaries had brought her back to the old dining-room, transformed, like her own life. Yes, she had done well to come and pass one night here alone. There was a dull pain and longing at her heart, which would not be stifled by all her cheerfulness and determined admiration. To-morrow, all would be better.

When to-morrow came, she told herself that all was better. She allowed herself to think of nothing but the impression Elise's purchase would make upon her, and she spent the morning in unpacking and finding homes for her own effects, while marveling anew at the completeness of every room, the details of which Mrs. Redmond had found means to superintend, even from the other side of the continent.

The new lady of Beech Knoll was capricious, and, knowing her to be capricious, it did not astonish Rebecca to see her, about noon, enter the grounds in a buggy driven by a strange, middle-aged man. As they approached, she could see that Mrs. Redmond was chatting with him, or rather to him, in a vivacious manner, and she drew back a little from the window, thinking that it might be the stranger would come in.

No. Elise stood a moment on the step and spoke some last words to him, then he raised his hat and drove away.

Miss Redmond hurried to the door and opened it. " Welcome home ! " she said cheerily.

The young woman who had so unconsciously stirred Snowdon to its depths looked not about at her new purchase, nor spoke a word. She stood for a moment looking straight into her sister-in-law's calm eyes, with a penetrating gaze most disconcerting to sustain. She was a glorious specimen of womanhood, tall, straight, and graceful, with a glow of health upon her face, and pleasant, blue-gray eyes, which, with her bronze hair, rough from curliness, seemed to express the force and vitality which formed such a contrast to the pale, slight woman before her.

" You do welcome me ; you are a good little woman," she said, stepping over the threshold, catching Miss Rebecca in her arms, and kissing her.

" It is all beautiful, Elise," began Miss Redmond nervously, a little perplexed by her sister's strange manner.

"I dare say. I will look at it in a minute. First, Rebecca Redmond, sometimes familiarly known as Sister Bec, I have a confession to make."

Miss Rebecca looked up into the brilliant face which smiled down at her, and then her glance dropped to her imprisoned hands.

"I waked up this morning feeling small, humble, mean. I do not remember ever to have felt so before, and it is not a pleasant sensation."

"What has happened?" Miss Redmond looked up.

"I have been stupid beyond compare; selfish, absorbed in my own plans, blundering along, regardless and forgetful of your feelings until last evening. Then, it suddenly dawned upon me why you wished to come out here alone. It suddenly came to me how dense and indelicate I have been. O Rebecca, I am so ashamed! Don't speak yet. I am always headlong about everything. I have always loved Beech Knoll. The happiest weeks of my childhood were those I spent here. One reason I married Mr. Redmond, when he was so kind as to wish to take charge of me and my cares, was because he was associated with this place. When I decided that I must spend some time in or near Boston, I grasped at the idea of buying Beech Knoll. I thought it would be such a pleasant surprise for you. Yes, I am ashamed of it

now, but I really did. I took pains that it should
not be known here who had bought the place, for
fear some of your old acquaintances might write
you and spoil my surprise. Fancy that! Then,
knowing that a poor sort of people had lived here
of late, I proceeded to have the place made habita-
ble ; then I brought my precious news to you. Oh,
how well you received it, you brave little dear!"—
a hearty kiss here on Miss Redmond's thin cheek.
"How kind and good you have been to me! It
needed your timid little request to come out and
get things ready for me to take the scales from
my eyes. Now, first, I wish to apologize for all I
have made you suffer, and then I wish to beg
you, earnestly and sincerely, not to stay here with
me. You have sacrificed yourself to me so much
and so long, I refuse to be selfish any longer."

There was a little flush on Miss Redmond's
face. "How like you, Elise, to ignore all you have
done for me," she returned. "Do you wish me to
leave you here?"

"When you know I am being unselfish for once,
why do you ask me that?" was the rather exasperated reply.

"Then, if you please, I won't leave you."

"And you will forgive me for being dull and
arrogant?"

Rebecca smiled. "My child!"

"It comes from my having had no home but
schools all my childhood and girlhood. Does it
not?" asked Elise anxiously

"The good things of life were to come to you later. Come and look at the result of all your brain work."

Mrs. Redmond continued to look, not at her new home, but into her sister-in-law's face.

"We can sell it," she said doubtfully.

Miss Redmond laughed. Nothing could so have banished her lingering pain as this contrition in the girl she had learned to love dearly.

"Let us not sell it," she said, "until you have tired of it. You will weary of living here before I shall."

Elise kissed her again impulsively. "I am a lucky woman!" she exclaimed; then she slid an arm around Miss Rebecca, and together they crossed the broad hall and entered the parlor.

"Is it not strange," she said gravely, "that this is the first home I ever had?" She looked all about. Even her precious pictures were safe and well hung.

"Those people have done well," she said. She had glanced into every room in the house before, finally, in her own, she laid off the hat and jacket she had worn since her arrival.

"I can hardly realize that we are going to stay," she said then. "We have been birds of passage for so long. I trust you do not feel that you are spoiled for a domestic life, Rebecca. I was saying to the minister, as we came along, that I expected to learn all the domestic virtues from you now."

"So that was the minister?" said Rebecca.

"Yes. When I reached Snowdon, there was no conveyance at hand, and this gentleman, happening to see my dilemma, offered to bring me to Beech Knoll. His name interested me at once. It is Terriss, and while I am waiting for my luggage will be a good time to tell you why that name interests me."

Poor Rebecca nodded. So long as she was not required to tell why that name interested her, she was willing to listen to any disclosures.

Elise seated herself near her. "When I was quite young," she began, "my father adopted an orphan boy, whose parents he had known in their lifetime. As you know, I was very little with my father, but his letters never failed to mention Terriss, and were always so full of interest in the boy's abilities and progress that I wonder I was never jealous of him. We knew one another but very little. I remember him as a singularly nonchalant, indifferent sort of boy, but, separated as we always were, it is little wonder that we were not attached to one another, as adopted brothers and sisters ordinarily are. The last year or two of my father's life, he, who had always been an absorbed business man devoted to his numerous financial interests, seemed to become more engrossed than ever. His letters were fewer, and now they ceased to mention Terriss Chester. I thought little of that, for I had learned to take it as a matter of course that I should not have my father's confidence." Mrs. Redmond sighed. "My father gave me what he believed to be every possible advantage, thinking — or at least I always hope that was his idea — that when I had completed my studies, we should become acquainted and enjoy one another. That was not to be; and when his sudden death recalled me, I had a secondary shock to sustain in finding that Terriss had disappeared, no one could tell me why or whither. It was known that he and my father had quarreled and parted. That was all. I did not realize how serious was the trouble until my father's will was read, and I was discovered to be his sole heir.

"I was greatly surprised and troubled. As soon as Mr. Redmond came to me, I told him all the circumstances, and begged his help in discovering Terriss and trying to assist him, even if I should not be able to persuade him to accept what I could not help feeling was his share of the property. Mr. Redmond dissuaded me from the step very earnestly. He represented that a young man who could have forfeited the affection of so devoted a guardian had better be left to follow the path he had chosen. He reminded me that I was a very young woman, not fit, perhaps, to judge of the fault of which Terriss had been guilty, and that it would be very indiscreet in me to look into a case which my father had had all opportunity for understanding, and of which he had left so decided a proof of his condemnation. In short, your brother made me feel ashamed of what he termed my quixotism, and I yielded to his persuasions, and let the matter drop; but the subject would not drop *me*. Every morning and every night, I would think of the disappointment that came to that proud, careless boy, who had been taught to expect a brilliant future, and I would wonder whether my inertia in the matter was right. Whatever Terriss was, he might, doubtless, become worse. Why was it not my duty to find him and see if my influence could be of use to him in any direction?

"Nearly six months ago, I heard that Terriss Chester was in Boston, and I determined at once to buy Beech Knoll. All sorts of fancies floated through my head of possible reconciliations and righting of wrongs, for I cannot get away from the suspicion that Terriss suffered a wrong." Elise's brow contracted. "I know that my poor father was hasty and hot tempered. If I could once be certain that he did not wrong the boy by disinheriting him, I could let the matter drop gladly; for it is not in the nature of things that I could feel an attachment to him. We were complete strangers even before the trouble came."

"Well, Elise," said Miss Redmond, "is *that* at the bottom of this experiment?"

"Not quite," returned the other, with an arch smile. "I have always secretly yearned for Beech Knoll. I only needed something to decide me."

Miss Rebecca shook her head. "Your life has been like a butterfly's, Elise, and there is no artificial sunshine here in winter to warm you. I fear you will not survive one season."

Mrs. Redmond's cheeks flushed. "Perhaps I do not like to be a butterfly," she replied. "I wanted a home and something to do. I wanted this home, and I believed my work lay here."

Rebecca felt inclined to smile, but she refrained. She saw that her sister was deeply in earnest.

"I think you are perfectly right to search for this young man," she said. "I do not see how a woman of heart could do otherwise. Perhaps Richard's advice to you was wise, but I cannot see it so."

"I am so glad that is your feeling," returned Elise, pleased and surprised. "Frankly, I feared it would not be, else I should have told you my determination before we left California. I had decided not to be dissuaded, and so concluded not to touch the subject until circumstances made it necessary. I should not have spoken to-day, but that I was eager to have you know that I had some slight excuse for my selfish absorption and forgetfulness of you; and you have forgiven me, have you not?"

"Fully," said Rebecca.

"So now I am really very happy and hopeful," continued Elise, rising and moving to the window. "To think that in a few months we shall see the charming autumn foliage, and then will come one of the New England snowstorms, such as I have not seen for years."

"Yes, that is one thing you can look for confidently," returned Miss Redmond.

Her sister drew a hand slowly over the soft, silken window drapery. "You believe in Providence implicitly, even in the smallest details of life, I believe," she said abruptly.

"I do," replied Rebecca quietly.

"I should like to believe whatever you do," continued Elise, "since one is to judge of another by the fruits of his life. It seems to me — yet I thought myself perhaps superstitious for thinking so — that Providence showed approval of my plans in sending that Mr. Terriss to the station to bring me home."

"Yes?"

"What is very unusual for me, I felt a singular attraction toward the man. I should not have guessed he was a minister. His dress was not conventional, and he has no mannerism of speech. I like him. I cannot say why. I felt glad at once that he lived in Snowdon, even before I knew his name or profession. Well, I really am in a quandary as to how to commence operations. What should you say to my taking Mr. Terriss' name as my excuse, and going to him with my story, and asking his advice? Should you consider that 'following the leadings'?"

Miss Rebecca reflected. "Perhaps," she replied. "But why not write this boy a frank letter, and ask him to call upon you, or to appoint a place where you can meet; then I can go with you to see him."

"I have not his address, in the first place. In

the second place, he is not a boy any longer, you know. He may be a great, gruff, black-bearded ruffian, for all I know to the contrary."

"Oh, misery!" ejaculated gentle Miss Rebecca, much disconcerted. "I see you have thought a great deal about this, my dear. I wish I could help you, but I 'm afraid, if he should really turn out to be very big and at all ugly, I might not be of so much assistance as this Mr. — this minister you have met. He did *not* look like a minister, I must say, but Phyllis told me that was the new man's name, so I suppose it is all right."

"Oh, yes, it is all right, I am sure. His eyes settled that for me at once. Who is Phyllis?"

"A girl whom I left here almos a baby ten years ago. I met her, grown up, on the street yesterday. She said Mr. — the minister was a jewel, or else Roxana did," Miss Redmond was becoming rather fluttered and red-cheeked. "I think there could be no harm in going to him for his advice. The coincidence of names certainly would suggest the thought, even if he were not going to be your minister."

Elise gave a little laugh. "That speech gives me a realizing sense that I have a local habitation at last. My minister! Yes, Mr. Terriss gives one the feeling that he is thoroughly human and companionable. I like the idea that he is my minister. If he has anything to teach me, I shall like to learn of him. At any rate, I will go to him to-morrow."

"Not wait for him to call first?" exclaimed Miss Rebecca deprecatingly.

"No, not wait for anything. And you are coming with me, poor little Rebecca; you must come with me. You are the oldest resident, after all. He has only been here a year. You ought to call on his wife."

"Has he a wife?"

"I suppose so. Ministers always do have, I believe, and more particularly naughty children than they are able to support."

"Tut, tut, Elise!" returned Miss Redmond.

"You will come with me, children or no children, won't you?"

"I shall always go with you, Elise, whenever you want me," replied Miss Rebecca, with a little, unconscious sigh.

CHAPTER IV.

ONCE AGAIN.

EARLY on the following afternoon, Rebecca escorted Elise to the old parsonage.

To Miss Redmond's surprise, in response to her ring the door was opened by Mrs. Sherritt.

"Why, Miss Rebecca, this is good and neighborly of you, and no mistake," exclaimed the latter, in a gratified tone; "but it is exactly like you, and I might have expected it. Mrs. Terriss, poor woman, never bein' able to leave the house, folks must come to her; but how did you find out so quick?"

"I did not, Roxana, — I did not know about Mrs. Terriss. This is Mrs. Redmond, my sister; and, Elise, perhaps you remember Mrs. Sherritt, Dr. Joy's housekeeper, and my good neighbor always."

Roxana nodded in rather a cautious way, and gave Elise's cordial hand the loose shake of the uncultured.

"I do not remember Mrs. Sherritt," said Mrs. Redmond, smiling pleasantly as she entered the corridor.

"I am so glad you happened to be here, Roxana," pursued Miss Rebecca anxiously, "for Mrs.

Redmond wishes to see Mr. Terriss on business, and you will know whether it would disturb him just now."

"I guess not," replied Roxana, closing the door behind them. "Come into the parlor and wait a minute, and don't let on, please, Miss Rebecca," she added, lowering her voice, "that you did n't lay out to see Mrs. Terriss, for it 'll chirk her up and please her mightily to think you cared to come. Time hangs heavy with her sometimes. It 's natural it should, you know."

"Perhaps," said Mrs. Redmond, "Mr. Terriss would be so kind as to let me come to his study."

"I 'll see in a minute," returned Mrs. Sherritt shortly.

She was divided between gratitude to Elise for restoring Miss Rebecca to Snowdon, and a jealous dislike of her for being so far more beautiful, strong, and happy than the gentle, feeble Mrs. Richard of past years.

"She 's dreadful afraid some time 'll be wasted neighborin', at any rate," she thought, with some resentment, as she showed the visitors into the parlor, and then withdrew.

Rebecca looked sadly about her. Here was the same shabby carpet grown shabbier, the same dismal haircloth sofa and chairs, the same cold, small, marble table that she remembered. She looked beyond, where the door was ajar that led into the sitting-room, where Mr. Dunham, her old pastor, used to sit every evening in solitary contentment.

Mr. Dunham had been a widower, whose married children lived far away, and no feminine touch ever beautified the living-rooms of the old house where he dwelt among his books. Rebecca quite longed to pass into the next room so full of pleasant association, and see if it too had the same air as of old.

While she was absorbed in reminiscence, Roxana returned.

"Mr. Terriss would like to have you come up, Mrs. Redmond. You wait one minute, Miss Rebecca, till I show her the. way." Elise followed her guide, and in a few minutes Mrs. Sherritt returned.

"Now, then, Miss Rebecca, this way, please," she said, her face beaming with satisfaction as she threw wide the door through which Miss Redmond had been casting wistful glances.

Rebecca followed, and paused, surprised at the metamorphosis of the room she remembered so bare and poor.

A cheerful carpet of shades of brown and gold, a fire in an open stove, light furniture, and plenty of sunshine made a picture totally unfamiliar to the visitor. In the window stood an invalid chair, and in it sat a pale, eager-faced woman, whose piercing gaze people always found disconcerting until it became familiar. Mrs. Terriss had the combination, always striking, of flaxen hair and black eyes and brows, and these eyes, large and bright, seemed ever searching, ever questioning.

" Why is she not beautiful?" was Rebecca's
first, involuntary thought.

Roxana turned to her with a smile.

" This is Miss Redmond, Mrs. Terriss, the very
lady I was tellin' you about a little while ago, and
this is the first visit she 's made in Snowdon since
she came back, I 'll be bound."

" It is kind of you, Miss Redmond, as kind as it
can be," said the invalid, in a weary voice. " You
know, of course, I would come and see you if I
could ; but no doubt Roxana has told you how
feeble I am."

" I am very sorry for you, Mrs. Terriss," replied
Rebecca warmly, taking the chair Mrs. Sherritt
had placed for her. " How very pleasant your
room is! I must speak of it, because I remember
it such a different place in my girlhood. Roxana,
you remember too."

Mrs. Sherritt nodded. " I remember well
enough ; but Mr. Terriss fixed it all up till there
is n't a pleasanter room in town. Well, I must go
now, Mrs. Terriss. I leave you in good hands. I
think Lucindy 'll get along for a while now."

" Thank you. Do come again soon. You have
taught her to make bread at last, so I shall not
starve ; but do not leave us too long. Mrs. Sherritt has been such an assistance to us," continued
the invalid, after Roxana's departure. " The help in
Snowdon is so inferior that only strong, well women
could keep house here successfully, I am sure.
Mrs. Sherritt contrives to superintend our house

as well as the doctor's, or I don't know what I should do. She and Mr. Terriss between them manage to keep me alive," and Mrs. Terriss smiled faintly.

" Do you suffer much pain ?" asked Miss Redmond gently.

Mrs. Terriss closed her eyes, and lifted her delicate hands in an expressive gesture. " No one knows what I suffer," she answered, " no one but my husband. I have the best, the most devoted husband in the world," she added, warming into a sudden glow of enthusiasm.

"And have you long been an invalid ? "

" For many years. Ever since the loss of my only child."

Rebecca's conscience smote her for having made anything of her own trials.

" Dr. Joy comes to see me sometimes. His visits are a pleasure to anticipate, but there is little any doctor can do for me. My husband is my best doctor. Words cannot tell what he is to me. In fact, he constitutes my world ; but excuse the egotism of an invalid. Let us talk of something else. Are you glad to come back to Snowdon ? "

Meanwhile Mrs. Redmond was telling her story to an attentive listener. The room in which she found the minister was one of the barely furnished upstairs rooms of the parsonage, in which a desk now took the place once occupied by the bedstead. The ceiling slanted down to meet the windows on one side, and the opposite wall was filled with shelves of books.

The room below, in which Mr. Dunham had composed his sermons, was used by Mrs. Terriss as a bedroom.

"Of course, one room is as good as another to one who can come and go at will," she had said, when her husband had established her in her pleasant quarters.

Elise, after her first rapid glance at the surroundings, thought no more of them as she told the story she came to tell.

Mr. Terriss listened with the grave air habitual to him. His hair and short brown beard and mustache were thickly sprinkled with gray, and his deep-set eyes had the pleasant expression that had won Mrs. Redmond's confidence at their first meeting. He nodded and smiled, as she finished.

"It is your name," she added, "which has brought all this upon you. I thought I might need a man's help, and so I came to you."

There was almost a merry look in the minister's face as he leaned back in his chair.

"I hope you like a home in Snowdon under any circumstances," he said, "for your errand is not likely to require much time."

"You know Terriss, then," exclaimed Elise eagerly, a bright color tinging her fair cheeks.

"I do. It is hardly two weeks since I heard from him the other side of this story. He has been ill, and is in a hospital."

"Ah!" exclaimed Mrs. Redmond. "Is he — but excuse me, perhaps he is your relative."

"He is my cousin; but say whatever was in your mind."

"I was going to ask you if he is respectable; but I mean, is he worthy?"

"So far as I know; but we are almost strangers. He happened to learn recently that I was settled so near the city, and being rather lonely and depressed in the hospital, he wrote me, asking if I could come to see him."

"This is wonderful," said Mrs. Redmond. "I have thought and brooded over the matter so much, and imagined so many difficulties in the way of finding Terriss, that this sudden discovery seems almost too good to be true. Did he — of course he did — tell you the cause of the quarrel between him and my father?"

Elise's cheeks burned, and she bit her lip.

Mr. Terriss read aright the signs of apprehension in her face.

"You will be surprised," he said, "to learn how slight was the cause of the trouble."

"Do you think he told you the truth?" she asked quickly.

Mr. Terriss raised his eyebrows. "I hardly see how he could have any reason not to do so."

"Why, to preserve his reputation. If he is ill and unfortunate and needs your help, he would not willingly prejudice you against him."

"You have no faith in him?" asked Mr. Terriss, keeping his eyes fixed on his visitor's earnest, beautiful face.

She made a gesture of despair. " I do not know
him. I have not seen him since I was ten years
old. That is the worst of it."

" Well, I think he was telling me the truth."

" You do. What did he tell you? May I
hear ? "

" Certainly. He said that from the time he was
sixteen Mr. Beckwith wished him to enter the min-
istry. At first he made no decided objection, but
as time went on the idea became growingly re-
pugnant to him, and at last the matter became the
subject of the quarrel which separated them."

" Is that all?" exclaimed Elise, as her edifice of
vague and dreadful suppositions faded into noth-
ingness.

" That is all."

" And you believe him ? "

" I saw no reason to doubt him. I see none
now."

" Well, what shall I do?" Elise spoke rather
curtly. She felt extreme vexation with the boy
whose obstinacy had given her so much perplexity
and anxiety. It would have been easier to bear
had he given her father more reasonable ground
for complaint.

" Is he a successful man ? " she added.

Mr. Terriss smiled. " He has lost his position in
a banking-house by this illness," he returned, "and
is not yet able to think of finding another. In
fact, he admitted to me that he had been unusually
unsuccessful. Quite a sum of money which he had

saved was lost in the —— Bank failure, and the
little he has left is melting fast in his present
rather expensive quarters."

Mrs. Redmond's cold look did not soften., She
did not like the picture 'of the invalid pouring his
woes into the ear of his stranger relative; but a
sense of justice constrained her.

"He was brought up as the son of a rich man,"
she said. "It is hard for him. May I ask you to
take the trouble to write him, saying nothing of me,
excepting that Mr. Beckwith's daughter has communicated with you, and inform him of my wish to
give him his share of the property?"

"Since it is your wish, after much consideration,
I will do so with pleasure."

"I do not care to meet him if it is not necessary,
so do not tell him that I am here. Simply say, if
you will, that I consider that he ought to have a portion of my father's property, and that I am ready to
give it to him. My lawyer will attend to the rest."
Mrs. Redmond rose. "You are very kind to assist
me," she added, with a return of her gracious
manner.

"You may be sure that I am very happy to have
a hand in bringing better times to my cousin — a
second cousin only, to be sure, but we are a small
family, and must make the most of each other."

"I am very sorry," said Elise, as her companion
rose, "to learn that Mrs. Terriss is ill."

The cheerful light died from the minister's face.
He bowed slightly. "No more so than usual," he

said. "Mrs. Terriss is an invalid. I should like to introduce you to her before you go. It is a great pleasure to her to meet new people."

"Thank you, I should be glad to know her. She is receiving a call now from my sister, Miss Redmond."

"Ah, I am glad of that. I suppose, Mrs. Redmond, in the case of Terriss Chester, it is not in my province to remind you that you are doing an unusual thing, perhaps an unnecessarily generous thing, in giving up this property."

The haughty look came back to the fair face. "I shall relieve myself by doing so. There is nothing unselfish in it. If only it does good and not harm to Mr. Chester, I shall be entirely satisfied. I am more than fortunate to have found such a friend in the matter as yourself."

The minister bowed again. There was a graceful dignity about the man, despite his threadbare coat and shabby surroundings, which more than ever impressed his guest favorably.

She followed him downstairs and into the sitting-room, where comfort prevailed in such striking contrast to the rest of the house.

"Lily, I have brought you a visitor," he said. "This is Mrs. Redmond, who has come to live at Beech Knoll."

Rebecca straightened herself suddenly in her chair, and a mist passed before her eyes.

"And this, my dear, is Miss Redmond," returned Mrs. Terriss, her voice suddenly sounding far away to Rebecca; but the latter mechanically put out her hand to the one extended to her.

"Miss Redmond and I met once, many years ago," said the minister.

"Philip, I wish you would draw that shade down a little," observed his wife. "Mrs. Redmond will sit down, I hope."

"I thank you. I only came in to meet you this time, Mrs. Terriss. I shall call on you soon, if you will let me. We must not stay longer to-day."

"No, not to-day, Elise," echoed Rebecca. She did not know what more was said. She did not know how finally relief came, and they two were walking in the fresh air. She did not hear a word of what Elise said to her. There was room in her mind for only one idea at present. History had repeated itself, and she had stood face to face with Philip Terriss, heard his voice, and touched his hand.

CHAPTER V.

IN THE MIDST OF LIFE.

ROXANA walked in upon Phyllis, who was curled
up in her favorite corner of the sitting-room, reading.

"Well, I've seen her," she commenced, unpinning her shawl.

"Who?" asked Phyllis vaguely, looking up reluctantly from the interview between Romola and
her dying brother.

"Mrs. Richard Redmond the second," replied
Mrs. Sherritt, removing her hat.

"You do not like her," said Phyllis quickly.

"Who told you?"

"You did. I know you, Roxana."

"I do like her," returned Mrs. Sherritt, rather
ashamed of herself, and taking refuge in defiance.
"You ain't any mind-reader, Phyllis. To be sure,
she did n't seem just willin' to stop and visit with
Mrs. Terriss."

"Is that where you met her?"

"Yes; she came to see the minister."

Phyllis laughed. "Mrs. Redmond looked or
said something that you did n't like. I know that
perfectly well."

"Then I'm an ugly, touchy thing," observed

Mrs. Sherritt, her lips twitching in a smile. "She looked handsome, and she spoke civil; but Miss Rebecca was with her, and *she* stayed, in her quiet little neighborly way, to visit with Mrs. Terriss, while the young woman rushed off to the minister's study. It seems as though her soul must need attendin' to in an awful hurry, seein' she could n't wait for him to come and see her. However, it 's none o' my business."

"Do you think I dare visit her?" asked Phyllis eagerly.

"Oh, I guess she ain't as wicked as all that comes to. I was only jokin'."

"Nonsense! I mean, is she very elegant and — and proud? Does she look as though she would laugh at one?"

"Why, Phyllis Flower, I am surprised at you!" exclaimed Roxana, standing still to point her words. "Don't you know your folks are as good as any in the land? There are relicts up in the attic this minute that are most likely older and respectabler than any Mrs. Redmond could show to save her life. What was her father? Prob'bly began life with a pickaxe in a mine. All those rich California folks did. Your great-grandmother was related to the governor o' the State in her time. There 's a green brocade dress o' hers in the attic this minute, and if Mrs. Redmond should say anythin' high-headed, it would n't do any harm for you to refer to it. Dare to go and see her! You 're *goin'* to see her! I heard your uncle say he should call on Miss Rebecca no later than to-morrow, and you shall go with him."

"Oh, I am not sure I want to," said Phyllis. "What is Mrs. Redmond like?"

"Like? She's tall, and slim, and red-headed, with a goodish complexion," returned Roxana, shaking down the stove with a racket that almost drowned the words which Phyllis strained her ears to hear.

"Do stop that noise," begged the girl. "Is she young?"

"It feels more like spring than ever," remarked Roxana, rising from her knees. "I should n't wonder if, when this fire goes out, we did n't have to build it up again."

"Is she young?" repeated Phyllis. "Miss Redmond said so."

"Yes, she's young, and she's got kind of a bossin' way with her that old-fashioned folks think sets better on older people."

Phyllis repressed a smile. She knew Roxana had a predilection for doing all the "bossing" herself.

"You shall go with your uncle to-morrow," added Mrs. Sherritt decidedly. "You've been invited, and you sha'n't hang back. After you've been once, if you don't want to go again I won't say a word; only, do you hold up your head, Phyllis, and remember who you are."

Dr. Joy smiled in an amused fashion when his housekeeper informed him of her desires.

"You think it is time the little girl made her début, do you?" he said.

"Miss Rebecca asked her to come," returned Roxana; "and I will say for Phyllis," she added, in a lowered tone, "that she has been very sensible about all this Beech Knoll fluster, and it's natural she should want to see the place. Now, let her go decently and in order with you, and make a call, and that's all right."

Mrs. Sherritt personally aided at the girl's toilet on the important occasion. Phyllis wore a plain gray dress of thin and lustrous silk, a black straw turban, a gray and white shawl, and black silk gloves. Had she arrayed herself in the ancestral brocade, she could hardly have presented a quainter appearance; but in her own and Roxana's eyes her costume left nothing to be desired.

"Remember the governor o' the State," whispered Mrs. Sherritt, as she tucked her into the buggy.

"What was that?" asked the doctor, as they started.

"Roxana does n't want me to be shy," explained Phyllis.

"This is your first formal call, is n't it?"

"Oh, don't frighten me with that awful word!" exclaimed Phyllis, catching her breath. "There could not be any formality in Snowdon, could there?"

"No, I think not. Do you ever wish you could go away from Snowdon, little one?"

" I did until that night we spent in Boston. Oh, how noisy it was! I wondered, and I wonder still, how people keep their wits in such an uproar."

" Then you are quite contented ? "

" Oh, who is quite contented ? " replied the girl.

The doctor nodded. " I often wonder if I am doing right by you, Phyllis. I know I'm a near-sighted old man, mentally as well as physically ; and because I am satisfied with a fire and plenty of books and tea when I come in from a cold ride, I am apt to forget that you need something more stirring. It seems to me you never have young people at the house any more."

" No, the only girls I cared for are away at school."

Dr. Joy looked around at her sharply. " Why haven't you asked me to let you go away to school ? "

Phyllis shook her head. " I knew it cost too much, and, beside, I like my studies with you so much. I am not afraid I shall not be able to hold my own with them when they come back."

Dr. Joy continued to cast uneasy glances at his companion. " You seem always to be reading," he said.

Phyllis smiled. " A great mistake of yours, Uncle Doctor. Roxana sees to it that I do a variety of other things."

" Roxana is very fond of you, and she has taught you to be as handy as herself ; but I think

sometimes you ought now to have other and more
suitable companions.   How old are you?"

" Twenty, my next birthday."

" Impossible!" ejaculated Dr. Joy, with a great
start.   " Bless my soul!"

He directed a frowning gaze forward between
the horse's ears, and muttered to himself, —

" That settles it.   I must see Terriss as soon as
I can, and tell him.   I can't think of it."

" Can't think of what?" inquired Phyllis curiously.

" Oh, a favor he asked of me.   No matter."

" You ought not to refuse any favor to Mr.
Terriss."

" Well, I had something of that feeling myself,
and so I told him I would consider it; but I did
not remember then how old you were," and Dr.
Joy smiled.

" I shall get Mr. Terriss to tell me what it is.
He is lovely to me since I have been going regularly to read to his wife, and I am sure he will not
refuse.   Uncle Doctor, did you ever see so devoted
a husband?"

Dr. Joy nodded.   " The man is a marvel," he
returned.   " One who did not know that the debt
was all on her side would say that he was inces-
santly trying to make up to her for some sin of
omission.   There is enough unselfishness under his
shabby coat to fit out his entire flock, and have
some to spare."

" But Mrs. Terriss is remarkable, too."

" Admitted. Mrs. Terriss is a marvel, also."

" Uncle Doctor, I do not understand you. You have no right to smile in that horrid little way, whenever you speak of Mrs. Terriss. A doctor, too. Are n't you ashamed, dear ? "

" I 'll try to be, Phyllis. How will that do ? "

" Why, it will not do at all, unless you succeed better than you have in the past. You are so good and kind and sympathetic about everybody else that it puzzles me and provokes me to have you behave so about Mrs. Terriss."

" It is very difficult for stout people to be sympathetic," returned Dr. Joy soberly, "and I have grown far too stout the past year."

Phyllis leaned lovingly against him. " There cannot be too much of you, you know, only you are not so well, Uncle Doctor, and you must diet. Oh, we are almost there ! Have you seen her ? " and the girl sat up very straight and her eyes brightened.

" No, not for a dozen years."

" Oh, I do not mean Miss Rebecca ! There is nothing frightful about her. I mean Mrs. Redmond."

" No, I have not seen her. There is the house — spruce, is n't it ? "

Phyllis looked eagerly about her as they turned in at the gateway. There was a group on the drive at the foot of the steps. A lady on horseback was walking her steed up and down, while another lady and a man in a rough coat looked on.

"What a beautiful horse!" exclaimed Phyllis,
"and how that lady sits! There is Miss Redmond on the piazza. She sees you, Uncle Doctor."

Dr. Joy touched his hat, and the lady on horseback drew away to let the buggy approach, meanwhile looking inquiringly toward Rebecca, who
came smiling down the steps. "I am very glad
to see you," said the latter warmly. "Elise, this
is Dr. Joy and his niece Phyl — Miss Flower.
Mrs. Redmond, Doctor."

Mrs. Redmond bowed, her graceful figure bending in compliance with the restless motions of her
horse.

"My sister will take you into the house," she
said cordially. "I will join you soon. I have
just purchased this saddle horse, Dr. Joy. Do you
like his appearance?"

"He is a beauty, madam, and worthy of you,"
returned the doctor, with prompt politeness. He
dismounted with the deliberation of the corpulent,
and gave his hand to Phyllis, whose cheeks and
eyes were bright. "This little girl would give her
ears for his mate; but she takes an occasional
canter on old Sorrel here, and makes that do."

"You will try my horse some day, perhaps,
Miss Flower," said Mrs. Redmond pleasantly.

Phyllis was filled with confusion and wrath at
her uncle. It was provoking in him to make such
a blundering remark. Mrs. Redmond had been
forced at once into patronizing her. Such a young
woman, too!

Phyllis felt strangely shy and awkward as she passed into the house. Surprise at Mrs. Redmond's beauty, for which Roxana's grudging description had in no wise prepared her, mingled in her thoughts with resentment at her own embarrassment. Her heart beat fast as she followed Miss Rebecca and her uncle, after making some inarticulate answer to Mrs. Redmond's politeness. Here was the interior she had so ardently desired to see, and its beauty completed the subjugation which had been commenced.

A young woman who bought and furnished houses like this, who rode blooded horses, and who was never shy or embarrassed, was not a person to be affected by the green brocade, or the dignity of anybody's great-grandmother. Phyllis was reflecting upon this when the mistress of the house entered, her bright head uncovered and her habit gathered in one hand.

Rebecca looked from her to Phyllis.

"You must excuse me, my dear," she said to the latter, "for stumbling over your name. The idea, you know, of calling little Phyllis Miss Flower."

"When you left her a bud," said Elise, seating herself beside her caller.

Dr. Joy looked at the speaker with undisguised admiration. "I have a complaint to lodge against you, Mrs. Redmond," he remarked. "Do you know you have nearly ruined my practice by your enchantments?"

"It would be uncivil, I suppose, to call that a blessing to the community," replied Mrs. Redmond. "Tell me how, pray."

"By making Beech Knoll so interesting. Women that should have been at home studying their nervous systems have put on their bonnets and walked up here every day. Fresh air and exercise are mortal enemies to physicians. I am thinking of suing you for damages."

Elise smiled. "Let me advise you not to do so, for it will be an endless suit. I am as devoted to an outdoor life as when I was here twelve years ago; and I mean to set a constant example to the townfolk, now that I am really back in beloved Beech Knoll."

"I hope you will try your influence on our minister's wife," said the doctor.

Phyllis's tongue became loosened. "Uncle Doctor," she warned, "be careful; you will give a false impression."

"I made Mrs. Terriss' acquaintance yesterday," said Rebecca in her quiet voice. "She appeals very strongly to one's sympathy; yet she seems to have a lovely resignation in her trials."

"Yes," replied the doctor, catching his niece's anxious gaze, "I think she is entirely resigned to her situation."

Mrs. Redmond's fair brow wrinkled and she shook her head. "How marvelous that mortals ever can accept such imprisonment! I suppose everything has been tried for her?"

Dr. Joy started to speak, but his niece, not liking the expression of his mouth, interrupted —

"She has almost no use of her limbs, Mrs. Redmond. Mr. Terriss carries her back and forth from her bed to her chair."

Mrs. Redmond turned toward the speaker. "A very prepossessing man, Mr. Terriss," she said, "and no doubt a devoted husband. My sister knew him, it seems, many years ago."

"Yes, many years ago," said Miss Redmond, as they all looked at her; "so many that we have to begin our acquaintance afresh. Let me see, Dr. Joy, it is once in seven years, is it not, that we are entirely renewed physically? Phyllis, for instance, has nothing about her of the Phyllis I used to know — unless, perhaps, you still have a fancy for my seed cakes. How is that, Phyllis?"

"I am sure I have."

"Well, you shall see, at any rate. I made some this morning, just for Auld Lang Syne. It is long since I have had a chance to cook. Elise, may I take Phyllis and show her more of the house?"

Mrs. Redmond assenting, Phyllis rose, a prim figure, and followed Miss Rebecca from the room.

Mrs. Redmond observed the fond gaze with which the doctor followed her.

"Your niece seems to have been a pet of my sister's in the past," she remarked.

"Yes, poor little Phyl. Her orphaned condition always drew kind hearts toward her."

"But she has a father in you, I see."

"Yes, I have done my rather poor best for her. I am very glad you and Rebecca have come," continued the doctor, emboldened and attracted by his hostess' gracious manner. "I hope you will let that little girl visit here sometimes. I know well enough that she needs something beside what she gets at home. The woman who has had charge of her almost from infancy is a shrewd, sensible, good-hearted creature, who is devoted to her, but she is necessarily narrow. For years, Phyl has studied with me instead of going to school, and she is fairly well educated; but I assure you, Mrs. Redmond, she took my breath away to-day when she announced that she would be twenty on her next birthday. Where does time fly to? I am a plodding sort of an old fellow, and when I realize that Phyl is a woman, I find myself rather helpless. I suppose I knew she would become one if she lived; but the prospect was always a dim, vague one, like that of -- well, death. Her mother was my favorite sister. I want to do the very best thing in my power for the child. Perhaps you and Rebecca will advise me sometimes. I am glad to find I have some sense, too," continued the doctor more hopefully. "A friend has just been asking me to take a single man to board in my family. Well, I considered it. To-day, when Phyllis told me her age, I saw plainly enough that it would n't be a wise thing to do. Now, then, that was having my wits about me, eh?" and the doctor's round face beamed in self-congratulation.

" That was very wise in you, undoubtedly," replied Mrs. Redmond, with a quick, pretty nod. " Rebecca seems fond of your niece, and Rebecca is a friend worth having." She spoke in so graceful and cordial a manner that the good doctor did not perceive that his new acquaintance committed herself to nothing. Mrs. Redmond's experience had taught her caution. Much was always expected of her. She was accustomed to have her favor sought under all sorts of pretexts, and to be courted under many guises. She was no longer in danger of yielding an inch of territory, simply because it was begged of her ; but she gave Dr. Joy a frank gaze, the dimple dipped in her cheek, and he felt certain of her sympathy and comprehension.

Miss Redmond entered the room, bearing a little tray.

" You must try one of the seed cakes, Dr. Joy, and see if you think my hand has lost its cunning. Take a glass of wine with it."

" Not the w.r †hank you, Rebecca. There is a humming in my ₀ead in these days, if I try anything but water, that makes me believe I have a bee in my bonnet."

Phyllis sat down, and while her uncle ate a bit of the cake and chatted with his old friend, she lifted her eyes to her hostess.

" I am very much surprised that you cared to come to Snowdon to live," she said.

Mrs. Redmond raised her eyebrows. " You do

not like it, then?" she returned, her slow, musical
speech striking the girl as a great charm.

"I should like to see another place some time."

Elise looked at her with more attention.

"That is natural; but I have tried a great many
places, and you see I come back to Snowdon."

"But tastes differ," said Phyllis.

"Oh, yes, indeed," admitted Mrs. Redmond,
amused by the stiff reply. "Perhaps I shall find
that some of the charm of Beech Knoll has departed with my childhood, but I do not believe it
yet. Do you play lawn tennis, Miss Flower?"

"No," replied Phyllis, angry with herself because
she could not say yes, and consequently flushing.
Elise began to see that she was very pretty, and
that she was shy.

"I expect to have a ground laid out to-morrow.
I will teach you the game, if you like. I must have
some one to play with," she considered mentally.

"Thank you," returned Phyllis curtly. "I hope
you will come and see us, Mrs. Redmond. Uncle
Doctor, we must go," she added; and rose as she
spoke.

Her uncle imitated her movement rather reluctantly, and after a few more words the visitors
entered their buggy and drove away.

"What a quaint little creature," exclaimed Mrs.
Redmond, when Rebecca returned from seeing
them off. "Phyllis Flower. How the name suits
her! Poor little maid, dressed in her grandmother's
fashion, and so stiff and ill at ease!"

" She was afraid of you, perhaps," suggested Miss Redmond. " Her stiffness disappeared as soon as we left you. I showed her several of the rooms."

" Are there many of them?" inquired Elise, with a far-away look.

" What are you talking about, child? Rooms?"

" No, Flowers. I mean people," replied Mrs. Redmond abstractedly. "I forgot that there would be people here."

" Well, well!" exclaimed Miss Rebecca, bridling.

" Of course, *your* friends," returned Elise hastily, " any one you care for, I shall care for as a matter of course; but it has just occurred to me that perhaps Snowdon has a sewing-circle, and that it will expect to meet here."

She sank upon a divan with so dismayed an expression that Miss Redmond laughed in spite of herself.

" You did not ask my advice before you decided to come to Snowdon, remember. Yes, I think you may have to entertain a quilting-bee here in time."

" Rebecca, don't frighten me, or I shall invite a house-party."

Meanwhile, Dr. Joy, as they rolled along toward home, had turned to his niece questioningly.

" Well, Phyl, how do you like formal calling?"

" I hate it," responded the girl sententiously.

Roxana, coming expectantly to the door to meet them, was surprised at the weary, unhappy look on Phyllis's face.

"She did not enjoy herself, somehow," said the doctor explanatorily, "but I did. Snowdon has made an acquisition in that beautiful woman."

"She ain't any beauty, to my mind," said Roxana, looking anxiously at her darling. "Did you see Miss Rebecca?"

"Yes, and she showed me all over the house," replied Phyllis, coming into the dining-room and sitting down. "You never saw such a place, Roxana. It is like a palace. I never want to go there again."

"I thought so," ejaculated Mrs. Sherritt indignantly. "I knew you would not like that stuck-up woman. I ain't generally mistaken in folks and"—

Phyllis stopped her with an impatient gesture. "She was very pleasant and kind," she asserted. "It was myself who disgusted me. I was so stiff and tongue-tied. I should be ashamed ever to see her again. She wanted to laugh at me. I dare say she is laughing at me at the present moment," and the girl's cheeks tingled.

Dr. Joy, who entered the room in time to hear the last remark, laid his hand on his niece's head.

"All's well that ends well," he said kindly. "That is going to be a good place for you to visit, and you will laugh at this some day. I am glad Rebecca has come back. I believe I will go upstairs and lie down awhile," he added, turning away. "I am bothered with that giddiness again. Call me in time for tea. Promise me to be your sensible little self, Phyl, and don't sulk. Perhaps it was some of Uncle Doctor's awkwardness that made things go wrong, eh?"

Phyllis, in thinking over these words afterward, trembled to think that she might have shrugged her shoulders in silence, or otherwise have indulged the spirit of childish resentment which possessed her.

What she really did was to raise her eyes to the kind old face, and feeling touched by its expression, to throw her uncle a kiss.

"Dear Uncle Doctor, you redeemed the occasion. They are not laughing at you, if they are at me," she said affectionately.

He smiled faintly, and left the room; and an hour afterward Phyllis, prostrate on the floor beside his bed, was sobbing her heart out in gratitude for those loving words; for Roxana, when she went according to directions to call the doctor to their early tea, had found the good man peacefully sleep ing his last sleep.

CHAPTER VI.

IT was the day following Dr. Joy's funeral that Philip Terriss walked in at the gate of Beech Knoll and asked for its mistress. It was his first call, and he felt something of the qualms Rebecca had experienced as he entered the doors; also something of the same relief, as he saw how unrecognizable were the old rooms, where in his youth he had endured such enchantment and such pain. The resolute purpose which had led him back to the side of his *fiancée* had never faltered. He had long since won a habit of considering his wife and ignoring himself, which had become an armor against the assaults of the past or present.

He had seen that it was a blow to Rebecca to meet him, and he blamed himself for having surprised her. He had accepted the call to Snowdon as being a favorable place for his wife's health, with the belief that Rebecca had left the town forever. When he suddenly learned of her return, it did not occur to him that he might meet her before she learned his identity; yet the privilege of apologizing to her now would be denied him. Perhaps after all it was unnecessary. Little Rebecca, with her snowy hair and her calm eyes! How different she had been when last he saw her in this room! He was reflecting upon the past with a vague return of his old wonder at the cruelty of circumstances, when Mrs. Redmond entered the room.

There was some haughtiness in her erect bearing as she crossed to him; her long soft dress, of a dark green color, making her fair skin fairer and her chestnut hair warmer in tint. The visitor was not only the minister whose face and manner she liked; he was the relative of the person who had given her years of annoyance. He was her go-between in a matter which she was in scornful haste to have ended, and in spite of her realization that he was doing her a favor, she associated him perforce with her beneficiary, who in her own mind she had decided was a small-souled, ungrateful, and whining individual.

She gave him her lovely hand, however, and thanked him for coming.

"Had it not been for Dr. Joy's funeral," he returned, "I should have been here yesterday, as I received a letter from my cousin in the morning."

"Yes?" said Elise, seating herself near him and taking a screen to shield her face from the wood fire, which burned these May mornings in the little room where she received him. "Dr. Joy's death was a very sad event," she added. "Miss Redmond is at the house to-day. I believe Miss Flower is very much overcome."

"Yes;" Mr. Terriss nodded gravely. "Phyllis

has had a great loss, and like all young people she thinks now she cannot bear it ; but she will discover that human endurance is very elastic."

" Her uncle seemed very fond of her," said Elise.

" Yes, yes, indeed. It was a father's fondness that he gave her. They will miss him greatly. Mrs. Sherritt, the housekeeper, feels quite borne down by the responsibility left upon her, for the doctor was hardly more than a child in business matters, and has left nothing to speak of. She looks at the practical side, poor woman, although she sincerely mourns the doctor, to whom she was faithfully attached."

" Yes," returned Mrs. Redmond. " I believe I saw Mrs. Sherritt the day I called upon you. Do you say," she went on abruptly, " you have received a letter from Terriss Chester regarding my proposition ? "

" Yes, Mrs. Redmond. What I wrote him was something like this : The daughter of Mr. Beckwith has communicated with me as your relative, in order to make known to you her opinion that you are entitled to a part of the property you expected to inherit, and to express her willingness to give you the portion she considers fair."

Elise nodded coldly. " You conveyed the correct idea, Mr. Terriss. I thank you very much. The lawyers I employ in Boston are Deen & Farrington. I will see them very soon and " —

" One moment, Mrs. Redmond." The minister

changed his position. "Terriss thanks you very much, but he declines."

Elise drew her head slightly backward. "He declines," she repeated haughtily.

"Yes. He would rather not be under such obligation."

Mrs. Redmond's breath came faster. "Where is the obligation?" she demanded. "I fear, after all, you did not make it quite clear, Mr. Terriss. I am not doing this as an act of friendship to him. It is a matter between me and my own conscience."

Mr. Terriss smiled at the fire. "I am quite sure that I did make that clear," he replied.

"He must accept it," said Elise, repressing her excitement. "I have been bored — pardon the expression applied to a relative of yours, Mr. Terriss — by that person ever since my poor father's death, which may even have been hastened by his ward's obstinacy. I insist upon being able to dismiss him from my mind and life."

The minister looked into her shining eyes. "I am sure nothing need hinder you from that now," he said.

"Why, certainly I am hindered. Terriss can go on considering himself abused."

"How? Since you have offered reparation and he has refused it."

Mrs. Redmond looked down and reflected. "Perhaps," she said suddenly, looking up, "I ought to have offered him half. I will offer him half."

Mr. Terriss, who had been conscious of some amusement at the beauty's imperiousness, began to realize how fully she was in earnest.

"I think you exaggerate your duty in this matter, Mrs. Redmond. You are in no way to blame for the circumstances of the case. Had you and Terriss been so situated that you grew up together in the affectionate relations which sometimes exist between adopted brothers and sisters, it might be now that, even though Terriss had quarreled with your father, you could find it in you to offer him his share of the inheritance from a loving heart; and then he might accept it, but " —

Elise flashed a blue glance at the speaker. "Does he expect me to love him, indeed?" she exclaimed.

"Oh, no; not at all," replied the minister, trying not to smile. "I have hesitated about showing you his letter, because it was not intended for your eyes; also, because it contains unnecessary personalities like many letters written by idle persons; and I do wish that without seeing it you would consent to abandon your generous ideas, accepting my word for it that it will be useless for you to try to assist my cousin financially."

"Please do not put it in that way," returned Mrs. Redmond, striving for her usual calmness. "I simply insist upon giving him his rights, so that when the thought of him passes through my mind, it *may* pass through and not linger to vex me."

Mr. Terriss sighed. "I see it will be better for you to read his letter," he replied. "It will not make you more lenient toward him, but it will set your mind at rest."

"Then by all means let me see it," said Mrs. Redmond, holding out her hand for the folded paper which the minister took from an inside pocket.

He handed it to her, and she unfolded it. The writing was small and rather stiff. Elise's lip curled slightly as she remarked it. The following was the letter: —

—— HOSPITAL, *May* 12.

DEAR COUSIN PHILIP, — I have enjoyed the memory of your visit ever since its occurrence. Imagine the pleasure I felt to see your signature affixed to a letter which I opened this morning. Need I say that its contents amazed me? After these years of silence, that Elise Beckwith should have sought you instead of me, and should have made me, through a third party, so presumptuous a proposition, was indeed an astonishing discovery.

A mental picture of my guardian's daughter rises before me as I write. She must have been, perhaps, eleven years of age when I saw her last; and so I see her now. Arms and legs of an appalling length and thinness. Hair, red as flame. Movement and manner, awkward. But what is all that now that she is a great heiress? I will wager there are plenty to tell her that she is graceful as the slight, swaying reed, and that Titian would have dreamed of her hair. Alas for human nature, why does not that satisfy her! Why must she search me out in order to pose before an admiring public, and get her generosity woven into such a newspaper article as delights the wild and woolly West? No, cousin Philip. Will you kindly write to my would-be benefactress that I have recently expired in the —— Hospital, or, if you prefer, tell her in any shape which bests suits your standard of combined courtesy and truth that, when her father disowned me simply because he could not pare and shave off my corners to make me fit the mould he had chosen for me, I relinquished all claim or thought of the Beckwith dollars.

I am dressed to-day, but absurdly shaky. The doctor says I cannot work for some time. I have not forgotten your promise to try to find me some inexpensive boarding-place, and was disappointed that this letter contained no word on the subject.

Shall hope for another soon. By the way, please don't misunderstand me if I request you not to refer again to the subject of the Beckwith patronage. I am a Sybarite with regard to emotions, and that idea disturbs my equanimity.

Ever sincerely yours,
TERRISS CHESTER.

Elise, at the close of her reading, raised her eyes slowly to the minister, who was gazing at the snapping logs. She folded the letter slowly and carefully and passed it back to him.

" Are you satisfied ? " he asked with some anxiety, as he accepted it.

She gave him her most charming smile, and the dimple sank in her flushed cheek.

" Perfectly, thank you."

" He is not — not an unpleasant fellow, as you might judge he was from this," hesitated Mr. Terriss.

Mrs. Redmond made a deprecating gesture. " I am sure it is deceptive to judge of persons by their letters, and certainly Terriss seems to have developed into a decided character."

" Yes, so he has, no doubt of it," returned the minister, pleased and relieved.

" Do you think you may find board for him in Snowdon ? " pursued Mrs. Redmond.

" Well, I doubted, — on your account. If you would object " —

" You must remember I should not be myself at all to him," she replied archly. " I have changed my name, and if you do not betray me, do you think from his description of Elise Beckwith that he will recognize me ? "

Mr. Terriss gazed at her with dawning surprise. "Surely not. Do you mean that you could keep your identity a secret ? "

Elise raised her eyebrows. " Why not ? If you are going to bring him to Snowdon, do you not think from the tone of his letter that it would be less awkward for me to be simply Mrs. Redmond to him in case we should meet ? "

"But I am not willing he should retain that rough judgment of your motives," said the minister warmly. "I want him to know you. I want him to see how wrong" —

"No, no; trust me, Mr. Terriss, these deep prejudices are not easily removed. Please say nothing of me."

"Well, if you wish it," assented the other reluctantly. "Of course, you may never meet," he added.

"Perhaps not," returned Elise, and the minister began to consider that possibly her expression was too brilliant, her eyes too radiant.

"The question is," he continued, "of a boarding-place. My own house is not one where a stranger could be made comfortable, owing to Mrs. Terriss' inability. I asked Dr. Joy, a few days before his death, as to whether he would be willing to take Terriss, and he had not given me an answer. I can put it to Mrs. Sherritt, at any rate. She will know what decision to make. I feel bound to do the best I can for Terriss; and Mrs. Sherritt is an excellent cook." Mr. Terriss rose. "You have no objection to his coming to Snowdon, I understand?"

"Provided you keep my secret," replied Elise, with a spirited glance.

"I see no harm in doing so. As you say, it might be awkward. You will feel relieved now, I hope, Mrs. Redmond. You have certainly done your whole duty."

"Oh, Mr. Terriss, when can one feel that one's whole duty is done? Perhaps there remains even more due from me to your cousin. In any case, I thank you very much for your assistance in this matter. It might have dawdled along over weeks of time. Now, a few days have been sufficient for a decisive settlement."

She held out her hand to him, and he took it. "Mrs. Redmond," he said simply and earnestly, "I congratulate you on your tact and self-command. I had feared you would be vexed by this turn of affairs. If I can ever be of any service to you in future, command me. I wish you good-morning."

He went, and Elise stood in the centre of her dainty room, her breast heaving with its emotion. Her eyes and cheeks were still bright, but her mouth no longer smiled, and her hands clenched themselves. She had never been so angry in her life. At last she began walking up and down the floor. "Is it for this that I have left my friends?" she reflected. "Is it for this I have furnished Beech Knoll, have lain awake through long hours of the night, have poured out my heart's sympathy? Has my life for years borne a vague shadow, only for this?"

She caught sight of her reflection in a glass above the fire, and suddenly paused, approached, and looked into her own eyes.

"Is none of it true, Elise Beckwith?" she demanded. "Have you not through it all enjoyed the effect of your own generosity, posed for your own admiration, and patronized the unknown youth?"

Her cheeks tingled.

"He should not have been the one to tell me of it. That is too cruel," she exclaimed, turning from the glass. Then she rang the bell.

"Have them bring Star around," she said to the servant, for her mood must be changed before Rebecca's return.

CHAPTER VII.

THE MOTH AND THE CANDLE.

Miss Rebecca's first impulse upon discovering the minister's identity was to run away from Snowdon, but a number of practical questions arose to hinder that summary disposition of an embarrassing situation. First, where should she run to? Second, what excuse should she give for going there? Third, what would Elise do without her? Fourth, should she not make herself ridiculous in the eyes of the man who had given her such calm greeting?

"But he was prepared," thought poor Rebecca, "while I — I was cruelly unprepared."

The outcome of all her reflection was that she decided to remain where she was, and, according to her old recipe for endurance of trial, "live by the day."

Rebecca, without herself suspecting it, was a strong character; and when she had once made up her mind that it was best for her to settle down within walking distance of Philip Terriss and his wife, she repined no longer, but systematically turned away from her own tremors.

The thing that horrified her most, as revealing a wicked heart, was the sudden repugnance which

sprang up in her toward the pale invalid with
whom she had spent that quiet hour.

" The poor creature whom I would innocently
have robbed," she thought remorsefully. " I hope
I can help to cheer her life." Dr. Joy's sudden
death turned her thoughts with a shock into another channel, and for a few days she had heart
and hands filled with care of and for Phyllis and
Roxana. As Elise had said, she was with them on
the morning of Mr. Terriss' call, and as she was
coming away from the house, she met the minister
in the street. She felt a great bound of the heart,
which sent the color into her face, as he lifted his
hat and stopped.

" Good-morning, Rebecca," he said. " Are you
coming from Dr. Joy's ? "

" Yes."

" How are they this morning ? "

" The passionate stage of Phyllis's grief is passed.
She is like a subdued, gentle child, this morning,"
replied Rebecca. " Roxana, poor woman, feels
quite bewildered by her responsibility. She is beginning to wonder how they shall live, for it seems
Phyllis has almost nothing."

" I wonder if they would take a boarder," said
Mr. Terriss. " I was on my way now to ask
Mrs. Sherritt."

" I think they will be very glad to do so," replied
Rebecca earnestly.

" It is a cousin of mine, who wishes to come out
here."

" How fortunate !   I hope you will go and talk it over with Roxana.   Why should not Snowdon be a good place for summer boarders ? "

" I think it might," returned the minister ; then he lifted his hat and passed on, and Rebecca realized with a sense of relief that their first interview was over.

" I ought to have asked for *her*," she thought, with a pang of conscience.   She had not forgotten the civility.   She had neglected it purposely, and she knew it.   " He loves her, he is devoted to her. He has done his duty and he has his reward.   Let me do mine," she said to herself, as she hurried along the road.

She turned her thoughts resolutely to Roxana and her quandaries.   Supposing this proposed boarder should be — Why had she not asked him ?   Perhaps it really was Elise's adopted brother, who had turned out so strangely to be the minister's cousin.   She would ask Elise immediately ; but upon reaching home no Elise was there. She had gone to ride, the servant said.

In about an hour, Mrs. Redmond returned.   " I have had a glorious gallop," she announced, coming fresh and rosy into the joint sitting-room, where she and Rebecca spent most of their time indoors. " How are your poor friends ? "

" Adjusting themselves to the situation as best they may," replied Miss Redmond, looking up from her sewing.   " I met Mr. Terriss on his way there with some news that I think will cheer them.

He has a boarder for them. He said it was a cousin. I was wondering, Elise," in a lowered, confidential tone, " if it might be your gentleman."

Mrs. Redmond threw herself back in the laziest of postures on a deep divan among the large dull-colored cushions.

" I am not the possessor of a gentleman, my dear Rebecca."

" I mean your brother."

" Well, I presume he is a man and a brother in one sense. It is Terriss Chester, if that is what you mean."

" You don't say so ! " exclaimed Miss Redmond.

" There is not the least occasion for your looking radiant, Rebecca."

" Why, I think it is just like a story," answered Miss Redmond. " That you and this Terriss should be united after " —

" Re—becca, will you clip the wings of your fancy before it leads you further astray ! " Elise smiled. " Mr. Terriss has been here to tell me that Mr. Chester refuses the property."

Miss Redmond laid down her work. " Is it possible ! " she ejaculated. " How do you feel about that ? "

" Why should I feel at all? I have done my part in offering it. He has seen fit to refuse it. More than that he has shown an ungrateful,"—here Mrs. Redmond's voice trembled, — "a low bitterness toward the Beckwith family, which makes it impossible that we should ever be friends."

" Then, dear me, he ought not to come out here, and yet Roxana does need it so," said Rebecca, much troubled.

" Why need he know who I am ? " asked Elise, lazily switching her skirt with her riding whip, as she watched her sister-in-law's face.

" Why, sure enough! Why need he ? " Miss Redmond's eyes grew larger as she realized the scope of the other's suggestion. " He does not know your married name ; you said so. We need not say a word, and he could n't remember you."

" I think not," said Elise briefly, recalling the written description.

" It would not make you uncomfortable to have him in town ? " asked Miss Redmond doubtfully.

" I am perfectly willing he should come," returned the other, with an inscrutable smile.

" Well, it 's just as good and kind of you as it can be, dear," said Rebecca warmly. " It will be a help to Roxana. By the way, here is a letter I got out of the post-office. I laid it on the table so I should not forget it."

She handed the envelope to Elise, who glanced at the writing. " Probably a bill," she remarked, as she opened it. " Why, no, it is not," glancing at the beginning of the letter and quickly turning to the signature. " Why," with a laugh, " it is from Tony Bellows ; how did he find me ? "

" Bellows, Bellows," repeated Rebecca, looking at her pensively. " I do not remember any Bellows. Was he the one before the last ? "

Elise laughed again. She was accustomed to her sister-in-law's vague terms for her admirers.

"No. Don't you remember young Bellows, that comical creature that followed us around so when we were at Monterey? I did not know he had come back to Boston."

"There were so many creatures," said Rebecca plaintively, "and they always followed us around."

"But Tony was young and — I do not wish to be slangy, but he was *fresh;* a blonde boy, who wore six neckties a day. Oh!" becoming grave, with sudden recollection, "it was he who told me where Terriss was; and now he has found me, the troublesome fellow. Let me see what he says."

BOSTON, *May* 14, 18—.

MY DEAR MRS. REDMOND: —

A friend in San Francisco, whom I shall bless to my dying day, has told me that you have come to live in Snowdon, Mass. I immediately tried to find the place on the map. It was not there. Why in the name of all that is sensible should *you* choose to live in a place that is not on the map? Perhaps to bring the town into prominence. There, I meant that to be a graceful compliment, but I slipped up somehow. Take the will for the deed, please. Now, when are you going to let me come to see you? I tell you frankly that I shall come, and if you do not set a date I shall have to surprise you.

I have not seen Mr. Chester since my return.

I am sorry to find that he is ill, and has had to lose his position. I remember you took an interest in him, and the next time I see him I shall tell him that you are a near neighbor now, and would like a call from him for your father's sake, when he is able. Shall I?

I shall watch the mails eagerly until I hear from you. You cannot think how delighted I am at the prospect of seeing you again. Please address me at the bank. Ever faithfully yours,

A. BELLOWS.

"How provoking!" exclaimed Elise. "That blundering boy may give me no end of annoyance. I shall have to telegraph him in self-defense."

"Well, here's some paper," replied Rebecca briskly. "Do send him word. I can't help thinking of Roxana and how much she needs a few dollars a week."

Mrs. Redmond wrote and dispatched the following: —

MR. ANTHONY BELLOWS: —
Come out on morning train. Will meet you. Say nothing of me to Mr. Chester.

MRS. REDMOND.

The next day, Mrs. Redmond herself drove to the station to meet the expected guest. She had little fear that he would disappoint her, and smiled to herself as she pictured the surprise and delight with which the young man had probably received her flatteringly prompt reply.

The incoming train had scarcely stopped when the familiar, broad-shouldered figure stepped from it, and the delight Elise had fancied was plainly visible in the eager face, when he turned and perceived the fair driver of the smart new equipage.

"Mrs. Redmond, this is awfully good of you!" he exclaimed, hurrying forward and shaking the hand she offered him. "If you will wait one minute — I brought a handful of flowers" —

Mrs. Redmond smiled as he turned away. She knew Tony's idea of a few flowers, and was not surprised to see him return from a trip in the direction of the baggage-car with a formidable box, over which his blonde face looked gayly.

"Just the weather when flowers ought to grow if they don't," he remarked. "Beautiful, is n't it?"

"It is, Tony; but where *are* you going to put that Saratoga trunk? When will you learn not to get everything by wholesale?"

"Don't worry! plenty of room," returned Tony, balancing the box behind the seat, on the edge of the cart. "Now, this is fine," he added, taking the place beside his hostess, who turned her spirited ponies toward home.

"I am very glad to see you," returned Elise.

She found that she was very glad. Her associations with her guest were all of pleasant places, and no one could fail to be glad to see such an incarnated sunbeam as he was.

" What jolly little ponies ! " he remarked.

" Yes, they are pretty. I am not much acquainted with them yet. They are new. You will find everything new, except the house itself and some of the pictures."

" Of course you know I 'm still awfully puzzled as to why you are here at all ; but I can only congratulate myself that Snowdon is so near Boston."

" Why should n't one come here ? Does n't it strike you as a pretty town ? "

" Not bad ; but then all these villages are pretty enough. That explains nothing. It is n't even the season to go into the country to board."

" But I am not boarding."

" Great heavens, Mrs. Redmond ! " and the genial face fell. " You don't mean to say you are married ? "

" Oh, no, not married, only settled. I have bought a place and gone to housekeeping."

" Well, the mystery increases." They were driving rapidly through the business street of the town, and Mr. Bellows observed that every pedestrian turned to look after themselves and their equipage. " Do you remark that we are astonishing the natives?" he continued. " I feel as though I were making a triumphal entry into this peaceful hamlet. I am, too, you know. You have no idea how it puffed me up to receive your invitation so promptly."

His hostess smiled. " I might not have been quite so sudden with my summons, had it not happened that I was especially desirous that Mr. Chester should not know I was here ; and you threatened to betray me."

" Oh, come now, that 's too bad, Mrs. Redmond. I have been flattering myself for nothing, then."

" It is absurd for you to try to look plaintive, Tony," laughed Elise. " You never could, even when you were seven. By the way, you have no idea how surprisingly like your seven-year-old self you look this minute."

" I don't believe a word of it. I know you only pretend to remember me at that age for the sake of taking me down whenever you feel like it."

" I do remember you perfectly. Of course I do. Why, I was ten, you know."

" There you are, at it again. I don't see why you are always so determined that I shall remember you were ten."

" You had the prettiest yellow curls," continued Elise ruthlessly, " and when you were very good-natured, you used to let me brush them over my finger."

" I will let them grow again, if you will promise to do that."

Mrs. Redmond laughed. " Would n't you look comical ? "

" No funnier than those old cavalier fellows ; but we are way off the subject. I say it is too bad of you to get me out here in this glorious weather, feeling as jolly as a grig over my invitation, only to tell me it is on Chester's account."

" But I was just about to explain that I simply meant I would have written you instead of telegraphing, had it not been for Mr. Chester. You remember I told you that when a lad he was my father's ward. Well, I have learned since I saw you that he has bitter feelings against the Beckwiths, and I do not wish that he should know one of the family is here. The world is small; I may chance to meet him some day, and I should wish it to be as Mrs. Redmond merely. He does not know of my marriage, and he does not know me by sight."

" Then you mean " —

" I mean that you are never to speak of me to him, under pain of my eternal displeasure."

Tony nodded. " Agreed. Luckily, I missed going to see him yesterday, as I intended to do. Had I gone, I should certainly have told him all about you. Poor old fellow! he is down on his luck just now. If I had been here when he fell ill, I should have offered my services to the governor to fill his place in the bank until he was able to take it again."

" What a pity you were not! I imagine it will take some such exigency to force you into active service."

Tony flushed, pink as the flower in his buttonhole.

" I don't know why you should suppose that. Do you think I have not put in my time well since I left college ? "

" I think you have enjoyed yourself exceed‐
ingly."

" Is that any harm ? I have been seeing the
world as a part of my education. I am sure I
have met you in a good many parts of it."

Mrs. Redmond laughed. " True enough ; but
you see I have settled down now, and you must do
the same."

Phyllis Flower, walking to the village on an er‐
rand for Roxana, looked up from a dejected rev‐
erie at the sound of the horses' feet.

She forgot everything for the moment in admi‐
ration of the novel sight of the stylish equipage.
Instantly she perceived that it was Mrs. Redmond
driving, and that beside her sat a strange man.
The lady was smiling, her companion talking, and
the whole bright effect made Phyllis shrink from
being recognized, with the wish that she had
chosen another road.

As she was in the act of dropping her eyes,
however, she saw something which made her lift
her hand to attract Mrs. Redmond's attention.

The latter saw who it was who beckoned her,
and drawing in her ponies, turned them toward the
walk. The figure in black stood still and waited.

" Excuse me, Mrs. Redmond," said Phyllis, col‐
oring as she felt the stranger's eyes upon her,
" your baggage just dropped off into the road."

Mrs. Redmond looked bewildered a moment,
and Mr. Bellows turned around.

"It is the flowers," he remarked, lifting his hat.
"I will get them," and he jumped to the ground.

Mrs. Redmond laughed. "Thank you, Miss
Flower. Let me introduce to you my friend, Mr.
Bellows. He has just brought me a handful of
flowers from Boston, he says. I do not know
whose hand he is libeling, mine or his own."

"I am awfully obliged, Miss Flower," said Tony.
"You see, the box is so light we did not hear it."

"I do hope it is not broken," said Phyllis, has-
tening with him to where the box lay in the road.

"Not badly. String snapped, that is all. I
wish you would take some, Miss Flower. There
are a good many, and Mrs. Redmond does chaff a
fellow so," and Tony took out a handful of rich
La France roses and held them up.

Phyllis's eyes shone as she took them. "Ought
I to accept them?" she exclaimed. "How beautiful they are!" and she eagerly inhaled their fragrance.

Tony was delighted with her pleasure. "Are n't
they the loveliest things in the world?" he returned. "I am so glad you like them. I wonder if I can tie up this thing again;" and he fum-
bled at the broken string.

"Let me try," said Phyllis.

"Thank you. I'll carry it over to the walk.
The dust here will ruin your dress. Black shows
it so."

The girl's face fell at this reference. Uncle
Doctor had not been gone a week, and here she

had been feeling eager, young, happy again. Her
transparent face showed the sympathetic Tony that
something was wrong, and he stood by in troubled
silence while she deftly pieced and tied the cord.

"How cleverly you did that," he said, as she
stood up. "I 'm sure, I 'm awfully obliged."

"You are very welcome," she replied gravely.
"I thank you very much for the roses," and she
bowed to him, and then to Mrs. Redmond, who,
half turning in her seat, was watching the proceed-
ings with much amusement; then the girl went
quickly on her way.

"I know you are happier for that little *contre-
temps*," said Mrs. Redmond, as Bellows returned
with the box. "You have given flowers to a new
person, and I know the satisfaction that gives you,
you good-natured boy; but how do you suppose I
like to have my flowers presented to other people?"

Tony stepped into the cart. "Like seeks like,
you know," he replied. "Did n't you say her
name was Flower?"

"But you do not look happy, after all. What
is the matter?"

"I made that girl feel bad, somehow," returned
Tony, clasping the box for its safety as the ponies
started.

Elise smiled. "Oh, no; she is a stiff-mannered
little Puritan maiden, that is all."

Tony's face lit up happily. "Then she has n't
lost anybody lately, — any friend?"

"Yes, she has. Her adopted father, about a week ago."

Tony groaned. "That is what I was afraid of. That is like me, exactly. I never yet lost an opportunity of saying the wrong thing. I referred to her being in black, by way of bringing in a little pleasing small talk, and I saw the light go out of her face in a flash."

"Do not let that worry you," said Elise, smiling at his despair. "She is sensitive just now; but the roses will comfort her. Probably you are the first man who ever gave her any. Now, in a minute more, you will see Beech Knoll."

"Oh, that is the name! Did you buy the place on account of its name?"

"Wait and see," returned Elise briefly.

Soon they entered the broad gate, and the guest looked about him critically.

"Fishing?" he asked with interest, espying the sparkle of the river.

"I think so; but is it not attractive, with all these old trees, and the high and dry land? Do you still wonder?"

"But you are not a hermit, to be satisfied with scenery," objected Tony, unconvinced.

"Certainly not; else you would not have been invited here." Mrs. Redmond gave the reins into the hands of a man who was waiting, and preceded her guest into the house.

Rebecca rose from her seat by a window, whence she had been watching their approach.

"Oh, to be sure," she said calmly, as Tony approached her, his hand outstretched, " I do remember you. You are the one we met first in Italy, who turned out to be the brother of one of Elise's schoolmates."

" Had you forgotten me, Miss Redmond?" exclaimed Tony. " What an unlucky fellow I am!" but his face belied his words, for Elise had uncovered the box at last, and was looking love and admiration at the lilies and violets as she lifted them out.

CHAPTER VIII.

ROXANA'S BOARDER.

MRS. SHERRITT received the minister's proposition as to taking a boarder with prompt assent.

"That is one thing I ain't afraid to try to do," she said, a perceptible lightening of the anxiety in her face; "and I take it it's all right to put the doctor's house to any use I see fit, now the good man can't help us any more."

The minister glanced at Phyllis, who sat sober-eyed and silent, listening to the conversation.

"I suppose it is Phyllis's house now," he said.

Roxana followed the direction of his glance indulgently. "Yes, what there is, is Phyllis's; and I'm Phyllis's, you know, and it's my business to scratch around and see what I can find for her."

"What should I do without you, I wonder?" said Phyllis.

"You ain't called upon to wonder about that," responded Mrs. Sherritt gently. "About how soon, Mr. Terriss, would your cousin want to come?"

"Probably, the first day you could receive him. You know he may be a good deal of trouble at first. His meals would have to be served in his room, very likely."

" All right.   Let him come Saturday," returned
Roxana, stifling a sigh and clearing her throat.
" How are you getting on at your house?"

Mr. Terriss rose.   " We need a call from you,
Mrs. Sherritt, when you can spare the time.   How
I wish we could come and swell your family ! "

" I wish you could," replied Roxana heartily,
" but I have n't any place as comfortable for Mrs.
Terriss as the rooms she 's got.   If I could hear of
anybody better than Lucindy, you should have her;
but Snowdon 's an awful hard place to get help."

" You are a valuable neighbor, and we are very
grateful, I assure you.   Good-by, Phyllis ;" and the
minister held out his hand to the young girl, who
rose and put hers into it.   " I am glad a busy time
is coming for you.   Work is the greatest blessing
of our lives, and I know Roxana can count on you
to share her burdens."

His words gave Phyllis's thoughts a new bent.   It
flashed across her that she had been willing to let
Roxana do all the thinking, planning, and working,
herself content to do obediently what was required
of her, and nothing more.

Mrs. Sherritt looked reflectively out of the window after the minister's retreating figure.

" Well, I 'm in for it," she remarked.

" In for what?" asked Phyllis.

Roxana tossed her head.   " I was thinkin' out
loud, I guess," she continued.   " I was cogitatin'
on the queerness o' things in general.   How likely
it is that folks have got to do in this world just

what they hate most. I'll bet a cookie that Mr.
Terriss, for instance, would like a life with lots o'
variety, and that he is partic'lar about his victuals;
the facts bein' that he must live in the country and
take care of a sick wife, and eat Lucindy Bates's
cookin'. Now I would like to be delivered from
strange men, especially sick ones; and here I am,
a - welcomin' one right into my best chamber, and
calc'latin' to run my legs off, waitin' on him."

"I am going to do better, Roxana," said Phyllis
gravely.

Mrs. Sherritt looked at her in surprise. The
girl's eyes were hollow from weeping, and her
mouth had lost its ready smile.

"How can you do better, child? You are all
right."

"You always said I was lazy."

"Well, ye - es, perhaps, sometimes; but there
ain't a capabler girl in Snowdon. I've said that,
too. You're as smart as a steel spring, Phyllis."

Mrs. Sherritt's words of praise were rare; but
she felt very tender toward the girl at this time.
Phyllis colored faintly.

"Well, I want you to let me help you. I would
rather work than read now."

After this declaration, Phyllis could not refuse
Roxana when, a few days later, she asked her to do
an errand at the village, although she dreaded to
go out and meet kindly, pitying words and looks.

Upon her return, she found Mrs. Sherritt on her
knees scrubbing the kitchen floor.

" You ought to see the smart turnout that went by a little while ago," exclaimed the latter. " Mrs. Redmond has got a pair o' ponies that will make your eyes shine."

" I met them." Phyllis came close and held her fragrant roses before Roxana's face.

" For the land's sake, what beauties! " cried the latter, astonished. " Where did you get 'em ? "

" A box of flowers fell out of Mrs. Redmond's carriage, and I told her of it, and the gentleman with her gave me these."

" Well, I declare, how pleased the doctor would have been."

" O Roxana ! they made me forget him," mourned Phyllis. " For the first time since he left us, the sorrow went out of my mind when I saw these."

" Look here, Phyllis, you are on the wrong track," said Roxana kindly, looking up from her steaming pail. " You were a good child to your uncle, and he set uncommon store by you. In lookin' back, I take it you have n't anythin' to regret. Well, he went in the Lord's good time, and it was mighty hard for us to spare him ; but do you think it 's good sense or religion to hang on tight to your trouble? No, indeed. Let the grief slip away just as soon as it will. The love won't slip with it ; and that 's the part he would care to have you keep."

" Do you think he knows ? "

Roxana rose from her clean floor. " Any way,

we know that he was a good man, and it was his gain to go. Ain't that enough?"

Phyllis moved slowly out of the kitchen, and putting the roses in a vase of water she set them on a table beneath the picture of Uncle Doctor, into whose eyes she looked until her own filled with tears.

"There is no danger that I will ever love you less, dear," she murmured. "I did not remember you every minute when you were here, and if I seem to forget you now sometimes, it will only be in the same way that I did when you lived with us." She turned and went upstairs to the room which she had made it her business to prepare for the boarder. It was as clean and pure as soap and water and much beating and brushing could make it.

Phyllis had not exercised her imagination concerning the expected stranger. Her old habit of castle-building was no temptation to her in these days. She dreaded the advent of the invalid, and combated the feeling as a form of the laziness she had determined to forswear. She made his room look as inviting as her slender resources would permit, and, after some mental conflict, carried thither Dr. Joy's armchair, as being the best substitute for an invalid's lounge at her command.

Roxana followed her upstairs and looked about the room, nodding approval.

"Them roses would put a finishin' touch to the bureau," she suggested.

" Those are for Uncle Doctor," replied Phyllis quickly.

" He 'd spare one most likely if he had anythin' ,to say about it," remarked Roxana. "A flower or two in a sick-room does a body good."

Phyllis thought a moment, then went down to the dining-room, which was their living-room as well, and took a couple of roses from the vase.

" Uncle Doctor would like it," she said to herself.

The girl little suspected how far from approval of the whole undertaking Uncle Doctor would have been, so the simple preparations went forward, and at the appointed hour Mr. Chester arrived.

The minister met him at the depot and brought him to the house, where Phyllis and Roxana, feeling rather dreary and apprehensive, awaited him.

His appearance was surprising to Phyllis, but as to Roxana, let the stranger be short and fat, or tall and thin, let him be young or old, the same fortitude was required to take him in and welcome him.

He was haggard from the fatigue of the short journey, and he looked from Phyllis to Roxana and back again with a sombre, impatient expression in his dark eyes, which made Phyllis thankful to shrink into the background after the introduction.

" I was very glad to come, Mrs. Sherritt," he said curtly. " I should like to rest here a mo-

ment," and he sat down upon the haircloth sofa.
" Do not wait for me, cousin Philip."

" Oh, yes. Let me help you up to your room
presently," replied the minister.

" No. I do not need that at all. I wish to be
still awhile, then I shall be ready to go upstairs.
I do not need any assistance. Many thanks for
your good offices. Good-by," and Mr. Terriss
was forced reluctantly to take his leave.

Phyllis saw him go with a sinking heart. The
stranger's pallor and his quick, brusque speech
were far from reassuring. She was appalled when
Roxana spoke.

" I 'm goin' out to get Mr. Chester's tea. You
stay here, Phyllis, and when he feels like goin' up,
show him his room," and Mrs. Sherritt turned
energetically and left the parlor. Phyllis con-
quered a desire to grasp her disappearing skirts,
and lifted her glance to the figure leaning back in
the corner of the sofa. The stranger sat with his
thin hand over his eyes, and Phyllis sank noiselessly into a chair, almost holding her breath, in
the hope that he would not note the flight of time
until Roxana's return. There was something in
the dejection of his attitude and the nearly Span-
ish darkness of his hair and complexion that suggested to the girl her cherished vision of the misanthrope who was to inhabit Beech Knoll in that
long-ago time that preceded Dr. Joy's death.

She was gazing curiously at him, noting the
curves of his mustache and chin, when he languidly

dropped his hand and looked full into her frightened eyes.

"Who is the best doctor here?" he asked suddenly.   Then, the expression of the girl's face jog-
ging his memory, he continued in his feebly brusque
fashion, "Excuse me.   I know of your loss; but I
fear I may need a physician soon."

"A homeopath?"

"No! a regular physician," was the impatient
response.   "Excuse me again; I do not know
which school your father belonged to."

"Uncle Doctor was a regular physician," replied Phyllis slowly.   "There is another here.   I
can get him for you, if you like."

"Can't you send an errand boy?"

"I am our errand boy," replied Phyllis.   "I do
not mind going."

"I will see when I get upstairs," responded the
other.   "I will go now, if you please."

He looked so weary and pale as he rose that
Phyllis hesitated.

"Will you take my arm?" she asked bravely,
conquering her dread.

The stranger looked down at her curiously, and
smiled for the first time.

"Oh, no.   Lead the way, please."

He leaned heavily on the slender old banister
as they ascended, and midway on the stairs was
obliged to stop and sit down.

"Why didn't you let Mr. Terriss stay!" exclaimed the girl, looking back at him anxiously.

He muttered something under his breath. "This is very absurd," he said. "Wait a minute, I am dizzy, that is all. You are at liberty to laugh as much as you like, Miss Flower."

"Laugh!" exclaimed Phyllis, who felt much more inclined to cry. "I only wish I were bigger so you would be willing to let me help you."

Her hearty tone seemed to do the sufferer good. He pulled himself to his feet.

"Now, once more," he said; and this time he reached the top, and followed his guide into the room she had prepared.

The guest looked eagerly toward the neatly curtained window. "What direction is that?" he asked.

"South."

"Bless you," he responded.

Phyllis drew forward the armchair suggestively.

"Roxana will be here soon with your tea," she said.

Chester took off his overcoat, and sank into the armchair. "I hardly think I shall need a doctor. This is a very pleasant room, and you are very kind."

"I am glad you like it," returned Phyllis, and with a breath of relief she passed out of the door.

Roxana was mounting the stairs with a loaded waiter when she emerged.

"You might take it in, Phyllis," she suggested

The girl shook her head decidedly. " No, it is your turn. He nearly fainted on the stairs, and I'm afraid. I will sit here, and if you want me, you have only to call."

Roxana stifled a groan and passed within. The invalid's face lighted as he saw the food. His hostess drew a little table up before his chair, and placed upon it the creamed toast, tea, marmalade, and lamb chops which she had prepared.

" How very nice ! " said Chester appreciatively. "There is a wolf within me nowadays."

" Glad to hear it. You are all right, then ? "

" Oh, yes. I hope you believe I am considerate enough not to come out here and die on your hands. Perhaps, however, you will consider bringing with me a convalescent's appetite quite as outrageous."

" I sha'n't complain a bit, if you don't," returned Mrs. Sherritt, with a practical glance about her to see if her boarder had all the requisites. " I suppose you've got a napkin-ring somewhere."

Chester smiled under the combined influence of the chop and his entertainer's manner.

" Yes, in my trunk. I have not used it for years, though, because I lost my pleasant association with the giver."

" Better use it now, because I have n't got any to give you, unless it was Dr. Joy's, and I guess Phyllis would n't like that."

" Oh, don't trouble yourself. Any piece of rib-bon will do."

"No such slack way would do for me," remarked Mrs. Sherritt dispassionately. " If you 'll give me your trunk key, I 'll unpack your things for you."

Chester looked up, surprised. Roxana returned his glance coolly, strength and determination in every line of her plain face and figure.

"You — you are very kind." He took a key from his pocket and handed it to her. " I have no idea where anything is. One of the nurses packed for me."

Roxana took the key, and vanished behind the broad back of Chester's chair. He proceeded with his meal as the lock of his trunk clicked, and Mrs. Sherritt performed her self-imposed task.

In half an hour, the bureau and closet were neatly filled, and Roxana stood beside the empty dishes, a heavy silver napkin-ring in her hand. There was an inscription upon it, which read A. B. to T. C., but she did not glance at it.

" This is a good ring," she remarked, and slipped it upon the napkin beneath the eyes of its astonished owner, who, having enjoyed his meal, felt. more inclined for sleep than contention, and so submitted in silence.

" There 's a cane here," remarked Mrs. Sherritt, pointing to the head of the bed. " If you should want anythin' very bad and very sudden, rap with that and I 'll come. I think you 'd better go to bed and not try to do any more to-day." So saying, the housekeeper picked up the tray and left

the room, with a sense of having done her whole
duty.

"You waitin' here yet?" she remarked, observing Phyllis, patient and large-eyed, on the stairs.
"Don't you worry! Our boarder ain't goin' to
die *this* week. Come down to your supper."

CHAPTER IX.

A FEW days afterward, Miss Redmond looked in at the doctor's to see how Phyllis was faring. She remarked at once quite a new atmosphere in the house. The mournful anxiety which followed the doctor's departure was dispelled. Phyllis's face, as she answered the door-bell's summons, wore its old look of life.

"Roxana will be so glad to see you," she said, the stars showing in her eyes. "She needs comforting, and you always comfort her. You know we have a boarder."

"Yes, I know."

"It is wicked for me to laugh," said the girl, laughing nevertheless. "Poor Roxana!"

"Why, what is the matter?" asked Miss Redmond, walking out to the sitting-room, where Mrs. Sherritt, coming from the kitchen with a red and heated face, met her.

"If ever anybody was welcome!" exclaimed Roxana. "Sit down, Miss Rebecca, I 've got a minute to myself, I do believe. You know I 've got a man on my hands now."

"Yes; I called to see how you were getting on."

"Don't say one word!" exclaimed Mrs. Sher-

ritt, seating herself near her guest and lowering
her voice to a confidential huskiness. " He's been
sick ever since he got here, and what with his
havin' to eat five times a day. and needin' waitin'
on more or less, I'm about wore out. Phyllis has
done everythin' ·she could, but I don't want she
should bother around him, of course, and so I've
had to take the brunt of it."

" Dear, dear," said Miss Redmond uncomfortably. She could not help feeling somewhat responsible for Roxana's boarder. " You should have
sent for me. Let me see. His name is Chester,
I believe."

" Yes. He's pretty near drove me to makin'
poetry, it rhymes so handy with pester," responded
Roxana dejectedly. " He can't help bein' sick, I
suppose," she added reluctantly.

" Is he very — troublesome ? " asked Miss Rebecca; " I mean unpleasant — cross, you know."

" As two sticks," returned Mrs. Sherritt laconically. " Take a man gettin' up from a fever, and
headachy and fussy, and if it ain't a means o'
grace to take care of him, I don't know what is.
Mr. Terriss comes and stays a little while every day,
good man ; but, land ! he has his cup pretty full
at home. Phyllis has been to see his wife pretty
steady while I've been so shut up."

" I ought to go to see her, I suppose," said Rebecca slowly.

" Indeed, Miss Redmond, it's the kindest thing
you can do," replied Roxana heartily. " It needs a

housekeeper's head to look in there once in a while, to oversee things; but I 'm fixed just so I can't go. For instance, this afternoon I 've got to be here to watch the beef tea, and take it up at the right time."

"No reason why I should n't do it. I 'm not afraid of him," remarked Phyllis stoutly.

"'T ain't your work," said Roxana in a final manner.

Poor Rebecca saw her duty with sudden and disconcerting clearness. "I will stay and attend to it," she said, after a moment's pause.

"Miss Rebecca, you 're too good!" cried Roxana eagerly.

"Of course I will," said Miss Redmond, beginning to untie her bonnet strings. "Show me what is to be done."

Mrs. Sherritt sprang up with alacrity. Rebecca followed her into the kitchen and took her directions.

"I can stay two hours," she said, and Roxana, repeating her thanks, hurried away to put on her bonnet and shawl.

Miss Rebecca's heart fluttered as she heard the outer door slam. All Elise's careless suggestions as to the black-bearded ruffian into which her adopted brother might have developed returned to her now. "As cross as two sticks," Roxana had said.

"Phyllis," called Miss Redmond falteringly.

The girl came from the dining-room, and as she

appeared there sounded a mysterious thump, thump, thump! from the story above.

" What is that! " exclaimed Miss Redmond.

" Mr. Chester," sighed Phyllis.   " He wants something.   I wish you would let me go."

" No, indeed," replied Rebecca, with flushed cheeks.   Thump, thump, thump! came the summons again.

Miss Redmond hesitated no longer, but hurried up the staircase.   Only now it occurred to her that it might annoy the invalid to see a stranger appear in his room.   The thought was not an enlivening one, but it was too late to repent.   With the courage of desperation, she opened the closed door.

" Mr. Chester," she said, entering, " Mrs. Sherritt has gone out.   What may I do for you ? "

The sick man turned impatiently, scarcely glancing at his visitor.   " I should think you might see what to do for me," he replied.   " Lower that curtain so the sun will not lie directly upon my eyes."

Rebecca crossed the room and complied with the demand.   She watched the weary face as she drew the shade, in order to see when it was low enough.

" That will do, that will do," he cried brusquely. " It 's gloomy enough to lie here hour after hour without making it as dark as Egypt."

Rebecca went back to the door.   " I will bring you some beef tea in half an hour," she said.

" Humph ! " responded the sick man.

Miss Redmond stole downstairs and into the sitting-room, where Phyllis glanced up from some sewing she was at work upon. To her entire surprise, Miss Redmond sat down and began to laugh. She laughed until her delicate face was red up to the roots of her white hair, stifling the sound with one hand, and making hushing gestures to Phyllis with the other.

Phyllis smiled in sympathy. " Why, my dear, he is a perfect *bear*," whispered Miss Redmond rather hysterically.

" Poor Roxana ! It is a shame," said Phyllis. " I think her money is hardly earned. One good thing is, she is n't a bit afraid of him."

" And I am so relieved to find that I am not," said Rebecca, looking, nevertheless, very nervous. " When a person is ill enough to be in bed it would be ridiculous to be afraid of him, would n't it ? I believe, though, I will take his beef tea up a little before the time, for I am afraid I might get fidgety if I had long to think about it. Mr. Bellows, the young man who was visiting at our house lately, knows Mr. Chester " — Rebecca halted abruptly. Was she letting any cat out of the bag ? No, surely it was safe enough to speak of that. " He admires him," she continued. " It would be a good idea for him to come out and take care of him, I think."

" The young man who brought the flowers ? " asked Phyllis with interest.

" Yes ; such a good-natured boy ! I think he

would be an excellent contrast to Ursa Major upstairs."

Miss Redmond jumped up.   "Dear me! I
must hurry.   If he should thump again it would
confuse my wits so that I should be sure to do
something wrong."   She went into the kitchen, followed by Phyllis, and between them they prepared
the tray, looking like a couple of conspirators as,
with their heads together, they laughingly whispered their comments, apparently fearing that the
object of their remarks might hear through closed
doors.   At last Miss Redmond started forth on
her perilous mission, pursued by mischievous suggestions from Phyllis.   At the door of the sick-
room she composed her features with an effort,
and Terriss Chester, hearing her step and watching
the door with gloomy eyes, saw when she opened
it what looked to him a very pretty picture.   Rebecca's white hair brushed down in its accustomed
neat flat waves, her flushed cheeks, and her bright
eyes were far more pleasing than Roxana's colorless, drab effect.

"What is your name, if you please?" he demanded.

Rebecca smiled because she could not help it.

"I know you think me a surly fellow, and I
wish to ask your pardon in due form for speaking as I did when you came up before."   Chester
spoke in a grudging tone; but Rebecca detected
its weariness, and her kind heart pitied him.

"I am Miss Redmond," she said, "and I forgive you, certainly." She set the tray down on a stand by the bedside.

"I have had a wretched pain in my head ever since last evening," went on the sufferer, in gruff apology, "and as I have nothing pleasant to think about, the hours are interminable."

"Well, well," said Rebecca, completely at ease after this confession of weakness. "I know this is a tiresome experience for you, and you certainly must get very lonely. Can you help yourself to this bouillon, or shall I feed you?"

The gloomy eyes wore a gentler expression as the invalid replied, —

"I can help myself, thank you, Miss Redmond. Yes, it is lonely. I have wished many a time I had waited longer before leaving the hospital."

"You will be up soon," said Rebecca cheerily. "You must not be despondent. Shall I sit down a little while?"

Chester looked at her in surprise. This was a different class of good Samaritan from Mrs. Sherritt.

"You are very kind," he replied rather eagerly. "If you will sit down until I finish this, it will save your coming upstairs again." Rebecca complied. She was a pleasant figure in her soft black dress, and Chester appreciated it.

"I won't promise to hurry," he said, with the shadow of a smile. "You see my cousin, Mr. Terriss, makes the only variety in my day, and his visit was over at ten o'clock this morning, so

I have nothing to look forward to until to-morrow."

Rebecca smiled. "We have another mutual friend, Mr. Chester," she said. "His name is Bellows."

"Humph! The banker? He was my employer. I am very sorry I cannot say he *is* my employer."

"No; this is a young man. I think his father is a banker."

"Oh! Tony Bellows, perhaps."

"Yes. He was out here last week visiting my sister."

"Ah! I did not know he was in this vicinity."

"He has recently returned. He wishes very much to meet you again, so you will be likely to see him walk in here one of these days."

Chester smiled satirically. "His devotion to me will hardly bring him to Snowdon. Why should he talk of me to you, I wonder?"

To the speaker's amazement, his words sent a flood of color all over his visitor's face. "I — I" — she stammered. "Perhaps it was hearing that you were coming here to board. Of course it must have been that."

Chester regarded her with grave curiosity. What connection could jolly Tony have with this demure and gentle spinster? What attraction could it be that was strong enough to bring young Bellows to the quiet and countrified Snowdon? From what Chester had seen of the village and its inhabitants, it was the last place in the world upon which his vivacious friend would bestow so much as a passing glance; but why, above all, should Miss Redmond blush about him? The question baffled Chester. He went on sipping the steaming bouillon, while Rebecca plunged into speech to conceal her embarrassment.

"My sister knew him, that is my sister-in-law, Mrs. Redmond, when he was a child, and — he came out to see her."

"Ah?" responded Chester.

"Would n't you like me to read you something?" continued Miss Redmond, rising and going to a table covered with books, and wishing heartily that she need not have so guilty a feeling concerning Elise's secret.

"Would you really be so kind?" said Chester eagerly. "But why should I take your time?"

"I am entirely willing. I promised Mrs. Sherritt to remain until her return, and I would as lief read as do anything."

Half an hour later, Roxana returned. Phyllis beckoned her into the sitting-room.

"Where 's Miss Rebecca?" asked Mrs. Sherritt.

"I think we shall never see her more," replied Phyllis. "She entered the lion's den with the beef tea fully an hour ago, and has not emerged. I think he has taken her for dessert."

Roxana smiled. "She 's a lion tamer, that 's what she is. I expect nothin' else but what she 's makin' that poor fellow have the best time he 's known in a good while."

"Poor fellow! I did not know you felt any sympathy for him."

"I'm perfectly just," responded Roxana, unpinning her shawl. "He can't help bein' a man and not havin' any self-control, and he's havin' an awful slow time of it. He needs a missionary. All men do; and Miss Rebecca's a home missionary."

"Very well. I think you had better see if she has not shared the fate of that brother in Timbuctoo, who was eaten up and his hymn-book, too. She was frightened when she went upstairs."

"Fiddlesticks!" exclaimed Roxana, with the usual toss of her head. "Miss Rebecca's plucky enough when it comes to the point; but I've just left a poor worn-out woman, I tell you."

"Yes. Do you know, Roxana," Phyllis lowered her voice, "Mrs. Terriss isn't exactly a saint."

"Did you ever think," replied Mrs. Sherritt tartly, "whether it would turn you into a saint to sit in one spot day in and day out, alone half the time?"

"I do not believe it would make me snap at my husband, if he was Mr. Terriss," returned Phyllis slowly. "She did yesterday when I was there."

"Well, you've no call to judge her. Of course, she is only human."

"I do not wish to judge her. It disappointed me, that is all."

Roxana sighed. "You might as well learn early in life that it's a great mistake to set up human idols. Poor feeble human nature is terrible apt to disappoint anybody that expects too much of it."

Phyllis smiled. "It makes considerable difference to you whether an invalid is a man or a woman, I notice, when it comes to a question of indulgence."

"Maybe," returned Roxana noncommittally. "At any rate, I must let Miss Rebecca off now."

She left the room, and shortly returned, holding up both hands and laughing.

"She's tamed him, sure enough," she announced. "He's as pleasant as a lamb, and she's a readin' to him. She says she'll soon be through, and then she'll come down. As true as I live, he looks a great deal better. Now, if Miss Rebecca'll just cure him up for us, won't we be everlastin'ly obliged to her?"

CHAPTER X

WHETHER or not the fact was entirely due to Miss Rebecca's kind offices, it proved that that was the last day Mrs. Sherritt's boarder spent in his bed.

He dressed each morning and sat in Dr. Joy's armchair, and was able to enjoy the sunshine at his southern windows and the spring green of the large maple which grew close by. The busy minister came less regularly to see him, considering the need less, and the days, broken only by Roxana's business-like visits, were very long. Chester cast affectionate glances at certain painting paraphernalia, and wondered when his hand would be steady enough to hold the brush. Not quite yet, at any rate. In this tedious season, it was an unmixed pleasure to him that one day Miss Rebecca's prognostications were fulfilled, and Tony Bellows appeared at the door of his room.

Tony's liking for his eccentric acquaintance was sincere; still, it might not have led him to set aside a day, and actually to journey to Snowdon, for the sole purpose of beholding Chester's countenance; but, taken in connection with another visit to Mrs. Redmond, the idea was full of attraction. Also, he had not forgotten the pretty girl in the black dress, whose feelings he had hurt. He knew that Terriss was boarding in the same house with her. Altogether, the thought of paying him a visit was a pleasing one. He concluded, upon arriving at Snowdon, to go directly to the doctor's house. He had an uneasy sense that Elise would tease him less if, when he presented himself at her door, his visit to Chester was an accomplished fact.

Phyllis, answering the door-bell, was startled to behold the immaculate form of the stranger.

" The flower man," thought she.

" The Flower girl," thought he, and he raised his hat and smiled in his most sunshiny fashion.

Phyllis colored in a very satisfactory and becoming manner.

" Won't you walk in, Mr. Bellows?" she asked politely.

" I am so delighted to see you, Miss Flower," said Tony, his hat in one hand and a florist's box, moderate in size this time, in the other.

" Thank you," said Phyllis. " Oh, I understand — you have come to see Mr. Chester."

" I do want to see him, yes ; but — but — I have a few flowers here for him, and I thought perhaps you " —

" Yes, I will," said Phyllis with alacrity, as he paused. " Come into the parlor."

" Can I see you fix them? I would like to so much," said Tony.

" Certainly. I will bring the bowls and water

here." Bellows sat down and opened the box, while Phyllis brought the pitcher and vases. A sort of elation had taken possession of her at the first sight of the visitor. He was to her a glimpse outside the monotony of her life, a being associated with a charmed mingling of luxurious roses and Mrs. Redmond's magnificence, yet in himself not in the least frightful or overwhelming.

She drew forward a table, and they sat one on each side of it. Tony was relieved to see the bright expression of her face, and to know that she had forgiven him his unfortunate remark.

" You like flowers very much, " she said, looking across the mass of blossoms at him.

" And so do you, of course," he answered.

" Ah! " she exclaimed. " There are some roses like mine — those you gave me, you know."

" Yes; La France. You like that rose particularly ? "

"I think they must be the loveliest in the world." Phyllis lifted one caressingly. " They suit me better than I suit them."

" What do you mean by that ? "

" I can scarcely tell. I suppose I am too plain a person for them. Mrs. Redmond is the right sort to have them."

" Yes; what a queen she is ! " burst forth Tony impulsively. " The queen of flowers is hers by right."

Phyllis laid the rose down quickly.

Tony was the simplest of mankind, but his twenty-four years had educated him in certain lines of worldly wisdom.

"But she cannot have that," he added hastily. "That is for you."

"I am sure you brought them all for Mr. Chester," said Phyllis, with her demurest air.

"No, indeed. You will hurt my feelings if you will not accept one bud."

Upon this, delivered with a beseeching glance, Phyllis relented.

Roxana, hearing voices and stepping to the parlor door, stopped in amazement. On one side of a flower-laden table sat Phyllis, holding a deep pink rose to her lips and looking into the eyes of a blonde young man on the other side of the narrow table, who returned her gaze devotedly.

The girl heard her and turned. "Come in, Roxana," she said pleasantly. "Mr. Bellows this is my — this is Mrs. Sherritt."

Roxana came slowly forward. Tony rose and made her a low bow, which would have graced a formal drawing-room. Mrs. Sherritt looked at him sharply and nodded slightly.

"Mr. Bellows has come to visit Mr. Chester," explained Phyllis.

"I want to know!" said Roxana dryly. "It don't look much like it," she thought; then she added aloud, "Them are sightly blooms."

"Are n't they beautiful? I am going to put them in water for Mr. Bellows to carry up."

"Won't you take a rose, Mrs. Sherritt?" asked Tony, with his usual prompt cordiality.

" Well, if there 's one o' them pinks to spare," said Roxana, taking a carnation. " It does seem good to have one this time o' year."

Mr. Bellows might have tried in vain a long time, on any other line, to bring a smile to the housekeeper's thin lips, but she loved flowers with an ardor equal to his own, and left the room well pleased, inhaling the odor of her spicy blossom.

" Do you know," said Phyllis naively, while her busy fingers continued their work, " I was afraid when I saw you that perhaps you had come to see me. I do not know how to receive calls from young men."

" Indeed ! "

" No, we do not have any in Snowdon. Boys are born here, of course, but as soon as they can walk alone they leave town."

" How disagreeable for the girls ! "

" Horrid," admitted Phyllis frankly.

" Yet you would n't be glad to let me call on you ? "

" Not for anything in the world! I should n't know what to say. Nothing ever happens to me to talk about, and we do not know any of the same people."

" Mrs. Redmond ? " suggested Tony, amused.

Phyllis looked up at him and shook her head.

" No, indeed. I called upon her before — before I lost Uncle Doctor, and only yesterday she called upon me. We do not know each other at all."

"Why, that is strange! Ladies usually become acquainted quickly in the country."

Phyllis continued to shake her pretty head emphatically. "She petrifies me. I am mortally afraid of her."

"Are you?" said Tony eagerly. "So am I. Shake hands on it." He reached across the table, and Phyllis put her brown hand into his white one.

"You see she is so — she's such a magnificent woman, and she has such a — such a horrid way of looking thoughtful when she smiles at you," said Phyllis, "as though she understood you, and you amused her."

"Precisely," said Tony, beaming. "You have described it exactly. Shake hands again."

Phyllis gave her hand more reluctantly this time. "Is it Bostonian to shake hands so much?" she inquired.

"No. I am recently from the West, and it is a habit there, and I fell into it."

"Well, that is enough," said Phyllis demurely, withdrawing her hand. "Wait until we meet in the West. There! will the flowers do now?"

"Yes, indeed. Chester will be as much obliged as I am."

"No doubt," returned Phyllis, with a droll glance. "Don't you think his name lacks one syllable? He really should be called Chesterfield; but excuse me, he is your friend."

"Why, Miss Flower," said Tony, puzzled, "he is really a fine fellow, — a talented fellow."

" No doubt ; but the trouble is the same with all your friends : they frighten me."

" I don't, do I ? "

" Not a bit, because you have n't called on me, you know. I met Mr. Chester the evening he came, and I really do not know him, because he has been ill ever since, and I have not seen him ; but rumors of his amiable disposition and suave manners have reached me through those who have had the pleasure of taking care of him."

" Say, Miss Flower," said Tony, grinning at the mischievous face, " you are downright wicked, you know. How can you be sure I sha'n't tell Chester what you say ? "

Phyllis laughed. " I am not in the least afraid of you, remember. Now, shall I show you the way ? "

" Yes, if you are positively determined not to receive a call from me."

" I am, positively. I will take one vase and you the other. This way, please."

Phyllis preceded him upstairs, and arriving at the boarder's door, knocked.

A curt, deep " Come in " responded.

" It is a good thing for you that you have a peace-offering," whispered Phyllis. " Here, take the other bowl. You will want all the sweetness at your command."

" Then won't you " — began Tony ; but Phyllis turned the handle and then fled.

Terriss Chester, reticent, unsocial, disappointed

man that he was, had never more than tolerated the friendship of his employer's son; but, at the present moment, the sight of Tony's genial countenance was an unmixed pleasure.

" Why, Tony, my boy ! " he exclaimed. " Are you personating spring? I am glad to see you. Set down those flowers and give me your hand. This is extremely friendly of you, for, to tell you a secret, the days in Snowdon are forty-eight hours long."

"It seems to me a pleasant old place," said Tony, shaking hands heartily. " There are some drives about here worth seeing."

"Yes, yes, no doubt; and I hope I shall soon get out; but, for the present, the advantages of Snowdon are for me pretty much the advantages of any other bedroom, where a severe specimen of womanhood dispenses food to me five times a day."

" Yes, I met the severe specimen downstairs ; but there is another specimen here, a girl, — an awfully pretty girl."

Chester snapped his fingers. " The pretty girl, as well as the drives, is a pleasure deferred; but you have a friend here who has come twice to read to me. *She* is a girl that I appreciate. To be sure, her hair is white, but I am in love with her. Did you bring those flowers for me ? "

" Of course I did."

" Thank you. Well, I would pass half of them along to Miss Redmond, if I knew how to get them to her."

"To Miss Redmond? Why, I will take them. I was going there anyway."

"Oh, you were!" said Chester, eyeing his guest with lazy curiosity, and remembering Rebecca's incomprehensible blush.

The mate to it stole up over Tony's face. "Of course; I should not think of coming to Snowdon without calling at Beech Knoll."

"You are my rival, I am afraid," remarked Chester.

Tony shook his head. He was feeling deeply the burden of Elise's command. "It was kind of Miss Redmond to visit you," he said. "You look rather thin, but a few weeks of this country air will fix you all right."

"I hope so. I have a cousin here, and to-morrow, when he comes, I shall go downstairs again. I hope I am about through with this sort of thing. Who is it you visit at Beech Knoll, Tony?"

"Oh, all of them."

"Yes, I understand; but who are 'all of them'? What country maiden are you electrifying with your charms?" ·

"Not a single maiden!" replied Tony earnestly. "Miss Redmond is the only maiden there."

"Then what is all this blushing about?" demanded Chester, a gleam of amusement lighting his eyes.

Tony laughed. "Oh, there must be a deep and dark mystery about it, of course!" he said desperately. "When you get well enough, I will take you up there to express your thanks to Miss Rebecca, and then you can ferret it out."

"Tony, you have a bad conscience — but never mind. I happen to have learned that there is a widow at Beech Knoll. The faithful and severe Mrs. Sherritt has vouchsafed that information. Your candid face informs me that she is young. Very well, my boy, you have money enough for both, and I only hope your father won't forbid the banns."

Tony smiled. "This is a nice way to treat a fellow that has come all the way from Boston to see you," he remarked.

"I appreciate it, Tony. Upon my word I do. I am dreading the moment when you will spring up, take my flowers, and say you must be off for Beech Knoll. I adore Miss Redmond, but I don't think I can let you take the roses. It has just occurred to me that I will paint them. I believe I can do it, now. Do you see what a pretty vista I get from this window? I am going to make a sketch of that some day, too."

"Wait till you see the vistas at Beech Knoll!" exclaimed Tony enthusiastically.

Chester gave him his smiling, satirical glance.

"I will try to be patient," he replied; and then he proceeded to ask his friend concerning affairs in the city.

CHAPTER XI.

TIME did not yet begin to drag for the new mistress of Beech Knoll. She rode and drove a great deal. She watched the leaves unfold on her fine old trees. She held consultations with her gardener, and watched him carry out her plans. She imbibed greater health and beauty daily from the crisp air and sunshine, and Rebecca looked on well pleased. Elise's interest in her new home bade fair to outlast the spring.

She was out-of-doors when Tony walked into the grounds on his way from seeing Terriss Chester, and she came to meet him, a smile on her face and in her gray eyes. Tony told himself again that she was the loveliest woman he had ever seen.

"You see I did n't dare to wait until you sent for me," he explained. "I was afraid you might forget."

"You are always welcome," was the gracious rejoinder; "and you have brought me some more flowers, you kind boy."

"No, I — you see I wanted to bring some to Chester, and so " —

"Ah, certainly," said Elise, with a little nod. "You are on your way to him?"

"No, I have been there. He sent these by me" —

"Tony!" Elise stopped and looked at him accusingly. "Have you betrayed me?"

"No, no; upon honor. Chester sent these to Miss Redmond," was the eager response.

Elise broke into a gay laugh.

"She deserves them. It was very kind of him. You did not speak of me to him?"

"Not once; and you have no idea how hard it was with him catechising me all the time."

"Good boy; but why should he catechise you?"

"He's so broken up over Miss Redmond," exclaimed Tony, wiping his brow, heated by his anxiety to establish his innocence.

Elise laughed again. "I long to see Rebecca's face when she hears of it. Let us go in and tell her."

Tony, much relieved, followed her quickened steps into the sunny sitting-room, where Miss Redmond was reading.

"Rebecca, here is Mr. Bellows."

Miss Redmond rose to greet the young man, who smilingly placed the box in her hands.

"Did you know you had an admirer in town?" asked Elise. "Shame upon you for keeping it from me."

Miss Redmond grew crimson, and looked at the speaker with startled eyes.

"Open your box. Here, let me help you. See, lilies of the valley, carnations, heliotrope, ferns. He is generous."

"What do you mean, you children?" asked Miss Redmond.

"They are for you," said Tony, "with the regards of Mr. Terriss Chester."

Miss Rebecca smiled and grew grave. "How could the poor fellow get them?"

"This poor fellow brought them to him, of course," laughed Elise. "Everybody imposes upon Tony."

"I am very much obliged to you both," said Miss Rebecca. "I will put them in water on this table, where I can enjoy them all the time. How is Mr. Chester to-day?"

"He seems to be improving. He expects to go downstairs to-morrow. I do hope he will be able to get out-of-doors soon; then he will get well, of course. I hope some one will take him to drive. He says he has a cousin here."

Rebecca shook her head. "Mr. Terriss has no horse, and I am afraid very little money to hire one."

Elise looked from one to the other with the reflective, amused expression which Phyllis found so disconcerting.

"If you will drive my ponies, Rebecca, they are at your friend's service," she remarked presently.

"Elise, you know I could never do it in the world," returned Rebecca, with evident trepidation.

" If you would let *me* do it some day, Mrs. Redmond," suggested Tony.

" Certainly. To-morrow, if you like. I suppose your pressing business engagements would permit you to remain in Snowdon over night for such a charitable purpose ? "

" Now what are you always chaffing me about business for ? " demanded Tony, much aggrieved.

" Because you are so amusingly ornamental, *Tonychen.*"

" Well, I give you warning that I am going to be ornamental until the fall. There is n't any chance to begin to be useful until then. Here is summer coming on so, and I have accepted an invitation to Newport for August."

" Your reasons are unimpeachable, my child."

" I object to being called your child, and if this is all you have " —

" Tony, Tony, your face is of a color which makes your hair look very yellow, almost gaudy by contrast. Now calm right down, and tell me if you do not think I am admirable to put my carriage at the disposal of a man who abhors me, or would if he knew who I am ? "

" He would n't. That is all nonsense," said Tony sulkily. " I have a mind to tell him."

" If you do, *Tonychen,*" replied Elise dispassionately, " I will never speak to you again, and that is the literal truth. I do not choose that Mr. Chester shall be the crumpled roseleaf in my sweet summer. Fate insisted upon his coming to Snowdon, and I will even play the good Samaritan and help him to get well; but that is all."

"Perhaps I have blundered, then," said Tony, his eyes widening as a new, appalling thought struck him. "I promised to bring him to Beech Knoll to see Miss Redmond and the vistas."

"The what?"

"The vistas. He is an artist, you know."

"An artist and a cashier in a bank?"

"Why, even an artist must eat," observed Tony.

"Never mind," said Mrs. Redmond, with unexpected graciousness. "You may bring him some time," and she lowered her eyes this time as she smiled at some thought. "You will stay, Tony?"

"Oh, you know I will, as long as you will let me," was the impatient answer. "I saw Miss Flower again to-day," he added. "I had not promised not to speak of you to her, you know."

"You did not find that the subject interested her, I am sure," replied Elise. "I cannot get on with fair Phyllis."

"You frighten her," exclaimed Tony.

Mrs. Redmond smiled skeptically.

"You do really. She said so," continued Tony earnestly.

"I am afraid she is an affected little maiden, if she said that," returned Elise.

"That she is not," remarked Miss Redmond heartily.

"Oh, I am sure she is not," echoed Tony.

"Well, if you are sure of it, Tony, it must be

that she is not. I am sure no girl could deceive you," said Mrs. Redmond.

"Phyllis is a very nice girl," said Miss Rebecca soberly, "and a very dull life she has of it. Still she knows of nothing different, so perhaps it is not marvelous that she endures it well. I have asked her to come here some day. I am sure she would enjoy walking by the river and seeing the trees in their new dresses."

"Yes," said Elise, "and if she wished, she could take a ride. Her uncle said she rode. Ask her to come and spend the day with you."

Rebecca looked up, well pleased. "Thank you," she returned, "that is what I should like to do."

Mrs. Redmond frowned at her smilingly. "You waited for my permission, you foolish Rebecca? You know that is not treating me fairly. It is as much your home as mine. I will try not to frighten your friend more than my naturally terrible aspect makes necessary."

"Come, now," said Tony, "you are all wrong. She admires you immensely and all that. It is because of that" —

"Wait, wait, Tony, you are growing metaphysical. You will get beyond your depth in a minute more. We are wasting time this beautiful weather. Let us go and have a game of tennis."

The following day was a red-letter one to Mrs. Sherritt, for her boarder came downstairs. Moreover, he came without assistance from any one, and was so much encouraged as to his condition

that Phyllis told herself he looked positively genial when he came into the parlor where she was
awaiting him.

"Happy to see you again, Miss Flower," he
said cheerfully.

"I congratulate you on getting out of that room;
you must be very tired of it."

"I am, heartily, and am sure Mrs. Sherritt is
quite as much so."

"You will be getting as far as my house one of
these days," observed Mr. Terriss, who had followed him into the parlor. "My wife will be
pleased to make your acquaintance."

"And I to make hers. I feel ashamed to chafe
so at a short imprisonment, when I think of her
fate."

"It is indeed a hard one," said the minister
quietly, that subtle cloud falling over his face
which always settled there when he mentioned his
wife outside her presence. "Well, I will leave
you now, Terriss. I hope this is the beginning of
the end, and that you will commence to enjoy life
again. Good-by, Phyllis. What a sweet rose you
have there! I noticed it the instant I entered the
room."

"Isn't it beautiful? It is for you, Mr. Terriss."
The girl started up and took the flower from the
vase. The minister demurred, but Phyllis insisted, and he was forced to accept.

"Thank you; I will take it home to Mrs. Terriss."

"No," returned Phyllis decidedly; "it is for you." She came close to him and drew the stem through his buttonhole, and he smiled.

"You make me look like a gay young man."

"I should like to. Now promise me that when you get home you will put it on your desk and not on Mrs. Terriss' table."

"Why, Phyllis" —

"No, no. Variety is the spice of life. Promise!"

"Well, I promise," said the minister, half laughing, yet seeing himself in fancy enter his house in a secret and guilty manner, and tiptoe up the stairs to keep that lightly demanded promise. It gave him an unwelcome glimpse of the fact that he was the object of feeble tyranny, and his thoughts on the homeward walk were less cheerful than usual, in spite of the fragrant breath of his rose.

Entering his front door quietly, he was about to carry out his programme, when a sound of choking and sobbing in his wife's room startled him.

Hurrying down the narrow corridor, he threw open the door, and a strange sight met his eyes. His wife was convulsively weeping, her body half supported in Rebecca Redmond's arms, while Lucindy Bates, open-mouthed, stood by, wringing her hands helplessly.

"Your husband has come, Mrs. Terriss," said Rebecca. "Try to control yourself for his sake."

"O Philip, Philip!" cried the invalid hysterically. "Oh, how I suffer, how I suffer!" and she flung herself out of Rebecca's arms into those of her husband, who had knelt on her other side.

The minister looked into Rebecca's eyes for explanation, but Miss Rebecca shook her head in despair. She had seemed on the eve of succeeding in calming Mrs. Terriss before her husband appeared; now the cries grew to shrieks, and the uncontrolled woman stiffened throughout her body.

"You can stop this, Lily, and you must. It will make you ill," said the minister sternly.

"She's a goin' to faint, sir," said Lucindy excitedly, as Mrs. Terriss set her teeth and closed her eyes. "When they holler it kind o' flustrates me, but if she'll faint, a tumbler o' cold water right in the face is just like magic."

"Don't you dare," gasped the sufferer, opening her eyes and fixing them wildly upon the handmaid, who suddenly set down the goblet she had raised.

"That is right, Lily. Control yourself," said the minister.

"Oh, I will, I will," moaned his wife. "Miss Redmond has been so kind, so kind to me. Thank her, Philip."

"I do thank her," said the minister, low and gravely, not looking at Rebecca.

Her face was as grave as his own. "I will go now," she said, rising quietly. "Mrs. Terriss will want to rest."

"Tell him first, tell Philip first," said the latter, hrowing her arm over her husband's shoulder.

"I am not sure that I fully understand,' said Rebecca, and her calm voice was soothing to hear after the querulous one of the invalid. "Your wife sent for young Dr. Ramsey, and he came, and during their talk he said — I did not get here until he was leaving, but I understood from Mrs. Terriss that he underrated her illness in some way."

Mrs. Terriss raised her head with surprising energy. "He said that he could not discover that there was anything very wrong with me!" she exclaimed.

Mr. Terriss was silent, the grave, harassed look still on his face.

"Dr. Ramsey is rather young and inexperienced," he said.

"So I told him. I drove him away, — I drove him away, and I am glad I did." Her voice trembled with excitement.

"Do not talk of it now," said Mr. Terriss firmly. "I thank you very much, Miss Redmond. Do not let us detain you any longer." He raised his eyes to hers for one moment, then lowered them again to his wife's trembling form.

Miss Rebecca carried a heavy heart with her down the pleasant street. She was puzzled, too, and doubtful as to her duty.

A smart rattle of horses' hoofs and a bright voice interrupted her troubled reverie.

"Good-morning again, Miss Rebecca," cried Mr. Bellows, stopping his team beside her. "Are you going anywhere that I can take you? I am very generous with Mrs. Redmond's horses."

" My destination is the same as yours," replied Rebecca. " I like walking, but I do not mind driving when it is so easy as this."

Tony jumped out and helped her in, and in a few minutes they drew up before Phyllis's door.

Phyllis herself and Terriss Chester saw the equipage from the parlor window.

" Mrs. Redmond's carriage," said Phyllis, her eyes sparkling. " Miss Rebecca does not usually come in such style."

" Mr. Bellows is her coachman, I see," remarked Chester. " He must be quite intimate at Beech Knoll."

" Yes, he visits there often," returned Phyllis, watching while Tony tied the horses, and then walked beside Miss Rebecca up the path.

" Why, Mr. Chester, I am glad to see this," said Miss Redmond as she entered the parlor. She shook hands heartily with Terriss, who rose to greet her. " I enjoyed the flowers you sent me so much. I am not accustomed to such pretty attentions from young men."

" You mean you will not receive them," said Tony, turning from his cordial greeting to Phyllis. " She tried to run away from me this morning, but I caught up with her on the street. Chester, I have come to take you driving behind the best little team between here and Boston."

" Why, thank you; I had not thought of going out so soon."

"Of course you had n't. You did n't know what was in store for you. Mrs. Redmond has been kind enough to lend me her carriage for the purpose, and it will do you all the good in the world."

"Oh, it will, I am sure," said Phyllis, so earnestly that Mr. Bellows wished circumstances required him to extend the invitation to the family in turn.

"I advise you to go. The air is not chilly," added Miss Redmond.

"I want to go badly enough," said Chester, "but I am as fidgety as an old woman when I think of being possibly put back to bed. Will you come and read to me, if I am, Miss Redmond?"

Rebecca promised, so Chester went. Phyllis watched them drive away.

"How nice it looks," she said, sighing. "O Miss Rebecca, why can't we all be rich?"

"We all may be in some direction," replied Miss Redmond.

"You mean something moral, I know," pouted Phyllis. "I do not want to be rich in contentment and those things; I want real bad riches, horses and carriages, and new dresses."

Miss Redmond smiled. "You make me doubtful whether I ought to do the errand I came to do."

"What is that?" said Phyllis, turning toward her eagerly.

" I came to ask you to spend a day with me next week; but you will see carriages and horses, will ride a horse if you choose, and you may see new dresses. Are you better off not to see these things?"

" I do not care whether I am or not. I shall come, if you ask me."

" I never thought you were at all a discontented child," said Miss Rebecca thoughtfully. " You have such health, and have had such a sensible bringing up. Why should you not be happy every minute? To be sure, your life is quiet."

Phyllis shook her head. She could not explain how Mrs. Redmond and her belongings, including her guest and his roses, had opened to her vision a new world of possibilities.

" I hope you will invite me, Miss Rebecca," she said naively.

" Well, I do, child. Come next Wednesday. Where is Roxana?"

" In the kitchen. Shall I call her?"

" No. I will go to her."

Roxana was peeling potatoes at the sink when Miss Rebecca went in.

" Don't let me disturb you, Roxana," she said, drawing a chair into a convenient position and sitting down. " I went in to see Mrs. Terriss this morning."

" I thank you, Miss Rebecca; I take that as a favor to myself," said Roxana earnestly. " What's the news? Any?"

" The young doctor had been there, Dr. Ramsey, and he said something to displease her. When I arrived, he was just going away; and as soon as she saw me, the poor lady broke down completely in hysterics."

Roxana washed a large potato vigorously. " Well, I s'pose that young whipper-snapper hain't got good sense yet. Most likely he thinks he's goin' to regulate the whole medical profession. If anybody's excusable for bein' hysteriky, it's a woman fixed just the way Mrs. Terriss is, that can't hardly move."

" Roxana," Miss Redmond glanced toward the door and lowered her voice, " the circumstance which is so strange that I scarcely know whether or not to speak of it to you is that when I entered Mrs. Terriss' room, she was standing as erect as you are this moment, by the mantelpiece, on the other side of the room from her chair."

Roxana paused, and looked full into the eyes of her companion. " That young greenhorn must have carried her across. She can't move her limbs. Mr. Terriss carries her around like a baby."

" So I have heard," replied Miss Rebecca, slowly ; " but she walked back to her chair beside me, scarcely leaning on the arm I gave her."

Roxana stared in silence a moment, then she took her hands out of the water, and crossing to the door that led to the dining-room closed it, her eyes round with amazement.

" Does Lucindy know this ? " she asked, coming back.

" No; Mrs. Terriss made very little noise until after she was in her chair again. Then the girl came in."   -

" Well," said Roxana, sitting down, " I am beat."

" What shall we do ? " said Miss Rebecca. " Something must be done."

" Land o' liberty, you don't s'pose she *likes* to set there till she most takes root, do you ? What on earth is the explanation of it ? "

" I think she must have come to believe that she is helpless. There have been such cases, you know."

" Well, my way would be to go in there and say, ' You can walk all right, if you only think so, Mrs. Terriss. Come out and see what a good sunny kitchen you 've got.' "

Miss Rebecca sighed. " She would only be as angry with you as she is with Dr. Ramsey, who, I think, must be very simple or else a genius."

" Well, he ain't any genius, just put that *down ;* but he 's put me in a muddle, I know that. I can't do for Mrs. Terriss and feel as I have done."

" Roxana," said Miss Rebecca earnestly, " I have not told you this to set you against her. Think how terribly she is to be pitied in her delusion. We must help her, if we can. I doubt if, at this moment, she realizes that I saw her outside her chair. I *must* help her, for her own and her husband's sake. It must be my work, else why was I led in at that moment to see her? O Roxana, I dread it. Help me to the best way. Help me to think it out;" and to Mrs. Sherritt's consternation Miss Redmond bowed her head on the edge of the sink, and burst into tears.

CHAPTER XII

A GOLDEN MORNING.

WITH the ability to come and go as he would, even within the narrow limits of the house and dooryard, life became again a thing worth having to Terriss Chester. He could read, he could paint, he could walk until his slender stock of strength was consumed, and then he could sleep for an hour; and he began to feel the slow return of his old energy.

" He does seem to have a realizin' sense o' the trouble I've took for him," Roxana confided to Phyllis, "and that's more than most men would feel; but I just long for the dear, happy time when he can go off to the minister's and stay, say half a day. A man around the house all the time always was awful wearin' to me."

" You will not have it to bear long," said Phyllis. " He has come straight up since the drive with Mr. Bellows, and there is a look in his eyes when he stands at the window or on the steps like that of a wild creature in a cage. When he can escape, he will go. He has been asking me all about the walks near here, and the woods. How lovely it must be to know how to sketch as he does ! "

"But laws," said Roxana prosaically, "how his paints smell! I will say, though, them dark red roses he did look just as though you could pick 'em right up, and it's a good thing he can amuse himself that way just now, secin' he can't knit."

Phyllis laughed. The picture of their deep-voiced, gloomy-eyed boarder engaged in knitting was particularly amusing; but she did not reply. It was Wednesday morning, and she was hurrying to get ready for the anticipated day at Beech Knoll. She suddenly grew solemn as she stood before the glass. "Roxana, can't I have a new dress?" she asked, studying her reflection.

Mrs. Sherritt paused, arms akimbo. "What's the matter with that one?" she asked kindly. "Nice, good, gray silk. 'T ain't every girl o' your age has a silk dress, and that was your mother's best."

"Isn't it too old for me, or something?" returned the girl. "I think I look better in my calicoes; and my hat is a fright compared to Mrs. Redmond's."

"I like your looks first-rate," said Roxana comfortingly. "Don't you fret. Mrs. Redmond has style and fashion; but you've got a whole row o' great-grandmothers."

"I wonder if she would exchange," remarked Phyllis audaciously. "I would give a great-grandmother apiece for a bonnet and dress like the ones she wore here."

"Phyllis Flower, I'm surprised at you," exclaimed Roxana, horrified.

The girl ran to her and threw her arms around her neck. " What is the matter with me ? " she murmured. " I used to be the most careless, contented creature in the world, and now there is a buzz of longings all through my head, and I am always expecting something, I do not know what."

Roxana looked at her gravely, then took her hand and led her across the room to where hung a photograph of Dr. Joy.

" All those feelin's are ungrateful to *him*, Phyllis," she said quietly, " and they ain't the best part o' your nature, either. He did his best to train your mind, and I 've done mine to make your body healthy and useful. Don't tell me you ain't enough of a person to overcome this restlessness you tell about. It has n't got any great hold over you yet, and do you nip it now, right in the bud."

Phyllis stood silent and flushing. " I do not know where to begin to nip," she said at last.

" Begin whenever you feel discontented," returned Roxana. " If you once began to count your blessin's, you would be surprised. Of all things on earth, don't be mean. It 's mean to envy, it 's mean to grumble, it 's mean to feel cast down 'cause somebody else is set up. Take Miss Rebecca, a disappointed, tried woman, if ever there was one. Supposin' she looked long-faced because her lot is different from that sister-in-law's. The best thing I know about Mrs. Redmond is the way Miss Rebecca seems to be fond of her. She may be a very good woman, but I mistrust all her

fine doin's have sort of upset you. Now you're
goin' there to-day. Do you go *armed*. Supposin'
you ain't dressed in the latest style. You'll appear better behaved, if you don't think about it
and don't feel bad about it. 'T ain't anythin' to
feel bad about. You are a good-lookin' girl, Phyllis, and you know how to talk and behave, and
you're goin', because you are invited, to see Miss
Rebecca. There's one thought that'll always give
a person meekness and dignity both. It is this:
I am just as dear to the Almighty Father of us all
as anybody else, and I ain't any dearer to Him
than everybody else. When you see Mrs. Redmond this mornin', you think o' that, and it'll lift
your mind right up off your hat."

Mrs. Sherritt was unusually stirred, and it was
long after Phyllis had set forth on her walk before her mind settled to its ordinary calm.

Things were slipping out of their accustomed
grooves and running wild. Mrs. Terriss either
self-deceived or a hypocrite, and Phyllis — what
was the matter with Phyllis? Would Roxana
have sufficient penetration and worldly wisdom to
meet and control the girl under new conditions?

She went with a mind distrait to her boarder's
room, carrying the beaten egg she gave him in the
middle of the morning, into which he always poured
a spoonful of some liquid from a flask, while Mrs.
Sherritt averted her eyes.

He looked up from his book as she came in.
"This is the last time you must do this," he said.

"I will come to the table for my meals hereafter, and take only the same number as other people. I just saw Miss Phyllis pass out of the gate."

"Yes. She has gone to spend the day with Miss Rebecca. It is a great treat for her."

"Miss Rebecca appears to be a universal favorite," replied Terriss.

"Yes, yes," said Roxana rather abstractedly. "Miss Rebecca can stand anythin', prosperity or adversity. She was just the same in the old days when money was close, as she is now when it's plenty."

"She has inherited property?"

"No, her brother married it, and then died, and she lives with the widow. You haven't seen the widow?"

"No, but I hope some time to see her and thank her for the pleasant drive I owe her. Do you like that little rose-piece, Mrs. Sherritt?" for Roxana had absently taken up the water-color as she stood, one hand on her hip.

"Well, I did yesterday when it was pinned up across the room," she returned; "but now, close to, why they might be anythin'. I guess you hain't had lessons very long, have you?"

Chester gave a sudden smile. "I was going to ask you to accept it, if it took your fancy," he said.

Roxana looked pleased, but puzzled. "Well, let me put it up where it was yesterday and see," she remarked, suiting the action to the word and then retreating from the sketch, while the artist looked on, highly entertained.

"There, there, now," she exclaimed, keeping her eyes fixed on the flowers, "a body can most begin to smell 'em. I do say it's clever of you to give it to me," and she walked back and took down the sketch, which she held by one corner while she continued : "You was speakin' o' Mrs. Redmond. You must n't repeat it, Mr. Chester, if I tell you somethin'. That woman or girl, whichever you've a mind to call her, —'sometimes she seems about eighteen and again she's the grand lady, — well, she's made me a great deal o' trouble. I want to ask you what may seem a queer question ; but you're a city man, and you most likely know. I want to ask you how Phyllis looked to you as she went out o' the gate."

Mr. Chester was puzzled. "I could not see her face."

"No matter about her face. What did you think of her general looks, — her clothes ?"

"Mrs. Sherritt," smiling now, grimly, "I am the last man in the world to know anything about a lady's dress."

"Could n't you even tell if she looked — well, in the style, as people call it ? "

"No," said Terriss promptly, "she did not look in the style."

Roxana's face, which had been unconsciously wistful, fell.

"Could you tell what was the matter?" she asked. "You see, Mrs. Redmond *is* in the style, or I suppose she must be, and Phyllis wants to be, too. If you could give me any idea " —

Terriss stirred restlessly. "I could n't, to save my life. Why don't you ask Mrs. Redmond?"

"Not for the world," responded Roxana.

"Buy a fashion book," suggested Chester.

Mrs. Sherritt looked contemptuous. "Do you suppose I 'd turn Phyllis into one o' them wasp-waisted simpletons? I see," she continued, with a sigh, "you don't know any more about style than I do, except that you know it when you see it. I s'pose it's right enough Phyllis should have it, if it don't cost too much. I don't like to bother Miss Rebecca. She has her own style and sticks to it through everythin', but 't ain't natural Phyllis should be willin' to."

"It is to be regretted," said Terriss, beginning to be less bewildered and more amused at the situation, "that Mr. Bellows had not been in my place. He could have given you some practical advice. He has spent his life among devotees of fashion, while I have only observed them from afar, vaguely."

"Oh, I would n't ask that young chap, even if I had him here," replied Roxana shortly. "Well, we 'll see, we 'll see," and she turned and left the room.

Terriss smiled to himself over the conversation. That he should be applied to for advice on the subject of woman's dress was a contingency he had never thought of. This Mrs. Redmond seemed to be a person of consequence. She had captivated the city youth and the country maiden alike. It was certainly an odd circumstance that such a woman should elect to live in Snowdon, and the fact seemed to argue a retiring nature.

"Probably she remains here but little of the time," he thought, lighting a cigar to assist his lazy meditations. "The fact of her being a novel effect among these people proves that. As for Tony's judgment — well, at all events the Redmond family have placed me in their debt. It is hardly becoming that I should gossip about them, even to my own thoughts."

He rose and, putting on a light overcoat and taking his hat, went downstairs into the spring sunshine. He walked down the street, his hands behind him, and as he went his thoughts wandered away from Mrs. Redmond to the practical affairs of his own life. He would willingly remain in this country spot as long as his finances would permit. How long would his finances permit?

He was considering this problem in mental arithmetic when a lady mounted on horseback appeared in the street. An experienced horsewoman is always a pleasing sight. Terriss postponed his calculations to enjoy the view of this one. Time was not precious to him as yet.

The lady's horse had been coming at a great pace, but now she quieted him, and it was almost at a walk that she approached. Chester, indifferent at first, gazed with fully awakened interest as he realized that a glorious living picture was, by a kind freak of fortune, passing his way.

The shining hair and the exquisite coloring of the lady, the dark green habit, perfectly fitting her graceful outlines, the arched neck and proud step of her coal black steed, formed an apparition positively startling in such a place, and seemed to make of the village street some royal avenue.

The lady for one moment let her gray eyes rest full upon Chester's face. Involuntarily, his hand went to his hat. She lightly touched her horse with the whip. Chester's hand fell. It was over.

What had happened? His heart beat. His head seemed to whirl. He suddenly stopped and turned. No one was in sight.

As for the lady, her heart was beating too. The gray eyes shone. She knew she had seen the man whom she had come thousands of miles to serve, and who had so roughly repulsed her. For the first time in her life, she had coolly planned to be observed; had chosen the street and the hour; and recognizing by the slow gait and the general appearance of the convalescent that her object was attained, had reined in her horse and passed deliberately in order to see and to be seen.

She had obtained a good view of the pale face and tall figure, had seen the light leap into the dark eyes, and her cheeks glowed as, fully satisfied, she cantered briskly down a side street.

Terriss Chester walked back toward the house with a quicker step than he had used since his illness. He strode through the parlor and out into the low-ceiled dining-room, where Roxana met him, looking up in surprise.

"What's the matter?" she asked involuntarily.

"Nothing. I — I have just been taking a short walk. We were talking about Mrs. Redmond this morning. Has she — has she golden hair?"

"No, not exactly. Kinder reddish."

"Does she ride a black horse, and is she very handsome?"

"She rides a black horse that's as wild as a nightmare. She's a good-lookin' woman,—straight and healthy-lookin', kinder pale, but I guess that may be the color of her skin. Why?"

"Nothing, nothing," replied Chester hastily. "I have seen her, that is all, and I — well, that's all, Mrs. Sherritt. Thank you;" and he disappeared.

Roxana looked after him meditatively. "There's a new disease cropped out in Snowdon," she muttered. "It's Redmond fever. Scarlet fever's nothin' to it; and if I don't miss of it, my boarder's struck down now."

CHAPTER XIII.

TRAILING ARBUTUS.

WHEN Phyllis came home, late that afternoon, the boarder looked at her with a new interest. Her face was all alight with the pleasure of novel experiences.

" I have had a beautiful time, a perfect time," she said, as she seated herself opposite Chester at the tea-table.

Roxana hovered about, with her usual close attention to their wants, waiting upon the table, and throwing in an observation from time to time, maintaining, as had always been her custom, an air of equality, reminding one that she was fully entitled to a seat at the family table, provided she chose to take it, only she never did choose to do so.

She regarded Phyllis now with an air half pleased, yet doubtful.

" Miss Rebecca made you have a good time, eh ? " she questioned.

" She was good to me, as she always is, but Mrs. Redmond did the most to entertain me."

" You like her better than you did ? "

" I know her better. I am not afraid of her any more, and she is *so* lovely ! She showed me piles of foreign pictures in a great stereopticon, and described them so that I feel as if I had made a European tour; and she let me ride her horse. Oh!" exclaimed Phyllis, leaning back in her chair, "I cannot eat anything."

"I dare say you made a pretty substantial dinner up there," observed Roxana.

"Such a dinner!" sighed the girl. "I did not eat very much of it, though, it was so pretty to look at;" and again she drew a long breath of enjoyment.

"Well, *you* didn't have any of it, Mr. Chester," said Roxana. "Why don't you eat something?"

"I am doing very well. I am enjoying Miss Phyllis's retrospect with her."

"I want you to go to Beech Knoll as soon as you can, Mr. Chester," said Phyllis earnestly. "I feel as though it would pour strength into any one just to walk about on that soft grass, and sit by the river, and lie in a hammock in the cunningest little sheltered place Mrs. Redmond has among a clump of trees."

"Phyllis Flower, you're stark crazy! Mr. Chester won't lie in any hammock yet awhile, unless he wants to be sick again."

"I think, Mrs. Sherritt, you and I dread that about equally," remarked Terriss, smiling at the housekeeper's consternation.

"You're lookin' first-rate to-night," returned Roxana more mildly.

She was right; but the reflection of Phyllis's

glowing countenance in the boarder's face was a short-lived brightness. He sat by the parlor window for some time after tea and read in the long twilight; but his author might have been Mother Goose instead of Ruskin for all the sense Chester obtained from his pages. They were illustrated pages, illumined by his own fancy; and on each leaf the picture was of the same regally graceful figure.

Phyllis flitted about the room, humming a little tune. He observed that she looked at him stealthily before slipping off an apron she had put on to preserve the gray silk; then she jumped into a chair and hung the apron scarf-fashion over the corner of a picture.

Chester smiled. He knew that out of the corner of his eye he was beholding the evidence of evolution. "Do you like the effect?" he asked, without looking up.

Phyllis whipped the apron off the picture and jumped lightly to the floor, blushing brightly.

"Yes, I do," she said courageously, "and I believe that up in the attic I can find something that will do better than an apron."

"Of course you can," said Chester with a nod. "The attics of New England are proverbial treasure-houses."

"I wish you wouldn't laugh at me, Mr. Chester," returned Phyllis wistfully.

"I'm not laughing at you. I am envying you," he replied curtly.

She came nearer, and sat down on a low stool and looked at him.

"Envying me! What for?" she asked, surprised and curious.

"For your courage. Why don't you fret and mope because your parlor is n't like Mrs. Redmond's? I should, in a parallel case."

"And that was the way I did at first; but now it is different. Mrs. Redmond filled me with despair at first; but now she has filled me with courage. Not that I talked to her about the parlor, but something about her while I was with her today braced me; and I thought, why should n't I learn of her? I have common sense and time, even if I have n't much money."

"Sensible," returned Chester. "So Mrs. Redmond's programme is first to fill one with despair, and then with courage, is it?"

"That was the way I took her," explained Phyllis simply. "I suppose she has been the same all the time; but you are n't feeling well, to-night, Mr. Chester. Don't you want me to read to you?"

Chester smiled. "You have come to believe that is a panacea for all my woes, I believe. I thank you, but my eyes are too strong now to excuse my robbing you of your time."

"I know how stupid it is here for you," said Phyllis timidly. "I do not wonder you grow depressed."

The other looked at her in some surprise. It

was a totally novel experience to him to receive feminine sympathy, and in his present mood, and from this humble little girl, rather soothing.

"I fear any place would be stupid to me where I had only myself for company," he returned. "I am a failure, Miss Phyllis, and a failure is always disagreeable."

"Dear me! do not say such a thing," said Phyllis, genuinely shocked. "How can a man decide that he is a failure before his life is half over?"

Chester shook his head gloomily. "I see my future as plainly as if I had already lived it. It is a foregone conclusion. An automatic performance of one work while my heart is in another, for the indefinite period of my life."

He seemed to forget Phyllis as he finished, looking out into the darkening village street, chafing to-night more restlessly than usual at his circumstances, his slow-coming strength, his poverty, his baffled hopes. The sore sense of self-dissatisfaction which was his constant companion seemed to increase with sudden vehemence. He threw himself back in his chair, and his eyes fell again on his silent companion.

"I suppose you know, Miss Phyllis, an old bachelor grows more selfish every day. I have been imposing upon you simply because you are good-natured."

"Do not mind me," said Phyllis earnestly. "I am so sorry you feel this way about your circumstances; but if Mr. Terriss cannot make you look

at them differently, of course I cannot." She
sighed. " I suppose it cannot be true," she added,
in a lower tone, "but it *does* seem as though, if
one had health to begin with, money would buy
every other blessing in the world."

" Yes ; but one may pay too dearly for money,"
replied Chester, thinking of the offer he had refused within a month. He had had time enough,
since coming to Snowdon, to think over what that
refusal had lost him, and what acceptance would
have gained him ; but he had not been tempted to
regret his course.

" Yes, indeed," returned Phyllis, with a wise
nod, " one might pay too dearly for money ; and,
Mr. Chester, there are so many things to enjoy in
the world without it, especially in springtime," she
added, with enthusiasm.

The following day, Chester concluded to try his
powers further than he had yet ventured to do.
The morning was fresh and beautiful ; the leaves
were large on the maples, and the birds were singing at their house-hunting as they flitted from tree
to tree in the warm sunshine.

" Indeed," thought he, as he stepped out-of-doors,
" Phyllis is right. There is a great deal to be
enjoyed without money in the springtime."

He hesitated a moment when he had reached the
street. Perhaps the first use to make of his liberty
should be to pay a visit to the minister and his
wife. The sights and sounds of the morning, how-

ever, drew him too strongly. Phyllis had showed
him the shortest route by which to reach the unin-
habited, wooded part of the village. He had his
sketch-book under his arm, and his hesitation was
brief. He walked down the street in a direction
opposite to his cousin's house. He passed by the
spot in the road where yesterday the beautiful
horsewoman had appeared to him as though in a
fleeting vision, and the same warmth of wonder
and admiration flashed through him. He resented
the pertinacious effect of the fair stranger.

"It is all a part of the same weakness," he
thought. "This wretched fever has robbed me
of mental balance as well as my balance at the
bank."

He walked faster, with the instinct of one in the
hopeless endeavor to escape from himself, reckless
of the strength he was expending. The houses
grew farther apart, and at last a soft line of wooded
country met his eye. He followed a green ribbon
road which led within the shade, and breathed a
long sigh of satisfaction as he found himself among
the pines and oaks. A flat rock invited him to
the rest which he began to need, and he seated
himself and looked about him. The sight of a little wooded slope, at the foot of which flowed a
brook, caused him to forget his fatigue, and taking
his block of paper, to make a rough sketch of what
he saw. Afterward he rose, and coming closer to
the little murmuring stream, drank of its crystal
water; then he turned and walked deeper into the

wood. He observed with delight a spray of the trailing arbutus, and gathering it, drew it through his button-hole. The air was life-giving; the lone-liness and beauty of the woods most grateful; but without warning, all this Arcadian charm was broken by a most unfitting and exasperating sensa-tion. Mr. Chester realized all at once that he was only a convalescent, and that Roxana's good care had formed in him a habit which could not be sud-denly broken with impunity. It was the hour when an egg-nog customarily appeared before him, and this morning, as an effect of the exercise and the bracing air, he felt the need of it far more than usual. In short, Mr. Chester all at once became conscious of extreme weakness and gnawing, even to the extent of faintness. This, in view of his situation, caused him some anxiety as well as vex-ation.

"I will turn back to the brook," he thought, "and from there find my way to the nearest house."

Suiting the action to the word, he attempted to retrace his steps, but though he grew constantly weaker and more annoyed, no brook met his view. He stood still and listened. No gurgling sound rewarded him. Nothing but the sleepy swaying of the tree tops and the "chipping" of the bright-eyed squirrels broke the stillness.

He had to smile even in his vexation. This strip of forest, which in his days of health it would be a morning's stroll to traverse from end to end, now seemed a labyrinth to his weakness. After fifteen minutes' further effort, he rested himself perforce. "The sooner the birds begin to cover me, the better," he muttered. "I don't see any way out of this." A rustling in the bushes near by attracted his notice. He turned and beheld a woman's figure, simultaneously with her discovery of him.

The newcomer uttered an involuntary exclamation of surprise, and turned hastily.

"My good woman! Don't be frightened. I am "— but Terriss Chester spoke no further. A black mist swam before his eyes. He put up his hand as if to brush it away, and fell over on his side.

The stranger saw his fall, and being an individual of good muscle and good nerve, thought better of her intended flight. Although her heart beat quickly, with the thought that the man might be really a tramp, and his faint a feint, she approached slowly until she saw his face. Its pallor left no room for further doubt, and in a moment she was on her knees beside him. She looked around in perplexity. There was no water to be had.

She rubbed his hands vigorously. It was all she could think of to do; but the swoon was not a deep one, and in a minute the stranger's eyelids fluttered. The girl took off her broad hat and fanned him hopefully. The color came back slightly to his lips. With a dread of his awakening came a realizing sense of the absurdity of the position.

"The story of the Sleeping Beauty reversed," she thought; for the stranger's features were symmetrical enough to deserve the term of beauty.

In a moment, Chester's eyes opened. He gazed a moment with a dazed expression at the flushed face of the brown-robed figure bending near him, then a light of joyful amazement sprang into his eyes, which suddenly gave his face its identity to his companion. She started at the recognition.

"Where are we?" he breathed.

"Do you feel better?" asked Elise, rising, and speaking as coolly as her surprise would permit.

"Pardon me for frightening you," said Terriss slowly, raising himself until he leaned against a tree trunk. "I thought perhaps I had died."

"I hope you are not disappointed," returned his companion, held in her place by the sight of his weakness.

"Not so long as you do not vanish."

Mrs. Redmond thought this a little daring, but the gravity of the other's white face was not to be denied.

"I was just questioning myself as to what would happen to you if I should vanish."

"I think my hallucination would probably become fact."

"Do you feel so very ill? How came you to overtax your strength so imprudently?"

"A child ought to be able to do what I have

done. Do not let me trouble you any longer. I shall rest here awhile, and then I shall go back. Only tell me which way is toward the village."

Elise indicated the direction, but still hesitated.

"One moment, Mrs. Redmond," said Terriss, rising slowly, still looking at her, his eyes beginning to shine in his pale face. "Perhaps it will be long before I have an opportunity to speak to you again. I thank you for the drive you gave me."

"You know who I am, then," returned the other, surprised.

"Yes, I saw you, riding — when? Why it was yesterday. It seems much longer. My name is Chester. You lent Tony Bellows your horses for my benefit. I thank you."

Elise stood, her bright head still uncovered, her hat hanging from her hand. She had read admiration in so many faces. What was it in this countenance which impressed her with an intensity as of white heat? Was it her secret knowledge which lent force to the effect this man had upon her?

"Yes, I know who you are," she said slowly. She waited a moment, and he forgot everything, while hanging upon her words. "I think," she continued, "that as my house is rather near by, you had better come with me."

Had she held out her lovely hand and offered to lead him into the celestial regions, Chester could not have accepted with greater gratitude.

" You could not possibly get back to Mrs. Sherritt's in time for dinner," she added.

"Oh, no, not possibly," returned Terriss.

Elise smiled at the simplicity of his manner. " I suppose it would be rude to ask you why you had not more common sense," she said.

Chester shook his head. " It is strange," he replied. " But the morning was beautiful, — and I have met you."

" Well, we will go. Do you feel strong enough to walk now ? "

" Yes. Oh, yes." This enchantress had not only exorcised by her glance his restlessness and self-distrust, but he felt that wherever she led it was as though the magnet said to the needle, " Follow ! " He could follow and know nothing of weakness.

" I see you have been more fortunate than I," she said, as they walked on. " You have found some arbutus. My errand this morning was to search for it, but it has escaped me thus far."

" No, you have found some," said Terriss, " if you will take this little spray. I think if we turn back I could find for you the place where it was growing."

" Turn back ? By no means," answered Elise. " It seems you require a sober, common-sensical person to remind you that you are weak. Hereafter, I advise you to invite Mrs. Sherritt to accompany you in your rambles."

Chester received this humorous suggestion with

the same wistful, shining look that he had worn since his waking. His head felt light; the whole adventure through which he was passing seemed at least improbable. There was a tranquillity upon him which was as unnatural as the rest. If he should waken now in Roxana's best chamber, it would surprise him less than to have this transcendent good fortune continue.

"We are nearly there," said Elise encouragingly, putting on her shade hat as they came out into the sunshine. "There, you see the roof of the house yonder among those beeches."

"You live there?"

"Yes; that is Beech Knoll. Really, Mr. Chester, if you grow any paler, I shall insist upon your sitting down and waiting until I can send you some wine."

"No; let me come with you," he answered quietly.

There was a gate which led into the grounds at the rear of the house, and this Elise opened. Her companion followed her within, and soon Rebecca had the surprise of seeing them advance together toward the side piazza, upon which, so mild was the day, the door stood open.

"Well, Elise is the most astonishing person," thought Miss Redmond, starting up. "One can never count upon her; but it is not often that she is as unconventional as this."

She came out upon the piazza, and was immediately struck by the guest's pallor. "Why, Mr.

Chester," she said anxiously, "this is a long walk for you. It has been too much."

Terriss raised his hat, and then sank upon a step that led up to the piazza. Mrs. Redmond smiled upon him and nodded.

"Faint as much as you like, now," she said cheerfully. "At the same time, if you could put it off five minutes, you shall have an armchair, and some lunch, and a good rest. Rebecca, take care of Mr. Chester a minute;" and she ran lightly up the steps and into the house.

"Faint!" exclaimed Miss Redmond, descending to the young man's side. "What is my sister talking about? I hope you have n't been faint."

"I have. I am very much ashamed of it," said Terriss, with a wan smile. "I shall not do it again."

"Well, I will not make you talk now," said Rebecca kindly. "Come into the house as soon as you are able, and you shall lie down."

Chester rose at once. "This giddiness is the most annoying thing that I have suffered from," he replied; "but I thank it for having brought me here."

Scarcely had Miss Rebecca placed him in the most comfortable chair in the cozy sitting-room, when the door opened, and Mrs. Redmond appeared with a small silver salver, on which were wine and crackers.

"Take some of this," she said, "and in a few

minutes we will have lunch. You do feel better already, I am sure."

Chester looked at her, lovelier even in the simple brown gown than she had been on the high mettled horse, and forgot, simply forgot, to answer.

Rebecca regarded him, and recognized the well-known symptoms.

" O foolish young man!" she thought. " How much better you would do to look the other way. Hopeless, worse than hopeless, even if you were not Terriss Chester."

CHAPTER XIV.

THE HELPING HAND.

Miss Redmond felt heavily the responsibility incurred by her accidental discovery of Mrs. Terriss' ability. Her last thought before sleeping at night and her first in the morning was of the invalid and her patient husband. Once the idea suggested itself to her of taking the minister into her confidence; but she dismissed it instantly. Surely she and Roxana between them ought to have sufficient wit to solve the problem. At last a thought occurred to Rebecca which she, with some misgivings and with flushing cheeks, laid before Mrs. Sherritt, who received the plan with acclamations.

"You've hit it, Miss Rebecca. I shouldn't wonder a mite if you had!" exclaimed the latter.

"The only trouble is, it is deception," said Miss Rebecca doubtfully.

"Law! What if it is? You go ahead. If we don't have anythin' worse 'n that to answer for at the last day, I shall be glad. Only think, Miss Rebecca, of Mr. Terriss! For one, I'd take some punishment hereafter for the sake o' givin' him a little easier row to hoe here."

Thus braced and encouraged, Rebecca set forth

for the parsonage. As she entered the gate, the minister was just coming down the steps of his house. His face illumined suddenly at sight of her, and he raised his hat courteously.

"I am always glad to see you coming here, Miss Rebecca," he said.

"Is Mrs. Terriss as well as usual?"

"About the same. She has seemed rather more depressed since the nervous attack of the other day, and she has often spoken of wishing to see you. I hope"— Rebecca was now standing beside him —"that your kindness and sympathy are broad enough to excuse that exhibition of weakness. Mrs. Terriss is weak, very unhappy in spite of the little I can do for her, and very much to be pitied."

"I believe all that," replied Rebecca earnestly, "and with all my heart I am anxious to help her."

The minister shook his head. "I ought not to discourage you," he said, "and every hour which you help her to pass less sadly is a blessing; but her help must come from within and not from without. She does her best," he added hastily,—"doubtless she does her best. Good-morning, Miss Redmond, good-morning;" and apparently forgetting that it would have been more according to the laws of hospitality for him to remain and usher the visitor into the house, the minister hurried down to the gate.

Rebecca did not look after him, but as she rang the door-bell, a little smile was on her lips. "I

am proud to have loved him, and no other man,"
she thought. "God help me now to help his
wife."

She found Mrs. Terriss looking exceedingly discontented in her neat and pretty surroundings.

"Good-morning, Miss Redmond," sighed the invalid. "It is a kind fate that has sent you to
break the monotony of my day. Mr. Terriss'
calls take him away so much. I should think people might excuse him when they know how I need
his society; but it is a selfish, unfeeling world.
So few are able to look beyond their own trials
and take those of others into consideration. Now
you, Miss Redmond, of course I appreciate your
kindness in coming to see poor, dull me, but after
all, you have nothing to detain you; you have
health, a luxurious home, no cares or responsibili-
ties, — an enviable lot altogether. I am sure you
cannot have a trial in the world."

"I have many blessings certainly," replied Rebecca calmly; "but do you know, Mrs. Terriss,
your deprivations haunt me much of the time?"
The invalid sighed, and cast down her eyes with
the modest air of one listening to a merited compliment. "And I am not ready to believe your
case hopeless, in these days of advanced skill."

Mrs. Terriss looked up with her strange, searching glance. "You ought to know, Miss Redmond,
that my husband and I would hardly settle down
to this trial were it an avoidable one."

"Yes, I did think so at first," replied Rebecca

firmly; "then I saw that settling down into a groove, if you are salvable physically, was ruin to you. Oh, look out there, Mrs. Terriss;" the speaker drew back the curtain and the spring sunshine streamed across the carpet. " What effort would you not make to call the privilege your own of walking across that grass and watching the flowers spring in your garden bed? Think of the glad surprise to your husband if he could come home some afternoon and find you standing at the door to greet him, if he could see you sitting opposite him at table after all these years. Would it not be like being born anew?"

The invalid stared at Rebecca with wide, startled eyes, and grasped the sides of her chair nervously.

" What do you mean by drawing these tantalizing pictures?" she cried. "Do you call it kindness to add to my misery by suggestions which can never be realized?"

"I believe they can be realized," returned Rebecca, with increased earnestness; " only you must long for it with all your heart."

"How dare you imply that I do not long to be well!" said Mrs. Terriss, frightened and angry.

"I do not say that. I believe if you thought there were grounds for hope you would be all eagerness. I *do* believe there are grounds for hope, and it has excited me. Will you put yourself in my hands for an experiment, Mrs. Terriss?"

Miss Redmond's cheeks were flushed, and her gentle gray eyes looked into the black ones with such earnestness that Mrs. Terriss shifted her position uneasily.

"What do you want?" she demanded ungraciously. "As you may imagine, I am weary of experiments."

"I want you to let Roxana come and rub your limbs every day for a week with a liniment I have found, and at the end of that time you will be able to walk from your bed to your chair with scarcely any assistance."

"I would rather not. I do not enjoy massage even from an experienced operator."

"But if I assure you that this will give you the use of your limbs?"

"Of course, if I believed that"—said the invalid, stirring restlessly.

"Then why not try it? It is a simple thing that cannot hurt you. Dear Mrs. Terriss, do trust me, try it. You will thank me so when you are walking."

"Well, well, I will try it," was the petulant response. "I confess I do not understand why you are so persistent."

"Not understand!" exclaimed Rebecca, so genuinely astonished that the ejaculation was involuntary. "I see you in prison and believe you might be free. Shall I not lift a hand to save you?"

That afternoon when the minister returned, he found his wife depressed and inclined to tears.

"You have not been alone many hours, I hope, Lily. I thought Miss Redmond would cheer you and make you feel better."

"Well, she did n't. I am disappointed in Miss Redmond, Philip."

The minister took his accustomed seat opposite his wife's chair. "Are you? I am sorry."

"Yes, she has not the refined nature I thought at first. Like most old maids, she must have her peculiarity, I suppose; but meddling is the last fault I should have selected for her."

Philip Terriss never contradicted his wife. He had long since learned to treat her as an unreasoning being, and ordinarily he listened patiently to all that she had to say on any subject. This one, however, he found unbearable.

"What have you been reading to-day?" he asked abruptly.

"Nothing. Miss Redmond quite unfitted me for everything. You have no idea what an eccentric creature she is, after all. Will you believe that she has some quack medicine that she is determined to try on me? It is only to be used externally, so I consented, in order to be rid of her; but she did fatigue me inexcusably."

"Something she wants you to be rubbed with?" asked Philip, looking gravely into the discontented face.

"Yes. Mrs. Sherritt is to do it; and in a week I am to walk."

"Walk!" exclaimed the minister.

" Oh, yes ; quite a miracle is to be worked, you see. I hope you will not be too disappointed when it fails."

He shook his head. "No, my poor wife, no," he said, in a low voice.

" O Philip ! " she exclaimed, extending to him her hand; "you are the only one who understands me, and yet you must always be going away and leaving me to the mercy of people who have no pity on my nerves, no regard for my condition."

So she went on for some time, bemoaning herself, her husband holding her hand and bowing his head above it while he listened, in an attitude which years had rendered familiar.

The current of the mournful tide was stemmed by the entrance into the room of Lucindy, who announced that a gentleman waited in the parlor to see Mr. Terriss.

The minister left the room, and soon returned with a stranger, whose appearance immediately turned Mrs. Terriss from the consideration of her trials, and set her to wondering if her hair was becomingly arranged.

The newcomer was a handsome man, and handsome men were rare as visitors to the minister's invalid wife. He was tall, overtopping Mr. Terris by half a head, and he had long, sombre dark eyes, and there was a dissatisfied expression in them and in his whole face.

" This is our cousin, Terriss Chester, Lily," said

the minister; and the stranger came forward to shake the offered hand.

" I have heard much about you, cousin Terriss," said the lady, fixing the stranger with her piercing, eager gaze. " You have been an invalid, too, but unlike myself you have had hopes of health, which are now realized. Are you quite yourself again ? "

" Not altogether, thank you, but I am on the road to health. I owe cousin Philip a debt of eternal gratitude for finding a place like Snowdon for me to convalesce in, and then for visiting me so often."

" So your opinion of Snowdon has improved; I am glad to hear it," said the minister.

Chester looked at him, and then away again. He had forgotten his many animadversions on the village before discovering what a jewel it contained.

" Oh, yes," he said hastily. " I have been out and have discovered its good points, — its woods, you understand, and its views, — and, of course, its very pure air. Very fine, very desirable, you know. Oh, yes, — I like Snowdon."

" There are some very pleasant people here," returned the minister, " when one finds them out."

" I am no acquisition socially," returned Chester, " but if the lady who found me out is a specimen of Snowdon society, you are certainly fortunate. You know who I mean — Miss Redmond."

"Yes, we know Miss Redmond," said Mrs. Terriss quickly. "You say she found you out?"

"I mean that I made her acquaintance in my sick-room, where she came to help care for me."

"Just a little officious, dear Miss Redmond," remarked Mrs. Terriss. "Well-meaning, oh, no doubt well meaning, and for that we should excuse her eccentricities. I wonder why it is, cousin Terriss, that unmarried women past middle life are so apt to be eccentric."

"I wish I had met more persons eccentric in Miss Rebecca's line," returned Chester, with his customary bluntness, regarding his hostess with an open expression of astonishment.

Mrs. Terriss smiled upon him with a look which made her face more eerie than usual.

"Your acquaintance is not so full of experience as mine, remember, cousin Terriss."

He would have spoken quickly, but the minister, sitting back in the room, slightly shook his head, and the guest, not entirely comprehending, took refuge in silence.

"Much as I have seen of Miss Redmond, my affliction has prevented my seeing her home," continued the invalid. "She is quite dependent, you know, on her sister-in-law, a person who certainly does not spend much of *her* time in visiting the sick. Every one says that their house is very beautiful."

"I was there yesterday," remarked Chester laconically, in the silence that followed.

"Oh, you have been there," said Mr. Terriss, his interest reviving at the thought that Chester had met his would-be benefactress. "You saw the lady of the manor, I presume?"

"Yes," returned Terriss shortly.

"Now, then," exclaimed Mrs. Terriss, with what was intended to be an arch manner, "your cousin Philip and I are much hurt that you visited Beech Knoll before coming to us. Are n't we, Philip?"

"I should not have thought of doing such a thing," said the guest uncomfortably. "It was accident. I had walked too far in the woods and overtaxed my strength " —

"Oh, a story, a story," exclaimed Mrs. Terriss, clasping her hands with a movement which ripened the guest's unpleasant impression into positive intolerance. "Do go on, cousin Terriss."

He shifted restlessly, and scowled. "A very short story," he returned. "I found I must seek the nearest house, and it proved to be — Beech Knoll."

"I am glad you have been there," said the minister, "because as a homestead it is the pride of the village."

"Yes, we forgive you," added Mrs. Terriss graciously, "provided in future you give us the greater number of your visits. You belong to us, remember."

The guest stirred uneasily under her smile and glance. "I am not a visiting man," said Chester shortly. "I wish I might be of service to you in any manner comparable to cousin Philip's to me, but I have not the faculty of amusing anybody, not even myself."

" Perhaps you are more difficult to amuse than I am. At all events, we must become better acquainted. Perhaps I prefer the conversation of a black-haired man to that of a white-haired woman as a diversion. Our tastes are not all alike, you know. Oh," as the guest rose, " must you go so soon ? "

" I do not wish to weary you," returned Terriss, drawing a breath of relief at finding himself upon his feet. " Cousin Philip, you need not trouble yourself to see me out."

But the minister insisted, and after shaking hands with Mrs. Terriss and receiving a parting injunction to consider their house his home, Chester strode out into the narrow hall. The thought occurred to him that, as it was so near the hour for the noon meal, it was strange his hostess had not asked him to remain. Each instant he feared Mr. Terriss would give the invitation, but no word came. The guest stood awkwardly a moment at the door, doubtful if he ought not to refer to his cousin's wife, and expecting at least that the minister would himself speak of her; but the expectation was not fulfilled. Mr. Terriss, as he opened the hall door, referred to the beauty of the season, and congratulated Chester on his so nearly restored health, all in his usual kind and simple manner;

and as Terriss parted from him, standing on the steps, the gloss on his shiny coat very evident in the sunlight, he felt a new respect for his cousin, not unmingled with awe at what he vaguely felt was not insensibility but a sublime patience.

"What do men do that sort of thing for?" he asked himself, fuming, as he walked homeward. "There was a time when cousin Philip was free. Why did n't something or somebody prevent him from tying himself to that uncharitable, vain, shallow appendage? Why could n't he have met Miss Rebecca Redmond, for instance?"

Thinking of Miss Rebecca was but a short step from thinking of Mrs. Redmond, and in a flash, Chester had forgotten Mrs. Terriss' restless eyes and faded archness, forgotten cousin Philip's weary lot, in going back to live over the two blissful hours of yesterday, — hours when he had been lifted above every adverse circumstance of life into an enchanted atmosphere, never to be forgotten. After his experience of the morning, he found it a thing to exult in that he was free, — free to adore, if only at a humble distance, the star that had dawned upon his horizon.

CHAPTER XV.

AND now there was a bond between Phyllis and the boarder which gave them a new interest in each other. Perhaps Chester was the one of the pair who chiefly benefited by their good comradeship, for, while the girl had only the effervescence of a new and pleasant excitement to express, a deep and abiding passion had taken possession of her friend ; and to him it was a blessing indeed to be able to speak his lady's name to sympathetic ears, and to hear it spoken by admiring lips. Not that his curt and unsmiling manner greatly changed. Phyllis little suspected how great a fire her lightly spoken words sometimes kindled. But she felt his interest in a subject of which Roxana was always shy, and so, when she was with him, the conversation was sure to turn upon Beech Knoll; and the one of the two who had acquired the latest bit of news concerning the family related it for the other's benefit. Although to a third person it might have seemed an excessively trivial fact to mention that Phyllis had seen the flutter of Mrs. Redmond's riding habit as she turned a corner in the distance, or that Mr. Chester had observed that the hedge of lilacs was in full bloom at the rear of the Beech

Knoll grounds, there was no lack of interest felt by this infatuated couple, either in giving or receiving such items.

Roxana observed their growing friendliness with complacency. " Phyllis won't get any harm from *him*," she thought; "and it's a nice amusement for 'em both to sort o' change around furniture in the parlor and hang up pieces of old silk here and there. Foolish, o' course, but harmless enough. Some day they 'll get sick o' such doins', and then I can cart the things off up attic again. I do think bringin' down that spinnin'-wheel beats all; but, thank fortune, I can keep my face straight and hold my tongue too, at the right time. It's worth a good deal to see Phyllis as bright as a new dollar, and old sober-sides, too, is comin' out of his shell more 'n I ever thought he would."

Roxana's leniency was heightened, moreover, by the important business she had on hand at the parsonage. Miss Redmond had gone straight from the minister's wife to Mrs. Sherritt, to recount her negative success, and on the day following, Roxana, early in the morning, before the hour for Mrs. Terriss to rise, presented herself at the invalid's chamber door with her usual cheery familiarity.

" Have you come to rub me? " inquired the sick woman from her pillow.

Roxana disregarded the clouded face and peevish tone.

"Yes, I have," she replied heartily. "I guess some good angel goes around with Miss Rebecca and points out things to her. Who else would ever have found out what to do for you?"

"Do you mean to say you believe she is right, Mrs. Sherritt? Don't tell me that a woman of your sense believes that there is a mixture which will make paralyzed limbs walk, and that the doctors have not discovered it!"

"I mean to say," said Roxana impressively, "that I believe that in this bottle is an ointment that, if you 'll only have faith, will make you walk in a week's time."

"What is the stuff?" asked Mrs. Terriss ungraciously, regarding the white, opaque substance which her visitor held forth to view.

"The bottle ain't marked," returned Mrs. Sherritt shortly. "All we 've got to do is to obey orders."

"Well," sighed the other resignedly, "I suppose I must consent, or else appear ungrateful; but remember, I tell you in advance that the effort is worse than a waste of time."

Roxana groaned in spirit, but set to work at her task with an appearance of unshaken confidence.

"I have met my cousin Terriss, at last," remarked the invalid, after a moment of silence.

"Who?"

"My cousin. Your boarder."

"Oh!"

"Yes. How strange that no one has told me how handsome, how distinguished, he is; but then, I suppose I ought not to expect that people will trouble themselves to make poor me acquainted with every interesting fact." The speaker sighed.

"I don't suppose any man looks very distinguished in bed," replied Roxana shortly, "and that's where I saw him mostly for a good while; and after he got out, I was too much relieved to care whether his nose was snub or long."

"Oh, his nose is well enough; but those eyes, those great, grand, gloomy eyes, and his straight, proud look as he steps!"

"I want to know!" remarked Roxana, her lips twitching.

"Do you mean to say you have n't observed it?"

"No, ma'am; but I 'm real glad you think he looks pickin' up. He was dreadful lantern-jawed one spell, but he eats everythin' now, and I 'm gettin' a good deal used to him. He draws and paints real nice," continued Roxana, with the air of saying what she could in favor of one for whom she was conscious of feeling no partiality. "He made a drawin' o' Phyllis the other day. She had some kind of a scarf around her head, but the instant I set eyes on it, '*Phyllis!*' says I. I knew it right off."

"An artist!" exclaimed Mrs. Terriss eagerly. "He ought to be one. He looks it. I am going to let him make a study of me. He could do it as well as not, for there I must sit, hour after hour, anyway. Would n't it make a touching little picture! He could call it 'Patience.'"

" He 'll have to do it this week, then, Mrs. Terriss, for you and that chair won't be such close friends after that," said Roxana firmly. "Just think how you 'll enjoy steppin' around your house and seein' to things yourself ; and by and by you 'll be comin' over to see me."

Mrs. Terriss did not appear to regard her words. "Where is Phyllis, and what is she doing of late?" she asked, interrupting.

"Oh, she is at home. She 's taken a notion to fix up the house lately ; and Mr. Chester, with lots o' time on his hands, is willin' to help her. There ain't a piece o' furniture settin' where it ought to be in the parlor this minute ; but law! I can stand that for a few weeks."

" And is the changing of the furniture all the harm that you expect to result from their spending so much time together?" asked Mrs. Terriss.

" Oh, yes."

" Then you are as much mistaken in that as in this farce of rubbing that we are going through. Don't you know that Phyllis, little inexperienced girl, will fall in love with that man, the first eligible man she has ever known?"

Mrs. Sherritt gave a great start and her sallow cheeks reddened. "No, I don't, Mrs. Terriss, I don't, not for one minute!" she returned, rubbing so vigorously that the invalid cringed.

" Oh, oh! be careful! you hurt me!" she exclaimed. " Well, you will find out that I am right, perhaps, when it is too late. Cousin Terriss

is just the Byronic-looking hero to attract a girl.
Mark my words ! "

"Oh, pshaw ! " said Roxana. " Phyllis ain't
goin' to be 'attracted,' as you call it, till she's
asked ; " but though she turned the matter off
lightly, Mrs. Terriss' words had alarmed her.
She even considered speaking to Phyllis on the
subject, but something restrained her. If there
were romantic possibilities in Roxana's nature, circumstances had not developed them. She had
married a man who was sordid and mean and dis-
sipated, who made her wretched until death relieved her of him ; so it was no defined delicacy
which determined her not to repeat Mrs. Terriss'
words to Phyllis. She said to herself that she did
not wish to put such thoughts into the girl's head.
She would wait, and, meanwhile, would not fail
to watch.

Her watching discovered only a very amicable
state of things between Chester and Phyllis, and
for once poor Roxana wished herself versed in lovers' ways, that she might tell whether the boarder's interest in her child's companionship were the
sort likely to interfere with Phyllis's fancy-free
condition.

But an immediate source of anxiety to Mrs.
Sherritt was Mrs. Terriss' attitude toward her
own possible recovery. As the days went by, she
found it continued to be impossible to infuse hope
or enthusiasm into the deluded woman. At last
there was but one day left of the prescribed seven.

Mrs. Terriss still smiled indulgently on her friends' folly. With her, the result of the experiment was evidently a foregone conclusion.

So Roxana put on her best bonnet and set forth for Beech Knoll. She felt that she must see Miss Rebecca. Phyllis offered to accompany her, but the housekeeper declined. "You stay at home," she advised, "and work on your new frock. You was set on havin' it; now stick to it till it's finished. I want to talk to Miss Rebecca about a good many things that would n't interest you. Mrs. Terriss is one of 'em."

"Oh," replied Phyllis; "I suppose that means you think I ought to go to see Mrs. Terriss oftener. What 's the reason," asked the girl, tying Roxana's bonnet-strings, "that men do not like Mrs. Terriss, when women do so much?"

"It's likely I can answer that question, ain't it?" remarked Mrs. Sherritt irritably. "How do you know men don't like her? What business have they got to like her? Mr. Terriss does, that 's enough."

"Like her! I should think he did! She says he worships the ground she walks on."

"I hope he likes her better than that," retorted Mrs. Sherritt. "That would be mighty little."

"Well, Mr. Chester really dislikes her, *dislikes* her. Is n't it odd? Uncle Doctor did n't like her, and did n't trust her."

"Phyllis Flower, you 're gossipin'! Ain't you ashamed o' yourself?"

The girl laughed lightly. " I do not count what I say to you, gossiping. "

" Why do you say your uncle did n't trust her?"

" Oh, I must n't gossip."

" Tell me this minute ! I 'm in a hurry, and I want to know."

" He did not believe she was really ill. I do not know exactly what he thought ; but he used to say things that gave me that impression."

Roxana groaned. "Oh, dear, dear, dear, what a world ! " she exclaimed, shaking her head.

" Yes; I never could understand it in dear Uncle Doctor, the kindest of men," said the girl.

Mrs. Sherritt walked up the street, swinging one arm. "The kindest o' men. So he was," she mused. " He saw through her, and he must have thought it was n't any use to try to change things, so he never said anything. Well; I wonder if Miss Rebecca and me have got to give it up."

She walked on briskly until she came to the low iron fence which surrounded Beech Knoll, and upon entering the gate, beheld a sight which would have been thrilling to the others of her family, but which she sustained calmly. It was Mrs. Redmond stooping over a bed of flowers, from which she was gathering some bright geraniums.

She rose at sight of Mrs. Sherritt and said good-morning.

" Don't let me disturb you," said Roxana. " I want to see Miss Rebecca, and I 'll just go on to the house."

"Are all well at home?" asked Elise, for she saw the cloud on Mrs. Sherritt's face.

"They are very well, thank you. Mr. Chester's gettin' to be almost like other folks."

"I am glad of that. He was so over-fatigued the day we kept him here to lunch, I feared he might have hurt himself."

"No; he's picked up right along ever since; but I guess it taught him a lesson to be a little more careful. Well, good-mornin', Mrs. Redmond."

"Oh, I will come with you to find my sister," said Elise, walking along by her side. "What weather to be out-of-doors!"

"You're out a good deal, I guess."

"Yes, as nearly all the time as I can manage."

"I don't see how your complexion stands it so," remarked Mrs. Sherritt bluntly.

"It is fortunate," returned Elise, with an amused smile, "for although I have the average share of vanity, I could not sacrifice so much to looks as to remain indoors, or to look at Mother Nature through a veil."

"Shows her sense *there*," thought Mrs. Sherritt.

"Ah, Mrs. Sherritt, I am glad I have remembered something in time that I wished to speak about. I want Phyllis to come and play tennis with me. She would like to, but says she has no dress for it. I want to ask you if I may venture to offer her one of mine."

Roxana looked around at the questioning face

and let her eyes fall, uncertain how to respond. It was not easy to resist Mrs. Redmond in a gracious mood. "I guess we can fix her up one, if you'll tell me what she needs," she answered.

"But that would take a longer time. This suit I speak of I had to discard because it was too tight for me. It would be too large for Phyllis, probably, but could be quickly changed. As it is useless to me, and it would oblige me to have her able soon to play, I thought she might consent to take it. The principal thing in favor of the costume is that it is not too gay for her to wear now."

Mrs. Redmond finished by a questioning look, which elicited a grim smile from Mrs. Sherritt.

"I s'pose Phyllis would like it a sight better because you'd worn it. She'd rather have it than a new one, I s'pose," she remarked.

"Then I will leave it at your door in a day or two."

"I'd just as soon take it along," said Roxana. "I don't mind bundles."

"That would be very kind of you; and tell Phyllis to come and have a game the first day that is convenient. Ah, there is Rebecca; she sees us and is coming to let us in."

Miss Redmond opened the door, and shook hands with the newcomer, looking at her eagerly as she led her into the sitting-room.

"Any good news of Mrs. Terriss, Roxana?"

The latter turned involuntarily toward Mrs. Redmond, and hesitated.

"I have confided our plan to Mrs. Redmond. Do not fear to speak before her. I know by your face you have not good news."

Mrs. Sherritt sat down in the straightest chair the room afforded, while the others took seats near.

"No, Miss Rebecca," she said, crossing her hands in their Lisle-thread gloves. "Mrs. Terriss don't give me one bit of encouragement. She just acts scornful every time I speak of to-morrow, — that's the seventh day, you know, — and it's my opinion she won't try to step foot to the ground."

"Dear, dear," said Miss Rebecca.

"Knowin' what I know, I feel like sayin' a good deal more 'n 'dear, dear,'" remarked Roxana desperately.

Mrs. Redmond laughed low and lazily. "What do you propose doing next?" she asked.

"Ask the cap'n there," returned Roxana, with a nod toward Rebecca.

The latter colored. "I do not know what to do," she admitted, much troubled.

"Do you want advice? I am always ready with advice, you know," said Elise.

"Yes, I do," replied Miss Redmond, "if Mrs. Terriss refuses to make an effort. She has not refused yet, remember."

"But Mrs. Sherritt feels sure she will. First, Mrs. Sherritt, you tell me your opinion of what to do next."

"Well," said Roxana, "if Mrs. Terriss won't

try, and I'm sure she won't, she does act for all
the world as if it wa'n't of any consequence to
her whether she ever walked again or not, I'm
afraid I shall bu'st out and tell her what I think
of her."

Mrs. Redmond shook her head. "That is
hardly the best way. It would relieve you; but
she would never see you again if she could avoid
it, and you would lose your chance of helping
her."

"Well, it does seem wicked," said Roxana vigorously, "to leave her alone."

"I think so," returned Elise calmly. "If she
will not be coaxed out of her delusion, she should
be shocked out of it."

"I'm willin' to shock her out of it," said Mrs.
Sherritt promptly. .

"And the way to do it," continued Elise, "is
for Miss Redmond to tell Mr. Terriss that she
has seen his wife walk. A woman that can walk,
and won't walk, should be made to walk. Poor
creature!"

"Poor creature, indeed!" exclaimed Rebecca,
her cheeks very red. "I will not consent that her
greatest, her only comfort, her husband's confidence, should be taken from her. No, no, a thousand times no, to your plan, Elise."

Miss Redmond was greatly agitated.

"My dear Rebecca, that would be but a temporary result," said Elise. "I for one like Mr.
Terriss better than his wife."

"That's what I say, Miss Rebecca," added Roxana; "think o' the minister's side of it."

Poor Miss Redmond. There was little fear that she would not think of the minister's side of it. It was her trembling earnestness of desire not to do injustice to his wife that clouded her thoughts now.

"When in doubt, do nothing," she responded.

"*I've* always heard it, when in doubt, play trumps," said Roxana emphatically. "To tell Mr. Terriss what you saw that day would be playin' a trump card, and no mistake."

"And one which would probably win the game," added Mrs. Redmond.

"No, no, indeed," said Rebecca earnestly. "You do not know what you are saying. That would be a wicked interference between husband and wife. Nothing could excuse it."

She looked anxiously from her sister to Mrs. Sherritt, and apparently saw something in their faces which startled her, for she continued, with redoubled earnestness, "If you are thinking of opposing me and telling Mr. Terriss in spite of me, you are planning an unpardonable thing — unpardonable;" and to the consternation of Miss Rebecca's companions, she covered her face with her hands and burst into tears.

Her excitement, so unlike herself, and so disproportionate to the case, might have suggested the truth to any one more imaginative than Roxana; but the latter was incapable of such a wild flight of fancy as would be necessary to connect the minister with the hero of Miss Redmond's long-ago love affair, and Elise had never heard of the existence of such a romance. Mrs. Redmond rose and threw her arms around Rebecca.

"You dear little thing," she said caressingly, "rather than that you should shed a tear about the matter, I promise not to lift a finger to relieve the minister, and I am sure Mrs. Sherritt will do the same."

"I won't deny," said Roxana, "that I was calc'latin' to tell him ; but of course I should n't think o' disobeyin' you downright, Miss Rebecca."

"Promise me, then," sobbed Rebecca.

"I promise. There, I do promise," replied Mrs. Sherritt, reluctant, even in the midst of her dismay at this emotion, thus to seal her own lips. "I 'll let you know what happens to-morrow, Miss Rebecca," she went on. "Don't you fret over this one bit. We 've done the best we knew how, anyway."

"I thank you, Roxana," replied Miss Redmond, slowly recovering herself. "You have had all the hard work, and I assure you I appreciate your kindness very much indeed."

"There ain't any danger of your not appreciatin' folks," said Roxana, rising.

She had a moment alone with Mrs. Redmond when the latter gave her the tennis suit wrapped in a bundle.

"Too bad," said Elise, with a smile and a shrug.

"'T ain't in human nature to stand it," returned Roxana, in a low tone. "I ain't ever goin' to have any more comfort with that woman a dead weight on the minister's hands."

"What shall you do?"

Roxana shook her head. "Can't tell you; but I guess I'm Yankee enough to think up somethin'. Too much of a Yankee to give up, I'm afraid."

"Miss Redmond has tied your hands, I fear."

"Bless her good heart! She thinks she has." Roxana cast a shrewd look at Elise. "I put my trust in Yankee invention yet, Mrs. Redmond. I'll bid you good-mornin'."

CHAPTER XVI

ROXANA found herself an object of much interest when she came home that day. She would not talk until dinner was on the table, and Phyllis and the boarder were served; then Phyllis was full of questions, and Chester all attention. Mrs. Sherritt was too preoccupied with the main subject of her thoughts to do more than answer shortly, and Phyllis's astonishment at the housekeeper's compliance in accepting the tennis costume was almost speechless.

"I think you must have been enchanted too," she said at last.

"I guess maybe I was," admitted Mrs. Sherritt. "She put it, Mrs. Redmond did, in that kind of a way, that it looked sensible to take it and would have made me look simple to refuse it."

"Of course she did," laughed Phyllis, exchanging a glance of appreciation with the boarder. "Oh, I cannot wait to see it. Is it in that bundle?"

Roxana pressed a firm hand on the girl's shoulder, precisely as she would have done ten years before. "Sit still and eat your dinner," she said shortly. "Plenty of time afterward for the bundle."

Thus admonished, Phyllis took up her knife and fork and chattered on. How Chester blessed her volubility.

"What was Mrs. Redmond doing when you got there?" she asked.

"Pickin' flowers. I don't see how on earth her complexion stays so fair. She had some kind of a cap on her head that wa'n't a mite o' protection."

"Oh, she is a perfect beauty, and she always will be, and she can't help it," observed Phyllis; for which bit of gush the boarder lifted his eyes and sent her a glance which might have impressed even Roxana with its inflammable tendency, had she observed it.

It was lost on Phyllis also. She was glancing wistfully at the bundle on her own account.

"What else did she say?" she asked.

"She wants you to come some day soon and play tennis with her."

"Aha, Mr. Chester, don't you envy me?" cried the girl triumphantly.

"Never mind, Mr. Chester," said Roxana smiling. "She asked how you was, if she *did n't* send you any tennis suit; and, anyway, pretty soon it'll be you instead o' Phyllis that'll be goin' up to Beech Knoll."

"Why is that?"

"Because she's invited that young feller out here to stay a week, she said."

"What young fellow?" was demanded in unison, eagerly by one voice, sternly by the other.

"It's the strangest thing I can't think of his name. Phyllis, he came here once and gave me a pink."

"Mr. Bellows?" said Phyllis.

"Bellow is the name," returned Roxana, relieved.

Phyllis smiled meditatively at her plate. Terriss stared out of the window with a gaze which should have dyed the grass and foliage a more vivid green.

What, he wondered, was there in Tony to procure him such a superlative honor?

He could not restrain a "Humph!" of disgust, which caused Phyllis's face to rise questioningly.

"What is it?"

"I was thinking what a butterfly existence Tony's is."

"I s'pose it's fittin' enough," observed Roxana, "that one butterfly should amuse another."

"If you mean by that that Mrs. Redmond is a butterfly," returned Phyllis, "you are very much mistaken. Miss Rebecca has told me about some of the lovely things she has done in the way of charity. Not lazy charity either. Miss Redmond says she is too active and energetic to be willing not to know how her money goes. She does lots of good in the world, and does it very quietly."

"So much the better," said Roxana, nodding. "I liked what I saw of her to-day first-rate."

"I have finished," said Phyllis, pushing her chair back from the table. "Now for the precious package."

Mrs. Sherritt said nothing as the girl took the bundle in her lap and untied the string. Presently she held up to view a costume of soft woolen material, striped with gray and white, and as she beheld it, uttered a cry of delight. "O Mr. Chester! — and there's a cap to match! Isn't it lovely?"

The boarder came around the table and inspected the limp mass with puzzled eyes. It must be lovely, of course. She had worn it. "What is this scarf for?" he asked, touching the soft stuff with a reverent hand.

"That is the sash, I am sure," cried Phyllis joyfully. "Oh, I am so happy!"

"Go and put it on," he suggested, catching her excitement.

"Yes, go on," said Roxana. · She wished to be rid of the girl, in order to have an opportunity for speaking to Mr. Chester undisturbed. She felt the disappointment keenly of being debarred from advising with Mr. Terriss, and, as an alternative, it occurred to her that, two heads being better than one, her boarder might be of some use.

"Look here, Mr. Chester, I'm in trouble," she said, as soon as the door had closed upon Phyllis. "I've got mixed up in other folks's business kind o' unexpectedly, and I want to get some help, if you've got any to give. You bein' a relative o' the minister's, and *she* bein' taken with you, I thought I'd tell you, because I don't want Phyllis to know a thing about it, and Miss Rebecca won't let Mrs. Redmond and I do what we think best; so it's just *there*."

Mrs. Sherritt was usually so sensible and direct that Chester thought it must be the fault of his own perception that this address gave him no idea. Until he caught Mrs. Redmond's name, his face had been inattentive; but now, Roxana could not complain of any lack of interest in his countenance.

" Pardon me," he said, regarding her troubled face as she leaned on a chair-back opposite, " I did not quite understand."

Then Roxana told him in consecutive fashion Miss Rebecca's discovery, and what had been done in the matter up to the present day.

The boarder gave an exclamation of impatience. " Any one could perceive on first meeting her that the woman is a hypocrite! " he exclaimed.

" Miss Rebecca says she ain't. She says Mrs. Terriss thinks she's just as feeble as she appears to be. Kind o' self-deceived, as it were. Now the question is, seein' Miss Rebecca's little scheme has failed, what next? She's for lettin' it go; but I can't rest to do that, on the minister's account, and no more can Mrs. Redmond."

" Of course you cannot. To-morrow, when you go to make the trial of her ability, you might tell her, if you think it would do any good, that I am ready to make a portrait of her as soon as she can come to me here. You might tell her," added Chester with a grimace, " that I wish to do it."

" Well, that might work," said Roxana hopefully. "She certainly took an amazin' likin' to you."

"That is surprising, for I was so repelled by her that I feared I showed it very plainly."

"She liked the way you stepped off," explained Roxana.

"Well, we were of one mind there. That was the part of the call which I liked best, too."

"You please keep thinkin'," said Roxana; "but don't say a word to Mr. Terriss, or Miss Redmond would never forgive us."

"Mrs. Redmond interests herself in it, does she?" asked the infatuated boarder, lingering.

"Yes, indeed she does. You know everybody that knows Mr. Terriss thinks a sight of him."

"Yes. I think we will have to accomplish this, Mrs. Sherritt. Mrs. Terriss' fate is sealed. She will have to walk."

Whether the object was to be attained on the next day remained to be proved. Miss Redmond called early for Roxana, and together they sought the parsonage, where all the tender encouragement and hearty assurances they could lavish on the invalid were brought to bear. Roxana added the bait of the artist's invitation, to which Mrs. Terriss responded with the first smile she had worn during the interview.

"I am willing he should have my poor face, if he wants it," she replied, "but he will have to come here for it."

"He can't move his things, he says," returned

Mrs. Sherritt. "Just try, only *try*, Mrs. Terriss. Just lean on me and take one step, only one. I 'll catch you if you fall, you know I will; or shall I call Mr. Terriss? I hear him up in his study."

"Yes, call him; call Mr. Terriss," responded the invalid quickly.

"Perhaps you *would* feel safer," said Roxana soothingly. "I did hope we could surprise him, but if you want him now, you shall have him. Miss Rebecca, will you just step up to the study, while I tidy things a little more here?"

Miss Redmond started immediately. She was so much absorbed in her self-forgetful work of love, that she entirely forgot that it was her first visit to the minister's study. She knocked, and he opened the door upon the familiar face, grown so youthful again in its interest and brightness that he gazed into it speechless.

"Mr. Terriss," she said, catching her breath a little, "can you come downstairs a minute? The time has come for your wife to make the effort to walk, and she does not wish to try without you. You know of our experiment?"

"I do, Miss Rebecca," he answered, in a tone as unsteady as her own, "and have been entirely mystified by it. The very fact that the scheme originated with you gives me a respect for it; yet it surprises me beyond telling that you put any faith in the result."

"O Philip, don't say so!" exclaimed Rebecca almost tearfully. "I do put all faith in it, and I beg you to do so. If she sees that you do not hope, it will all fail. I tell you I believe, I *know*, she can walk this morning if she will try."

Carried along by her excitement, the minister followed her down the stairs.

" You will help?" she said, turning to him beseechingly, just before opening the door of Mrs. Terriss' sitting-room.

He nodded and they went in. Mrs. Terriss sat there, her cheeks flushed and an odd glitter in her eyes, which glowed darkly with some excitement.

" Philip," she said, in a hard voice, " I have sent for you to defend me against any further annoyance under the guise of friendship. Mrs. Sherritt I do not blame ; she has only carried out the orders of Miss Redmond. It is strange that Miss Redmond should take such an interest in my affairs, is it not?" Here the speaker turned her glittering eyes with a malicious expression upon Rebecca. " It was an entire mystery to me until last evening, when I heard something which throws light on the subject. It seems that she is an old flame of yours. You visited her family once in your college days. Now, of course, I understand it all. Her officiousness serves to keep her in your mind in the light of an angel of mercy. Miss Redmond, I " —

" Silence !" cried the minister, and there was silence.

His wife sank back in her chair, struck dumb by his voice and his transfigured face.

Roxana's eyes seemed starting from her head as she shrank back in horror.

Miss Rebecca's face grew white, nearly, as her hair. Her gentle eyes were fixed on the minister's wife, with a look in them as though the woman had stabbed her to the heart. They were all four motionless for a long moment, and no one spoke as Rebecca turned noiselessly and walked slowly from the room.

The sound of the closing of the outer door seemed to break the spell. Roxana hurriedly began gathering up her wrap and bonnet and gloves. Mrs. Terriss watched her anxiously.

"Mrs. Sherritt, don't go yet," she said, almost timidly, observing Roxana's averted face. "I said I did not blame you ; I am sure I thank you " —

Roxana turned, and stood gazing at her with the same wide, awe-struck eyes.

"Shame, *shame* upon you, forever and ever!" she said, with such solemn and concentrated energy that to the invalid's ears the exclamation bore an unpleasant resemblance to a curse.

Mrs. Terriss cowered, but seemed unable to remove her eyes from the stare that held them.

"I'm bound by promise," continued Roxana, "or I would tell, here and now, what made that angel who just went out try to help you as she has this week. If you really don't know, cast your mind back to the day Dr. Ramsey came to see you. What did you do that day, hey? What did you do just after Dr. Ramsey left the room, hey ?"

Roxana's lips snapped together in order to let out no more.

Mrs. Terriss trembled, and she looked more frightened and bewildered than ever.

" Nothing ; I — I had hysterics. I " —

Mrs. Sherritt looked at her with righteous indignation. " I don't know whether you really deceive yourself or not," she returned. " Miss Rebecca, whose shoes we ain't any of us fit to tie, says you do. She's got a sight more charity 'n I have, that's all ; " and Roxana caught up a small leather bag Miss Redmond had forgotten, and gave a furtive glance at the minister.

" I might have talked out as plain as I wanted to," she thought; " he has n't heard one word." Then she hurried out of the room.

Mrs. Terriss looked at her husband appealingly. His face had not relaxed its terribly strange expression, his eyes looking away, over her head. She began to whimper. It was frightful to feel such a distance between them. He did not seem conscious even of her presence.

" Come and hold my hand, Philip," she begged. " I feel so wrought upon by all this absurd fuss " —

But her husband did not hear her. He sank suddenly into a chair and bowed his head upon the table before him, convulsed by sobs. Once before in his life had he shed such bitter, hard-drawn tears. It was on the night before he went to seek his fragile *fiancée, t*o ask her to name their wedding-day.

CHAPTER XVII.

THE awe which had taken possession of Roxana at Mrs. Terriss' words was not dispelled by the time she reached home. She seated herself in the empty parlor, still bonneted and shawled, and looked before her with fixed eyes.

" Oh, my soul!" she ejaculated. " Oh, my soul! Miss Rebecca, dear Miss Rebecca."

All the touching little story which she had recounted to Phyllis came back to her, and assumed for the first time the hues of reality. She thought over, in a slowly appreciative fashion, what it must have been to Miss Redmond to find in her pastor her old-time lover, and, as she recalled the simple and quiet manner in which they had conducted themselves toward one another, Roxana's lips parted, and she became more than ever lost to her surroundings. New light broke upon her concerning Miss Redmond's extreme agitation at the suggestion to tell Mr. Terriss the truth about his wife. She saw the sensitive conscience, the delicate mind, in new clearness.

Her reverie was interrupted by her boarder's voice.

" Well, how did it come out ? " he asked, ap-

pearing at the door. " Did Mrs. Redmond attend
the *séance?* "

Roxana turned her eyes upon him with a dazed
expression, which she might indeed have brought
from one of the meetings usually designated by
the title he had used at random.

" What is it ? " she asked, endeavoring to recall
her thoughts.

" Did your patient walk ? "

Roxana shuddered. " No," she replied curtly.

" You look tired," said Chester kindly. " I am
very sorry for your disappointment."

" O Mr. Chester," and Mrs. Sherritt leaned
back in her chair; " that woman is a — I don't
know what to say she is," she finished abruptly,
realizing that she was on the eve of reviling a
member of the sex she loved to one of that sex
which, to use Mr. Gilbert's phrase, she considered
" nature's sole mistake." " I think I shall have to
be done with her," she added.

" Oh, Miss Redmond is responsible for this faint-
heartedness," said Terriss.

Mrs. Sherritt nodded. " Yes," she replied,
" Miss Rebecca is at the bottom of it."

" Mrs. Redmond will be firmer. She will restore
your energies. You have not tried me yet. I may
have a suggestion worthy to be followed."

Roxana only shook her head disconsolately.
" I 've got the heartache, Mr. Chester, a real, low-
down, discouraged heartache, and it 's all because
o' Mrs. Terriss. I can't talk about her any more

to-day. I want to know, if you 're goin' to walk this afternoon, if you 'd just as soon go to Beech Knoll as anywhere ? "

" I will go with pleasure," was the prompt reply.

" Miss Rebecca left her hand-bag at the minister's this mornin', and I brought it home. I want to get it to her."

Terriss' countenance displayed the most cordial concurrence. " It is a kindness to give me an errand," he declared.

" All right. I should be glad to send it; but when you get there, Mr. Chester, don't ask to see Miss Rebecca; if she feels as tuckered out as I do, she won't care to have any company to-day. I suppose you would just as lief see Mrs. Redmond ? "

Accordingly, after the noon dinner, Terriss set forth on his commission, very little of the invalid appearing in his springing gait. Arrived at Beech Knoll, a servant told him that Mrs. Redmond was out in the grounds, perhaps in the grove by the river.

Declining the maid's proffered guidance, he strolled toward the water, enjoying the sunlight, the sweet odors, and a bird song, which dissolved all their beauty in the glow of his anticipation. He reached the grove, and the sight that met his eyes made him pause suddenly.

Mrs. Redmond was there as he had expected, lying in a hammock as he had suspected, but what disconcerted him was the fact that she was fast asleep.

"The Sleeping Beauty in the wood," he thought, and in natural sequence the Prince's action occurred to him, and he smiled as he considered that what was chivalrous, romantic, fitting, in the hero of the fairy tale, would, if he imitated his example now, be unchivalrous and mean, not to mention being followed by condign punishment at the hand of the Beauty.

"So much for the difference between fact and romance," he sighed, but the smile remained on his lips as he seated himself in a rustic chair. Nothing in all the realm of fancy could be more charming to him than his present nineteenth-century environment, no enchanted bower of fairyland more tempting than Mrs. Redmond's grove of beeches, and certainly no princess of story could have looked lovelier, sleeping, than the lady before him.

A light gray shawl was spread over the hammock. The cushion that supported her head was covered with dull, deep red silk, and as she lay, one hand beneath her cheek and the other dropped upon the shawl, she made a picture which caused Chester's hand to seek his pocket involuntarily for the block of paper which always accompanied him. He made a rapid sketch, but in his eagerness to get another he started to tear off the sheet, and, although he took pains to remove it quietly, the sound wakened the sleeper. She turned slightly, opened her eyes, closed and opened them again, started violently, and spoke.

" Mr. Chester ! "

" Excuse me, I fear I wakened you," he said apologetically.

" What do you mean ? How long have you been here ? "

There was vexation in her voice, and Chester's cheerfulness faded.

" Not very long," he said meekly. " Perhaps fifteen minutes."

" Fifteen minutes ! It might as well have been fifteen months."

" I wish it had been," responded Terriss devoutly.

" Well, it was very impertinent in you, very."

Chester rose, looking perplexed. " What should I have done ? " he asked.

" Gone away, of course."

" But I wanted to see you."

" Very well, you saw I was asleep."

" And I was perfectly willing to wait," returned Terriss quickly.

Elise smiled impatiently, and bit her lip. " I am not well. You will have to excuse me to-day. Good-afternoon, Mr. Chester."

Terriss looked at her, his eyes full of surprise and reproach.

" This is Miss Redmond's bag," he said. " I came to bring it." He laid it on the chair he had vacated. " Good-by," and he turned and walked away.

Elise immediately rose from her helpless posture. "Is the man half-witted?" she thought. "Does n't he know that I have to get out of this miserable hammock?" and with a sweep of her skirts, she put first one and then the other of her slippered feet to the ground.

Terriss, walking along, quite wretched from disappointment, heard her voice.

"Mr. Chester."

He turned. She was sitting on the edge of the hammock, her back against the netting, gently rocking herself to and fro. He looked at her, and as she did not speak again, he walked back.

"Is n't it a wonderfully warm day for the season?" she remarked. "Is that the reason Phyllis did not come with you?"

"No. Mrs. Sherritt wanted her at home this afternoon. Oh, Phyllis wanted me to thank you for the tennis suit. It looks very pretty on her."

"It would be more gallant for you to say she looks very pretty in it."

"I am never gallant. I have not had any practice. The dress belonged to you, and that is all I think of when I see it."

Elise smiled. "Upon my word, very well for a beginner. Is it your pleasure to practice on me?"

"I fear I shall have to, if on any one, for there is no one else who will ever teach me now."

She colored. "Oh, fie! you are too open. An artist should understand better keeping himself in perspective."

" I was putting myself in perspective as fast as I could when you called me back. What did you wish ? "

" Why, to see you, of course, after you have come so far."

" Then will you tell me why you sent me away ? "

" For the same reason that I called you back."

" Why was that ? "

" You will have to guess."

Terriss reseated himself, taking Miss Rebecca's bag on his knee. " I was always very slow at guessing," he said, the serenity returning to his face.

" Toss that bag over here out of your way. Perhaps you can tell me some particulars of this morning's experience at the parsonage. My sister came home with such a headache she could scarcely speak beyond telling me that the experiment was a failure."

" Mrs. Sherritt was more depressed when she returned than I ever knew her to be. Probably they had counted more on success than they realized."

" It is a case that interests me very much," said Elise. " I hope it is not going to be left in this way."

" It shall not be, since you wish it. From my impressions of Mrs. Terriss, I should have said that perhaps the less locomotion she was capable of, the better. However, you wish her to walk, and so some way must be devised to accomplish it."

Chester looked directly at her as he spoke, with

the unconscious worship in his eyes which she found so novel.

They had met several times now, and on each occasion she had observed that he never seemed desirous of making a good impression upon her, but always wore the same docile air of adoration, quite as though what she thought of him was a matter of no moment, but that his subjection to her was an inevitable matter of course. It was her first experience of an admirer who exacted nothing, who seemed not even to think of himself. It was very pleasant flattery, certainly, but it took away all the satisfaction of overcoming resistance which she had anticipated on the day when his letter to the minister had angered and wounded her so deeply. As she looked at him now, he was so different from her mental picture of the writer of that letter, she could scarcely credit the fact of his identity. Where under that placid, gentle exterior dwelt all the resentment and obstinacy he had manifested?

"Have you sketched much of late?"

He smiled and touched his sketch block. "It was because I tried to tear off a leaf from this that you waked," he said.

"Why, what was there here worth sketching?" asked Elise quickly and suspiciously. "Have you taken my grove?"

"I shall not answer you, unless beforehand you promise to spare my life."

"Then you have done something more impertinent," she exclaimed, coloring. "If you were base enough to sketch me, you must give it to me at once."

"You are not really angry, are you?" He asked it with so much simplicity and anxiety that it was with difficulty she forbore smiling.

"Indeed I am; and if you wish to be forgiven, you will show me that sketch immediately."

"Well, I will destroy it," and he began tearing the leaf.

"No, no, I wish to see it." She extended her hand imperiously.

He passed it to her in silence, and she studied it eagerly.

"Did I really look as peaceful as this?" she asked.

"You looked very peaceful."

"It is not — not becoming to people to be asleep," she said, still flushed and resentful, and speaking with some embarrassment. "You had no right" —

Light began to dawn upon Chester as to the nature of his offense, but he was too earnest a slave to feel any amusement.

"It is very becoming to you," he said. "You fulfilled my idea of the Sleeping Beauty. This sketch is nothing, but I could do it. I could make a portrait of you."

"You have really a gift for getting likeness. I recognize myself here. Why did you not cultivate your talent instead of adopting a business life?"

In answer to the careless question, Elise saw the face before her change. The eager, happy light faded that had made it young, the eyes grew gloomy, the whole countenance expressed sullen endurance and discontent. The writer of the offensive letter of refusal was before her.

"That is a long story," he replied; and now she understood how Rebecca could have been startled by his surly manner. "But it can be made a very short one. Necessity and poverty compelled me."

"That was hard. It is a wonder you did not prefer to remain in the profession you loved, even though it kept you poor. That seems to be the artist spirit."

"Poor? I shall always be poor. I have no interest in making money; but I preferred to get what time I could for my art work and do it for love, rather than be a mediocre painter, obliged to do work he loathed to obtain bread and butter. Of course I shall never do anything worth doing. I know that well enough."

Elise felt a little thrill of compassion for the speaker.

"Not even if you do my portrait?" she asked lightly.

The dark eyes that had been gazing out toward the water turned back to her.

"Do you mean to let me try?"

"I believe I will. Of course it will be on a business basis."

He smiled. "You mean you want to pay me for it?"

" Yes."

" I would rather you did not."

" Why ? "   The question was short, and asked in a tone which recalled Terriss to realities.

He bowed slightly.   " Forgive me.   You must remember it is a very unusual occurrence for me to receive an order for a portrait."

" An ability to make really fine portraits," said Elise, " would have given you something better than a hand-to-mouth living."   Her heart hurried a little as she decided how to continue.   She felt she must draw him out, yet she feared to be moved to anger against him by what he might say of her father.   " I am sorry you happened not to be able to study," she added.

" Especially as I grew from childhood almost to manhood with every expectation of having the means to do so."

Mrs. Redmond's heart pulsed faster.   " That certainly made it doubly hard," she said gently.

" It did.   I have never been man enough to rise above the disappointment."

But he had been man enough to refuse her money, and Elise remembered it now, realizing how sorely tempted he must have been.   " Have you lost your parents ? " she asked, to lead him on.

" Yes; but a male orphan of thirty-five summers in tolerable health can hardly be considered a pathetic object."

" That depends upon circumstances.   I am an orphan of twenty-seven summers, and sometimes

I feel the loneliness to be more pathetic than I did at seventeen.   Your people had money and lost it, I suppose."

" A very common fate," said Chester.

The evasive reply and succeeding silence showed Mrs. Redmond that at least it was not a relief and satisfaction to him to revile her father to any chance listener.

" You are not inclined to talk about yourself," she remarked, smiling.

He smiled in his turn.   " As a matter of fact, I am a very uninteresting subject, even to myself."

" Mr. Terriss told me, I believe, that you have lived in California most of your life.   I have friends there.   I wonder if you know any of them. The Smalls.   Do you know any of the Smalls ? "

" Yes, there were some Smalls who lived near us," replied Chester, in a manner which betokened a supreme indifference to that family.

" The Smalls, and the Haydens, and the Beckwiths," continued Elise.   " They lived near together, and I knew them all."

Chester looked up with a gleam of interest. " You knew the Beckwiths, Mr. Aaron Beckwith's family? "

Again Mrs. Redmond's heart beat fast.   His eyes were fixed upon her, and it seemed to her he must recognize her.

" I knew Elise Beckwith.   I went to school with her," she answered.

He looked away again, his thoughts evidently far distant.

" Did you ever hear her speak of her father's adopted son ? "

" Yes, I have," replied Elise faintly.

" I knew him," said Terriss curtly.

" Did you ?   I believe Mr. Beckwith was devoted to him."

" Indeed ? "

" Yes.   I used to think it rather remarkable that Elise never seemed to be jealous of him.   It was perfectly evident to me, from what she said, that the father's heart was more bound up in that boy than in the daughter who was his own flesh and blood.   Did it not speak well for the boy and girl both, that the one should have been able to command such loyalty, and that the other should have been so willing to give it ? "

" Did you ever hear what became of the boy ? " asked Terriss.

" I went abroad soon after those school-days."

" The devotion of Mr. Beckwith for his adopted son was not so deep as to prevent his sending him adrift when a difference of opinion arose between them."

" Oh ! "

" All the plans and ambitions which that boy had been encouraged to expect to carry out were laid low in a day, and he dismissed without a dollar beyond what he had in his pocket.   Not an unprecedented situation for a boy, you will say.

True ; but this boy, though not entirely lacking in independence of feeling, had been full of ardent hope to progress in the art he loved. It was his very life, and the disproportion between his offense and its punishment embittered him."

"Naturally," exclaimed Elise, thrilled by his tone and manner almost to forgetfulness that she was joining in blame of her father. " It was not right! It was not right!"

The excited and sympathetic tone made him turn his eyes back to her with the old expression. "How did we come to talk of this?" he said. "Let us never do it again."

" But I must. It interests me so. Do you not believe that, had Mr. Beckwith lived, he would have recalled you?"

" Me?"

Elise colored furiously. "Your manner made me suspect" — she said, "made me certain that you yourself are that disappointed boy."

Chester laughed. " Your knowledge of human nature probably prevents you from crediting me with showing so much feeling for another."

"Not at all. I have a very high opinion of human nature; still, I think you are the boy. You know women have strong intuitions and often correct ones."

" The boy disappeared long ago," rather moodily. "I am what he left behind him."

" And the girl — Elise?" asked Mrs. Redmond softly.

He looked up. "You have seen her since I have, if you knew her in her teens."

"And have you never had sufficient interest in her to seek her?"

"No, I never took any interest in her. She was so much younger than myself, and so seldom at home, it was not to be expected."

"Yet she took an interest in you. She was the more generous of the two."

"I fancy she still piques herself on her generosity."

"Why?"

Chester raised his eyes, a humorous look in them. "Perhaps you still correspond with your school friend. I must not answer your questions."

"I do not correspond with her," returned Elise, feeling her color rise.

Terriss sighed reminiscently. "I dare say she is a dashing young lady, at present; but I remember thinking her an extraordinarily awkward, unattractive little thing."

"Was she indeed?" Mrs. Redmond's eyes looked very resentful as she put the question.

"Yes," returned the other absently; "she had this bright red hair, and hardly any flesh on her poor little bones."

"Ah! Did you never read your Hans Andersen when you were a child, Mr. Chester? Did you never read of the Ugly Duckling? I can assure you that when I knew Elise, and she was eighteen, she was not considered the worst-looking girl in school." The speaker's voice shook a little, in spite of herself. "For my part, I wonder you feel no tenderness in the remembrance of that plain little motherless child, whose indifferent father had eyes only for yourself, whose lot it was to be sent year after year among strangers, and whose child- ish heart would have responded so gladly to a few kind words from you, in whom she felt all a sister's pride."

Terriss gazed at the speaker in surprise, and when he discovered that there were actually tears in her eyes, his dismay knew no bounds. "I have hurt you in some way!" he exclaimed; and his honest despair must have alleviated a wound to his companion's *amour propre*, had it received one.

"Yes, you have," she returned. "I do not like to think you heartless, and the way you speak of Elise Beckwith is so different from her manner of speaking of you."

"Why did you not say you loved her?" asked Terriss, perplexed by her reproach.

"I hope you would still have been honest, if I had."

Chester looked at her gravely. "Mrs. Red- mond, I have led a lonely enough life. Be sure, I have thought, many a time in these after-years, of Elise, and longed for her friendship. It was a pleasant thought to me that somewhere in the world was this girl who, had events turned as they promised, would now be calling me brother."

Elise, woman-like, shrank inwardly at these cor-

dial words.   There was much which she must forgive before consenting to a reconciliation between
her actual self and her father's adopted son.   His
next words thawed her momentary stiffness in a
glow of unpleasant surprise.

"But lately an event occurred which changed
my feeling entirely, and deprived me of any desire
to renew what could hardly at best be called an
acquaintance."

"And what was that, please?" asked Mrs.
Redmond, in so imperious a tone of demand that
her companion looked at her a moment in silence.
Then he shook his head.

"You are too much a partisan," he said.   "Let
us change an unpleasant subject."

Elise controlled herself.   "I see you think me
a little impertinent in wishing to hear the whole
story."

"You could not be impertinent.   Nevertheless,
I prefer not to call upon myself any more such
flashes of your eyes."

"Be it so," she replied carelessly.   "A man is
not obliged to criminate himself."

"I beg your pardon.   There is no question of
self-accusation here."

"Then, if you are so confident, why not proceed?
Since I now know both the characters, the story
interests me."

"Very well, I will.   Your friend, Miss Beckwith, offered me money."

"Yes?"

" Yes," emphatically.

" Well?   Go on."

" Go on?   Is not that enough ? "

" Enough for what?   It was certainly very nice of her, and very natural, too."

Elise looked undauntedly into the dark eyes, although their expression of amazement and displeasure was not pleasant to endure.

" Well, you are even more partisan than I expected.   Still, you do not understand yet.   This girl, instead of making any friendly advance toward me, or allowing me to make her acquaintance, sends me through a third party an offer of money. You " — his hard tone changed, and he finished apologetically — " you did not understand."

Mrs. Redmond blushed brightly.   " I " — she hesitated ; then finished abruptly, " I believe she meant well."

Chester shrugged his shoulders.   " That never counts for much, you know."

" It ought to," said Elise, tears again in her eyes.   Her heart was beating fast, and she felt bewildered and confused, in strange contrast to her usual self-poise.   Amid the tumult, she realized that this repeated display of feeling would be likely to arouse suspicion, and that she must leave the subject.   " Very well," she continued, " you are so certain that you do not misjudge Elise that I see it is useless for me to argue with you.   At the same time, I believe she has always been more generous to you than you to her.   I believe in my own sex, you see."

Terriss nodded. "I might bring you to regard her motives as they look to me, but I am content not to try. I felt very hot over the matter for a time; but now the most indifferent being to me on earth is Elise Beckwith."

This was said with a look which belied the words so utterly that Mrs. Redmond laughed. She was as near to a hysterical condition as a woman of her strength can come.

"When is my portrait to be commenced?" she asked abruptly.

"Oh, when you like. To-morrow?" eagerly.

"I rather expect Tony Bellows to arrive to-morrow. Why, what is the matter? You do not look so rapturous in the prospect of seeing your friend as you should."

"I had forgotten for a little while that he was coming," returned Chester; then he paused. He perceived that he should appear as absurd to resent Tony's advent as he would to sulk because a cloud floated between him and the sun.

"When may I come, then?" he asked quietly.

Elise looked at him curiously, almost inclined to believe that, should she declare her identity, that worshiping face would still say, "Command, and I obey;" but she would not risk it quite yet.

"Come Monday," she replied.

"Very well. Meanwhile, I will study Mrs. Terriss' case."

"Oh, yes. All Snowdon will lionize you, if you succeed there."

CHAPTER XVIII.

THE OLD BRIDGE.

WHILE this talk was going on, Miss Rebecca sat in her room behind locked doors and pondered. After the horror of the first shock of Mrs. Terriss' accusation, she felt the benefit of the strength and temper which years of self-control and orderly performance of duty had given to her character. A frantic, desperate, girlish misery was impossible to her now, and although the fresh wound was a deep one, she rose to an endurance of it; even more, to a height above it, from which she could look down, as it were, upon her own suffering and calmly consider it. Nothing more humiliating than this could have come to her. All her woman's nature cried out in pain at the insult she had received. She even hesitated a moment before the tribunal of her own conscience, asking whether, by ever so little, there was truth in the invalid's accusation; but the answer came quickly: Not guilty. She felt herself fully exonerated from the charge. No self-interest had insinuated itself into her genuine effort to bless. The realization was a great support to her, and mitigated the force of those poisonous words which seemed to echo over and over in her ears. At last, worn out by excitement and

exertion, she lay down upon her bed and fell
asleep.

It was twilight in the room when she awoke,
and for a minute she felt bewildered. Why had
she been sleeping at this hour? What had happened? With a rush, memory returned to her.
Some one in the village knew of the bittersweet
episode of her youth, and discovering that the
minister was the hero of the story, had informed
his wife, and the latter had used her knowledge in
a cowardly and cruel fashion.

"It was a poor return," mused Rebecca, — "a
poor return ; but she does not know."

She lay still, musing. Her thoughts went back
to that old time, and she did not attempt to divert
them. At last she rose, obeying an impulse, and
catching up a wrap went quietly downstairs and
out of the house. She walked down the slight
declivity that led to the river, then moved along
its bank until she came to a huge willow-tree. At
sight of it, her heart contracted, giving her a sensation of faintness.

One step more and her foot touched the bridge.
She walked out upon it, and stood at the railing,
looking down into the murmuring water. Farther
on, the river would rush swiftly to turn the busy
wheels of the manufacturer, but here its voice was
hushed, — hushed as on that night twenty years
ago when last she stood here.

As she leaned upon the railing, the music of the
wavelets and the sighing of the night winds amid

the branches of the old trees mingled with the thoughts to which, for once, she yielded without a struggle. It was as though the hurt she had received gave her the right to relax her firmly imposed self-denial.

The measurements of time fell away. The warm summer breeze touched her cheek gently. She was a girl again, her heart swelling with its love, yet nerved to its sacrifice. The unspeakable mingling of joy she would not have missed, and agony wellnigh unendurable possessed her. Giving the reins to memory, she indulged in the unwonted luxury of living over once again her springtime.

Sooner or later, she could not tell how long she had been standing there, another step sounded on the bridge, a man's step. It came nearer. Rebecca did not stir from her position. Involuntarily and unreasoningly she spoke, —

" Philip."

The man drew near and paused before her.

" Rebecca," he returned, and a thrill of eagerness pervaded his tone.

In the waning light she could distinguish his pallor and the expression of his face. Instantly her dream had fled. She was back in the present, and true to her habit of self-forgetfulness, forgot her own wound in a rush of compassion for him.

" Do not take it so, Philip," she said, with faltering gentleness.

" It seems too good to be true that you are here," he returned quietly. " I do not know why I came,

nor when I started.   I suppose I came to rest myself near you."

They stood side by side in silence for a minute.
Rebecca strove for calmness.   She felt the hopelessness of his mood and realized that she must be
strong; but the enervation of her mental self-in-
dulgence had been a poor preparation.

"It is the same sort of evening," he said at
last.   "Just as cool, just as quiet.   Oh, the blessed
night!   Rebecca, this is rest.   If only the sun
might never rise for me again — to be near you in
the coolness and the dark, and to have the end
come here, on the old bridge, where the coura-
geous young fellow that I once was laid down life
and hope twenty years ago!"

A sob rose in her throat, and she could only say
again, "Do not take it so, Philip."

The man turned and looked at her.

" Did I do right?" he demanded, with an acute
change of tone.   "I have never in all these years
dared to ask myself the question until to-day.   It
meant madness to doubt."

" It is madness to doubt," said Rebecca, and her
voice grew firm.   "You did right, nobly right.   I
have always honored you for it.   I honor you now
for it.   Everything is right."

"Everything is wrong," he returned dispassionately.   "Everything has been wrong since
that night."

" It seems so to you," said Rebecca gently, "but
it has been right, really right.   Do not question it,
even in your thought."

" As to the occurrence of to-day," he continued, in the same tone, weary almost to indifference, " there is nothing for me to say."

" No, there is nothing," she replied quietly. " Is there anything you think I had better do ? "

" Have you thought of — going away ? " he asked.

Rebecca smiled faintly. " You have been thinking of it too. Yes; talk about our old friendship is likely to become general in the village; I have considered going away."

Philip seized her hands, and she felt his tremble. " O Rebecca, I could not bear it ! " he exclaimed, a thrill of suffering in his tone. Tears sprang to Rebecca's eyes, and her heart beat suffocatingly. She could not speak ; but it was only for a moment.

" You could bear it, you will advise it, if it is best. Philip, listen to me. Remember, when we were two weak young creatures, how in this very spot we had strength given us to do what was honorable and right. Have the years not made us stronger ? We are more, not less, sure than then of receiving help when we ask for it."

Happily for mankind, a good habit is as masterful as an evil one. Philip Terriss had controlled and constrained and denied himself for twenty years. Rebecca's intuitive appeal fell upon ear that could hear.

He dropped her hands and turned away.

" Forget my hasty words. Do not let them frighten you or affect your decision," he said.

Rebecca looked at him with troubled eyes.

" Go, if you fear at all the gossip of idle tongues," he continued. " It is little enough they can find to fasten upon."

" And if I should decide that it is best not to show fear of them " —

" Then stay."

" And — you ? " said Rebecca faintly.

" I ? You need not think of me."

" You must tell me," said Rebecca resolutely, " while we are here alone with God and conscience, if, so far as you are concerned, you can ask me to stay in Snowdon."

" Yes, stay," he replied. " Struggle and endurance, struggle and endurance, that is life for me at best."

" Philip ! And you are a minister ! "

" Yes, and what of that ? Why should clergymen be put in a cruelly unnatural place ? A struggling, tempted minister is a struggling, tempted man, able to derive no more strength and help from his theories than any other human being derives from his. It is the amount of truth we have *lived* that helps us in an emergency, not the amount of truth we know."

He looked at Rebecca's white hair, gleaming under the black lace thrown over it, and smiled bitterly. " I sometimes wonder," he added, " if I should know what to do with happiness if it came to me."

She glanced up at him, and it would have helped

him to catch the soft radiance in her eyes. " You will know when it comes."

" When it comes ? " he repeated.

" Yes, it is coming, of course. What matter whether in this world or the next? It is all life, you know, and meanwhile there is always enough work to do and real satisfaction to be found in it. That, Philip, you must admit is a helpful truth, for you are living it every day."

" Yes, Rebecca, yes." There was an utter absence of elasticity in tone and manner. " Of course you will come no more to my house," he added, after a moment of silence.

" No more, of course."

" That must be. My wife has forfeited all claim."

" Philip, forgive her," said Miss Redmond, with timid appeal. " No one could live the life she does without becoming morbid. She sees things in a distorted fashion. Tell me you forgive her. It was her love for you " —

" Rebecca! " the minister interrupted sharply. " Yes, you are right," he added gently, " you are always right. I think I shall see the situation correctly after a time. Just to night I can't think about it. When she accused you to-day, something within me seemed to snap. If hearts ever broke, I should think mine had. Some resistance, some grip that I had on things yesterday has gone."

The quietly spoken words sent a desolate chill through Rebecca's heart. She was silent, for there were no words that she might speak to comfort him.

The river murmured and sang. The willow dipped its tassels deeper in the water as the wind arose.

"Stale and unprofitable," said Philip musingly. "Surely no man ever had greater cause than I to look back on life and say, to what good?"

His companion turned to him suddenly. "I cannot listen to that," she said. "You have fulfilled the duties of your profession conscientiously, and you have made your wife happy. You have succeeded in your undertaking, *succeeded*. Think what that means, Philip! You should be humbly thankful, *happy* this night, instead of downcast. You have shown yourself a hero in the battle of life, and do you say to what good? Do not disappoint me so. It is not your inmost feeling. I refuse to believe it." Her earnest tone changed to one of anxiety. "You are shivering. Come, you must not stay here longer. You must go home directly."

"Yes," he replied, taking her hand in his cold one, "this leaf is turned. I must go — home. We leave the old bridge together to-night, Rebecca. We did not before. You went, I stayed. Do you remember?"

Rebecca looked at him with yearning compassion. "The bridge has been made over since that night," she said gently. "It is not the same bridge. We are not the same people. We must not remember too much. You yourself once called my attention to one of the best rules of life I have ever had. ' Look up and not down ; look forward and not back ; look out and not in ! ' "

" Forward and not back," repeated Philip as he relinquished her hand, and they advanced upon the soft, damp turf. " Good teaching, good teaching. My inclination is to look a long way forward, as it is to look a long way back."

At the graveled walk, they parted. Nothing save a simple good-night passed between them, and Rebecca stood still to look after the minister's figure, walking heavily toward the gate.

When it disappeared, she caught her breath in an involuntary, tremulous sigh, and began to move slowly toward the house.

She was conscious now of feeling bruised and tired from the strain, and as though she must have a long interval of rest and stillness to restore her inner tranquillity.

What then was her disappointment on entering the house to hear a bright, hearty voice in the hall. " Don't trouble yourself. I 'll find somebody, never fear. Just take this box, will you, and give the roses a drink."

Tony, of course ! Tony, bringing a flower-laden breeziness with him, forming with his youthful, happy noisiness the most striking contrast that could be found to the overstrained man with whom she had just parted.

She shrank back with the idea of concealing

herself, but at that moment Tony turned from the maid into whose hands he had intrusted a box.

"Why, Miss Rebecca, I'm awfully glad to see you," exclaimed the cordial young fellow, advancing and shaking her hand heartily. "It seems a year since I was here before. Now don't say anything cruel. Mrs. Redmond would, but you won't, I know. You have some mercy on a fellow."

"You are one of the last beings on earth who should appeal for mercy, Mr. Bellows."

"Oh, don't call me Mr. Bellows. You know we settled that the last time I was here."

"Did we? So we did. Well, it is much easier to say Tony. I never feel quite so old and slow as I do when you are about. Go into the parlor, and I will call Mrs. Redmond."

"Not yet. Not quite yet, Miss Rebecca. I have been thinking of you all the way out from town, and who knows if I will have another opportunity to see you so quietly alone."

"Thinking of me?" said Rebecca, leading the way into the dimly lighted parlor. "I wonder why."

"Because," returned Tony ruefully, "you are just as good and kind as you can be, and I knew you wouldn't snub me if I told you. No, let us not have a brighter light. I like this very much, if you do."

Rebecca sat down obediently in a chair the young fellow drew forward for her.

"It will be such a comfort for me to talk it

over," he continued. "In the first place, I must ask you outright, Miss Redmond, if you would have any feeling as to your sister-in-law's making a second marriage?"

"None at all, I assure you."

"Then oh, Miss Rebecca," he burst forth, "do you suppose she would marry me?"

"*You!*" exclaimed Miss Redmond, in such genuine astonishment that poor Tony colored even in the darkness up to his yellow hair.

"Oh, come now, don't take it that way," he protested.

"But you are — she is older, several years older than you."

"Age has nothing to do with her any more than it would have with any other goddess," burst forth the lover. "I do adore her so, and I can't get over it, and I can't forget her, and I shall never change," finished Tony, volubly replying in advance to the time-honored advice he feared to receive. "She doesn't care for anybody else, does she?"

"I imagine not; but I am certain, Tony, really certain" — began Miss Rebecca kindly.

"I shall ask her anyway," he interrupted obstinately.

"You will astonish her very much, and you will put an end to the pleasant relationship between you."

"You are extremely certain what answer she would give me, aren't you?"

" And you are also in your inmost heart," returned Miss Rebecca. " There would be something unsuitable about the match which you can feel and see."

He was quiet a minute, then he spoke again.

" A very queer thing happened to me once, Miss Redmond. A young lady, a very nice girl in every way, proposed to me."

" That *was* a queer thing," remarked Miss Rebecca dryly.

" But she was a *very* nice girl and a good girl," said Tony eagerly. " Never mind. All I speak of it for is because I remember how neatly I thought I got out of it. I told her she was surely mistaken in believing that she cared for me, because love always begets love, and I did not love her."

" That *was* neat," admitted Miss Rebecca.

" But it was a lie. Have n't I proved it to be a lie, since I adore Elise, and she is indifferent to me ? "

Miss Redmond smiled. " It would certainly be impossible for Mrs. Redmond to return the affection of all the men who have believed they adored her," she remarked.

" Do you imagine for one minute any of those others felt as I do? I have come out here with my mind made up to tell her the truth, and prudent or imprudent I shall do it. I know I shall not be able to be in her presence five minutes without doing so. I " —

" Well, well, Tony, what in the world is the matter ? " questioned Elise gayly, coming into the room.

Mr. Bellows gave a guilty and violent start, and sprang to his feet.

" Oh, Mrs. Redmond, I came a little sooner than I expected. You don't mind, I hope. I have n't inconvenienced you ? "

" Not at all. We are delighted," returned the hostess, giving him her hand. " We have really looked forward to having a sportive young person about again."

" Thank you," said Tony, stiffening into extreme dignity, and growing warm at the laughing tone.

" Yes, you shall turn Beech Knoll into one big playground, and I shall invite that pretty little girl, Phyllis Flower, to come and play with you. Speaking of flowers, the roses you brought me are exquisite. But why are you in the dark in here ? Was it Rebecca you were addressing in such stentorian tones ? "

" Yes — I — I " — stammered Tony, evidently quaking.

" I heard only enough to make me immensely curious. You were going to tell somebody something before you had been in her presence five minutes ; and, judging by your tone, when that somebody hears the something, her blood will run cold. Are n't you going to tell me about it ? I am just as safe a confidante as Miss Redmond."

" I — I can't tell you. That is, not now," hesitated Tony, conscious of his own absurdity and fuming proportionately. "It was n't much of anything — that is, you will know some time."

"I think I will go upstairs, if you will excuse me," said Miss Redmond, rising.

Tony seized her arm. "Oh, stay awhile longer," he said, trying to use a jovial tone, which succeeded only in being desperate.

"Yes ; we will have a light so we can see one another," remarked Elise. "You can't plead sleepiness so soon as this, after your nap of this afternoon, Rebecca."

Tony took advantage of his hostess' move to call the servant, and turned to Miss Redmond.

"I can't say anything while she is in this mood, of course," he muttered impatiently.

"Very wise," returned Rebecca, smiling. "If you will be advised by me, you will keep her friendship exactly as it is."

CHAPTER XIX.

MR. BELLOWS' CONFIDENCE.

"Roxana, you *must* tell me what is the matter with you," cried Phyllis imperiously. "I have spoken to you three times without being able to get your attention."

"Maybe I 'm gettin' deaf, Phyllis," replied Mrs. Sherritt with a start. "Old age will come to high or low, spry or slow, if they live long enough."

"Oh, don't give such an excuse. Only look in the glass at your eyes. They have been just as round and scared as that ever since you got home from Mrs. Terriss' that day. I doubt if they have closed since. You never kept a secret from me before. I think you are too unkind. Now do tell me what happened at Mrs. Terriss'."

"She would n't step foot to the ground. I told you that, and that 's all I 've got to tell."

"Miss Rebecca will tell me," remarked the girl, with a determined setting of the lips.

"Phyllis Flower, look here." Roxana grasped her arm with a force that made her wince. "If you want to be mortified and ashamed to the last day of your life, do you ask Miss Rebecca about that day. If you want to disobey and displease me more 'n you ever have since you was born, do you speak to Miss Rebecca on that subject."

Phyllis stared for a moment with parted lips. It seemed incredible, but there were actually tears in Mrs. Sherritt's eyes.

"Well," she returned after her long scrutiny, "I am simply burning with curiosity."

"Burn, then," retorted Roxana, loosening her grip to dash away the gathering tears, and going briskly about her housework.

"Sha'n't I ever know?" asked Phyllis.

"I pray you won't, but perhaps you will."

"Never from you, though," said Phyllis.

"You can rest assured o' that," replied Roxana shortly.

Phyllis made a little *moue* of disgust, and skipped across the room and out of the open door with such vigor and abandon as very nearly to cause a collision between herself and an individual in the act of ascending the steps.

If her startled cry was scarcely sufficiently repressed for good manners, she was to be excused, since anything so gorgeous as Mr. Bellows in his tennis costume had never before been observed at the entrance of any of the staid old dwellings of Snowdon. He wore trousers of white flannel and an uncommonly blazing "blazer" and cap, making an effect so surprising that Phyllis, in her quaint little pink calico gown, could only stand, after the first retreat, and stare, and gasp, —

"Mr. Bellows! Oh — why, Mr. Bellows! How do you do? Won't you come in?"

"Thank you, I will, just long enough for you to

get ready to return with me. I am commissioned
to bring you, and under no circumstances to take
no for an answer," returned Tony, shaking hands
and looking appreciatively at the girl's brown
eyes, clear complexion, and short dark waves of
hair. Miss Redmond had been depressing, discouraging, on the evening of his arrival, certainly.
She had actually succeeded in persuading him to
lock his feelings in his bosom so far through his
visit; but the weather was beautiful, and the be-
comingness of Phyllis's pink gown raised his cork-
like spirits a degree higher than they had been for
many a day.

Roxana, hearing the approaching voice, appeared at the parlor door.

" Who " — she began, and paused. Tony's
canary and crimson stripes arrested her. He
bowed low, cap in hand, and Roxana responded
with a slight nod, while her eyes never forsook the
amazing coat.

" Mr. Bellows, you know, Roxana," exclaimed
Phyllis eagerly. " Mrs. Redmond wants me to
come and play tennis. Of course I can go."

Mrs. Sherritt would have required a heart of
flint to withstand the intensity of appeal thrown
into the closing words.

" Oh, by the way," remarked Tony, " Mrs. Redmond sent an invitation also to Mr. Chester."

" Go up and ask him, will you, Roxana ? " asked
Phyllis. " I will go at once and change my dress.
I will not detain you long, Mr. Bellows," and she
left the room.

Mrs. Sherritt climbed resignedly to her boarder's door, and knocked.

"Come in," was called in an unusually cheerful voice, and she entered. Chester merely glanced up from the collection of tubes and brushes scattered about him. "Have you come to see why I am spending so much valuable time indoors? I wish to have everything all ready in case Mrs. Redmond should send for me. I suppose Phyllis told you that I am going to paint Mrs. Redmond's portrait."

"She 's sent for you now," said Roxana shortly.

Terriss looked up eagerly.

"No, you can leave your paints and things this time. She wants you should come and play tennis. That young man Bellow is downstairs, lookin' as though he 'd just come out of a circus ring. If I ever saw the like, my name ain't Sherritt."

"Oh," with a decided falling of the countenance, "Tony has arrived, has he?"

"I should think he had. A body needs blue spectacles to look at him with comfort. Phyllis is hurryin' up to go. She 's sent for, too."

"Very well," said Chester, returning to the examination of his brushes. "Please ask them not to wait for me. I will follow after a time."

Roxana nodded, and took her way to Phyllis's room. The girl was in the act of slipping on the costume in which her soul rejoiced. The corners of Mrs. Sherritt's mouth twitched down in a repressed smile of gratification as she regarded the pretty picture. Phyllis tied the long soft sash of gray silk, then turned about for inspection.

"You look very well," said Roxana, in that moderate and cool tone which she deemed wholesome for the young and flighty. "I did think them stripes o' yours was some showy yesterday, but good land, since I've seen that chap in the parlor there, you look modest enough."

"Oh, he is *elegant*, Roxana."

"Elegant, eh?" responded Mrs. Sherritt dryly. "May*be;* but all the same, if you should see anybody on your way up there that looks as if he might be the fool-catcher, my advice is that you screech for help."

Phyllis laughed, threw her arms around Mrs. Sherritt's neck, and pressed her blooming cheek to the sallow one.

"Dear old Roxana!" she exclaimed, an exultant, rich sense of life possessing her; "it is too bad that I have all the fun."

Roxana patted her with a sparing caress. "Yes, it *is* too bad that I can't go and race around in the hot sun and bat a ball against that big red and yeller butterfly; but I'll try to bear it."

"Will you truly have a good time, Roxana?"

"Of course I will. It'll be a regular treat to have you and Mr. Chester both gone. I haven't read 'The Lamplighter' yet, this year. I wouldn't wonder but I'd sit down and begin it, after things are all quiet."

"Yes, do," returned the girl, releasing her. "Any message for Miss Rebecca?"

" No, not a word," replied Roxana decidedly. "Don't say a word to her about me."

" You are n't vexed with Miss Rebecca? That is n't the secret, is it? "

" No, ma'am, it ain't. When I 'm vexed with Miss Rebecca, it 'll be time to put me in a strait-jacket. Mr. Chester 'll be along presently. He ain't quite through fixin' his paints, and he don't want you to wait for him. You are gettin' to feel pretty well acquainted with Mr. Chester, Phyllis?" finished Roxana, an unpleasant remembrance floating up to her of Mrs. Terriss' prognostications.

" Oh, yes. Much of the time I feel that I have known him always," returned the girl ; " but sometimes he goes away from me, — seems all shut up, you know."

Mrs. Sherritt watched the unclouded face as Phyllis bent over a drawer looking for her gloves. " If that ain't a heart-whole girl, I never saw one," she thought ; but she decided to press the matter a little. " We shall miss him some when he goes back to the city," she remarked.

" We shall indeed," said Phyllis absently. " Roxana, where do you suppose my gloves are ? "

" A fig for Mrs. Terriss! I might have known she could n't have a sensible idea." This comforting thought flitted quickly through Roxana's brain ; then she fell to scolding Phyllis vigorously for being guilty of such a lapse from order as to mislay her gloves.

A few minutes later, the girl came into the parlor and joined her gay cavalier, who looked his approval of her appearance.

Roxana stood at a window and watched their departure. " Red and yeller, catch a feller," she murmured. " I kinder hope Phyllis won't meet anybody she knows, and yet she looks as pretty as a pink, if I do say it. See that Bellow man look at her! Yes, look, young feller; there ain't a better lookin', nicer girl on any avenue in Boston. I ain't one bit afraid to have you look at her, from her little silky curls that I brushed around my finger when she was a baby, down to her feet. Phyllis has got nice feet, and I have n't ever let 'em be stunted or pinched. They 're a good shape, and she springs along on 'em exactly as Mother Nature meant she should. She 'll keep you at it, young man, to keep up with her," and Roxana turned away from the window with a low, slow laugh, as the young couple vanished from her sight.

It was no wonder that Mrs. Sherritt had been able to read admiration in the pose of Tony's head. He looked his companion over quite openly.

" That is the prettiest little dress I have seen in a long time," he remarked, gazing approvingly at the cap set jauntily on the short, shining hair.

" I am glad you like it," responded Phyllis, as carelessly and promptly as though it were not a total novelty for her to have her clothes remarked upon by a young man. It was a delightful thing altogether to feel sure she was correctly and be-

comingly dressed, to be escorted by a splendid being from Boston, and to be going to Beech Knoll.
That the sun should shine, the breezes blow, and
the birds sing, seemed only proper recognition on
the part of Nature of so ideal a set of circumstances. "My dress is very deceptive, though,"
continued Phyllis. "It is a prophetic costume.
It indicates what a very skillful tennis player I
intend to become .at some future day. For the
present, I play ridiculously."

"Never mind. Only get Mrs. Redmond to take
you on her side. Her playing carries anybody
along," and Tony finished with a sigh which testi-
fied to the depth and soundness of his lungs.

Phyllis laughed. "Is that so very sad?" she
asked; "or are you still so afraid of Mrs. Redmond that she is a solemn subject to you?"

"I — I am somewhat afraid of her still, I admit.
Such a glorious woman as she is would inspire any
man with that homage, that admiration, that has
something of awe in it."

"I am not in the least afraid of her any more,"
said Phyllis rather brusquely. It was the first
time praise of Mrs. Redmond had failed to please
her. "I find she is much too kind and sensible
and noble to inspire fear when one knows her."

"Ah, noble! Noble is the word!" exclaimed
Tony eagerly. "You have it, Miss Flower: noble in face, noble in form, noble in movement, noble in character, in aspirations. Ah!" and Tony
finished with another prodigious sigh.

Phyllis broke into a little mocking laugh. " I begin to think your name is very appropriate, Mr. Bellows. Be kind enough not to blow me off the sidewalk."

" I beg pardon ? " asked Tony vaguely.

" Why those tremendous sighs ? "

" Did I sigh ? Well, I háve reason enough. I have no right to bother you with my affairs ; but this one absorbing thought I find it difficult to keep from everybody except the one person I ought to tell it to. I know you would discover my secret long before to-day is over. Miss Flower, you know Mrs. Redmond perhaps better than I do ; does it seem to you she would be a very difficult person to propose to ? "

" To propose to, Mr. Bellows ! "

" I am sure I do not see why it should astonish you so," returned Tony, nettled. " Miss Rebecca received the suggestion in the same way. Now, when you know that Mrs. Redmond is a woman that everybody falls in love with, why should it be so amazing that a man should propose to her ? "

" I don't know," said Phyllis shortly. " Perhaps it is because she seems such a self-sufficient person. We all admire her : I do, you do, Mr. Chester does " —

" Oh, Chester does, does he ? " asked Tony quickly. " Well, he would n't if " — He checked himself with a thrill of dismay at his narrow escape from indiscretion ; " that is, I did not know that Chester ever admired anybody. How is he now ? "

" Quite well."

" About time for him to be going back to town, I should think," remarked Tony carelessly.

" Oh, I don't know. He does not seem to think of such a thing."

" Well, it is very strange," said Tony irritably. "I don't see why he should want to hang about here. I don't see what the attraction can be."

" That is because you are not artistic, Mr. Bellows," replied Phyllis quietly, but with a little sparkle of amusement in her eyes. " Mr. Chester finds the most charming views about here, he tells me, — especially in the region of Beech Knoll."

" Ah! goes up there, does he? Well, well, that is odd, all things considered."

" Why is it odd? You seem to think it well worth while to travel the distance from Boston for the pleasure. It is certainly not strange that Mr. Chester should enjoy strolling up there for an afternoon now and then, or to stay to a cozy lunch."

Tony writhed. " Well, Mrs. Redmond has her reasons for allowing it, I suppose, but Chester is a gruff old chap, — never saw any society worth mentioning."

" Yes," said Phyllis, beginning to enjoy the situation. " I imagine he will be going quite regularly after a time. She has asked him to paint her portrait."

" No! " ejaculated Tony.

" Oh, yes. I dare say, however, they will not begin it until after you have gone," returned naughty Phyllis demurely.

"Yes, they shall, certainly," said Tony. "I would like to see it go on. I will be present at the sittings, you know, and liven things up a bit for them both — read aloud, or something."

Phyllis gave him a mischievous glance. "Philanthropist!" she exclaimed. "Still," she continued, "even though Mr. Chester admires Mrs. Redmond so much" —

"Are you sure he does? Oh, you 're mistaken. As a model, he does, perhaps ; but nothing more, nothing more. Chester 's incapable of it."

"Did you not just say, Mr. Bellows, that she conquers every one? He does admire her. We often talk of her; but it never occurred to me before that he could think of proposing to her."

"Proposing to her! Ha, ha, that would be rich! Ha, ha, ha! Oh, preposterous!"

"Well!" exclaimed Phyllis, in an offended tone. "Then perhaps Miss Rebecca was excusable in thinking a proposal from you would be preposterous."

"I? Oh, that is a very different matter. If," with another sigh, which seemed to come from the depths of his being, — "if I only knew how she would take it."

Phyllis tossed her head. "If I were a man, I would never risk proposing until I knew certainly how I should be received. I have always thought so."

"You have, eh?" said Tony, much interested. "But do you think a woman ever really lets a man know how she feels toward him, that is, as a usual thing?" he added, qualifying his speech as the remembrance of his unique experience returned to him.

"A true, noble woman is always transparently honest," announced Phyllis loftily.

"Well, I don't know. I've always thought, 'Trust her not, she's fooling thee' was a pretty straight tip. Perhaps you're fooling me now. Say, do you know that dress is awfully becoming to you?"

Phyllis's thin scarlet lip curled, and she held the back of her neck very straight. "Shall I tell you why you admire this dress so much?" she said quietly. "It belonged to Mrs. Redmond. She gave it to me."

Tony impulsively seized one of the ends of the soft gray sash and carried it to his lips.

Phyllis flashed her eyes upon him, brilliant as two brown diamonds, and pulled the silk from his hands with sudden energy.

"Kiss Mrs. Redmond's clothes upon herself as much as you please. You shall not touch them upon me."

Tony stared at her aghast. There was no mistaking the sincerity of her resentment; and how brilliantly pretty she looked! It suddenly dawned upon him that the little country girl was an individual, and not one who would take kindly to the role of makeshift to a love-lorn swain. He reviewed mentally the talk with which he had so far entertained her, and tersely characterized himself as a "chump."

Phyllis, herself surprised by her unusual access of anger, breathed a little fast.

"There is Mrs. Redmond coming out of the gate to meet us," she said as Elise appeared, arrayed in white, with glimpses of lilac here and there as she walked.

The hostess approached and took Phyllis's hand cordially. It was her peculiarity, and one her friends soon learned, that she did not include a kiss in her greetings.

"You looked like a dove and a tropical bird coming up the street," she said, " but how brilliant and far from meek the dove looks! What witty sallies have you employed, Tony, to light her up so successfully?"

Tony could not answer. He felt crushed, and not all his gorgeous coloring could give him aught but a dejected and drooping appearance as he followed the ladies within the broad gates.

CHAPTER XX.

ELISE.

When Terriss Chester arrived at Beech Knoll, he found Miss Redmond only. She was sitting on a gauze-inclosed piazza, with a novel in her hand.

"You find me lazily employed, Mr. Chester," she said, rising to greet him. "In my young days, if a well woman of my age had been discovered in her own home at this hour reading a novel, she would at least have had the grace to be ashamed of herself."

"Which you have not?" asked Chester, shaking her hand.

"No, I think I am infected with the vacation spirit which is becoming rampant among American women in summer. At all events, I find it very easy to drift into idle habits now. Mrs. Redmond and her guests disappeared a little while ago. I will go with you to find them, if you like; but perhaps you are tired from your walk?"

"Don't humiliate me, Miss Rebecca! Tired from that walk in these days?"

He seated himself in one of the wicker rocking-chairs that stood about, and Miss Redmond looked at him critically.

"True enough. How you have changed!" she said.

"Yes, what a traveling advertisement I am for Snowdon! Persons anxious to dispose of property here should hire me to show myself to possible purchasers, with a description of my personal appearance six weeks ago."

"I will suggest it to Mrs. Redmond, when she becomes tired of Beech Knoll."

"Are you expecting her to become tired of it?"

"I did think she would at first, since her object in coming" — Miss Rebecca stopped, suddenly dismayed, and blushed. "Yes, I did at first, but she does seem so perfectly contented that now I have my doubts."

Chester looked at the speaker curiously. What an odd little woman she was with her starts and her blushes! He did not trouble himself to speculate long upon the cause of her behavior. He admired her genuinely, and she possessed a most attractive added charm in the fact of being Mrs. Redmond's constant companion. In sitting thus with her on the quiet, shaded piazza, he enjoyed a pleasure more distinct than he could hope for while sharing his hostess' society with Tony and Phyllis.

"I believe she cannot become tired of it," he said. "I am beginning to see that I need not hope to weary of Snowdon. Do you forgive me for sitting here and keeping you from your book?"

"I am glad to have you," replied Rebecca. She could not explain that her book was but a weapon of self-defense, a something to steady and direct thoughts that were wayward after her sleepless night, — a night spent almost wholly in her precious attic chamber.

"I ought to go back to Boston. I feel better than before my illness. I was beginning to look about me wildly for some excuse for remaining here which I could offer myself, and yet retain a little self-respect, when Mrs. Redmond rescued me."

He smiled at Rebecca with such a youthful and radiant look that she pitied him. There is but one emotion in the universe whose power gives the beauty she recognized in his face. She regretted to see it. Miss Redmond was a woman who felt for all persons with whom she came in contact; but she felt a special interest in Terriss Chester. From the day when she had reluctantly offered to wait upon him in his illness, she had unconsciously been in an attitude of defense of him toward Elise. She had an uneasy suspicion of the latter where her adopted brother was concerned. Miss Redmond had sufficient penetration to perceive that her sister's pride had been wounded by the failure of her plans. She had never felt altogether comfortable concerning Elise's motives for keeping her identity secret. The latter was capable of inflicting a punishment without realizing its severity. For some reason, Rebecca felt an intuitive impulse to shield Chester from her.

"I do not know what you mean," she replied.

"Mrs. Redmond is going to let me try to make a portrait of her."

"That is, after all, a waste of time for you," · answered Rebeca rather brusquely.

Chester laughed in happy amusement. "I did not suspect you would be unkind enough to dub my efforts a failure in advance."

"Even if it succeeds, what is that to you? Painting is not your profession."

"Alas, no," replied Chester; but he still looked absurdly content. Miss Redmond did not like to see it.

"It would be a pity for you to lose some good business opportunity by lingering in Snowdon," she said.

"Little danger of that, and" — he looked at his companion gravely now, but the light still shone in his eyes — "that vacation spirit you mentioned is an enticing sprite. There is not so much happiness offering along life's way that one can afford to turn one's back upon it when it comes."

Rebecca returned his look. "No — yet some happiness, sweet for a day, leaves months, years, of bitterness behind it. Are you so especially fond of portrait-painting, Mr. Chester?"

Chester understood her, and knew that she understood him. He believed in her goodness, and he felt her friendliness for him. He leaned toward her.

" This particular portrait, yes," he said slowly; " but you think I would do better to leave Snowdon ? "

" Vastly better," was the earnest response. Miss Redmond might have been excused for blushing now, but she did nothing of the sort. She looked with her sweet calm eyes straight into Chester's, quite unembarrassed, rather relieved, by his comprehension.

He drew a deep breath and shook his head. " I prefer to stay and take the consequences."

" It is because you do not believe in the consequences, then," said Rebecca. " Do you remember the fairy tale in which one prince after another travels the same road to perform great deeds and win a lovely princess, and how one man after another fails and is turned into a black stone by the wayside ? I feel an interest in you, Mr. Chester, and that is why I take the liberty — I know it is a liberty — of telling you that there are a number of black stones lying beside the road you are traveling."

Terriss rose and walked to the piazza rail. " Do you mean that you believe her heartless ? " he said.

" No. She has a warm heart and a good one; but it has never been won. There was never any pretense that my brother won it. She has never meant to be cruel to any one, but life, facts, are cruel sometimes."

Chester stood silent for a time by a pillar around

which a clematis twined. He spoke at last, quietly. " I thank you, Miss Rebecca. I have never in my life attained any object upon which my heart was set. I needed your words to remind me of that, and yet they come, in one sense, too late. This strange experience, which arrives early with most men, has come to me now for the first time, and I fear it has come to stay. No, I am dishonest when I say I fear it. I am glad of it to the bottom of my soul. It is the only thing I have ever been deeply and fervently thankful for. Let me live in paradise — a fool's paradise, of course — while I can ; and," he smiled a little now, " when like my predecessors I am changed into a black stone, you will have the consolation of knowing that you did your best for me."

Rebecca gave him her kindest look. " No power can change you into something dark and lifeless if your love is true," she said. " You will always be the better and nobler for it. You know the knight did finally come who stood all the tests."

" And he won the lady," said Chester ; " but do not be uneasy. I know such hopes are not for me."

" No ; that was a fairy tale," sighed Miss Rebecca.

The soft breath had scarcely mingled with the air when an apparition of yellow and crimson stripes stood before the piazza.

" Miss Rebecca — Why, there he is now !

What's the matter with you, Chester?" inquired Tony, much exasperated. "What did you suppose you were invited here for?"

"There, Tony, give me the privilege of scolding my own guest," and Elise came deliberately into view.

Chester sprang to open the piazza door for her. "Have I committed some awful blunder?" he asked.

"Should think you had," returned Tony, too much nettled by a complication of trials to hold his peace. "You were invited over here for a morning game of tennis, and it is twelve o'clock this minute."

"I really beg your pardon, Mrs. Redmond," said Chester, with such sincere dismay that Elise laughed. "I did n't understand" —

"Never mind," returned the hostess. "We have the whole afternoon and a part of the evening before us. You know what spending the day means in the country. 'Come as early as you can, and stay till after tea!'"

"Humph! as early as you can," grumbled Tony. "Keep three people waiting for you all the morning."

"Tony!" Elise looked at him in smiling wonder. "What is the matter with you to-day? Go this minute and find Phyllis. She is practicing still, and she will get a sunstroke. I am not sure that you have n't one already. You had better cool your fevered brow in the brook as you pass."

It was indeed unusual for Tony to be so ruffled. He himself was not quite sure what ailed him. The morning beginning so fairly had somehow been a complete failure. Mrs. Redmond had patronized and Miss Flower had ignored him. There was tangible consolation in the fact of having been able to fasten wrong upon Chester, and in grumbling at him for his misdemeanors. He walked the more freely for it, his head well up and his gay cap pulled down to shade his eyes. Striding across the brook, he advanced to the tennis court, where he expected to find Phyllis, who had insisted upon being left alone to get more accustomed to her racket; but she was not visible.

He stood still and called aloud. There were the remains of righteous indignation in his voice. " Miss Flower ! "

No answer. He turned about and looked in all directions for a glimpse of gray color, but in vain.

" *Miss Flower !* " There was a wider sense of injury, a more startling *sforzando* of peremptoriness in the repetition.

A lazy low laugh answered him from the other side of a clump of shrubbery a few feet away.

" Oh! " said Mr. Bellows, much disconcerted, advancing a few steps and beholding Phyllis leaning back in a rustic seat. " Why did n't you answer ? "

" I was rendered speechless at first by admiration of your lung power. "

" I began to think you had gone home. "

"If I had, your voice would have reached me, and I am sure I should not have dared disobey it. What has happened ? "

" Chester has come."

" Oh, is that all ? Why did n't you stay and guard your interests ? "

" Mrs. Redmond sent me to find you."

" Very well, you have found me. Now, good-by."

Phyllis's tone was provoking. She looked exceedingly pretty as she leaned back in the high-backed seat, her hair in silky rings on her damp forehead, and Tony looked into her saucy eyes with sulky dignity.

" Are n't you coming ? " he asked shortly.

" Thank you, no. I am not tired of life. I won't risk myself with you in your present mood."

Mr. Bellows sat down upon a rustic chair underneath the same large maple which sheltered Phyllis.

" I abominate selfishness, I must say," he answered.

" Whose ; mine, or your own ? You are not in the least agreeable just now. I do not want you here bluing the atmosphere."

" I am speaking of Chester," announced Tony, with painful distinctness. " He has simply spoiled the morning."

" And so in revenge you are going to spoil the afternoon ? " laughed Phyllis. " I should suppose you must be hungry, if I did n't know that lovers are never hungry. Good-by, Mr. Bellows."

"This is the first cool spot I have found in an hour," remarked Tony, ignoring her remarks as a childish ebullition unworthy serious consideration.

"Well, then, if you won't take a hint, I expect you to forget for the time being that you are a lover, and be agreeable."

"Pretty place, is n't it?" said Tony, looking about him critically.

"Ye-es," replied the girl hesitatingly. "I will admit it, if you make the proposition without any calculation as to the future proprietor."

Her tone upset Mr. Bellows' foreign gravity. He laughed reluctantly.

"I surrender, Miss Phyllis," he said, and he suddenly left his chair and took the place beside her on the rustic sofa.

"You were much better off where you were," suggested Phyllis. "This is rather narrow for two."

"Not when one of us is nobody's lover," returned Tony audaciously, restored to his customary gayety by restoration to good terms with Phyllis, whose disfavor he had been made to feel uncomfortably.

They had sat an hour in idle summer-day talk, and the girl had been pleasantly flattered almost into forgetfulness of Tony's startling confidence, when Mrs. Redmond and Terriss Chester interrupted their tête-à-tête.

"I would not let Mr. Chester come alone lest he should be as unsuccessful as you were, Tony," explained Elise. " To think that you were unable single handed to bring home one little girl like Phyllis ! "

She shook her head eloquently, took Phyllis's hand and drew it through her arm, and together they mounted the slope, followed amicably by the two men. Mrs. Redmond was secretly well pleased at the absorbed manner of the pair, and their involuntary start when she disturbed them.

Last night Rebecca had said to her, the last thing before retiring, " I am afraid you are going to have trouble with Tony, Elise."

" Trouble with that infant ! " with scornful incredulity.

" It won't help matters a bit to call him an infant," returned Miss Redmond. " I am afraid you will have to deal with him, yet."

So there was gratification in finding the young man so well entertained just now. To do Elise justice, it was no satisfaction to her when the princes of the present time became transformed to dull black stones for her sweet sake.

CHAPTER XXI.

THE CRASH.

THE dinner-table was laid on the inclosed piazza. Elise led her guests to it soon after arriving at the house. It was sweet with Tony's roses, and, outside the wire gauze, the vines and trees embowered the party.

The dinner was different from that which regaled Phyllis on the occasion of her last meal at Beech Knoll. It was a man's dinner this time. She ate dishes whose ingredients she could not even suspect, and wondered at the familiarity with which the others of the party discussed them.

It was a very gay little company. Tony looked often at Chester, asking himself what power had transformed the sullen, curt man into the responsive, light-hearted being he beheld. He suspected the cause, yet postponed the jealousy which should consume him to a more convenient and unpleasant season; half conscious, too, of wondering at his ability to do so.

Occasionally, Chester caught Rebecca's eye, with a half-apologetic look, which amused her even while she felt more than ever sorry for him.

"Now, no tennis for a few hours," said Mrs. Redmond, as they rose from the table. She led her guests to the broad veranda at the front of the house, shaded by a great elm which had been set out there by Miss Rebecca's great-grandfather. Tony lit his cigar, and the ladies disposed themselves in the beribboned chairs.

"This is a beautiful place," announced Chester, his eyes taking in the sparkle of the river half concealed by the luxuriant green.

Elise smiled. "Tony, is the conundrum as to why I settled here answered for you?" she asked.

"It is pretty. You will never stay here in the winter, though."

"O Mrs. Redmond!" exclaimed Phyllis apprehensively. "Tell him you will."

Elise shook her head. "I will not bind myself."

"But *you* would stay, Miss Rebecca?" asked the girl.

"I am Mrs. Redmond's shadow. I suppose I should follow her of necessity," replied Rebecca.

"Oh, dear," said Phyllis, with so dismayed an intonation that the others all smiled.

It gave the girl an unpleasant surprise to waken to the fact of the blankness that awaited her. Mr. Chester would go, never probably to return. The movements of Mrs. Redmond and Miss Rebecca were dependent simply on the caprice of the former, and, in the event of their departure, of course Snowdon would no more be gilded by the presence of Mr. Tony Bellows.

A strange sensation rose in Phyllis at the latter consideration.

" I cannot bear him," she thought vehemently.
" What did he ever come here for ? "

She looked across at Tony, sitting on the railing, and found him smiling questioningly at her,
his cigar poised between two fingers.

" What is it, Miss Flower ? " he asked. " You
look as though you had lost your last friend."

" Mrs. Redmond is my last friend," she retorted.
" I do not like to consider losing her."

" Take my advice," said Tony sagely, "and set
your affections on something more stable. Mrs.
Redmond may be *en route* to China a month from
now."

" Don't malign me. It will take me a long
time to extract all the sweetness from Snowdon,"
remarked the hostess.

The young fellow looked at her with slowly
crimsoning earnestness. " Especially since you
supply it by your presence faster than you can
draw it away," he said.

It was a point-blank bit of flattery at best, and
was delivered with a dogged determination that
made it amusing to the recipient. She laughed
spontaneously.

Chester regarded Bellows compassionately. His
erstwhile jealousy of the latter's favored position
as guest vanished as he recognized the touch of
feeling that made them kin. Here was another
candidate for the doleful procession of petrified
hearts which marked the difficult road to that of
Mrs. Redmond.

Phyllis blushed more violently than Tony. "Silly thing," she thought, in a tumult of resentment. "Why can't he wait until they are alone to say such things?"

She started up from her chair and ran down the steps across the lawn to where the croquet was set out, and began to knock the balls about. Miss Redmond rose and went into the house.

Tony's face did not reflect Elise's amusement. He continued very red and grave; his forgotten cigar paled on the railing beside him. Terriss felt the atmosphere oppressive. He glanced across at Phyllis.

"I take that as a challenge," he remarked, deliberately rising and going down the steps to join her, leaving the two together.

"Shall we go and play too?" said Elise lightly.

"No," returned Mr. Bellows shortly. "Did it ever occur to you, Mrs. Redmond, that it is not particularly pleasant to me to be laughed at and ridiculed by you?"

Elise again gave her low, appreciative laugh. "Then you shouldn't put on grown-up airs, Tony. You tempt me beyond my strength."

"Be in earnest for a little while," he broke forth, the sullenness disappearing from his face and a look which Mrs. Redmond had good reason to dread taking its place. "I"—

"Yes, yes, you are right, Tony," she interrupted more seriously. "You are so good-natured that you have spoiled me. Surely you do not need consolation in good earnest for being young, the most glorious condition you have ·to be thankful for. To be twenty-four, to be healthy, to have an income, to be pleasant to look upon, why, it is better than to be monarch of kingdoms, you lucky boy — man, I mean, excuse me. Ten years from now, you will like to be called boy. Wait, and see. But you will be young then still, while I shall be a woman of thirty-seven, envying you."

"Mrs. Redmond, listen to me." Tony was pale now, and his pallor became him.

Elise met his eyes kindly. "No more personalities," she said pleasantly. "I like our friendship so much, and personalities threaten it so."

He looked at the ripples of her hair, the curve of her handsome mouth. The steady light in her eyes turned him cold. He gazed into them wretchedly. "Is there not one atom of hope for me?" he said simply.

"It is a great pity that you should have to ask me that, and surely I need not answer it in words. You know how greatly I like you. Who else in the world would be in my house in the position you occupy now? There is only one sort of friendship I could have for the man whom I select thus, and that is a very cordial one. I hope you will always care for it, Tony."

He was standing near her, an excited, set expression on his face. As his averted eyes came back and met hers, she smiled faintly, and held out her hand.

With a sudden movement he fell into the seat beside her, took the hand, and bent his head over it.

Mrs. Redmond looked apprehensively toward the croquet ground, and her fears were realized. Terriss Chester, through the opening made by the broad flight of steps, was witnessing the rather suggestive tableau ; but she did not withdraw the hand held in a painful grip.   Terriss wheeled about quickly, and looked no more.   There was a straining and reddening of Tony's neck, one final, torturing pressure of the coveted hand, and it was released.   When the young fellow looked up, his eyes were moist.

"You have been very good to me," he said, in a rather choked voice ; then he rose.   "I think I will go and take a walk," he added briefly.

Elise watched him as he swung across the lawn down toward the water.   "What a nice boy he is!" she thought.   "Some woman will draw a prize in Tony Bellows one of these days."

She looked again toward the croquet ground. It was unfortunate that Tony's destiny had led him to choose broad daylight and a public spot for his declaration of feeling.   It was unusual for Mrs. Redmond to question how any act of hers would be regarded by another ; but she paid Chester that compliment now.   It annoyed her that he had seen Tony holding her hand.   Since the conversation with him regarding Elise Beckwith, Mrs. Redmond had not been able to think of Mr.

Chester complacently. His unfeigned contempt of her financial offer, and the mode of it, abashed her to an extent which she assured herself was unreasonable. Each time his remarks recurred to her she grew so warm that she was fain to press her hands to her flushing cheeks, and each time she shrank with stronger dread from the possibility of his learning her identity. So far, all had proceeded quite as a couple of months ago she would have said she desired. He had come to Snowdon, and had, by his homage, virtually retracted every scornful word of his letter to the minister. He hung upon her words and looks, and had agreed to accept her money in payment for the picture. She could make that payment include the property she wished him to have, could sign the paper Elise Beckwith Redmond, then haughtily turn her back upon him, and leave him to recover from his surprise. He would probably refuse the money. Very good ; but how would he sustain the discovery that he had been led as Elise Beckwith pleased, had been as wax in her hands? How would he recover from his love of her? Ah, that was a question too easily answered. Elise knew that the man loved her. Now she was honestly satiated with admiration. Why was it a disagreeable consideration to her that the shock to Terriss' confidence would surely destroy his passion for her? She had never before desired to continue to inspire love in one of her admirers.

It was old habit, obstinacy, pride, she told herself. Almost as far back as she could remember, she had longed for Terriss Chester's good opinion. She could not now submit willingly to feel that he had a right to look down upon her, that he did look down upon her.

Oh, why had she not been frank in the beginning? The deception she had practiced was at best so undignified. What explanation of it could she give him when the time came? It was liable to come at any moment. Her secret was shared with three persons, and a natural unthinking remark from either would divulge it. Surely, Elise thought, her scheme for punishment of Terriss' presumption had reacted upon herself most disagreeably. The lofty and calm supremacy of her mental bearing had been jarred daily of late. Thoughts seized her at odd moments, making her heart beat and her cheeks flame: considerations of the way her patronage had affected its recipient; of the way she had encouraged those who would bring Terriss to Snowdon; of her unworded plan to win his admiration as a balm to her pride. What would he think of her when he knew all, and considered the way she had drawn him on to speak of her child-self, and his relations with her father? In short, Mrs. Redmond had altered to her own consciousness, and had become an absent-minded, guilty, starting creature, whom she detested. She counted not at all upon the unquestioning devotion which, so far, Terriss displayed toward her. He was an upright, honest man,

scornful of subterfuge, disdaining even to conceal
his love for her. She thought the pleasure she
found in dwelling upon the look that came in his
eyes when they met hers arose from her certainty
that it would be short-lived ; and when she came
to herself, in the midst of a reverie, to find that she
had been lost in enjoyment of this picture, she drew
herself together with a sharp exclamation of surprise and contempt for her own weakness.

She had invited him here to-day in a spirit of
bravado. She suffered more from him absent than
present. It was solace to her wounded pride to
rest in the sunshine of his approval, and to see his
spirits rise higher with every kind word and look
she gave him. For the time being, the discrowned
queen felt restored to her throne.

She sat there alone on the piazza, her eyes following the game of croquet, her thoughts wander-
ing sometimes to Tony, whose disappointment she
rated at about its real worth ; but dwelling mostly
upon the man who, in all his varied movements,
sedulously kept his eyes from seeking the veranda.

At last both Phyilis's balls had hit the stake.
Chester threw down his mallet with some laughing
remark, and looking toward the house, saw that
Elise was alone, and suggested to Phyllis that they
should join her.

The girl made some excuse, and Terriss approached alone.

"You found it pretty warm work, I imagine, at
this hour," remarked Mrs. Redmond.

"I found I had too experienced an opponent," he replied, coming up the steps, and removing his hat as he seated himself. "I hope you have pardoned my late arrival this morning," he continued, after a pause. "I was interested in getting my materials in order, so that, as soon as you are ready for a sitting, I may begin your portrait, — study, sketch, or whatever it turns out to be."

The flattery in the speaker's eager, repressed manner and his honest eyes was the sweetest Elise had ever tasted. Sweet, because shortly to be forfeited, she told herself.

She kept silence a little to enjoy it. The fear, almost grief, that accompanied the enjoyment might have taught her something, had she been accustomed to think that some time her own heart would be discovered.

A humming-bird, darting beneath the roof of the piazza, poised for a long moment near her head, as though attracted by the rose she had tucked in her hair, but flitted away like a beam of light at her admiring ejaculation.

"What a bold midget!" she exclaimed.

"He is accustomed to regard roses growing in the sunshine as his own property," replied Chester.

She searched for a light retort in vain. "As to the picture," she said, "I suppose there is no especial hurry."

"Excepting that I must not stay here much longer."

" What are you going to do when you return to the city ? "

" Hunt for a situation."

" How long will it take you ? " asked Elise naively.

Chester laughed. " Any time from a week to a few years."

" Oh ! " she exclaimed. She rebelled against the idea of the uncongenial routine life he had led for so long, and against the indefinite continuance of it.

" As I am open to almost anything, anywhere from Maine to the Golden Gate, it ought not to be a matter of very much time," he continued.

" Don't you care at all what you do ? " she asked, rather awed by the total lack of interest in his voice.

" Very little, — so it gives me enough to live upon."

" That ought not to be the height of your ambition," she returned, adopting the tone of a mentor. She felt quite experienced and superior as she spoke. " You do not wish to go drifting about all your life, accomplishing nothing but eating, sleeping, and snatching a little time to paint. You will marry, and " —

Chester laughed again roughly. " Yes ; what a delightful life a woman would have with me ! You can see what a prize I am, and what a tempting offer mine would be. If I should ever become so beside myself as to commit such folly, and you should hear of it, I beg now, being in my right mind, that you will order somebody to have me shut up in the nearest asylum."

The bitter, careless expression again transformed his face. His suddenly angry words raised a tumult in Elise. A great and awful light broke upon her. As unhesitatingly as he had repudiated her money offer in the face of his ambitions and lifelong desires, so surely would he, in spite of all love and longing, repudiate herself. His keen sense of failure would never allow him to ask her life of a woman who possessed everything he lacked. What but the word of the woman herself could convince him that himself alone outweighed all the material superfluities she longed to bestow upon him; and how could the woman speak that word!

There was a ringing in Elise's ears as the questioning despair tore its way through her. She, the heiress, the belle, the beauty, the loftily inaccessible Mrs. Redmond, knew in one appalling, sweet instant, that her hour had come. She herself was the woman who longed to speak that impossible word.

Chester did not turn his eyes toward her still, pale face, and the silence had not been broken, when Miss Rebecca came to the door.

" Elise, Elise," she called unsteadily.

Mrs. Redmond looked up. She saw that her sister wore a street dress and a bonnet, and carried a small satchel.

"Mrs. Terriss has sent for me," said Rebecca. "I think I shall not be able to come home to-night. Don't be anxious about me. I will send you word to-morrow."

Mrs. Redmond tried to arrange her disordered thoughts. She looked vaguely at Rebecca, and leaned forward in her chair.

"Do not disturb yourself," said Miss Redmond hastily. "Good-by, Mr. Chester," and she disappeared.

Terriss did not even turn at her farewell. He was looking now at his hostess, full and earnestly. The devil-may-care look in his face was replaced by one hard to read.

Mrs. Redmond's breath came fast under the gaze she could not now meet.

"She called you Elise," he said quietly. "It is not a common name."

Here was the extremity. Mrs. Redmond's heart leaped into her throat. She was so frightened that she was calm, and there was a particularly haughty expression on her white face. She did not speak, and he studied her still, and, searching his memory, wondered at his own dullness.

"Are you," he said slowly, "Elise Beckwith?"

Her face was that of a beautiful statue, except that her eyes met his.

"Yes," she said distinctly.

It seemed to her an eternity that they both sat there in silence. At last he rose slowly, hat in hand. Her eyes drooped. Unconsciously she raised her chin. Her body rebelled, by its attitude, against the depths of her humiliation.

" I thank you for the hospitality you have extended to me," he said, quietly as ever ; then he bowed toward her unseeing eyes, and descending the steps, went down the path and out of the gates of Beech Knoll.

CHAPTER XXII.

A BITTER CUP.

Miss Rebecca had hailed the first moment when she could with propriety leave the piazza. She felt more than ordinary need of the nap it was her habit to take in the afternoon, so she sought her own room, and exchanging her organdie gown for a dressing sack, lay down on the bed and closed her eyes. The monster of wakefulness which had presided at her side all the previous night left her in peace now. The breeze rustled through the trees outside her window, and blew the muslin curtains. All disturbing thoughts seemed stilled in the quiet of the summer afternoon, and without waiting to be coaxed, sleep visited her eyelids.

She dreamed that it was found necessary to remove the old bridge. People said it was unsafe. Philip Terriss seemed to be among the workmen who were destroying it. One after another they directed heavy blows at the supports. Each resounding thump sent a pain through Rebecca's heart.

"Oh, don't don't!" she cried. "What is it?" she added, wide awake now, and aware that some one was knocking loudly at her door.

" It 's me, Miss Rebecca, Roxana."

" Come in, it is n't locked."

The door opened, and Mrs. Sherritt entered.
" You were asleep.   I 'm sorry," she said, in a
hurried, excited manner, foreign to her, " but I
knew there was company here, so I came in the
back way, and the girls said you might be up here.
I 've come to tell you Mr. Terriss is sick.   He 's
a very sick man, or I never saw one.   I can't go
there and help 'tend to him.   Now the question is,
can you ? "

Mrs. Sherritt had sat down in the nearest chair.
A red spot showed in each of her sallow cheeks.
Miss Rebecca, half lying, half sitting upon the bed,
looked back at her, her face nearly as colorless as
the pillows that supported her.

" It is impossible," she said.   " You heard what
Mrs. Terriss said to me that day."

" Now you ain't goin' to mind that crazy talk,
are you ? " asked Roxana appealingly.

Miss Redmond paused and seemed to meditate.
After half a minute, she spoke.

" There was some truth underlying what she said,
Roxana.   You are my faithful friend, and it is
necessary you should understand.   Long ago, here
at Beech Knoll " —

" Yes, Miss Rebecca," Mrs. Sherritt interrupted,
her face coloring to the very roots of her hair.
It was the most embarrassing moment of her
life.   " I know about it.   The first Mrs. Richard
told me."

Miss Redmond's eyes brightened, and her delicate lips grew tense. "Could it have been through
you, then, that Mrs. Terriss" —

"*Miss Rebecca!*" Roxana fairly shouted the
exclamation, and started to a standing posture.
"If any one thing could make me feel worse 'n
everythin' else in this world, that does."

"Forgive me," murmured Miss Redmond con-
tritely.

"I did n't know her husband was the man until
yesterday," continued Mrs. Sherritt. "I'd forgot
the name, if I ever knew it, a dozen years ago;
but for *you*, Miss Rebecca, that I'd guard and
defend till I dropped, — for you to accuse me o'
bein' a Judas, that hurts; hurts me through and
through."

"Oh, I am ashamed Roxana, I am indeed!"
exclaimed Miss Rebecca. "Forget it. If you
knew all I have passed through in the last twenty-
four hours, you would not wonder my thoughts and
judgment go astray. It was a momentary, wild
guess. I spoke too soon."

She pressed her hands to her eyes, looking so
frail and small in her white surroundings, that Mrs.
Sherritt experienced another revulsion of feeling.
A glow of affectionate compassion possessed her.
She came and sat on the foot of the bed, and patted one of Miss Redmond's ankles with her kind,
hard hand.

"That's all right," she said; "forgive me for
botherin' you. I've sifted that business to the

bottom, and it seems that great gump Lucindy's
to blame. Her ma remembered that Terriss was
the name o' the young man that visited you in the
old days, and some imp o' darkness put it into
her head to wonder if the minister might be the
same person. She talked it over to Lucindy, and
o' course *she* had to tell Mrs. Terriss. I don't
believe Mrs. Terriss was perfectly sure she was
right when she said that shameful thing to you. I
think she was kind o' guessin'. She was mad because we kept at her, and she wanted to hit back.
Anyway, I 've stopped up the leak, I guess." Mrs.
Sherritt smiled grimly. " I 'll bet there ain't anybody that could get Lucindy Bates or her mother
to talk on that subject to 'em after this. The
folks in this town are fond o' you, Miss Rebecca.
Well," she added, in a different tone, "there 's one
big bit o' news I meant to tell you as soon I got
here. God's ways ain't our ways, and Mrs. Terriss is walkin' around lively. It puts me in mind
o' some o' the cures we heard the Chicago fire
made."

" Why, Roxana ! " Miss Rebecca dropped her
hands and stared at her informant.

" It 's as true as a gun," said Mrs. Sherritt,
nodding cheerfully. " I went over there and seen
for myself. It was this way. Mr. Terriss was out
walkin' last night, and come home late. He was
kind o' dazed like, I guess. At any rate, he did n't
come to his wife's room to say good-night as he
usually does. She was lyin' awake, a bad con-

science, I guess, and she felt bad to think he did
n't come to her, and then she noticed how queer his
steps sounded, goin' upstairs ; most as if he 'd taken
too much.   Perhaps 't was n't him at all.   She got
so scared thinkin' it over she could n't go to sleep,
but laid there guessin' and thinkin' till, just the
darkest, lonesomest time o' night, she began to hear
talkin'.   She could n't make out anythin' except
that it was a man's voice, and it come from the
minister's room.   She was pretty well scared, but
she thought maybe he had the nightmare.   She
says she must have stood it fifteen minutes, and it
seemed like fifteen hours, before she rang the bell
for Lucindy.   She 's got a contraption the minister
fixed, so she can pull a string and ring a bell at the
head o' Lucindy's bed.   Well, she pulled it, and she
pulled it, till Lucindy came, her teeth chatterin',
and her hair on end.   It seems the minister's
talkin' had waked her up too, and she began cryin'
and sayin' she was awful scared.   Mrs. Terriss
scolded her and told her she was a silly thing, that
the minister had the nightmare, and that she was
to go upstairs right off and wake him up.   Lucindy 's afraid o' Mrs. Terriss, so she minded her, and
put on a dressin' gown and went up ; but in five
minutes she was down again, cryin' and takin' on.
She said Mr. Terriss had n't minded her knockin',
so she went in.   There was a lighted lamp on his
bureau, and he was lyin' on the bed all dressed
but his coat, his eyes was open, and he was talkin'
wild.   ' He 's goin' to die, Mrs. Terriss, he 's goin'

to die, sure,' she said, and boohooed away at a great
rate.   Well, it was then the miracle happened ; or
we should think it was a miracle, if we did n't
know what we know.   Mrs. Terriss sat right up
out on the edge o' the bed, and made Lucindy help
her into her clothes.   'He 's goin' to die without
forgivin' me,' she said, and she said it over and
over.   She did n't say anythin' else only that, Lucindy told me, and she said it more 'n twenty
times.   Well, she pulled on her wrapper and
jumped right up and made for the door.   She went
through the sittin'-room and the hall, and Lucindy
says it turned her cold to see her catch the banister and start upstairs.   Lucindy kind o' boosted
her by the arm, but she says it 's her opinion Mrs.
Terriss did n't know she was there.   By the time
they got to the room, the minister had stopped
talkin', and he was asleep and breathin' awful
heavy.   Lucindy says Mrs. Terriss knelt down
side of him, and talked wild to him.   I would n't
let her go on tellin' me what she said ; that kind
o' talk ain't our business.   Well, as soon as daylight come, Lucindy went for the doctor, and the
middle o' the mornin' some time, not over five
minutes after Phyllis started for here, she come
after me.   I went over, and I 've been there till
now.   We 've got Mr. Terriss fixed down in his
wife's room, and he 's got brain fever, and the doctor don't pretend to say he 'll get well.   O' course
he may."

Rebecca's breath came in quick pants.

"Now you know, after the other day, I would n't be the one to ask you to go there and wear out your strength and feelin's, if Mrs. Terriss had n't just beseeched of me."

"Has she no memory, no sense of fitness?" asked Rebecca excitedly. "How can she think I will come?"

"Well, it's just here," replied Roxana dryly. "The minister talks a good deal, and he don't talk about anythin' only just you and Beech Knoll, and the river, and the bridge, and the summer weather. Everythin' he's kept shut up for twenty years is just a bubblin' over and runnin' like a mill stream. He's restless and sufferin' and crazy as a loon. Mrs. Terriss knows, if anybody else comes to nurse him, this town won't hold the gossip and wonderment that 'll fill it from end to end. *Now* do you see?"

Poor Miss Rebecca turned her head on the pillow and closed her eyes. Her thoughts all seemed stunned. Only a bit from one of Elise's songs sang itself to her heart.

"Oh, that we two were sleeping under the church-yard sod,
    With our limbs at rest, 'neath the quiet earth's breast,
    And our souls at home with God."

She opened her eyes at last and regarded Roxana. "I suppose you would not let me take care of your house and you go to the parsonage," she said tentatively.

"Now, Miss Rebecca," replied the other in gentle reproach, "you know you could n't milk cows and do the chores I have to 'tend to."

"Then I do not see that I have any alternative, do you?" asked Miss Redmond.

Roxana smiled, and waited, and watched her.

In a minute, Rebecca rose from the bed.

"I'll pack your bag for you," said Mrs. Sherritt, immediately restored to briskness. "We hain't any time to lose." Miss Redmond produced the satchel from the closet, and her neighbor proceeded to fill it while Rebecca dressed. "Just tide 'em over till the craziest of it has passed," continued Roxana energetically. "Mrs. Terriss is weak and not much use, but I'll be there all I can, and Lucindy's so stupid and so scared it'll be safe enough to have her around."

Miss Redmond said her brief farewell to Elise, and then they set forth. Rebecca dreaded so to arrive that the walk had never seemed so short. However Mrs. Terriss might force herself to appear, how could she feel otherwise than hardly toward her rival? The prospect of being shut up with her to listen to Philip's wild talk was as painful a one as could be offered to Miss Rebecca, but she had the heart of a heroine, and she advanced to meet her fate, outwardly calm.

When they reached the parsonage, Roxana opened the front door noiselessly and went in. Miss Redmond followed, her heart beating almost to suffocation.

Roxana went down the corridor and opened the door into Mrs. Terriss' sitting-room. The invalid chair stood empty in the window, and Mrs. Terriss was lying on the lounge, her face ghastly pale and her eyes closed. Mrs. Sherritt put a warning finger on her lips and turned to Miss Redmond, but at that moment the minister's wife opened her eyes and saw the arrivals.

With one determined effort she drew herself into a sitting posture on the side of the lounge and tried to stand, but fell back in weakness. She cast a dry-eyed, appealing gaze at Rebecca, and held out both her hands.

Miss Redmond glided across the room, took the hands, and seated herself beside her. Roxana disappeared into the bedroom.

Mrs. Terriss spoke in a low, level voice.

"No words can tell you how I appreciate this goodness of yours," she said. "You forgive my misjudgment, my wicked speech?"

"Fully. Never speak of it again," said Rebecca.

"It hurt — it hurt his feelings," continued the wretched woman, speaking with dry lips, "more deeply than one could imagine. It was that, happening to come when he was on the eve of breaking down with illness, which makes him talk wildly now of you and your home, — for he does," she added explanatorily, still fixing Rebecca with that wild appeal. "I sent for you to prevent scandal. People might think his raving meant something serious; but you know, *you know* what a husband he has been. You know how he loves me."

"I know," said Rebecca, with solemn earnestness, "that few women in all the world are given such devotion as has come to you."

Mrs. Terriss pressed the hands she held excitedly.

"It has been my temptation," she continued feverishly. "He was not a demonstrative man, only so true, and deep, and faithful. I found that when I was weakest, most needy, he showed most his love for me. I was frail from girlhood. I craved expressions of my husband's love. I longed always to be in his mind, under his care. I allowed myself to become more and more of an invalid, because dependence brought me happiness. Do you see? I did not see it myself until to-day — to-day," she repeated with a dry sob, "this wretched day. I walked in the night," she continued, concentrating her despairing eyes again on Rebecca. "I walked; I went upstairs. My spirit must go, so my body had to follow. If he needed me now, I could go in there to him, but I am so weak — weak. I only quake and tremble when I try to rise. I " —

"You have said enough now," interrupted Rebecca quietly. "It is only a waste of your strength. This is the beginning of a new life for you. The scales have fallen from your eyes, and you will no longer seek your happiness selfishly."

"No, no," murmured the other, "and you will stay with us. You are so strong, and firm, and wise. You and the doctor will save him. I will spend the rest of my life for him. He shall be the

one to receive, and I to give. We will be so happy,
so happy! Give me your arm. I must go in there
with you at first."

Rebecca did not contradict her. She thought it
best to let her try her powers as far as she felt
inclined.

Mrs. Terriss rose slowly and tremblingly, leaning
heavily on the smaller woman, and then walked
with unexpected firmness to the bedroom door.

They went in, and the dim light revealed the face
on the pillow. The lips were repeatedly framing
the one word, "Rebecca, Rebecca."

Mrs. Terriss bent over the sufferer. He looked
at her, then turned his head wearily away, without
stopping his murmured appeal.

Miss Redmond, obeying the motion of Mrs. Terriss' hand, took up a position on the opposite side
of the bed. The minister's eyes fell upon her.
His voice died away.

"White," he said at last. "Your hair is white.
Why did you change it? I will stay here by the
river. I can rest better. Beech Knoll and happiness. All outside is misery."

Mrs. Terriss fixed her miserable eyes on Rebecca's.

"You see how it would sound to any one else, —
to one who did not understand," she said.

A strength not her own came to Rebecca's fluttering, shrinking soul.

"I see," she answered, with a calmness that
amazed herself. "While this fancy lasts, I will
stay with you."

The sick man never removed his eyes from her face. "We did right," he said. "I suppose we did. I can't think any more. You will have to do the thinking, Rebecca. It is all life, and life means endurance."

Roxana drew closer to the door toward which she had moved.

"Take Mrs. Terriss," said Miss Redmond to her, "and make her comfortable on the lounge. There is need but for one of us here at a time."

Mrs. Terriss suffered herself to be led out.

"This is embarrassing for Miss Rebecca," she said, as Roxana helped her down upon her pillow. "I appreciate her goodness in coming."

Mrs. Sherritt swallowed the lump that had risen in her throat.

"I'm real glad you do," she said kindly.

"Did you notice what a strange caprice Mr. Terriss showed in turning from me and staring so at her? It seemed to give point to his ravings." Mrs. Terriss tried to smile as she asked the question.

"Just what folks out o' their heads 'll do," replied Roxana recklessly; "turn against their best friends every time."

"Truly?" asked the other eagerly.

"Oh, you can count on it every time," replied Mrs. Sherritt emphatically. "Now you do as Miss Rebecca does, and consider his talk just like the wind that blows; and when he gets his senses, don't never tell him of it, 'cause it would make him

feel flatter 'n a flounder. I 'm goin' to pull these
shades down, and do you shut your eyes up and go
off to sleep. The doctor won't be here for an hour
yet, and you 'll get a good nap. You keep up
your strength, and you 'll be able to spell Miss Rebecca a good deal. I shall keep one hand in my
house and one hand here, as it were. Good-by,
Mrs. Terriss. We 'll live to laugh at this. Good-
by."

She gave a smiling nod and passed out of the
room and out of the house, but on the steps a
great sob overcame her. She ran down into the
yard and around the side of the house, and there
had the heartiest cry she had indulged in for years.
She did it thoroughly, and finished it, before march-
ing out of the gate and down the street. Not
another tear fell, although neither that night, nor
for many nights to come, was she able to put out
of her mind that picture of the wife that was and
the wife that might have been, gazing with miserable eyes across the prostrate figure that divided
them.

CHAPTER XXIII.

THE EARLY TRAIN.

SOMEWHERE along the banks of the cool river, the rejected suitor found means to drown his mortification and excitement; for when he returned to the house, he was the Tony of old, the feverishness that had marked his manner all through this visit having disappeared. Had Mrs. Redmond accepted him, he would have been a proud and elated man. He had for a long time been carrying a glorified picture of her in his mind, and had built castles in the air innumerable, in each one of which she was to reign beside him; but her manner, even more than her words, in their recent interview, had contributed to guard the sensitive pride belonging to his youth, and he was nearly as proud of her distinguished friendship as he was of having dared to ask her for something more.

When he ascended the slope leading toward the house, he perceived Mrs. Redmond still sitting as he had left her, alone. Chester and Phyllis had disappeared.

It was an embarrassing moment to him, but he put a bold face upon it. He thought it a little unlike Elise that she did not help him out by accosting him as he approached.

" How soon is that long-expected game of tennis coming off ? " he asked, coming up the steps, then was startled to observe the pallid change on his hostess' face.

" It will not come off," replied Elise, palely smiling. " All sorts of things have been happening in your absence. I have grown suddenly and miserably ill, unheard of for me, you know; Rebecca has been sent for post-haste to the minister's, and has gone ; Mr. Chester has departed ; and last but not least, Phyllis is lost. I was just wishing you would appear and take charge of her for me."

" Of course I will," replied Tony, much disturbed. " Don't you want a doctor ? Let me go right off for one."

" No, no indeed. This is some passing annoyance."

" At least you will go into the house. I do not want to frighten you, but really you frightened me when I came up just now."

" If it were not for Phyllis, I think I should disappear indefinitely. You see how I treat you, Tony ; I might even leave you to a solitary tea, if I do not feel better."

" By all means. You must think no more about me than if I did not exist. As for Miss Flower, I promise to make everything right with her. Now please leave it all to me and go in at once."

Mrs. Redmond looked gratefully into his face, full of kindly intention and concern for her.

"You are very good," she said, rising, and at that moment Phyllis appeared around the corner of the house — Phyllis, with a hotly beating little heart and an *insouciant* face, deciding that she could not have chosen a less opportune moment for her return, for Tony was tenderly supporting Mrs. Redmond's arm as she rose from her low chair.

"I am so glad you have come," said the latter.

"Why? Are you ready for tennis? I have been to the stable; startling confession, is n't it? but I wanted to see Star." _

She looked closely at Elise as she spoke, observing her pallor and putting her own construction upon it.

"I am ashamed to say I am obliged to excuse myself," replied Mrs. Redmond. "I do not feel up to tennis this afternoon."

"You do not look up to it," said the girl promptly. "I think Mr. Chester and I had better leave you to rest. Where is he?"

"He is already gone. He went some time since."

Phyllis's eyes sparkled angrily. "Then it was very rude of him," she said. "He might have waited for me."

"I am so annoyed at everything," said Mrs. Redmond hurriedly. "I hope you will pardon it that our day has turned out so badly."

"If Chester had waited, I should not have had the opportunity to walk home with you," remarked Tony.

" Thanks," returned Phyllis airily. " I would ever so much rather you would n't. Don't mention my disappointment, Mrs. Redmond, and do not wait. I am sure you need to lie down."

" Yes, say good-by and go right in, Elise," added Tony. It startled Phyllis in spite of herself to hear him use the familiar name. " I will promise to place Miss Flower safe in Mrs. Sherritt's arms."

Phyllis rebelled inwardly, but controlled herself. She too had seen the tableau presented awhile back on the piazza. If, as appeared now to be the case, Mr. Bellows was Mrs. Redmond's accepted lover, it would be a mistake to rebuff him ; so she made her farewells and started down the avenue, leaving Tony to decide for himself whether to follow her.

He soon made his appearance. " Why should n't we have one game before you go ? " he suggested, as he fell into her quick step.

" Please excuse me," said Phyllis. " I feel lazy this afternoon."

" And so do I," returned Tony. " Have you noticed, Miss Flower," with lively interest, " how apt we are to feel alike about things ? "

" I cannot say I have," returned Phyllis, walking with such conscious swiftness that she was distinctly annoyed by the fact that her companion kept abreast of her without effort.

" Why, I have noticed it from the first. Singular you have n't," he continued cheerfully.

No reply from Miss Flower.

"There is one difference between us, I'll admit," said Tony; "you are very moody."

Phyllis laughed, and then grew instantly grave.

"I have n't asked to be analyzed, you know, Mr. Bellows, and as to that, I'm sure you've been in forty different moods to-day."

"Well, which one did you like best?" asked Tony innocently. "I've shown you all shades, from the conceited ass of this morning to the present specimen of meek good nature, who is suiting himself to your breakneck speed without a murmur, in spite of the condition of the thermometer."

"Oh, excuse me," said Phyllis, a little disconcerted, suddenly moderating her pace. "I had no idea I was tiring you," she added loftily.

"I am a more fragile flower than you think, while you — you are " —

"Be careful," interrupted the girl. "If you were meditating a pun on my name, let me warn you that our acquaintance is at an end."

"Then I was n't. I never thought of such a thing. It would never do to forfeit your acquaintance at a time when I may become totally dependent upon you. Mrs. Redmond really looks to me as if she were going to have an illness."

"And do you think I will take care of you for her? You seem to have returned to that morning mood which you just described so aptly. I trust Mrs. Redmond is not going to be ill, and I do not think she will be. She is very strong."

" Yes, she is strong," said Tony meditatively ; " strong and — well, she is Mrs. Redmond, that is all."

" Very sensible of you," observed Phyllis, " to use a form of flattery which no one can disagree with."

" I hope you are not annoyed with her," said Tony quickly. " You could not doubt that her indisposition was real."

" You are really too foolish," returned Phyllis impatiently. " What a spectacle I should make of myself, annoyed with Mrs. Redmond ! "

" I think there must be illness in town," said Tony. " Miss Rebecca has been called away to somebody. It is rather forlorn for Mrs. Redmond."

" Yes," replied Phyllis stiffly. " You must let me know to-morrow, if she is not better."

In vain Tony tried to change Miss Flower's relentless mood. When they reached her door, he was still without the shell of reserve in which she had incased herself.

" It is n't my fault that Chester went off in his usual absent-minded fashion this afternoon, instead of waiting for you," he observed, standing a moment at the gate. " If my insistence upon walking home with you has really annoyed you, I beg your pardon."

He gazed at her with open reproach as he spoke.

" Oh, I am not in the least vexed with Mr. Chester," returned Phyllis airily ; " and of course,

I am very much obliged to you. How much longer do you remain in Snowdon?"

"That depends on Mrs. Redmond. If she is not well, I shall relieve her of the care of me."

"Well, then," replied Phyllis, with a super-cheerful smile, "I will say good-by," holding out her hand. "I may not see you again for ever so long, I suppose."

"Oh, I see," he said, a light breaking over his face. "You never invite anybody to call. I was on the point of feeling hurt. Still, a man might come at his own·risk."

"The risk is great," returned Phyllis. "I do not advise him to come."

Tony turned away, considerably piqued. Phyllis, after her good-by, went up the walk, humming a tune, stopped to pick an unusually white pansy, then entered the house and ran up to her own room. There the song ceased, the pansy dropped to the floor, and the girl covered her face with her hands and burst into tears.

With every sob she asked herself why she was crying. She did not know; and no amount of self-catechising could elicit an answer; so she finished the foolish performance as soon as possible, and tried, with cold water, to make herself presentable to Roxana's observant eyes.

As it happened, however, those eyes of Roxana's were in a more noticeable condition than Phyllis's own, when the latter went downstairs to set the table for tea. Phyllis started at sight of the housekeeper, with a stronger impression than ever of the world's topsy-turvy condition.

"Roxana, why Roxana, you have been crying!" she exclaimed involuntarily.

"Yes, I have," returned Mrs. Sherritt without looking up. "Mr. Terriss is at death's door, Phyllis."

"Oh, no!"

"Indeed he is, and as for sparin' that good man after Dr. Joy, there ain't any way o' reconcilin' ourselves to it that I see. Seem 's if we needed to remember all the teachin' that Dr. Joy ever gave us. 'Keep up your spirits,' he used to say to me, time and again. 'Every bit o' cheerfulness we show helps other folks to be good-natured;' and he made me promise once, that if he died before you did, you should n't be dressed in mournin'. He said you could n't live bright and happy as you ought to be if you was dressed in crape. I declare, I hope it ain't wicked to wish he was here now to pull Mr. Terriss through this. I 've minded him about the crape, but as for bein' bright and happy such times as these!" Roxana made a hopeless gesture.

Phyllis shook her head and began setting the table. "Oh, let us hope! Surely *everything* won't go wrong," she said. A couple of hours later, she grew less sanguine. It was a blow, both to her and to Mrs. Sherritt, when Mr. Chester announced to them that he must leave Snowdon the following morning. Roxana had confidently counted on another month of those convenient weekly payments. Phyllis thought nothing about the loss of income, but his going meant much to her. She had never seen him so grave and silent since his recovery. She put two and two together, with a conviction of the truth. Now she thought she understood why he had forgotten her in a hasty exit from Beech Knoll. He met her in the hall that night, as she was going to her room, and held out his hand. " I thank you very much, Miss Phyllis, for all the kindness you have shown me. I shall never forget the trouble you and Mrs. Sherritt have taken for me."

" If I have taken any trouble for you, I am entirely unconscious of it," she returned seriously. "I am very, *very* sorry you are going. Why do you go when your cousin is so ill? "

He returned her gaze uneasily. " I know it looks unfeeling," he returned, after a moment's hesitation. " I reconsidered a little when Mrs. Sherritt first told me ; but what can I do for him? Nothing. And I cannot stay here. It has become impossible."

Phyllis caught his eye, and flushed in her earnestness. " I am so sorry, so sorry," she said impulsively. " You should have been the one to succeed, not Mr. Bellows."

Her color was reflected in the dark face looking back at her. " Thank heaven, I was not such a fool as to try for success," he returned. " So Bellows succeeded, did he? I thought otherwise. Well, so be it. It is all one to me."

" But it is not to me," said the girl hotly. " It is a very unwelcome thought. · He is intensely disagreeable to me, and not worthy of her at all."

" A man is worthy of all he can win, Miss Phyllis, and Tony is a good fellow," returned Chester shortly.

All the same, the next morning when he arrived at the dépôt barely in time to catch the out-moving train, it was a disagreeable surprise to him, on opening the car door, to come face to face with Tony Bellows, and to perceive instantly that the only unoccupied seat in the car was by his side.

" What, you going in ? " exclaimed the young fellow pleasantly. Chester hesitated, but there was no reason why he should refuse the place which his friend's hospitable hitch toward the wall made larger for him.

" Yes. I thought I'd go this morning," said Terriss, taking the seat. " I did n't expect to see you, though."

" Mrs. Redmond is a trifle under the weather, and so I thought I would relieve her of me, as Miss Rebecca is away."

" H'm. Sorry to hear it," mumbled Chester, stopping the passing news-agent and buying a " Herald."

Tony, his transparent face betraying his disappointment at this unsocial proceeding, reluctantly followed his example.

" Yes, I took tea in solitary state last night, and after roving about the piazzas, and reading, and

frightening the owls with my improvisations on the
piano, I became so thoroughly tired of myself that
I determined, if Mrs. Redmond continued invisi-
ble this morning, to take the first train. She did,
and here I am."

"Ye-es?" returned Chester abstractedly, running his eye over the headlines of the paper he had
unfolded.

"Did you — ah — leave all well at your abid-
ing-place?" inquired Tony.

"What? Oh, yes, — yes."

"When are you going back?"

"Never — that I know of."

"What? You 've left for good?"

"Yes. I have accomplished what I went for,
why not?"

Although apparently Chester was scanning the
printed page busily as ever, he was wondering at
the carelessness with which his friend could leave
his *fiancée's* home on the score of *ennui*. The
blood pulsed faster through his veins at the thought
of that quiet house, the sunlight sifting through
the beeches on the lawn; the murmurous flow of
the river, and the privilege owned by the man beside him of lingering about the enchanted spot,
sure of a welcome from the lady of his heart when
she should appear. He himself would never see
that paradise again. It exasperated him to the
verge of outbreak that the unconscious Tony should
sit with folded paper in his lap, and drum upon the
window-sash with his fingers.

"Miss Flower is an odd combination," remarked the latter at last, with the air of a connoisseur. "I do not know that I like her altogether."

"She has the advantage of you there," returned Chester grimly. "She does know that she does n't like you altogether."

"Indeed!" ejaculated Tony. He unfolded his paper now with some energy, and the frowning eagerness with which he interrogated its contents rivaled Chester's own.

The latter had cause to congratulate himself on the effect of his bluntness, for he was disturbed no more until Boston was reached, and might think or read to his heart's content; but the combined skill of the news-gatherers was thrown away upon one Bostonian that morning. The whole current of Mr. Bellows' thought was changed. More baffling and exciting than any political situation to him was the question why Phyllis Flower should not like him. She was an obscure, unfashionable blossom, while he, although all varieties of conceit and vanity were abominations to him, was forced upon consideration to acknowledge himself a cosmopolitan charmer. Tony enjoyed being liked. He always had been liked. It gave him a sense of soreness to recall Phyllis's silky rings of hair, and her wide-open, brown eyes, and to know from an uncivil but impartial third party that she did not like him. He wished she knew how well he danced. He wished she knew how rich he was (in prospect). He wished she but faintly guessed his popularity among girls who would be sure to look down upon her from an immeasurable distance.

"Idiots if they did," he ejaculated mentally, suddenly going over to the enemy. "She is as sharp as one of her native briers. Give her a few weeks among that set, and enough money to keep up her end, and she would distance them all."

Chester's elbow gave him a slight accidental nudge. The temporary glow of enthusiasm faded. He scowled again at the "Herald," and ran his eye in business-like fashion down its columns.

He had turned, from force of habit, to the base-ball news; but the recorded fact that the Chicagos had defeated his favorite team the previous day failed to stir his blood as usual with loyal wrath, for he read between the technically descriptive lines that Phyllis Flower did not like him.

CHAPTER XXIV.

"GO, LITTLE LETTER."

MRS. REDMOND felt an infinite relief when Tony and Phyllis had left her alone with her own thoughts. She hastened to her room and, locking the door, sat down to look her situation squarely in the face. One certainty overpowered all others. She loved Terriss Chester. He was a commonplace enough individual. He had done nothing to win her affection save to show his own in a fashion the reverse of brilliant or masterful. He had not proven himself a power among men, had not surmounted and moulded the circumstances of his life, but rather had drifted on in a self-distrustful, ambitionless fashion which was not admirable.

"No matter, no matter," cried her heart passionately. "I love him."

She had been intensely mortified and humiliated, but it was not in Elise's nature to remain crushed. She was masterful by nature. Had she been a man, circumstances would have been well-nigh powerless to conquer her. She had done wrong to deceive Terriss. She would acknowledge it. She was no timid young girl to fear making an advance. Terriss had admired her, — her belief that he loved her had suffered a shock in the fact that

he could treat her offense with such cold anger.
Surely he would forgive her and learn to love and
trust her again.   At all events, all that made life
worth having to her now was this hope ; and to
sit quietly and leave her destiny to chance was not
possible to her.   A thousand considerations chased
one another feverishly through her brain as she
seated herself at her desk and drew writing materials toward her.   Oh, the relief of pouring out her
heart on the insensate paper, knowing that it was
in her power to send or to withhold the message at
the last !

   She wrote and rewrote, considered and reconsidered, her strong will and full heart pleading
with its object until she had worked herself into
the belief that he must see and feel wholly in sympathy with her.

   " The money ! The hateful money ! " she thought
wildly.   " It will stand in the way ; " and then she
recognized that if she revealed too plainly her
feelings he might impute her boldness to a realization of her wealth and his poverty.   How he had
spoken of Elise Beckwith's indelicacy in the past !
How would he consider this ?

   She covered her flushed cheeks with her hands
at the thought ; then suddenly in a panic began
tearing the written sheets into small fragments.
She realized now that the early evening shades
were falling, and remembered that she had dismissed the maid who knocked on her door for orders at tea-time.

From below she could hear vagrant snatches of melody, and knew that Tony was beguiling the tedium of his lonely evening at the piano.

But these discoveries were ripples upon the deep, rushing river of her thoughts. Again she covered her face with her hands and pondered. The old worshiping look in Terriss' eyes seemed to confront her and plead with her for her own happiness.

"I will not leave it so. I cannot. I *must* be the one to speak. He will not. Perhaps he thinks he cannot." She drew paper toward her again, and wrote : —

TERRISS, — Pride would suggest that I make no apology for the deception I have practiced toward you; but I cannot listen to it. I am wretched under your displeasure. I confess that for some time I intended to punish you for your cavalier treatment of Elise Beckwith; but that intention perished long ago, and I would have been glad to acknowledge my identity, but that a great dread restrained me. A dread of what? Forgive me, come to me, and perhaps you can guess.   E. R.

Her whole heart went out to him as she wrote, and her soft beauty as she hurriedly folded the letter and sealed it in its envelope would have inspired an artist less engrossed in her than Terriss Chester. The note was so cold and guarded in comparison with its predecessors that she enter-

tained no misgivings as to the advisability of
sending it. She rang for a servant and gave orders that a man should ride with it at once to the
post-office, preferring this means of communica-
tion, for some unexpressed reason, to the direct
road to Roxana's door.

The sweetness of relief and the sanguine hope-
fulness she experienced when she heard the clatter
of horse's hoofs down the avenue, lasted throughout the night, giving her pleasant dreams and
meeting her in the morning at the first moment of
waking. But, alas, for the garish light of day, it
brings out defects in such honest, unsparing clearness !

The defects in Elise's little scheme began to
obtrude themselves suggestively before she had
left her bed. How shallow and flippant her whole
course would be sure to look to Chester! The
suggestions began to be tormenting. His confidence in her was entirely undermined. Was it
likely he would permit himself to be whistled back,
perhaps to be duped in some new direction? How
unwomanly, how daring, had been the implication
with which that horrible note had closed ! The
suggestions had become torture. Elise could only
bury her face in her pillow and exaggerate her
own indiscretion and Chester's cold surprise and
contempt, regardless of time, until her maid appeared with a scribbled word of sympathy from
Tony.

" He says, ma'am, perhaps he 'd better take the
early train for town," said the girl.

"Yes. Give him my regrets and good-by," returned Mrs. Redmond, and as soon as the maid's back was turned she buried her face again in her pillow; but not for long. True to her nature, which refused to be quiescent under suffering, Elise began searching for a device to escape this new humiliation. Strange to say, the simplest method presented itself last, namely to get the letter out of the office before Chester could.

As soon as this possibility did occur to her, she made a hasty toilet, ordered her carriage, drank a cup of coffee, and started on her way to the village. Her horses were good ones, but to-day it seemed to her they crawled. She deeply injured the coachman's feelings by her criticisms, and by the time they reached the office, there was a general scattering in the street before the foam-flecked team.

She dismounted before the horses had fairly stopped, and found herself trembling as she stood before the little window.

"I will take Mrs. Sherritt's mail," she said, forgetting that she had not asked for her own. The postmaster looked vacantly into her excited face.

"Oh — Mrs. Sherritt's," he said, at last.

"Yes, would you kindly hurry a little?" she continued, an unsteadiness in her proudly authoritative voice.

The functionary pushed up his spectacles, and took from the shelf a package of letters, which he commenced deliberately to look over, one by one.

Mrs. Redmond gazed at the package with bright, eager eyes, longing to take it into her own deft hands.

The postmaster began slowly shaking his head as he neared the last envelope.

"Nothin' this mornin'," he said at last.

Elise's breath came fast.

"Not for Miss Flower — or — or Mr. Chester?" she asked.

"No, nothin' for Phyllis. Mr. Chester's mail ain't goin' there no more. It's got to be for-*ward*ed to Boston."

Mrs. Redmond's heart gave a great leap; but she realized that she was in a gossiping little village, and her wariness did not forsake her.

"I hope I am in time, then," she said. "I mailed an invitation to Mr. Chester last night. I am obliged to retract it. Be kind enough to hand it to me."

"Sorry I can't, ma'am. That invitation's bound to get to Mr. Chester 'fore night. It's on its way to Boston now."

Elise grasped the dingy railing. Her disappointment was poignant, and for the moment made her ill. Her thoughts, however, were nimble. How would it be to telegraph Terriss not to open her letter? No. That would but make a bad matter worse. Better to rely on her own ability, when she saw him, to contradict by her manner the interpretation he must put upon her written words.

She moved out of the post-office and entered her
carriage like one in a dream, only awakened by
the furious hurry into which the driver at once
urged the horses.

" William, not so fast. Drive slowly," she ordered, and unmindful of the coachman's astonished
and injured countenance, relapsed into her reverie.

Terriss would come. She felt sure of it. He
had left Snowdon hurriedly, driven away by her
falseness ; but he would come at her entreaty. He
would feel so much as that indebted to her. How
could she bear it ? She loved him. How could
she bear to see him and to face his criticism of
her ?

Suddenly her eyes brightened. She leaned forward and addressed the driver. " Turn back,
please," she said. " I wish to go to Mr. Terriss'."

Arrived at the parsonage, she looked hesitatingly
at the darkened front of the house, and then proceeded around to the back door, where she appeared, an astonishing vision, to Lucindy.

" I did not wish to disturb any one by ringing
the bell," she announced to the gaping hand-
maiden. " How is the minister this morning? "

" He 's awful dangerous," replied the girl, wag-
ging her head solemnly.

" I wonder if I could see Miss Redmond a moment. I will wait in the dining-room. You go
quietly, and if you can get a glimpse of her, tell
her I am here."

Lucindy dropped her dish towel and obeyed.

People always did obey Elise. She had not waited many minutes when Rebecca appeared, looking more spiritual and transparent than ever, but bringing with her an atmosphere of calm which was grateful to the caller's highly wrought condition of mind.

The latter advanced and took her sister's hand. " I hear the news is not hopeful this morning," she said.

Miss Rebecca shook her head. " No," she replied softly.

" I have come to see if you will not take me as assistant, — let me bring a bag and stay as many days as I am needed."

" No, dear child. We don't need you."

" You look very worn already," said Elise abruptly.

" Yes, because I have been up all night; but now Roxana is here, and I am going to sleep."

" Good little Rebecca," said Elise, looking at her wistfully. " You had better let me get a nurse to do this work for you. I don't know why I should allow you to wear yourself out in this way."

" I wish to — I wish to. Say nothing against it, dear. Have you heard how wonderfully Mrs. Terriss seemed resuscitated by the excitement?"

" Yes, the servants were speaking of it this morning. So this illness has solved one of your problems?"

" Yes, but I am fearful of the effect upon her of

so much effort. It seems to be a relief to her that I am here. It is clearly my duty to stay."

"Dear, good Mr. Terriss," said Elise. "It is easier to give you to his service than it would be to another's. Do you really think he cannot live?"

Such a look as Rebecca gave her out of those gentle eyes; such a suffering, frightened, patient look!

Mrs. Redmond was moved to give her a rare embrace.

"I am keeping you selfishly from your sleep," she said. "You faithful little sister, he will get well if good nursing can compass it. Is there any doctor, anybody, anything, you would like sent for? Please make use of me, if you can."

Rebecca wiped away the bright, slow-gathering tears. "You can do nothing, Elise. I have told the doctor to send for any one he will. He knows that no effort is to be spared. Good-by — good-by."

In her carriage again, Mrs. Redmond felt more rueful than before. Rebecca would not have her. That highly respectable avenue of escape was closed to her. Still, escape she must, even if but temporarily, the consequences of that mad letter; — that dreadful letter that took so much for granted.

Another idea occurred to her, a pleasant one, evidently, for she smiled as she gave the driver an order to proceed to Miss Flower's.

CHAPTER XXV.

"O HEART! ARE YOU GREAT ENOUGH?"

It is seldom in this world that a deeply coveted good actually comes to one at the time the craving for it is strongest; yet to Terriss Chester, the man of many disappointments and scant success, such rare fortune was on its way.

The remainder of the afternoon of the day on which he arrived in Boston was spent in search of a room, in which for few enough dollars per week he might have the privilege of storing his trunk and valise, and, by night, himself. The daylight he proposed to use for some time to come in a more or less declared search for a situation.

The room found and the hard bed slept in, Terriss considered that for the first time in his life he fully realized what an exceptionally lonely and comfortless existence his was. He reviled the lack of adaptability, the reserved and ungenial disposition, which had prevented his finding a single good comrade among the chance acquaintances of his many years of clerkship. He realized that these months under Mrs. Sherritt's conscientious supervision had given him a taste of home-life which by contrast made his fate more distasteful. Loyal little Phyllis! She had been a friend, philosopher, and guide not to be despised. Despised indeed! To be sadly missed and keenly desired. Chester had been too absorbed and confused in his hasty leave-taking of Snowdon to think much about Phyllis; but sitting on his trunk in his bare room that next morning, he thought of her. The bright sparks in her eyes and the feeling in her voice when she gave him her spontaneous sympathy came back to him now as a sweet remembrance. It was pleasant to think about Phyllis, and it was safe. Some time he meant to go and see her again. He drew a deep sigh, put on his hat, and went out to find a breakfast somewhere, and to study the advertisements in the papers. Some of these he answered during the day, and he called at several business houses to see if there were a chance for him; but when at night he lit the gas in his uninviting room, he had found no niche into which he might possibly fit.

He always remembered that night afterward. It was very hard to get to sleep, and he struggled so not to think about Elise. He tried to amuse himself by recalling Roxana's oddities, and soothed himself with a recollection of Phyllis and her naive girlish friendship. He calculated possible business chances; debated whether it would not be better for him to leave Boston and to go where there was more room. In vain. Mrs. Redmond was queen of his thoughts that night, and would not be deposed. He ceased struggling after a time. He deliberately yielded to the pleasing torment, and allowed his imagination to dwell upon the tones of her sweet, low-pitched voice, the natural, graceful poses of her royal head, and upon the fiery gold of each silky thread of her hair when the sun blazed full upon it.

How her throat and arms gleamed from the thin summer fabrics she wore! How proud and untender she was, yet womanly too! A woman who had not yet found the master of her heart, but was sovereign of herself as well as of all around her.

Yet Phyllis had said that Tony— It was strange how little lasting effect that statement of Phyllis's had had. Tony Bellows master of *that* woman's heart? Impossible. And yet she was going to marry him; Phyllis had said so. She doubtless had her reasons. Tony was good looking and rich, and of course her ardent admirer. All men must be that who had eyes to see and ears to hear. It made small difference to him. It was all over; and in Chester's hopelessness and the blankness of his lot compared with the heaven of his imagination, there seemed to him something not inapt in Miss Rebecca's simile of the black stone by the wayside.

A clod he felt himself when wearied out he fell asleep; a clod he felt himself when he awakened in the morning, and heavily rose and started upon another day. While at breakfast, he thought of the bank again. He had so far refrained from visiting the scene of his old employment. He did not wish to appear to be thinking of a situation there, and any place connected with Tony had grown obnoxious to him. Nevertheless, habit is strong, and he inclined to seek the spot of all in town most familiar to him; where at least there were faces that he knew. Then it suddenly occurred to him that he had left word at the Snowdon post-office to have his mail forwarded to the bank, that being the only address at his command. Here was a reason for carrying out his desire, and shortly after breakfast, he turned his steps toward the familiar locality.

Chester little suspected that when he crossed the marble threshold of the fine building he had sought, he was leaving his old life behind him. In spite of himself, his sensitive independence suffered in coming here at all. He was so conscious that he would be glad of the opportunity to reënter the old treadmill, that it seemed to him this hankering must be apparent to his fellow employees as soon as they saw him. Consequently his dark face wore an especially forbidding expression, and his tall figure was drawn up in its most unapproachable attitude.

His pleasant surprises began at the moment of entering the bank door. Some one looked up, and recognizing him, said, "Hello, there's Chester." A friendly hand grasped his, another and another pleasant nod and kindly word greeted him, and made him feel that after all he was a human being among human beings, and not entirely isolated

from his kind. Before he realized it, he was talking companionably with his old acquaintances
about his illness and recovery, and some twenty
minutes passed before he remembered the errand
that had brought him.

" Any mail for me ? " he asked then, and somebody handed him Elise's letter. He took it mechanically and slipped it into his pocket, quite
preoccupied by the fact that his old employer was
advancing to shake hands and say a cordial word.
Altogether, nothing occurred during his brief visit
to annoy him, and he left a few minutes afterward
with a glow of pleasant feeling, in which, for the
moment, the cold facts of his aimless condition were
forgotten. He had not yet had time to recollect
that there was no particular objective point toward
which his swift footsteps were tending, when, on
putting his hand in his pocket, it struck the edge
of an envelope.

" Ah, surely, I have a letter," he thought, and
drew it forth.

The handwriting was large and unfamiliar, the
postmark Snowdon. He tore open the envelope
without a suspicion of the writer's identity.

The opening word, his own name, without prefix,
surprised him. He walked slower, as he read, and
finally stood still on the sidewalk when slow comprehension arrived at certainty by means of the
initials that signed the page. A hurrying pedestrian was cleverly collided with and unpleasantly
jarred by this sudden standstill of Chester's, and

looking angrily at the offender with an impatient exclamation, met the most rapt and ecstatic gaze he had ever seen in a man's face. Chester forgot to apologize; he smiled vaguely, and moved on.

He had not comprehended the letter fully yet, and he knew it; but Elise had written to him, and kindly. He looked about him to see where he was. There was a restaurant a few steps away, and it was not likely there would be many persons in it at this hour. He entered, and seated himself at a remote table, rested his arms thereon, and holding the letter firmly with both hands, began to read again.

A waiter hastened to his side. Terriss looked up at him as though a waiter were the most extraneous object possible to imagine in a restaurant. He closed the letter between his hands, too, as though suspicious that the man had designs upon it.

"Your order, sir," said the functionary.

"Oh!" Chester reflected. At last he thought of ice cream, and that being a delicacy abhorrent to him he ordered it, and being left in peace returned with epicurean delight to his feast, which he discussed, one phrase at a time.

"Terriss. She uses my name." Then reading on: "She foregoes her pride. She acknowledges her deception, and regrets it. A great dread restrained her. A dread of what? Forgive her, — come to her" — Chester's breath came fast with excitement. "She thinks I was angry with her, when I was only ashamed, *ashamed* to have tried her patience so far; to have criticised and blamed her so boorishly. I felt that the best return I could make for her long and courteous toleration was to take myself off. How cold and haughty her face looked, royal always and never so royal as then! 'You have learned the truth,' it seemed to say, 'and now, surely, you can ask no more of me.'"

His deeply flushed face bent lower over the letter. " Forgive me, — come to me, and perhaps you can guess."

They were sweet, appealing words, and he read them over and over with a deep enjoyment, before his thought expanded to a breadth of comprehension in which their full import could come to him.

He read still again, "A great dread restrained me. A dread of what? Forgive me, come to me, — and perhaps you can guess."

Terriss' hand grew unsteady, for a tremendous thought, nay conviction, mastered him. His face grew pale. "My God! she loves me." Whether the exclamation was mental, or whether he spoke aloud, he did not know, and the name of the Deity was no irreverence on his lips. In his unsuccessful encounters with fate, he had doggedly and stoically pursued his way with little thought of the hand of a ruling Power in his affairs; but this sublime gift seemed only possible from an omnipotent Being, and in his exalted gratitude, his first impulse was acknowledgment.

He rose unsteadily and pushed his chair back.

The waiter was at his elbow. The untouched ice cream was melting and overflowing the sides of the saucer.

"There's your check, sir," observed the watchful one, indicating the slip of paper. Chester felt in his vest pocket and pulled out a dollar bill, which he handed the man, and then moved out of the place with a fixed gaze which gave some excuse for the philosophical shake of the head with which the waiter looked after him, his condemnation of Chester's supposed condition being tempered by the fee he had gained.

There was no doubt in Terriss' mind as to his next move. "Come to me," she had written. Of course he should go. The first train which he could get to Snowdon arrived there at seven o'clock. The time on the way would have seemed very long but for the letter which he held in his hand, and reread a hundred times, folding and placing it in his pocket occasionally, simply for the pleasure of taking it out again.

When at last his feet touched the platform at Snowdon, it struck him that much time had elapsed since that wretched day when last he saw it, and it seemed, too, that he could not be identical with the hopeless and aimless man who took that morning train with Tony Bellows.

Tony Bellows! Chester laughed aloud. It was the first time he had thought of his friend since this wondrous metamorphosis of the whole world.

He strode along the road to Beech Knoll at a

swinging pace, luxuriating as he went in conjuring up different possible images of Elise as he should find her. Whether indoors or out, occupied or idle, mattered little to her lover, so that he saw her at last, and received proof from her sweet lips and eyes that he was awake and sane.

He passed Mrs. Sherritt's domain with a glance, and hurried on. Beech Knoll at last. He entered the gates, went up the avenue, and approached the piazza. No sign yet of his lady. He mounted the steps and rang the bell with an eager hand.

A maid opened the door and gave him a smile of recognition.

" I should like to see Mrs. Redmond," he said confidently.

" She 's not at home, sir. I 'm sorry." The gratuitous addition was doubtless elicited by the change in the visitor's face. The maid had always considered Chester a handsome gentleman, and when she opened the door just now, she had mentally remarked that he was handsomer than ever.

" Where is Mrs. Redmond ? I will find her."

" Oh, she 's left town, sir."

" Left town ! " echoed Chester blankly. " Where has she gone ? "

" We don't know, any of us. She made up her mind suddenly, and went off."

" I would like to see Miss Rebecca, then."

The maid shook her head. " She 's at the parsonage, helping with Mr. Terriss. He 's very sick, you know, sir."

"Oh, yes." Chester reflected a moment. "Thank you," he said, then turned away.

His disappointment was great, but there were deeps to his happiness which could bear this draught upon it and leave him blissful still. The letter lay warm against his heart, and an idea came to him at which he smiled meditatively. Elise had written impulsively, then, frightened at her own temerity, had run away. Such an action was not like Mrs. Redmond, to be sure, but then neither was the letter, and the letter was a fact. He put his hand in his breast pocket to touch it and make sure.

"I will go and see Phyllis," he thought. It would be a real pleasure to see Phyllis; but at Mrs. Sherritt's a lesser disappointment awaited him. Ring, knock, and wait as he might, no sign of life could be evoked from the silent house.

"Is the town bewitched?" he thought. "But I must not leave without going to inquire for cousin Philip, and there I shall see Miss Rebecca."

Arrived at the parsonage, he found a written card tacked up at the entrance, which warned all persons not to ring, but to go around to the back door.

Chester followed the latter injunction, and absent-mindedly forgetting to knock, pushed open the kitchen door. He was greeted by a stifled shriek from Lucindy, who, sitting in the shadows, was greatly startled by the sudden appearance of the tall stranger.

"I beg pardon. I should have knocked. I came to inquire for Mr. Terriss."

Lucindy, who had retreated into a corner, came slowly forward at this placable address.

"Oh, I'm that nervous," she gasped; "what with folks out o' their heads, and dyin' in every room in the house, I jump at a shadder. I did n't see 't was you, Mr. Chester."

"Is Mr. Terriss dying, do you say?" asked Chester, shocked.

"He's dreadful bad," averred the girl; "and now Mrs. Terriss, she's got an awful fever, and we're scared about her too." Lucindy wiped her eyes.

"I am very sorry to hear this," said Chester. " I wish there were something I could do."

" They've sent to Boston for a nurse," replied Lucindy, shaking her head. "Miss Rebecca and Mrs. Sherritt, they've got their hands too full now."

"I suppose I would better not ask to see Miss Rebecca," remarked Chester.

"I don't believe she'd come down," replied Lucindy dolefully. "Mrs. Redmond, her sister-in-law, was here yesterday" —

"What? Yesterday?"

"Yes; an' Miss Rebecca could n't see her; an' Mrs. Redmond she had me give her a paper an' pencil, an' wrote her a note. I can give you one," suggested Lucindy, "if you want to write."

Chester reflected a moment. How narrowly he

had missed finding Elise ! but he would not trouble Miss Rebecca at such a time.

" No," he answered. " Just tell Miss Rebecca that I called to inquire, and give her my sympathy. Good-evening," and Terriss moved out of the door and down the uncertain back steps. He could not get back to Boston to-night. There was nothing to do but to find a supper and a bed at the Snow-don House, and perhaps in the morning he would return to the parsonage and get Elise's address from Miss Rebecca.

Further meditation, however, in his luridly-pa-pered room in the country hotel determined him not to do this. Now that his ideas were calmer, he saw matters in a clearer and more comprehensive light. The difference between his own and Elise's financial position, which had utterly faded from his mind, recurred to him. It would be better, before he followed her, to have some occupation in view. He sat in one of the small, uncomfortable chairs that furnished his room, and thought for hours, rose-tinted. thoughts, of the past and future. He reconsidered the episode of Elise's offer of the money, with tender leniency. Only the highest, most womanly, of motives, of course, could have influenced her. Shame upon him, that he could ever have. believed otherwise. He dwelt with gen-tle remembrance on the memory of Aaron Beck-with, and, for the first time in fifteen years, called him " father " in thought. The autocratic man would once have been very happy to foresee this.

How lovely Elise had looked that day in the grove, when she defended her childish self with such spirit and compassion! Terriss chafed in self-condemnation, as he recalled his own observations; but he took out his letter once more, the panacea for all wounds henceforth.

He forgot that he was thirty-five, and had never been given to sentiment, and he fervently kissed the paper where her hand had rested, and slept with it beneath his pillow that night.

CHAPTER XXVI.

ANYWHERE! ANYWHERE!

ON the morning, three days ago, when Terriss Chester bade good-by to his entertainers, they stood on the steps to see the last of him.

"Well, *that* chapter's ended," remarked Roxana. It was her sole comment on the boarder's departure, spoken with a comfortable consciousness of having done her full duty by him.

"It was a very pleasant chapter," returned Phyllis, looking after Jake Harvey's conveyance with a disconsolate little face.

"Yes, he did very well," said Roxana. "I'm sorry he couldn't stay longer, for every little helps us to make both ends meet. Now, Phyllis, let's make short work o' the dishes, for I've got to hurry to the parsonage and see how things are goin'."

"Go right away, if you like. I will do everything."

Roxana regarded her hesitatingly. The gravity of the girl's face troubled her a little.

"Maybe she *has* been a little touched by him," she thought. "Girls will take freaks. Maybe I've had about enough board money from Mr Chester, after all."

"All right," she returned. "You look some down in the mouth, and it 'll stir you up and make you feel better to do some extra work. Nothin' like it for the blues."

"Roxana is a good woman," thought Phyllis, left alone, and beginning to clear away the breakfast things. "I wonder if I shall ever come to the time when I shall think as little about self as she does."

All was emptiness to Phyllis this morning. She no longer desired to go to Beech Knoll, even if she were invited. She felt that there was nothing to look forward to, nothing to mark the monotonous, uninteresting days; no spice in Roxana's society, truly and gratefully as she loved her. There would be no more exchange of thoughts with Terriss Chester, no more interviews — this she hoped, at least — with Mr. Bellows.

"If I saw him coming in that gate now, I would run out by the back door and hide, rather than meet him," she thought; then she gazed a little at the gate, but happily no Tony appeared to drive her to that extreme of inhospitality.

"To think that he should be Mrs. Redmond's choice;" thus her musing ran as she moved into the kitchen, and filling the dish-pan from the steaming kettle, began the serious business of the morning. "I have heard her say she is older than he. No, I could n't do that," shaking her head virtuously. "It is a very strange choice for Mrs. Redmond." Here Phyllis heaved a sigh. "I shall see no more of her, of course. No doubt they will be married soon, and then they will have as little use for their native land as other bridal pairs with money enough to leave it."

Phyllis lost herself a moment in reverie, while she turned a goblet over and over in the hot water. At last two great drops gathered in her eyes, and fell with a splash into the steaming pan. " What have I to live for? What can I do in my poverty and obscurity? Why was I born to vegetate in this little forgotten corner of the world?"

It was the climax of all her vague longings and discontent, and for a moment she yielded to it with abandon; but Dr. Joy's and Roxana's love and labor had not been quite in vain. There was a substratum of solid sense in Phyllis's nature which revolted against such cowardly surrender. She set her lips determinedly, held back the glasses with one hand, and with the other tipped the dish-pan until all the tear-mingled water had run away; then refilled the pan, washed, scalded, and wiped the dishes after Roxana's most approved method, and by the time the last platter had been set in its place on the shelf, she had regained her poise and her self-respect.

" I will not be dependent upon any one," she thought, her eyes shining and her cheeks glowing. " I am Phyllis Flower, young, strong, and well. I am glad I am alive, and I am going to enjoy myself every minute, whether I'm sweeping a room, or reading a book, or taking a walk."

A sudden thought made her cheeks flush. "That is all I look out for, — that I shall enjoy myself. Roxana is n't so, nor Miss Rebecca. Never mind, I won't think, nor dissect myself. When I am old as they, perhaps I shall be as good. For the present, all I know is that I will not long to see Mr. Chester, nor Mrs. Redmond, nor wish to leave Snowdon, nor wish to have money. In short, my lot is precisely what I would like to have it."

Phyllis gave a little independent toss of her head as she finished her soliloquy, and set about restoring order in the boarder's deserted room.

She was still occupied in washing crockery and brushing furniture, when, happening to stand near an open window, she saw Mrs. Redmond's carriage stop at the door. For an individual whose lot left nothing to be desired, and whose state of mind was one of abounding content, Phyllis felt an astonishingly eager start of pleasant excitement.

She threw down brush and duster, and ran downstairs to open the door. Halfway down, she recollected herself, and changed her headlong rush into a subdued walk. "I am perfectly independent of everybody," she reminded herself, and with a strange pang she remembered, too, that Mrs. Redmond was engaged now, and had probably come only to apologize further for the disappointment of yesterday. By the time the front door was opened, it was a sedate and quiet Phyllis who greeted the caller decorously, and invited her into the parlor.

"I am glad to find you," said Elise. "I did not wish to be thwarted any farther this morning;" and she laughed with a bright, restless air, unusual to her.

"Yes, I am all alone to-day," replied Phyllis. "Roxana is devoting herself to Mr. Terriss."

• "Sister Rebecca, too," returned Elise, becoming grave. "Poor man, I fear there is little hope, according to what Rebecca told me this morning."

"His wife will die, if he does," said Phyllis.

"It is not so easy to die," returned Elise skeptically. "So far, his illness acts like a tonic upon her."

"It is all terrible," said Phyllis, feeling pale and cold, and wondering why she had not thought more already about the sorrow at the parsonage. She took a melancholy satisfaction now in emphasizing it.

Elise looked at her steadily. "Do you know, Phyllis, what I do with trouble when it is beyond my power to alleviate it?"

"Bear it, I suppose."

"Oh, no indeed. I run away from it."

Phyllis smiled faintly. "Lucky you, then."

The color showed suddenly in Mrs. Redmond's cheeks. "Mr. Chester has gone, has n't he?" she said abruptly. "I heard it in the village. It relieves me for some reasons."

"You need not have feared his troubling you, if he had stayed," burst forth Phyllis, becoming warmly defiant

Her companion's face looked very girlish. "O Phyllis, did he tell you?" she ejaculated, leaning forward with a self-forgetful eagerness of attitude and expression which considerably impressed her companion.

"He told me he could not stay any longer," returned the girl slowly.

Elise leaned back, and the light died from her face. Phyllis's mystified look proved more clearly than her words that she knew nothing.

"I dare say, then, Tony had him for company to town," she went on quickly.

"Has he gone too?"

"Yes, very sensibly. I kept my room this morning, and he fled. Very likely I should still be an interesting invalid, only, as I say, I made up my mind suddenly that Beech Knoll, even Snowdon itself, was overhung with trouble, and I would run away from it."

"You are really ill," said Phyllis, looking at her closely.

"No; only I did not sleep much last night, and my little attack of yesterday has left its traces. I went to Rebecca to see if I could be allowed to help nurse Mr. Terriss; but she promptly vetoed that plan so now for my alternative; and I want you to run away with me, Phyllis."

"Me? Oh!" exclaimed Phyllis, alert and alight at once.

"You would like to?"

"But how could I leave?"

Phyllis's hands were unconsciously clasped. Mrs. Redmond was much amused by her radiant face.

"Where should we go to?" the girl asked breathlessly.

"I don't know," replied Elise, "do you?"

"No, unless Boston."

"No indeed, not Boston," returned Mrs. Redmond emphatically.

"Then I don't know, either," said Phyllis, smiling. "Do you think Roxana will let me go?" she added eagerly.

"Why, you delicious little goose, what authority has Roxana over you? When she returns this afternoon, simply say to her, ' As long as I cannot help you at the parsonage, Roxana, I am going away on a little trip with Mrs. Redmond.'"

"Oh!" exclaimed Phyllis, catching her breath. "I haven't nice enough clothes, — except my tennis suit."

"You can almost live in that wherever we go."

Phyllis's eyes danced gleefully. "I must confess, I felt a little lonely this morning. I expected to miss Mr. Chester very much."

"He did not expect to leave so soon, did he?"

"No; he went " — The girl became suddenly grave. "He went because he couldn't stay."

Mrs. Redmond laughed, not very merrily. "An excellent reason, really."

Phyllis eyed her somewhat resentfully. "He went because he was very unhappy," she said distinctly.

"He went because he was very angry," returned Elise, her heart beating fast. "You did not read him aright, that is all." Then she added gravely, "Mr. Chester is deeply offended with me."

"You misjudge him," returned Phyllis warmly. "He is far from everything egotistical and narrow-minded."

"Yes, I think that too. He is right to be indignant with me."

Phyllis looked at the speaker in surprise at this humility. "I cannot see it so," she returned. "Had you not a perfect right to prefer Mr. Bellows?"

Elise smiled. "You misunderstand me. I should be very sorry to have you suppose that I think Mr. Chester jealous of my friendship for Tony."

Her friendship. Phyllis thought this an odd way to speak of her *fiancé*.

"I cannot explain to you just now Mr. Chester's ground for displeasure," continued Mrs. Redmond. Were it not for the letter she had written, she might have confided in her friend; but the reaction from that rash act was an impulse to lock her secret closely in her breast.

Phyllis's cheeks began to redden in mental defense of Terriss. At last her feelings drove her to expression. "What you take for displeasure is something very different, Mrs. Redmond," she said boldly. "Mr. Chester and I have had such a good time together admiring you!"

Mrs. Redmond flushed suddenly and seemed to find nothing amusing in this naive flattery. The questioning, expectant look she bent upon her companion gave the latter courage to proceed.

"I imagine he did not realize his own feelings until yesterday at your house. I felt so sorry for him last evening when he told me he must go. I feared you had been unkind to him; but when I told him — I could n't help it, Mrs. Redmond — I told him I wished he could have succeeded instead of Mr. Bellows, and he replied that he thanked heaven he had not tried, I " —

Elise, sitting close by the girl, seized her wrist. "How did you dare!" she exclaimed, her eyes flashing with indignation.

Phyllis was frightened, and wished with a beating heart that she had not spoken.

"You did very, very wrong," said Mrs. Redmond, making an evident effort to control herself.

"I think not," returned the girl with desperate courage. "He was wretched. There was no one else to say a kind word to him."

"You made a great mistake. He was not unhappy. He was angry. Did his reply not enlighten you? Thank heaven he had not tried!" Mrs. Redmond repeated this in a hard voice, and her blue-gray eyes flashed angry fire upon Phyllis, who quailed, and wished with her whole heart that she had not taken up the cudgels for Mr. Chester. "Do you say you thought me engaged to Tony Bellows?"

" Ye - es," stammered Phyllis, looking at her friend with fascinated, frightened eyes.

Mrs. Redmond gave a short laugh and loosened her hold upon the girl's wrist. " Let this teach you a lesson, Phyllis. I am not engaged to Mr. Bellows. You were very foolish to suppose it, and wicked to speak of it."

" He told me he was going to " — began the girl.

Her companion set her teeth, and muttered some epithet which it was happy for Tony he did not hear.

Phyllis looked at her reproachfully. " He held your hand," she said, catching her breath ; " I saw him kiss it. He lifted you out of your chair," — she caught her breath again, — " he called you Elise," she sobbed, and burying her face suddenly in her hands, the girl broke into stifled weeping.

" Phyllis, Phyllis, don't ! " exclaimed Mrs. Redmond.

Excited though she was, she felt condemned for her own harshness. She laid her gloved hand on the other's arm. " Please listen to me," she said. " Don't cry."

Phyllis was excessively ashamed of her weakness, and not a little angry with her guest for causing her to make such an exhibition. She controlled herself as quickly as possible.

" I did not think of making you cry," continued Mrs. Redmond, when her companion was quiet. " It is always extremely annoying to me to know that my affairs are talked over by any one, and perhaps I am somewhat arrogant in expecting them to be more sacred from discussion than those of other people. I am really sorry to have hurt your feelings. You will forgive me, and think no more of it, won't you?"

She took Phyllis's hands, and looked at her with an expression more of kindly authority than of supplication.

"I promise not to scold you in No Man's Land, or wherever we find ourselves a few days from now."

"Oh, I think perhaps we had better reconsider that," said Phyllis unsteadily.

"Now, Phyllis, don't be resentful. You would not be, if you suspected what a bitter experience underlies all this annoyance of mine. Mr. Chester is angry with me justly enough from his standpoint, so you see it was somewhat trying to me to learn that you had been wishing to give me to him."

There was simply no resisting the smile with which Elise added this.

"Then does n't it matter that I made him believe you were going to marry Mr. Bellows?" asked Phyllis, mollified but doubtful.

Mrs. Redmond blushed desperately. She was thinking how soon Terriss would know that report to be false.

"Nothing matters," she said hastily, "so that we go away quickly. I am a woman of one idea, you see. Could you be ready in time for the early morning train to-morrow ? "

" Oh, no, really I 'm afraid I could n't," said Phyllis, dismayed at the idea.

" The next morning at farthest, then," said Mrs. Redmond, rising. " You will hear from me to-morrow again."

Chester would hardly report in person so soon as to-morrow, even if all were as she wished it. At any rate, the risk must be run. She wanted Phyllis very much as companion and shield from her own thoughts, and she would wait for her.

Late that afternoon, when Roxana returned, Phyllis had some ado to draw her face into a suitable expression to greet the tired look the housekeeper had brought from the parsonage. There was no especial change in Mr. Terriss' condition, so Roxana said.

She seemed disinclined to talk, as though the sorrow she had left still weighed upon her spirit.

Phyllis insisted upon her remaining seated in a rocking-chair while she made tea and set the supper-table. She found it somewhat difficult to approach the subject uppermost in her mind, and uncomfortable misgivings assailed her as to the propriety of leaving Roxana to come home tired to an empty house after her fatiguing neighborly offices. Certainly no such airy announcement as Mrs. Redmond had suggested was possible now.

" And how have you got on all day by yourself?" inquired Roxana, her head leaning back

against the old chintz cushion, while she watched
the girl's neat movements about the table with a
sense of satisfaction.

"Oh, I have accomplished a good deal. When
you go upstairs to the spare room, you will believe
Mr. Chester's visit to have been a dream. Mrs.
Redmond has been here to see me, too."

"H'm. What'd she have to say?"

"She thinks of going away for a trip."

"Where now?" inquired Roxana dryly.

"She isn't sure."

"H'm. Anythin' so she keeps goin', I s'pose.
A pity she couldn't change places with the Wan-
derin' Jew."

This was not encouraging. Phyllis had thought
her request well-nigh introduced, but now it looked
as remote as ever.

"I wish there was something I could do to help
you, Roxana, so you wouldn't get so tired," she remarked.

"Oh, a good healthy tired ain't anythin' to be
afraid of," returned Mrs. Sherritt. "I'm bein'
lazy now just because it's a pleasure to see you so
handy about things, Phyllis. The only thing that
bothers me is, I s'pose I'll have to do night work
before this sickness o' Mr. Terriss' ends one way
or the other. I don't want you should stay alone
in the house nights. I was calc'latin' to ask Miss
Rebecca if you couldn't sleep awhile at Beech
Knoll. I guess you could anyway, even if Mrs.
Redmond does go traipsin' off."

Phyllis paused with the bread-knife halfway down through the loaf, and the bright, eager look returned to her face.

"Oh, Roxana, she has invited me to go with her!" she said.

"I want to know," returned Mrs. Sherritt. "Why did n't you say so?"

"It seemed selfish to go and leave you to get your own tea."

"And you want to go, I see," said Roxana, smiling musingly. "You 're just dyin' to accept an invitation to go off to nowhere in partic'lar."

Phyllis did not reply, but she looked questioningly at the housekeeper, and the knife remained motionless in the loaf.

"For how long, I wonder?" asked Roxana.

"I don't know. I think not for long. Would you care, Roxana?"

"Oh, you can go. You 're under foot just now," was the careless response; but that evening, after the tea things were put away, Mrs. Sherritt approached the girl and gave her a long hug. Roxana's caresses were at best somewhat trying to endure, her bony structure not being, one might say, comfortably upholstered; but Phyllis knew what they meant, and bore them when they came not only with good grace but appreciatively. Mrs. Sherritt might declare carelessly that she was entirely superfluous, but Phyllis well knew that the very light of day would be clouded for the good woman until her return.

" I 'm goin' to run over to the parsonage once more, Phyllis, before I go to bed. I won't be long. I 'm kinder uneasy not to see 'em fixed for the night," she said, releasing her.

" But it is raining, Roxana, and dark as pitch."

" Oh, I 'll take the lantern. You go to bed, if you want to. I 'll take the key to the back door. Good-by till I see you again."

CHAPTER XXVII.

OUT OF THE WORLD.

On the morning of the same day, when Roxana reached the parsonage she had found matters in a sad condition. The sick man's ravings continued, and his wife could not be kept from his side. Mrs. Sherritt, when she entered the room, saw Mrs. Terriss, deathly pale, at the foot of the bed, her great burning eyes fixed on her husband's face. Miss Redmond was moving about noiselessly as a spirit, fulfilling the various requirements of her office, and Roxana looked at her in amazement, and with some remorse at the thought that she had coerced her into a position of such unique discomfort and difficulty.

"This is martyrdom," she thought, as the pleading voice of the minister murmured on in words which, if Miss Redmond were not become wholly indifferent, must pierce her soul, while the wife listened, bending her searching glance first on her husband, then furtively on his nurse.

Mrs. Sherritt determined to bring the dreadful scene to an end. "Mrs. Terriss," she said, in a lowered voice, coming close to her, "I'm here to give you and Miss Rebecca a rest. You must both go out of here now and lay down."

"Miss Rebecca can go," returned the other quietly.

Roxana exchanged a few words with Miss Redmond, then the latter left the room.

Mrs. Terriss looked at Roxana with a smile which sent an unpleasant creeping sensation down the latter's spine.

"You think still this raving is nonsense, as meaningless as the wind that blows?" she asked, pointing at her husband.

"Come, now, Mrs. Terriss, you're tired out," said Roxana soothingly. "Do hear to me and go and lay down!"

"No, this is not meaningless. Philip is saying what he feels, perhaps for the first time in twenty years," continued the other unheedingly, her scorching gaze on the unconscious face.

Mrs. Sherritt had never suspected that she possessed nerves, but her hands grew unsteady now.

"Dear me," she returned coaxingly. "Don't it prove you're all wrong that Miss Rebecca can stand it? Look how calm and collected she is the whole time."

"I do not know if she loves him," returned the quiet, cold voice, "but he loves her."

"Now Mrs. Terriss, you're just overstrained. Look back along the years. What have Mr. Terriss' actions been? What has he done?"

The other nodded slowly. "I know what he has done, — know it for the first time. I know — I know."

"You must go and rest," said Roxana desperately. "You've got to do it. You'll be down sick, too."

The great black eyes rolled heavily toward her.

"I will go," was the quiet reply.

Roxana led her into the adjoining room.

"Will you lie on the lounge?"

"Anywhere."

Mrs. Sherritt covered her carefully, and then returned to the sick-room, a painful pulling at her heartstrings.

After an absence of several hours, Miss Redmond came back.

Mrs. Sherritt accosted her anxiously.

"You haven't had rest enough. Go back, Miss Rebecca. Sleep longer, if you can. I'm goin' to stay here all day. The night's enough for you. I'll relieve you o' *that* work, later."

Rebecca, after some demur, obeyed, and Roxana all the afternoon passed in and out between Mr. Terriss' room and the sitting-room where his wife lay. Mrs. Terriss did not ask again to visit her husband. Once when Roxana went out she found her standing by the window, where a slow drizzling rain was beginning to beat against the pane.

"How long the day is," she said, turning her colorless face toward Mrs. Sherritt. "It seems as though night would never come."

"You can't sleep in the daytime?" asked Roxana kindly. "O' course you sleep better at night?"

Mrs. Terriss turned back to the window. " I shall to-night," she replied.

It was five o'clock when Roxana at last gave back her charge into Miss Redmond's hands. She left the parsonage with great reluctance. It seemed a terrible thing to leave Rebecca to work and endure alone. Mrs. Sherritt was thankful that the latter did not seem to suspect Mrs. Terriss' changed state.

Roxana ate her supper and had her talk with Phyllis, but she could not put from her mind the despairing sorrow and the unmurmuring martyrdom she had witnessed to-day. Her uneasiness grew instead of abating, and she felt that she could not go to rest to-night without one more sight of the arrangements at the parsonage ; so, as was said above, she lighted her lantern, for the evening was dark and still rainy, and set forth.

There was a desolate chill in the air as of untimely autumn, and Roxana wished she had worn a warmer wrap, but she moved sturdily along to hasten her circulation, and began to calculate the advisability of a stove in Mr. Terriss' room.

When more than half the distance to the parsonage had been traversed, suddenly a muffled figure approached her from the darkness, made blacker by the circle of light around her own feet.

" Could you tell me," it said breathlessly, " the way to the bridge, — what they call the old bridge ? "

" There 's quite a number o' bridges," replied

Roxana, startled. " You ain't more 'n a block
from one o' them now, right down that street
there. Did you want to cross to Highfield? because if you do " —

But she was talking to the heavy, rain-beaten
air. The shrouded figure, with a stifled cry, had
sped away in the darkness.

Roxana stood still, mystified and amazed.
" What poor crazy thing was that? " she queried,
starting again on her walk. " I guess, by the way
she cried out, I scared her more 'n she did me."

Her sturdy, even tread had carried her several
rods when, cogitating on her surprising encounter,
a horrible thought suddenly struck her.

Many years had elapsed since Mrs. Sherritt
had supposed she could run; but she turned and
ran now, — ran with the nightmare sensation of one
in a dream, who feels, despite all strain and effort,
that he is making no progress. Turning down
the street she had indicated to the stranger, she
stumbled headlong over the road, swinging her
lantern aloft to fling the light ahead. Joy! She
saw the fluttering cloak just approaching the
bridge. She strained every nerve, and with a last
leap caught the figure in her arms. It turned and
struggled with her, — struggled with wonderful,
desperate strength. Roxana's breath was gone.
The lantern fell to the ground and rolled on its side.
She contented herself with merely hanging her
weight upon the miserable creature, who beat and
buffeted her to get free. At last, exhausted, the

stranger ceased her efforts. "How dare you stop me!" she gasped with laboring breath. "Let me go."

"Never, Mrs. Terriss, never. Thank God!" panted Roxana.

"O cruel, wicked woman!" cried the other, with a faint, last struggle; "why should you thwart me? I have only this left."

"You have all eternity," exclaimed Roxana. "You can't die even if you want to. Throw yourself into the river, and what then? A change o' worlds. You'll have the same heart, the same mind, the same self there as here. You wouldn't go uninvited into a lady's parlor. Would you force yourself unasked into the presence o' the King o' kings? O Mrs. Terriss, thank God with me for his mercy in sendin' me to save you. For Christ's sake, see the truth. You ain't through yet with what's been set for you to do. When you are, He'll take you. Poor dear! poor dear! Things wouldn't be made plain if you went now. Wait for your time, and they will be."

With a bitter groan the wretched woman hid her face on Roxana's shoulder, and the latter caressed her with whole-souled loving-kindness.

"You're chilled to the bone and shiverin'. Come home, and we'll fix you warm and comfortable. Your head's kinder turned with all you've been through, but it'll come out all right. We haven't taken enough care of you. You've got lots o' good friends, and plenty to live for."

Roxana picked up the lantern, and with one arm around the trembling form, the two began their difficult progress. After a long and weary effort, they reached the house, and then Mrs. Sherritt commenced her active labors. She actually carried Mrs. Terriss up the narrow staircase, and calling Lucindy to bring hot mustard water, made up a bed with well-aired sheets, and soon placed the sufferer within. Mrs. Terris's teeth chattered in a severe chill, and Roxana was thankful to remember that Phyllis was going away, for the parsonage now needed another pair of hands and feet. She gave Lucindy explicit directions, and then went down to the minister's room, where all was still.

Rebecca was sitting at the foot of the bed, her head leaning against the framework. She looked up at the slight sound Mrs. Sherritt made, and came noiselessly out where she beckoned.

"He is quiet," she said. "What has been going on? I heard Lucindy talking. How did you happen to come back?"

"I wanted to see that you was all fixed for the night, and it's a good thing I did, for Mrs. Terriss has had a pretty bad chill. I've fixed her upstairs. I think she's asleep now. Have the doctor see her when he comes. I'll get over as soon as I can to-morrow. Good-night, Miss Rebecca, these are times, ain't they!"

She took Miss Rebecca's hands in her hard ones that still trembled. Rebecca seemed to her like some high saint in her unconsciousness of the stormy passions that had seethed near her all the day. The latter returned Mrs. Sherritt's look earnestly.

" Times that are only to be lived through by looking upward," she replied. " I remind myself often of those lines we always liked, Roxana. You remember, —

" ' With us is prayer,
And joy, and strength, and courage are with Thee.' "

CHAPTER XXVIII.

PHYLLIS waked the next morning to a consciousness that something delightful was in the air. For a confused moment, Mr. Bellows' smiling image audaciously intruded itself upon her attention. She considered it a moment with a new tolerance; then, in a flash, she remembered. Mrs. Redmond had invited her away, and she was going. If the idea had seemed pleasant when it was first suggested, now it was entrancing. Phyllis thought it was really wonderful what a load was lifted from her mind by the discovery that her charming friend was not going to make so unsuitable a match.

Soon after breakfast, Mrs. Redmond's coachman drove up in a buggy, bringing a note which summoned the girl to Beech Knoll, and she hurriedly prepared herself for the drive.

"Keep your head steady, Phyllis," warned Roxana. "Like as not Mrs. Redmond 's given up the whole thing. You can't depend on a highty-tighty person like that."

"Oh, my head is steady," returned the girl, running outdoors and stepping into the buggy. She did not believe that Mrs. Redmond had relinquished her plan, and waited hopefully for further developments.

The neatness and quiet elegance of the Beech Knoll grounds struck her afresh, as the buggy turned in at the gate. It *was* strange that the mistress of it all cared to leave it. Phyllis was ushered into the little apartment which was Mrs. Redmond's favorite sitting-room, and in a few minutes a footfall sounded at the door. She turned and saw, not her hostess, but Miss Jones, the village seamstress, and the very individual who had taken such a vital interest in Beech Knoll in the days previous to the appearance of its owner.

" Well, Phyllis Flower," she said, holding up both hands, her wiry little curls trembling from her emphatic speech, " if you have n't fallen on your *feet*, goin' off with Mrs. Redmond, and she so pleased with you, and — Oh, here she is."

Mrs. Redmond appeared, smiling a good-morning; over her arm was a mass of white lace and ribbons. " We start to-morrow morning, Phyllis ? " she said interrogatively.

" Yes," assented the girl joyfully.

" We are going to a little resort I know of, not too fashionable. I went there sometimes when I was a school-girl. You will want one evening dress. Here it is."

" O Mrs. Redmond, I can't take your dress! " exclaimed Phyllis, her forehead crimsoning.

" I told you how it would be, Miss Jones," remarked Elise, with a smile and a shrug.

"Phyllis Flower, don't you go to flyin' in the face o' Providence," ejaculated the spinster, upon whose susceptibilities Mrs. Redmond had played with her usual skill. "Here's a new dress, Miss Redmond hain't never had on her back, and she don't want it, and there ain't time to make you a new one, not if you had all the mines o' Golcondy to pay for it with. Do you just take off your frock, and say thank you, too."

Mrs. Redmond met her friend's troubled eyes with a little reassuring nod and smile. "It is all right, Phyllis, you are my guest."

"Yes, but " — Phyllis was hesitating, when Miss Jones pounced upon her and began unfastening her dress, just as she had done in exasperating moments of the girl's fractious childhood, when it was a work of much coaxing to prevail upon her to be fitted.

One thing was certain: Miss Jones would not start any unpleasant gossip concerning a transaction which she herself forwarded so vigorously. Elise, the far-sighted, had counted on that.

Of course, Phyllis yielded. The filmy lace and the sheen of silk dazzled her imagination. Mrs. Redmond's kind tact soothed her scruples, and, more wonderful still, this self-same tact governed Miss Jones, who submitted, lamb-like, to follow Mrs. Redmond's instructions in making the necessary changes in the gown, and by evening it was reposing safely in Phyllis's little trunk, where the best of the young girl's earthly possessions were packed, ready for the start.

Perhaps in all Mrs. Redmond's varied wanderings, she had never been more entertained than during this short journey with Phyllis. At first the young girl's silence and gravity disappointed her; but she soon found that this manner only indicated an extreme enjoyment of a total novelty. She declined all offers of light literature with scarce concealed impatience. She could read at home. Now the panorama displayed through the broad windows enchanted her.

Arrived in Boston, Mrs. Redmond gave her guest a lunch, the daintiness of which even Phyllis's uncultivated palate dimly appreciated. She found herself looking around at the various tables in search of Mr. Bellows; fearing, of course, not hoping, that he might stray in here this August day. Again she realized what a relief it was to find that Mrs. Redmond was not intending to marry so unsuitable a man. Beautiful Mrs. Redmond, with her quiet air of experience and command! Phyllis looked at her, and fell more than ever under the spell of her charm, which communicated itself to every article she touched, used, or wore.

At last the girl looked up from the discussion of some delicious form of frozen cream. " Now please tell me, where are we going?" she said.

" Do you really wish to know?"

" Yes, only the name of the place."

" We are going to Deep Lake."

" How cool it sounds!" observed Phyllis with satisfaction.

" And it is cool, and very pretty. It will be rather late when we arrive, but I know exactly what we shall see from our windows to-morrow morning. I could not get the rooms I wanted. My freak came too suddenly."

" Oh, they know you are coming, then?" replied Phyllis.

" Yes, indeed. It would not do to risk having no place to lay our heads."

" How thoughtful you are! " said Phyllis simply.

Mrs. Redmond smiled. " What did people do before telegraphing was discovered, I wonder? They certainly could not carry out their caprices as comfortably as we are doing."

" We *are* very comfortable," replied Phyllis earnestly, lifting to her lips a frozen cherry, and wishing Roxana could taste it.

It was too dark when the train stopped that evening at the lonely station for Phyllis to gain any idea of the landscape. As they stepped from the car, she saw only the little square wooden building which did duty for a dépôt. Beyond and about it, all seemed to be woods and rolling fields. A long open stage was backed against the platform, and into this they climbed, and the horses started.

" Deep Lake again," said Elise. " I wonder if it has changed as much as I have in all these years."

" Up, up, up," observed Phyllis, referring to their road, when, after a long pull, the horses stopped to rest. "I should think the lake might be deep."

"Oh, smell the grass!" exclaimed Mrs. Redmond. "They must have been mowing this field. The aftermath is the sweetest of harvests."

Phyllis breathed the night air with tranquil satisfaction. "Very nice, but it only smells like Snowdon."

"Only!" repeated Mrs. Redmond. "Wait till you have roamed about as much as I have. Then you will know that this world offers nothing so restful as just this sort of soft summer night, with all its chirping insect sounds, and the pure, life-giving fragrance of new-mown hay permeating the air. How it mingles with the scent of firs! Yes, this is a little better even than Snowdon, Phyllis," and Mrs. Redmond took deep breaths of delight as the horses moved on.

They went, after a time, at a good pace along a level road, for they had a light load with only the two ladies for passengers. At last the gleam of a white painted fence showed through the dusk.

"Here we are," remarked Elise.

The horses knew it, too. Nearly home after the last trip of the day, they turned in at the opening in the white fence, and sped up an avenue lined with tall trees; and soon lights began to glimmer and music to sound on the sweet air. It seemed all a dream to Phyllis: the arrival, the pleasure of the landlady at discovering in Mrs. Redmond the Miss Beckwith of bygone summers, the moving through a laughing, talking bevy of people on the piazzas, the ascent to the bedrooms. Her eyes looked very bright in her flushed face when she stood alone with Mrs. Redmond in the latter's apartment.

"Well, here we are," remarked Elise.

"Just listen to that music," was Phyllis's reply.

"Pretty, isn't it?" assented Mrs. Redmond. "You will have the benefit of it even more in your room," and she threw open the door of the adjoining apartment.

Phyllis hurried to the open window and listened. The little orchestra was performing selections from a popular light opera, and through the windows of the assembly room across a narrow driveway, she could dimly perceive the dancers who were moving through a quadrille to its strains. It was all wonderful and strange to Phyllis. After the long drive under the starlight through the stillness of the fields and the dense woods, this sudden discovery of the crowd of gay folk amidst the light and the music seemed to her like enchantment.

Mrs. Redmond came to the door. She felt tired after the heat of the day and the long ride, albeit infinitely relieved and safe, and was about to condole with her guest upon the disturbance outside which might, for a time, hinder them from sleeping; but one glance at Phyllis's starry face and listening attitude silenced her. She turned back into her room with a smile. Condolences were evidently not in order.

Phyllis had no idea at what hour the exhilarating music ceased, nor when at last she fell asleep, so subtly were her dreams joined to the pleasant, novel, waking sensations which preceded them.

She had a vague expectation, upon opening her eyes the following morning, that the same music, the same stir and bustle of a gay crowd, would be filling the air. She was astonished to see the sunshine, turned in her bed with a start, and listened. What perfect stillness ! a stillness noticeable even to Snowdon ears. A couple of months earlier, how the robins and thrushes and catbirds sing at Deep Lake at this hour of early morning ; but now only an occasional note sounds here and there.

Phyllis sprang out of bed and hurried to the window. Before her lay a long, gently declining hillside, covered with soft grass and fine old trees, and at the foot, Deep Lake itself sparkled quietly in the morning sunshine. The lovely sheet of water lay, as it were, in an irregular green bowl, the edges of which were high, tree-covered hills. The girl stifled the exclamation of pleasure which rose to her lips out of regard for her friend, whose door stood ajar.

" But why is not every one out looking at this view ?" she queried mentally, her eyes feasting on the undulating line of distant forests and the varying greens which a rainy season had preserved in almost June-like freshness.

Her room looked south and west, and from both sides she could distinguish the roofs of cottages among the trees. "It is quite a village, after all," she thought innocently, having yet to learn the ways of summer resorts, and that these little abodes were adjuncts of the hotel.

Presently a rheumatic old bell, out of sight on some adjacent building, commenced to ring laboriously, a prefatory creak of its ancient joints preceding each clang of its tongue.

"The rising bell," thought Phyllis with satisfaction. "Now I shall soon see all the people again." She dressed herself, wondering somewhat that the appointments of her room were as little luxurious as those of her own apartment at home, and questioning how Mrs. Redmond could endure such privations. It was another of the many things Phyllis had to learn, that in summer time persons of wealth run, like a stampeding flock of sheep, away from their accustomed comforts, and spend their money on annoying inconveniences for a stated length of time, which, if it be for the purpose of augmenting an appreciation of home, certainly serves its end.

She was quite disappointed that, even when her toilet was completed, there was no sound of stirring in her neighbor's room. There began to be a banging of doors about the hotel, and an occasional loud voice on the verandas. She unpacked her trunk, touching with a new reverence and exultation the white dress. Perhaps some evening she, clothed in its beauty, would be one of the figures in that enchanted scene which last night she had dimly perceived.

Her trunk was empty before she heard her name sleepily pronounced in the adjoining room. She hurried to the door.

"What are you doing in there?" asked Mrs. Redmond.

"I have just finished unpacking."

"It is a shame we could not get into a cottage. This house always was the noisiest place in the world. I am too cross to say good-morning."

"Did I disturb you?" asked Phyllis, dismayed.

"You? No, indeed. You must have been very quiet; but why did you get up with the lark?"

"Why, it is late," said Phyllis earnestly. "The rising bell rang ever and ever so long ago."

Mrs. Redmond smiled and drew her watch from under her pillow. "The rising bell for the laboring class, perhaps. Yes," opening the watch, "just as I thought, it is seven o'clock. It will be two long hours before half a dozen people will appear in the dining-room."

"Two hours!" echoed Phyllis, aghast. "Why, at home I should be wiping the dishes for Roxana by this time."

Mrs. Redmond laughed at her sincere dicomfiture. ".We shall change all that. There are none of the down-hill paths quite so broad and easy as that by which one glides into the habit of a late breakfast; but I will take pity on you this time, and let you get a cup of coffee before you faint quite away."

" Roxana does n't let me drink coffee," said Phyllis simply.

Mrs. Redmond laughed again. " Oh, you *are* such a quaint little thing ! " she observed.

" How can they be willing to miss these glorious mornings ? " asked Phyllis, still wrestling with her problem.

" They must miss something," returned Elise, " and you seemed to think last night that the evening was too good to miss. Be thankful they all agree to be still at the same time so one can get a little sleep."

" I put on my tennis dress," said Phyllis interrogatively.

" Yes, that was right. I am quite proud of you in it. Run out on the piazza, and I will join you as soon as I can."

Phyllis found much during that first day to excite her wonder. How could the pretty ladies, who clustered in knots on the shady side of the piazzas after breakfast, enjoy life in the stiff, tight dresses they wore ? She looked commiseratingly on a few whom she took to be lame, and afterward found that their hobbling gait proceeded only from the small size and height of heel of their dainty shoes. Here, amid such lavish beauty of nature, they seemed to have eyes for nothing but one another's clothes ; while as for exchanging a chair against the wooden side of the hotel for a seat on the grass under the spreading oaks, with the water rippling before them and the commingled scent of clover and pines perfuming the air, the idea never even occurred to them.

Many among the various groups gave her more than a passing glance. An extremely pretty girl who had never before appeared at Deep Lake was sure to attract attention. Mrs. Redmond found a couple of her schoolmates among the cottagers, who were very cordial to her and her young companion, and took pains to introduce them whenever opportunity offered.

Phyllis was glad to escape as soon as possible from the hotel and explore the shore of the lake. Mrs. Redmond had done more wisely than she knew when she invited the girl's companionship. It was a charming diversion to see Phyllis enjoy everything so thoroughly, and without her Elise, with her zest for outdoor occupation, would have been somewhat at a loss here for a congenial spirit.

They rowed on the lake, rode horseback, and played tennis with the young girls. Men were, of course, almost entirely lacking. Deep Lake was, however, sufficiently near a city to draw a supply of the valued sex at evening. There were a number of young men whose summer vacation consisted in these short runs into the pure air of the pretty resort.

Mrs. Redmond and Phyllis had been at the hotel a sufficient number of days for the latter to feel quite familiar with its pleasures and as blind as ever to its possible drawbacks, when one evening there appeared among the dusty pilgrims on the stage the optimistic countenance of Mr. Tony Bellows.

The arrival of this six o'clock stage was always the interesting episode of the day, especially on Saturday, when the influx of husbands, lovers, and friends was greatest.

Elise, on this particular Saturday, was sitting among her acquaintances on the piazza, and glancing up with languid interest as the tramp of horses approached, immediately met the eager gaze of Tony, who had singled her out at once from the bright-hued group, and was watching for her recognition. Almost before she realized that it was indeed he, he sprang from the stage and hurrried toward her.

" Did n't expect me, did you ? " he said, shaking her hand with a painful grip and grinning cheerfully.

" I should not be sure it was you now but for your trademark," replied Elise, glancing at the florist's box which Tony was embracing in one arm.

" Fresh as daisies, I assure you," said the young fellow gayly. " They are packed with the greatest care. You will wear them to the hop to-night, won't you ? "

" Yes, indeed. I thought you were in Newport by this time."

" I expected to be ; but Mrs. Ingraham is ill.

They had to retract their invitations. As soon as I knew of it, I wired you to find out if you were well enough to bear the infliction of another call. Miss Rebecca answered that you were at Deep Lake. So you see," Tony tapped his broad chest vivaciously, "I am at Deep Lake too." He smiled with such genial assurance that Elise would have been obliged in any case to smile in response; but she could no more help being glad to see him than she could fail to like sunshiny weather.

He handed her the box.

"I shall have to divide with Phyllis, of course."

"What!" Tony looked all about expectantly. "Is she here?"

"Why, yes. Did n't you know it? She is enjoying herself hugely. For her, Deep Lake is an ultra-fashionable and wholly ideal spot."

"Then I 'm sorry I came." It was astonishing how the vanishing of Mr. Bellows' white teeth and the down-curving of his straw-colored mustache could becloud his visage.

"Ah, you do not like my little Phyllis?"

"Your little Phyllis does n't like me, — so that bear Chester took the trouble to inform me when we rode into Boston together the other morning. I think his breakfast had not agreed with him. He was as surly as a beast in a menagerie."

"Don't call him names, Tony," said Elise, coming near, her face flushed. "He could not help being very angry. I think it is better you should know. He found out that last afternoon who I am."

"Who you are," repeated Tony, for the time entirely forgetting his friend's momentous secret.

"Yes, — that I am his adopted sister. You know I told you he had quarreled with my father, and was bitter against us."

"And do you mean to say he blew out at you?" exclaimed Tony, incensed. "Wait till I see him. I'll " —

"Oh, no, nothing of the sort," interrupted Elise impatiently. "He behaved in the only way I could have expected. He was very polite."

"He must have been. Do you think I don't remember the way I found you that afternoon — white as a ghost? He is too rough a diamond. He needs a little polishing such as I can give him."

"Tony Bellows, do you wish to make me sorry that I confided in you? Don't you say a word to him. If I cannot tell you things that I tell no one else, and do so in safety, why let me find it out at once."

Tony shook his head and smiled admiringly. "You always get your way, and your scolding is flattery, and your flattery is scolding, and I don't see how you do it. Hang me if I do."

Elise bit her lip. "Well I intend to have my way in this case, I assure you. Now we must find Phyllis. It is all nonsense about her not liking you. At least, if she doesn't, it is your own fault. From what she tells me, I judge you have taken a blundering course so far to win her favor. It seems you have been praising another woman to her. Goose!"

Elise smiled, and Tony blushed furiously.

"I — well " — he stammered.

"Yes, I know all about it. You are accustomed not to try very hard to win a girl's favor ; but this is a different girl from those of your world. All the life she has seen is that of books. She reads George Eliot, and obeys Roxana, and never saw a stylish gown until mine dawned upon her vision. Now do not be too nice to her. She won't understand you if you flirt with her, and I won't have it."

"Oh, look here," ejaculated Mr. Bellows, much injured ; "you would be doing better to lecture the other party. She is as full of nettles as a burr. I can't come near her without getting pricked."

Elise laughed. "I am delighted to hear it. Don't venture too near, then. I think I know you pretty well, Tony," she said, becoming serious and speaking earnestly. "You are no conceited jackanapes to think every girl in love with you, but it will be like you, if you are amused here, to see a good deal of Phyllis, and please remember one thing, — some sorts of burrs have sweet hearts within. If you imagine she does not like you, it will be the mannish way for you to try to find hers ; but it will not be the manly way. I have my eye on you, Tony."

She had, indeed, both eyes, and Tony blushed and looked foolish, and tried to meet her look and could n't. Certain remembrances of the way the thought of Phyllis and her unflattering dislike had haunted him, and certain vague plans he had formed for conquering her, rose up now with a subtle power that made his ears tingle.

Mrs. Redmond took pity on him.

" To show my real confidence in you, I will let you go down now to the Spring House and get her. Tell her we are going in to tea immediately. Don't stop to philander."

Tony looked over his clothes, and mumbling something about being brushed first, entered the house.

Elise stared straight ahead of her, a look in her eyes that filled them only when she was alone.

" There is one pain," she murmured, " that is ceaseless, merciless, when it once attacks. If so weak a mortal as I can defend Phyllis from its pangs, I will do so."

CHAPTER XXIX.

SUNSET.

THE illness that had seized upon Mrs. Terriss proved to be a dangerous complication of difficulties, which speedily reduced her to a condition more critical than that of her husband. The doctors who consulted concerning her case were perplexed by her apparently apathetic mental state. The only thing for which she showed any desire was Rebecca's presence. This seemed so unnatural to Roxana, that the latter watched uneasily until she proved to herself that the sick woman showed a uniform and touching gentleness and gratitude to Miss Redmond.

The professional nurse arrived from Boston, and proved to be a kind and adaptable person, willing to assist in either sick-room ; so the three women divided the work among them. Mr. Terriss continued irrational for many days, his mind reverting persistently to his youth ; and Roxana, while this state lasted, was indefatigable in mounting guard in his room in Rebecca's absence, and managed that the strange nurse should wait upon him only in his quiet intervals.

One day Rebecca entered Mrs. Terriss' room, after hearing the discouraging verdict of the physicians upon the latter's condition. The invalid called her feebly. " They say there is no hope for me, don't they ? " she asked, as Miss Redmond came close to her.

" No, indeed," returned Rebecca quietly. " They hope, and we all hope."

" Yes, I know," replied the sick woman. " While there is life there is hope ; but they believe I am going to die, I saw that they did, and they are right. Rebecca," she stirred her hand and Rebecca took it, meeting the heavy, wistful eyes. " Philip will know how I loved him, when I follow him even there. He will know that I could not live without him."

" Live for him," said Rebecca, gently stroking the hand she held. " He does not grow worse. Perhaps he will prove stronger than the fever. You are too despairing about him. He may get well. Can't you determine to recover for his sake ? Can't you look forward to brighter times ? "

Mrs. Terriss kept her eyes fixed with the same expression on Rebecca's face. " It is too late," she said, in her faint, colorless voice. " I have no strength." Then she was quiet again.

Rebecca made a movement to rise. The other pressed her hand slightly. " Stay with me," she said.

For some time, silence reigned ; then the sick woman spoke again.

" You believe Philip will get well ? "

" I think he may ; but you should not talk any more now."

The wife did not appear to hear the admonition. "Philip has had a hard time," she continued. "I see it now, although he has hidden it as long as he could — as long as he could. If he lives, you and Mrs. Sherritt will look after him and take care of him?"

She waited, and looked so wistfully at Rebecca that the latter bowed again.

"You are unselfish and good," said the sick woman slowly. "Remember, when I am gone, that I learned to know it, and to appreciate you."

She said no more that morning, and in fact never again was able to speak a loud word. Rebecca seldom left her, and Mrs. Terriss' eyes followed her about the room, as though her presence were a tangible comfort.

All the world outside the parsonage soon seemed very remote to Miss Redmond. Tony's telegram to Elise was brought to her, and she dispatched a reply without consideration as to whether Mrs. Redmond would wish the young man to follow her. This question did occur to her afterward, but weightier matters prevented it from disturbing her; and it would certainly have been a waste of time to worry over it, for Tony at Deep Lake proved to be the right man in the right place.

On the evening of his arrival, he went down the hill to the Spring House, according to Elise's request, in search of Phyllis. The latter was not in the little pavilion, however, but standing on the shore of the lake, whose bosom was darkening.

The sky was opal with sunset tints; a robin's note fluted across the water. The scene and the hour were so beautiful that Phyllis was regretting that duty to her hostess demanded of her that she should reascend the hill, when she became conscious of some one's approach in the stillness.

She wondered which of her fellow-boarders had done so unconventional a thing as to come here at this time, but she did not turn her head; so Tony came and stood quietly beside her, rather puzzled, in his offended pride, as to what tone to adopt toward her, and deciding to take his cue from her manner.

She looked up, and beheld the unsuitable Mr. Bellows. There was evidently something too broad and ennobling in the natural beauty surrounding them to admit of the indulgence of petty human prejudices, for she was certainly wholly and astonishingly glad to see him.

" Well! " she exclaimed, biting her lip and then smiling and holding out her hand. " How do you do ? "

Tony shook her hand. " Very well, I thank you. Mrs. Redmond sent me to ask you to come to supper."

If the unsuitable one had swept up a bucket of cold water from the lake and poured it unexpectedly upon her, it could hardly have surprised and dampened her more than this harmless speech.

She looked back at the evening sky. " Yes, I am coming in a minute," she replied shortly.

" I had no idea *you* were at Deep Lake when I came up," continued Tony stiffly. " I thought Mrs. Redmond was alone."

This was too much. Phyllis flashed a hurt, angry glance at him, which was lost, since he was inspecting the lake diligently.

" Else I should have brought you some flowers," continued Tony solemnly. " Mrs. Redmond says she will divide with you."

" Oh ! " said Phyllis.

" I suppose, of course, you are going to the hop ? " continued Tony, when the silence had become awkward.

" Yes, indeed," replied Phyllis vivaciously, with a thrilling recollection of the white dress, " only I can't hop."

" Oh, don't you dance ? " asked Tony, with evident disappointment. What a pity it was that he could not impress her with his ability in that line.

" No, I do not dance. A Boston girl came to Snowdon once, when I was a child, and she taught me to waltz; but I should not remember, of course."

" It is too bad. I hoped we should dance together."

The smiles had returned to Phyllis's lips. She began to remember that she had not treated Tony very well the last time they met, and to understand his present conduct.

This evening had been one long anticipated by Phyllis. It was to be the gala occasion on which

Elise had said she must wear the lace dress for the first time.

At supper, Tony sat at their table, and somehow Phyllis felt that life at Deep Lake, though novel and pleasant before, had but now for the first time become full. The music, which had been engaged for the evening, discoursed gayly all through meal-time. Tony's stiffness had vanished, and Mrs. Redmond almost forgot, for the moment, her chronic restlessness, questioning, and longing, in the amusement she derived from Phyllis's pleasure.

The table at Deep Lake was not one of its perfections; but Tony managed that night, by dint of experience and the necessary bribery, to evoke a festive little supper from the mysterious recesses beyond the dining-room; and when, to the strains of a rollicking operatic bit, he clinked his champagne glass against Phyllis's, Mrs. Redmond looked into the girl's starry eyes and experienced a little pang of conscience.

"Champagne, indeed!" she thought. "This is all champagne to Phyllis. I hope she will retain a taste for Snowdon and spring water."

But Phyllis only thought, "What if Roxana could look in here now!"

Supper over, they stood awhile on the piazzas talking, and strolled about under the trees; but Phyllis had an objective point in view. It was the white dress. She was glad when the moment came for Mrs. Redmond to take her upstairs to their rooms, there to prepare for the grand occa-

sion. Through her anticipation of the dancing,
and the lights, and the music, a new delight had
loomed larger than them all; and this was that
Tony Bellows would see her in that beautiful gown.
She hummed one of the gay tunes the musicians
had played, while she made her toilet by the aid
of a kerosene lamp. Phyllis had never dressed by
any artificial light more brilliant, so she felt no
lack. She was not a slave to frizzes, so much
heart-rending anxiety was spared her. The making of that toilet was an undivided pleasure, and
the gazing at herself in the mirror when it was
finished was another.

The soft, graceful folds of the gown, and its
dainty puffs of sleeves, from which her slender
arms showed bare and round, took her attention
far more than the study of her familiar face; but
to-night her eyes were so bright, her lips so scarlet,
and her smile so happy, it did not seem quite the
everyday Phyllis that smiled back at her.

"I am pretty — I am, I am!" she thought ex-
ultantly, yet it was of Tony and not of herself she
was thinking.

At last Mrs. Redmond opened the door. "Ready,
Phyllis? Let me look at you."

The girl went forward very conscious and happy,
but as she crossed the threshold, she forgot herself
wholly by reason of the vision that greeted her.

It was a marvelous dress that Elise wore, a pale,
iridescent gown, which, I suppose, should be respectfully termed a "creation." At all events, it

suited the woman who wore it, and it clothed her, instead of, as in so many cases, her being subservient to it. A string of pearls surrounded Mrs. Redmond's throat, and she wore no other jewelry. It was a tribute to the ascendency of her own loveliness over that of millinery'that Phyllis, the little country girl to whom evening dresses hitherto had been unknown, looked straight into her friend's face.

" How beautiful you are ! " she ejaculated.

" Fine feathers make fine birds," replied Elise, smiling. " If we were to have a competition in complimenting I' could say some very nice things too," and she approached and looked Phyllis over, well-pleased. " You are very real and unspoiled," she added, gazing kindly into the girl's eyes. " I hope you will remain so."

" You have remained so," returned Phyllis simply.

" No." Elise shook her head slowly. " I am spoiled and imperious. I expect always to be obeyed, always to have my own way."

" But it is such a pleasant way. People are glad to give it to you."

" No, I do not always get it. I am suffering now because I cannot get it." She turned her face aside with a pretty gesture of despair. " I am wretched, wretched! " Her white chest rose and fell quickly, and her companion looked at her in distressed surprise. The exclamation was evidently genuine.

"Oh, tell me why, Mrs. Redmond. Tell me what you mean," she replied anxiously. "Let me help you. Perhaps I can. Try me."

Mrs. Redmond bit her lip and threw her head up as though she would toss aside her thoughts. "You do help me," she answered. "Perhaps you will never know how much you have been to me here. Do not let what I said disturb you. You do me the greatest possible kindness when you enjoy yourself thoroughly. Now let me see if you are quite ready. You have no fan." She turned to her trunk, which was indeed a veritable wonder-box, and produced a fan of soft, deep, white feathers. "Keep it," she said, placing it in the girl's hand; "it belongs with your dress."

Phyllis laid her cheek caressingly against the soft mass. "You keep me constantly thanking you," she said. "Now I am ready indeed."

"Then we will go down. Tony will be waiting for us. You had better take this white scarf for sitting on the piazzas." Mrs. Redmond threw an embroidered wrap about her own shoulders, then the two descended to the parlor.

Mr. Bellows, walking on the veranda enjoying a cigarette, saw them through a window. He stopped, and his eyes lighted with pleasure as they fell on Phyllis.

"I said so," he thought triumphantly. "Hold her own! She's the prettiest girl I know." He threw away his cigarette, and entered the house.

The consciousness Phyllis had expected to feel

under his gaze failed to trouble her. She was far too occupied in admiring him. Snowdon swains never wore full-dress, and Tony in his dress-suit was quite the most immaculate object her eyes had ever rested upon.

Yes, Mr. Bellows was quite an important person, she decided in her own mind. Tony would have been charmed to know how her respect for him was growing. It continued to grow during the evening to an uncomfortable extent. She had the opportunity to see the favoritism displayed for him by all the young women at Deep Lake. A week ago she had yearned to be one of the number in that enticing ball-room. Well, to-night she had the privilege. Was it a privilege, since Tony was evidently the best dancer in the room and she could not be his partner?

She watched furtively the pretty girls with whom he danced, and saw that they were pleased with his attentions, and responded to him with a manner far different from her own. Mrs. Redmond was his first partner, and Phyllis watched in delight and envy the way in which they floated about the room together, light as down, yet with pliant, smooth movements in which there was no hint of a jerk or a jump.

" Was n't that delightful ? " she asked eagerly when Elise returned to the seat beside her, Tony fanning her assiduously.

" Yes. Tony is simply perfect when it comes to a matter of dancing," replied Elise.

Mr. Bellows bowed his blonde head with exaggerated gratitude.

"Why have you not been teaching Miss Flower to dance all this time?" he asked reproachfully.

"Why, indeed! Phyllis, why did n't you ask me?"

"I did n't know I should wish so *much* to dance," was the girl's reply, given with so much naiveté that her companions both smiled.

"How many will you let me have, Mrs. Redmond?" asked Tony.

"I shall hardly dance again, I think. At any rate, there are too many pretty girls here for me to monopolize you. Take me across to Mrs. Sharpe a minute, please. I promised to speak to her to-night about something. I will be back soon, Phyllis. You have Mrs. Dayton on the other side of you. Mrs. Dayton, I am going to leave Miss Flower with you a minute."

Mrs. Dayton, an extremely stout lady, smiled expansively, and declared her pleasure in dear Miss Flower's society.

Tony escorted Mrs. Redmond to her destination, and then returned to Phyllis's side. The music began again.

"Who are you going to dance with this time?" she asked.

"You."

"But you know I can't," she said mournfully.

"Well, I mean I am going to sit here with you."

" Oh, how kind of you."

Tony took up her fan and waved it gently.

They watched the couples pass and repass for several minutes, Tony amusing his companion by his comments on the various pairs, and Phyllis entertaining him with bits of descriptions of her sister women as she had found them in every-day life at Deep Lake.

" Mr. Bellows," she said at last, seriously, " what is flirting ? What is it people do when they do it ? "

Tony smiled. " I should be delighted to show you, but Mrs. Redmond won't permit it."

" It is bad, then, is n't it ? "

Mr. Bellows looked rather puzzled for a minute. " Well, there are all shades, you know."

Phyllis shook her head doubtfully. " A good thing is good, all shades of it, and a bad thing is bad, all shades of it," she replied.

" You would be troubled to carry that out, I think. How about the champagne we had to-night ? "

" That is so, is n't it ? " exclaimed Phyllis, comprehending. " Yes, all champagne must be bad, then," she said firmly ; " but it is the nicest bad thing I can think of," she added, with a little smile.

" The same way with flirting," responded Tony dryly.

" Oh, I have n't thanked you for my flowers," said Phyllis, suddenly bethinking herself, and

touching the roses on her breast. " Mrs. Redmond
gave me all these."

" I should think you might spare one."

" What for ? "

" To decorate me, of course."

" Would you like one in your button - hole ?
Why certainly," and Phyllis, in view of any one
who chose to look, took a half-opened bud from
her corsage and placed it in Tony's coat, delighted
with the firm little elastic band she found, which
did away with the necessity for the ever-lacking
pin. A good many did choose to look. It was
not a matter of indifference to the Boston girls
present who put roses in Tony's button - hole.
Elise saw too. When that dance had closed, and
another begun, and still Mr. Bellows remained by
Phyllis's side, she thought it time to interfere.

Taking the arm of the man who happened to
be talking to her at the moment, she crossed the
room again and sat down on Mr. Bellows' other
side.

The latter turned to her. " Why do you not
dance ? " she asked.

" I am having a better time this way," was the
cheerful response.

" Well, you must n't do so any more. The
dancing girls here to - night consider you their
rightful prey. I do not care to have Phyllis quite
annihilated by glances. Go away at once, and do
not return until you have danced at least half a
dozen times."

" Really ? "

" Yes, really.   You know what I said to you
when you first came."

" Well, I have n't," replied Tony rather inco-
herently.

" How did that rose come in your button-hole ? "

" Well, if I must, I must, I suppose," and the
young man rose precipitately.   " *Au revoir*, Miss
Flower ; Mrs. Redmond thinks every man should
do his duty on an occasion like this."   He lowered
his voice and bent his head.   " If you watch the
young lady I am going to ask for the next dance,
you will receive a lesson in the art we were talking
of awhile ago."

" Can one do it alone ? " asked Phyllis.

" We-ell hardly."

"Then you are going to, too ? "

" I can't tell.   I may be driven into keeping up
my end."   He smiled and bowed and went away,
and it was after this that the little twinges of
jealousy and envy referred to before afflicted
Miss Flower, a wallflower indeed, and as discontented as she was pretty.

It was a new and disconcerting discovery that
she grudged Tony to these other girls; that she
did not care for the pretty dresses or the music,
because he was bending his head above another
woman's and smiling at her words.

Phyllis was frightened and resentful, but she
could not escape the truth.   Another and another
dance passed, and he did not return.   She had

heard nothing of Elise's low-spoken conversation with him, and although she told herself that she was unreasonable to expect him to sit and talk at a dancing party, she suffered from his absence just the same, and her lovely dress and the antici- pated evening were both together vanity. She had too much spirit to show this, however, and affected to be absorbed in watching the gay whirl, turning occasionally to speak to Mrs. Redmond with a bright smile, that accorded well with her heightened color; and Mrs. Redmond, being kept busy responding to the spontaneous homage paid her as the most beautiful woman in the room, would have been deceived by less good acting on the part of her charge.

Tony's six dances over, he deposited his last partner and returned to his allegiance, had Phyl- lis known how gladly, her wounds would have been healed.

"It is so warm," he said. "I wonder, Miss Flower, if it would be too cool for you on the piazza."

"Oh, I think not," replied Phyllis, with a very good assumption of indifference. "Would you like to go, Mrs. Redmond?"

"Thank you, no. You and Tony go, but do not stay long."

Tony placed the lace scarf about the girl's shoulders, and giving her his arm, they went out upon the piazza, where there was the same buzz of talk and laughter, the same passing and re-passing of couples, that Phyllis had discovered on the evening, so long ago it seemed, of her arrival. Now her dream was fulfilled. She was one of the figures in the scene, and her mood had changed. She was as happy as the happiest.

Her escort led her slowly to the further end of the piazza, where there was an inviting corner, retired, yet overlooking the water which shimmered in the moonlight. Tony knew all the resources of Deep Lake.

Long shadows lay across the hill. The night was enchantingly cool and quiet. To Phyllis, this escape from the glare and the noise and her own hot misery into such tranquillity alone with Tony was relief unspeakable.

He gave her a chair and seated himself on the piazza rail.

" Well, did you observe her ? " he asked laughingly. " Do you know now what flirting is ? "

" Yes, and I despise it. You did it too," returned Phyllis reproachfully.

Tony was pleasantly surprised at her tone. " It was only force of habit," he replied. " That girl is a great bore."

" Did you dance with six bores ? " asked Phyllis frigidly.

" Yes, I did," replied Tony heartily. "Mrs. Redmond made me. She thought my sitting there so long did n't look well."

"Oh, look well ! " repeated Phyllis scornfully. " How tired one gets of hearing that a thing does not look well! I wish people were n't so fond of criticising."

"You are safe for the present, at all events," replied Tony. "There is no one but me now to say whether or no you look well, and I tell you frankly that you do."

Phyllis smiled a little demurely. She was quite aware that she looked her very best, and at last it was worth while. "The moonlight is a great flatterer," she returned. "I have had a question on my mind to ask you for several days, Mr. Bellows," she continued. "I wish you would tell me why you thought it worth while to make me believe, — well, what you said about your feelings for Mrs. Redmond. You led me into the wildest blunders."

Mr. Bellows hoped the moonlight would pale the blush he felt mount to his forehead; but he answered firmly enough: "That was a mistake on my part. I believed all I said to you, and a great deal more."

Phyllis did not see the blush, and she felt another jealous pang.

"You have seen to-night how Mrs. Redmond attracts men and women alike," her companion went on. "You see the deference and attention that is always paid her, and the open admiration that follows her?"

Phyllis had not noticed anything of the kind, being far too preoccupied with interests of her own; but her silence seemed to give consent, and Tony continued.

" Well, she was always kind to me, having known me when we were children, and on my first visit to Snowdon the idea occurred to me that perhaps she would be willing to marry me. The idea intoxicated me, and I could think of nothing else until I went out there again, and then one day she brought me to my senses."

" Oh," said Phyllis, feeling uncomfortably warm ; " I did not mean to pry into your affairs. Excuse me for mentioning the subject."

" You had the right, since I made you my confidante before Mrs. Redmond showed me that extreme admiration and warm regard were what I felt for her, and all that I felt." Tony looked at the face of his companion, etherealized in the moonlight. " And now I thank her," he added, leaving his seat on the piazza rail and taking a chair beside Phyllis.

" You will not think any the less of me because I made that mistake, I hope ? " he asked in a tone which made the girl's happy heart leap, while intuitively she shrank deeper into her soft laces, and her pretty head bent as though the night dews weighed it down with the other flowers.

" Oh, no," she answered faintly.

Fortunately, pretty girls have no need of originality or brilliancy, especially with their lovers, and Tony was beginning to be a lover, and he was perfectly satisfied with this response.

CHAPTER XXX.

TONY OFFENDS.

WHEN considerable time had passed, and Tony and Phyllis did not return to the dancing-room, Mrs. Redmond's wrath began to kindle against the friend of her childhood.

She had put a constraint upon herself to dress and come here to-night, and to what end, if Phyllis were going to spend her evening star-gazing? Elise's state of mind regarding her own affairs since finding the too safe hiding-place of Deep Lake had fluctuated through all stages of hope and despair. Living over her summer's experience with Chester, there was much to make her confident that he belonged to her utterly. She was so accustomed to devotion: surely it was impossible that the one man her heart had ever gone out to should fail to meet her with a like depth and strength of feeling. A couple of days in this haven among the hills sufficed for the relief in her safety to evaporate, and she soon passed into a state of excited expectancy. Of course Terriss would manage to discover her whereabouts, and would follow her. When this result did not immediately come about, she began to think that he would write to her instead of coming, and watched the mails eagerly.

No letter arrived from him, and Rebecca, for a long time, was too occupied to write ; but when she did so at last, she mentioned the fact of Chester's call, and explained that she had not been able to see him.

Elise's spirits, just then depressed, rebounded at this, and she began to wonder how long she would be able to endure remaining at Deep Lake. She must consider Phyllis. She had brought the girl here to indulge a whim, and she must not cut her pleasure short selfishly. In this state of smothered feeling, she had immolated herself to-night on the altar of hospitality, and could ill brook the annoyance that Tony was causing her. She did not for a moment blame Phyllis, and she was not so occupied with her own engrossing hopes as to be thoughtless of the safety and peace of mind of her charge. She knew Tony's devotion to the pleasures of the dance, and that he should ignore the good floor and music for so protracted a stay out of doors suggested uneasy thoughts to her.

A young man was making eager attempts to entertain her at the moment when her restlessness reached its climax, and she suggested to him making a tour of the piazzas in search of the young lady she was chaperoning.

The consequence of this was that Mr. Bellows beheld, not long afterward, what he recognized as an avenging angel, despite the fact that those radiant beings are not usually represented enveloped in Paris wraps.

"We were just thinking perhaps you would wonder where we were," he remarked cheerfully.

"Do not let me detain you longer from the dancing, Mr. Lambert," said Elise to her cavalier, who bowed and accepted his dismissal, returning to the ball-room swelling with satisfaction in consequence of the number of minutes Mrs. Redmond had distinguished him by her society.

Mr. Bellows looked after the departing Lambert a little wildly, but he need not have feared for the present. Elise was too heedful of his companion to punish him now.

"It is midnight, Phyllis," she said pleasantly.

"Why, where has the evening gone?" exclaimed the girl. "Mrs. Redmond, isn't that scene like fairyland?"

"It is indeed beautiful," returned Elise kindly, looking down the shadow-strown hillside across the shimmering water. "What a solemn vastness the moonlight gives to our pretty daylight view! Do you care to go in and see any more of the dancing?"

"No, I think not, thank you. It makes me too envious."

Tony had risen upon Mrs. Redmond's appearance. Now he briskly brought forward a chair. "Won't you sit down?" he said.

"No, I thank you." The tone of the suave refusal conveyed nothing to Phyllis's unsophisticated ear, but it chilled Mr. Bellows' blood.

"I think, if you do not care any further for the

dancing, Phyllis, we had better leave this scene," continued Mrs. Redmond.

The girl gave an audible sigh. " I suppose so, but does n't it seem a pity ? " she returned.

Tony considered suggesting a claret punch, by way of lengthening the evening, but he thought of the probable slow passage of the last hour to Mrs. Redmond, and his tongue clave to the roof of his mouth.

" I suppose you will go back now, and dance with that green young lady again," said Phyllis to him as she rose from her chair.

" Shall I ? " he replied. " Do you wish me to ? "

" Oh, why should I care ? "

Whatever Mr. Bellows might have liked to reply to this, Mrs. Redmond's presence restrained him. He contented himself with pressing Phyllis's hand at the foot of the stairs which led to her apartments, and the girl ran up lightly, not afraid of any other girl, whether in green, blue, or pink.

Mrs. Redmond came more slowly behind her. She turned and gave the radiant young man one of the searching looks with which she understood the art of shriveling souls.

He clasped his hands beseechingly. " *Mea culpa*," he said, " if *mea* is n't too culpable ! "

" I am quite in earnest," she returned. " You will discover it later."

She felt that she ought to say something to Phyllis to put her on her guard, but when she reached her room, the girl rushed to her, threw her soft arms around her neck, and kissed her.

"Oh, how can I thank you for giving me all these good times!" she exclaimed.

Elise's own full, longing heart pleaded with her not to disturb this absolute content. Why put out the lights in those eyes, and introduce vague fears in place of this happy ardor? Let the child go to sleep to-night with all the glamor of her thoughts shining. To-morrow would be time enough.

"Mr. Bellows says he will teach me to dance this week," announced Phyllis, sparkling and beaming. "He says we can go into the ball-room any time we like, and then by next Saturday night I need not sit still."

"Oh, are we going to be here next Saturday night?" asked Elise.

The girl suddenly turned. "Are n't we?" she ejaculated anxiously.

"I had n't thought," replied Mrs. Redmond. "We will see."

But Phyllis was not to sleep that night quite unsaddened. She found a letter on her bureau from Roxana, and it said that Mrs. Terriss had died the morning before. She felt ashamed that her first thought, upon the reception of the news, was fear lest Mrs. Redmond should consider it necessary to return for the funeral, and that thus the visit to Deep Lake would be summarily ended; but Roxana did not suggest such a necessity, neither did it seem to occur to Elise; and Phyllis breathed freely again. Mr. Terriss was her favorite of the two, and Roxana said he was rational now at intervals, and that the doctors were hopeful about him.

On the next day, Mr. Bellows seemed determined to put off the *mauvais quart d'heure* Mrs. Redmond had promised him. He was simply exemplary in the impartiality with which he devoted himself to the two friends. The young lady in green of the night before, a Miss Plum by name, and an excellent tennis player, made the fourth in several games, and ruined them for Phyllis by the airs and graces which she lavished upon Tony ; but the carrying out of the dancing lessons consoled the girl somewhat. It was Mrs. Redmond who did the teaching however. Tony was relegated to the piano stool, where he played waltzes with inexhaustible patience and good humor.

Phyllis was an apt pupil. The little she knew already, her strong feeling for rhythm, and her power of imitation gave her, before many days, a tolerable facility in the art, in which she gloried as in the possession of an added sense. She never forgot the first dance she had with Tony, when Mrs. Redmond at last graciously declared her ready for that distinction. It was at the quietest hour in the day, when people were in their cottages, and few loungers were about the hotel. There was no one besides themselves in the ball-room. Elise played for them, and the two young people had undisturbed sway. It must have been a very poor dancer who could not enjoy a turn with Tony.

His powers of adaptation were limitless, and Phyllis, in the glow of youth and strength, found at last an ideal exercise.

"That is enough — enough!" exclaimed Mrs. Redmond, laughing and taking her hands from the piano. "Tony, your face nearly matches the stripe in your blazer. Phyllis, sit down this minute."

The girl was too breathless to speak, but her eyes replied triumphantly to Tony's compliments. Now let Saturday evening come. The minor dances of the other evenings were all very well; but the orchestra and the festal garments were needed to make her satisfaction complete.

But long before Saturday evening, Tony had offended again, and more than once, before Mrs. Redmond's watchful eyes.

One night, in their room, she approached Phyllis very kindly.

"My dear," she said, "I am your chaperon, and it is a part of every chaperon's duty to be disagreeable."

"How poorly you perform yours, then," replied the girl, looking at her affectionately.

"I'm afraid I do, rather. I have the greatest repugnance to spoiling your good time, you see; but Tony is getting too bad. I have scolded him, still he will flirt with you."

"Oh, no, he does n't," replied Phyllis earnestly. "One can't, alone, he says, and I don't know a thing about it, except what I 've seen Miss Plum do. Oh, I think she's horrible, the way she makes eyes!"

Elise smiled. "Miss Plum's natural advantages are not very great, but, you see, your eyes are all made; and when you look at a man, this is what he sees."

She took up a hand-glass with a quick movement and held it before Phyllis's excited face, so that the girl observed, perforce, the brown diamonds of which Mr. Bellows was beginning to dream.

She pushed away the glass gently and gazed earnestly at her mentor.

" What do you suppose Mr. Bellows thinks ? "

" I do not suppose Mr. Bellows thinks very often. He has been fanned along through life by favoring breezes as lightly as one of these Japanese butterflies."

Phyllis looked very serious, and the sudden vivid color died from her face.

" Do you suppose he means to flirt with me ? " she asked gravely. " Do you suppose he means to deceive me ? "

" He doesn't mean anything, my child," said Elise gently, for this pallor surprised and worried her. " That is the worst of it."

Phyllis moistened her lips. " And when we go away from here, it will be some other girl that he will talk to and look at as he does at me ? "

Mrs. Redmond felt as though she were pressing a knife into her friend, a two-bladed knife, which wounded herself as well; but she felt she must emulate the kind nerve of the surgeon. "Yes," she answered. "It will always be the prettiest girl, wherever he happens to find himself."

Phyllis gave a great, dry sob, and her face looked pinched. She saw facts in their true light for the first time. She knew that, from the moment Tony's box of flowers had fallen into the Snowdon street, she had thought of him day and night without ceasing. "Then what shall I do?" she said despairingly.

Her attitude and words broke down the control Elise was constantly imposing on her own excited feelings. She flung her arms about the girl's neck, and broke into repressed sobs. "O Phyllis, poor child, do you love him?" she exclaimed, shaken by the storm passing over her. "God knows if women ever recover from such things."

Phyllis was hardly moved by the tempest she did not comprehend, though she accepted Elise's embrace. Her wound ached, and numbed her to all beside. At last Mrs. Redmond's sudden access of emotion passed. She regained her self-control, and spoke again. "We will go home, Phyllis, to-morrow, if you like."

"No," replied the girl. "The one thing worse than what has happened would be for him to suspect it. I have talked so much about Saturday evening, I must stay and go through with it." Phyllis looked with sombre eyes into the flushed face of her companion. "If I can only be brave enough," she added. " I wonder how I shall get on. I believe I have never had anything to hide before."

Mrs. Redmond's smooth hand clasped hers. "You will get on," she replied. " It must have been foreseen from the beginning that women would need the art of dissimulation more than men, for they have it naturally. It is a very happy woman, Phyllis, who needs not at some time in her life to be an actress, and a clever one."

Phyllis proved to be sufficiently clever during the next few days for her own defense, and Elise, watching, for some time saw no need to interfere ; but as Phyllis retreated, Tony advanced. Had she been the artfulest schemer, she could not have devised a better plan than her own wariness for drawing him on. Tony could not understand how it was managed that his little arrangements were thwarted, one by one, and at last he was forced into certain ebullitions under Mrs. Redmond's very eyes, which gave her reason to utilize the first moment she found herself alone with him. Phyllis was making a gallant fight, and it thrilled her every fibre with indignation to see her so hard pushed.

There was a spreading oak halfway down the hillside, under which the three were wont to spend a portion of every day. On the much-anticipated Saturday, Elise advised Phyllis to lie down a time to be rested for the evening, while she and Tony took their books under the favorite tree. Phyllis

complied without question. She was waiting in
these days, — waiting for Monday to come, for
then they were going home.

Mrs. Redmond felt somewhat tremulous as she
went down the hill, escorted by the unconscious
Tony. Her splendid health was not entirely proof
against the inroads of suspense, hope, and doubt
of the past ten days, and her irritation, taking the
form of indignation toward Mr. Bellows, seethed
and pressed for outlet.

He arranged her comfortably in her favorite
spot, and himself lay down on the grass. "What
are you going to do," he inquired lazily, "read to
me?"

"No, I'm not," she returned shortly. "I am
going to talk to you about your utter, wicked
selfishness toward Phyllis."

Tony rolled over slowly, and looked into the
handsome, excited eyes.

"I warned you when you first came, and yet
you have gone on, doing everything you possibly
could to make that innocent girl care for you. It
is short-sighted, stupid selfishness, that I did not
think you capable of, Tony. How much satisfaction would it be to you, when you have gone off to
devote yourself to somebody else, to know that she
did care, — that you had succeeded in robbing her
of her peace of mind? Tell me that."

Tony looked somewhat surprised, but he gazed
eagerly and frankly into her challenging face.

"Why, I do believe you must think she likes

me a little, or you would not be quite so severe,"
he said slowly.

His accuser gazed at him with scorn and grief.

"This disappoints me!" she exclaimed.

"Upon my word, I've led such a life the last
week trying to find out that there's hardly anything left of me," observed Mr. Bellows art-
lessly.

"O Tony, are you really so egotistical, so shallow, so vain?" and suddenly bowing her face in
her hands Elise burst into tears.

Her companion looked at her aghast. "Mrs.
Redmond, Elise, what in the world *is* the matter
with you?" he exclaimed, utterly disconcerted by
this extraordinary display of emotion.

"I am ill," she answered, between her sobs,
"or I should not give way like this; but I'll have
you know that I am crying — with — anger at
you."

"You need n't, upon my word," said her companion soothingly. "Please stop, and listen to
me. You have n't given me a chance to say a
word in my own defense."

"Oh, actions speak so much louder than words,
Tony!" but she dried her tears more and more
successfully, and at last looked with tolerable calmness off toward the lake.

Tony began quietly, his eyes upon her averted
face.

"We both remember that I made a fool of myself at your house a few weeks ago, and I shall

always feel grateful to you for the easy way you let me down. You know that, don't you?"

" Well?"

" If — don't be angry — if you had accepted me, you know I should have been immensely proud and happy, and should always have remained so, don't you?"

Elise smiled faintly. " I won't discuss it with you, at all events."

" Well," continued the young man slowly, " I did not love you as I do Phyllis."

Mrs. Redmond raised her eyebrows and swallowed the lump that suddenly rose in her throat.

" Ah! You think you love Phyllis?"

"I won't discuss it with you, at all events."

The retort was so prompt that Elise smiled again.

" I know I cut an awkward enough figure in this affair," went on Tony, " but I am tremendously in earnest, and I cannot stop to care very much if I do."

" Indeed," said Mrs. Redmond, calm without, exultant within; " but what will papa say? His only son, the apple of his eye! Will he accept a little country girl for a daughter?"

" You are to attend to that part of it," returned Tony coolly.

Elise looked at him. " Would it be too presuming in me to inquire how?"

" I'll tell you. I've thought it all out. You would n't want to stay in Snowdon during the winter, anyway.   Take an apartment in town, invite Phyllis to be your guest.   Entertain a little, and invite my father."

Mrs. Redmond looked back at the lake with a smile.   " I have often heard you declare that there is nothing small about you, Tony.   You make me believe you."

" You know how my father has always felt about you for Lina's sake."   Tony lowered his voice at the mention of his dead sister.   " You will know exactly how to impress him favorably with Phyllis."

" Yes," Mrs. Redmond returned thoughtfully, "that is all very well.   Perhaps I might submit to your plans for old acquaintance' sake, but Phyllis is no puppet.   Do not carry your day-dream so far that you cannot wake up from it with a good grace."

" It has gone too far already," said Tony quietly. " It is a great thing to have your good wishes, Mrs. Redmond.   Will you give them to me ? "

" With all my heart," was the answer, spoken cordially at last.   " To tell the truth, I always thought you would be something of a prize as a husband, Tony."

" Yes, for some other woman," he replied, smiling.

CHAPTER XXXI.

"THE GOLDEN CLOSE OF LOVE."

SHORTLY afterward, Mrs. Redmond went back to the hotel. She knew it would be rather difficult to betray to Phyllis no sign of her discovery; especially as she longed to rekindle the light she had extinguished in the pretty face. She determined, at least, to encourage the girl to enter fully into the pleasures of this last evening, and on her way to the house concocted a variety of pleasant remarks calculated to raise her spirits.

Tony wandered off restlessly to the outskirts of the park, vaulted over the fence, and found himself on the border of a wooded ravine, into which he descended, tramping ruthlessly over ferns and moss and the various delicate growths of the silent and shaded spot. His thoughts were outrunning his quick march, and suddenly a tree trunk, rising with unusually inviting smoothness, tempted him to pause, and, after the fashion of scores of lovers before and since the time of Orlando, to trace thereon the letters of his beloved's name.

"P," he muttered aloud as he made the first incision with his knife; then added with a deliberate pause after every word, "stands for pretty, pert, provoking, precious, pet; and she is all that."

"Who are you libeling?" It was Phyllis herself who spoke. She was sitting on a moss-covered log, half hidden by some bushes. Her heart, which had nearly choked her at the sudden sight of Tony, beat so fast at his words that she spoke desperately, fearing that in a minute more speech would be impossible, and that he would discover her an eavesdropper.

Mr. Bellows looked about, and beheld the flushed, upturned face.

"You!" he exclaimed, taking an eager step forward and seating himself beside her. "What blessed magic brought you here, Phyllis?"

"My natural disobedience. Mrs. Redmond told me to lie down, so I preferred to take a walk."

"Well, I shall believe hereafter in the doctrine of attendant angels. What else could have determined me to come down here just now! We are as much alone as though we were a thousand miles from civilization."

Phyllis's face did not reflect the satisfaction which this consideration seemed to give her companion.

She rose quickly. "I must go back. Mrs. Redmond will wonder what has become of me."

Tony turned pale under his healthful tan.

"Wait one minute," he said. "I have something to tell you. Sit down once more."

"I can hear it quite as well, standing," replied Phyllis. One thing was clearly distinct among the whirling thoughts in her mind. She was not going

to furnish Mr. Bellows any more amusement.
Perhaps he had discovered her before murmuring
that audible confidence to the tree. It was quite
likely.

Certainly, Tony had not the air just now of being entertained. Phyllis wore a business-like,
spirited expression of face which was so far the
reverse of encouraging under the circumstances
that his heart felt like a lump of lead within him.
Tony was one of the "golden youth" of the day,
presumably spoiled, but he was manly enough to
feel as sincerely humble before this young girl as
though she were a princess, because he loved her
dearly, and felt in his simple way that his possessions of money and position would be worthless as
Dead Sea apples unshared by her.

As she would not be seated, he rose and faced
her.

"Answer me honestly, Phyllis," he said, "have
you been avoiding me lately?"

She hesitated. "Yes," she answered at last,
bravely.

"Why?" The direct question set the girl's
heart beating again until she seemed to hear it,
there in the green, sun-streaked silence.

"Because," she replied, looking into his grave
eyes with the courage which comes to a girl at
bay even though she is very much in love, "you
seemed too much inclined for the pastime that one
cannot play at alone. I thought I would make
way for Miss Plum, or some other experienced
girl."

Tony looked perplexed, then enlightened, then reproachful.

"Did you think I would flirt with you, Phyllis?" he asked, trying to take her hand.

She drew back from him and clasped her hands behind her, holding her head up with a proud air which could have been no more spontaneous had she been a princess indeed. "I think you will not," she answered.

Tony looked paler than ever. "I have lived over this scene in my mind hundreds of times, Phyllis. I did not think it could be so hard to speak. I do not understand how I have displeased you. At least you were very friendly to me once. I love you more than I ever dreamed I should love anybody. When you come in sight, every drop of blood in my body seems to rush on its way, and I feel twice as happy and twice as strong as I did before." He came a step nearer, and his face looked wretched. Before she could guess his intention, he clasped her to him fiercely and kissed her; then he released her as suddenly, turned his back, and leaned his head on his arm against the tree trunk scarred by his knife.

Phyllis caught her breath at the sudden attack, and a crimson flush stained her face and neck. Her breast rose and fell as she gazed with dark, full eyes, at the immovable figure.

He lifted his head after a time, and, turning, leaned against the tree, his face set, and his eyes gloomily meeting Phyllis's.

"I suppose you will never forgive me for that," he said brusquely.

Phyllis swallowed. "I am very sorry" — she began.

"I knew you would be sorry for me if it went this way. Never mind. Don't wait. Go back to the hotel. I will come presently."

The faintest of smiles played about Phyllis's lips. She half turned away. "Of course I must go if you tell me," she replied. "There is one thing you will know yourself capable of doing alone hereafter. You can propose and be rejected all by yourself."

Tony kept his eyes on hers. "I did not think you a girl to make game of a man," he said.

Phyllis gave a little shrug of her shoulders. "I think myself so lucky to get a word in edgewise at last that I scarcely know what I say. You are a great talker — Tony."

It was the first time she had ever called him by his name, and there was such a combination of sauciness and tenderness in her face that her lover walked to her as though drawn by a magnet.

"Have you anything to say? You know I am always willing to listen to you."

"Thank you," replied Phyllis, with exaggerated humility. "In acknowledgment, then, of your condescension, permit me to remark that you have not displeased me, and that I — still like you as well as I ever did."

"Ah!" sighed Tony with a deep, uncontrollable breath ; "but that never has been satisfactory."

"Then I will add that I like you very much," continued the girl demurely.

Tony's eyes began to glow. "Phyllis," he said, "I don't understand you. Is this the cat and mouse business ?"

"No," replied the girl, her eyes filling as he caught her hands, "this is solitaire. You have played your hand all through, and now I suppose I must play mine. Let me see, the proposal must come first before I can " —

Tony hung on her words, but the last one would not be spoken. After he had waited a second he clasped her in his arms again, tenderly this time, beseechingly. "Darling, darling," he cried, " was I mistaken ? "

Phyllis lifted her red rosebud of a face. "You were dreadfully mis " — but the rest of the word was lost.

Mrs. Redmond had had time to suspect all sorts of calamities to Phyllis before the girl returned. Indeed, she was just starting down the stairs, determined to institute a search which should set her fears at rest, when she came face to face with the missing one, running lightly up the staircase.

"Where have you been, you naughty girl ? " she asked, feeling something extraordinary in the air the minute she saw the glowing face.

For answer, Phyllis seized her and drew her into her room, and planted herself against the closed door.

" You were mistaken " (this time she gave the whole word successfully and with triumphant emphasis) ; " he was not flirting."

" Dear me," said Elise, sinking into a chair and regarding the starry eyes with an irrepressible smile. " Who would have thought it ! "

Phyllis shook her head. " No, he was n't. He is in earnest, and so am I, and — Oh, I am so happy ! " She ran to her friend and, falling on her knees beside her, laid her head in her lap.

" Then so am I," returned Mrs. Redmond, stroking her hair ; " very, *very* happy, and I congratulate you heartily. Do you know you are going to make a fine match, Phyllis ? "

" Of course I do," was the prompt response.

Elise smiled. She wondered how much the girl meant. " People will say I did well for you," she added.

Phyllis looked up. " How ? By not caring for him ? I do thank you so much for that," she replied simply.

Mrs. Redmond flushed. " No, you blessed child. The feeling Tony had for me was very shallow. People who marry on such sentiments make shipwreck. I referred to his prospects."

" Oh," said Phyllis indifferently.

" Have you thought that you will live in a fine house, and wear fine dresses and jewels, and have

as many horses as you like, and travel when you
please?"

The girl sat on the floor and looked up, her cap
set on the back of her curls.

"All that and Tony too!" she answered in an
awestruck tone which stirred Mrs. Redmond's risi-
bles again.

"Yes, and Tony's papa beside, a solid and
pompous individual."

"Yes," replied Phyllis soberly.   "Perhaps he
won't like me at first, but Tony says you will attend to him."

"Oh, I will attend to him," returned Mrs. Redmond, loth to disturb such placid faith.   "So you
have not taken your worldly good fortune into
consideration.   Happy Tony!"

"Yes, I have," replied the other, with a bright
nod.   "He is not going to dance with Miss Plum
once to-night, and he will not dance with any one
but you and me, and I'm not to dance with
anybody but him.   He will arrange it so that I
need n't."

"So we are going to the dance just the same?"
asked Elise, to whose mind the possibility had
arrived that she might now be spared that bore.

"Oh, we are going to the dance a great deal
more!" returned Phyllis gayly.

Mrs. Redmond concealed her disappointment
generously.   After all, in two days she would be
at home again.

"To-night is a great occasion," she answered.

"I shall wear my favorite white gown, and be as superb as possible in honor of you and Tony."

Very superb she was indeed, and more of a belle than ever in the ball-room that evening. She pressed Tony's hand and, looking into his radiant face, wished that he might give and receive all happiness in the life he was beginning.

She concluded to dance to-night since, by so doing, she would leave the newly betrothed couple free of care of her; but for all her determination, the hours seemed leaden. While she endeavored to fulfill the duties of her position, her thoughts were haunted by Chester's image, and the humiliating situation in which his neglect had placed her. Now that her responsibility toward Phyllis was greatly lessened, selfish considerations poured into her mind in an unobstructed flood. She recalled what seemed to her now the state of besotted enthusiasm in which she had sent that hateful letter. How thankful she was that she had not remained to bear its consequences! Chester had responded so far as to come to Snowdon; but in a perfunctory manner which she could picture to herself, else of course he would have made further search for her. Doubtless, she thought with crimsoning cheeks, he had been relieved not to find her, and had considered that he escaped easily.

Just as in some moods she had been able only to remember his devotion, and intuitively to rely upon it, so now she was fully convinced of his cold criticism or indifference, and she tortured

herself with mental pictures of his probable amusement at her fatuous exhibition of weakness, until
her hastened breathing set the diamond star upon
her bosom to flashing with a thousand lights.

"I cannot dance. Why force myself any
longer?" she thought. Her partner at the moment was the infatuated Lambert, and she excused
herself from him on the plea of indisposition.

"I am really not well," she said. "I think I
shall have to return to the hotel. I came for Miss
Flower's sake to-night, and I know Mrs. Dayton
will be kind enough to mother her for me if I ask
her. I have left my wrap at the other end of the
room."

The young man seated her after some expressions of sympathy, and then darted away. Next
to the pleasure of dancing with Mrs. Redmond
was the delight of executing a commission for her.

Elise breathed a little more freely ; but a sudden
turn of her head showed her something which sent
the hot blood to her face. Receding, it left her
faint and white.

Terriss Chester was standing in the doorway
and looking eagerly about the room. He had not
yet perceived her. She overcame with a strong
will the panic that beset her, and, recovering
quickly, was ready by the time he found her to
bow to him as a queen might acknowledge the
least of her subjects.

He seemed to feel no lack in her salutation.
With a luminous look in his eyes, he advanced to

her. "At last," he said in a repressed voice, clasping the unresponsive hand she gave him. She was so little prepared for the concentrated radiance in his face that her self-control seemed slipping from her.

"When did you come?" was all she could say.

"Just now. I have no dress-suit; I am not fit to come in here; but how could I wait? You will come with me?"

"Where?" asked Elise coolly, though the diamond star was speaking for her with myriad rosy and celestial lights.

"Out, anywhere." He smiled with such absolute trust and happiness that she felt shaken and bewildered.

Mr. Lambert approached with the wrap. Mrs. Redmond named the two men to one another, then she addressed the younger. "Mr. Chester will take me to the hotel," she said. "It is impossible for me to speak with every one who wished me to dance. Perhaps you will make my excuses where you see it to be necessary."

She gave the young man a smile which went directly to his head and set him stammering an eager assent, then she rose and took Chester's arm, pausing before passing out of the door to ask Mrs. Dayton to speak to Phyllis when she had opportunity, and kindly to look after her.

"I think she needs looking after," was the stout lady's smiling response. "Mr. Bellows is monopolizing her."

" With very good reason," returned Mrs. Redmond, in a significant, low tone. " We are not quite ready to announce it, Mrs. Dayton. You understand," and Elise passed on, leaving her acquaintance in a flattered condition of smiling surprise.

" You received my line, of course?" asked Terriss as they passed out across the piazza and down upon the walk.

" No, I have received nothing."

" Why, how could that be? After I first went back to Snowdon and found you were gone and that I could not see Miss Rebecca, I had my first moment of collected thought. I concluded that I should be a grain more worthy to approach you if I showed sufficient self-respect to have ceased to be a vagrant before I presented myself. I have worked since that day as I never worked before. No stone has been left unturned; but the time seemed so long, I grew desperate, and sent to Miss Rebecca for your address. She gave it to me, and I wrote you a few words. Soon afterward I stumbled upon the track of something promising, and secured almost a certainty of a good position. There remained to be obtained the assent of one man. I inquired his address, and found he was at *Deep Lake.* Imagine what I felt. Well, before I entered the hall to-night I saw him, and it is all right. I am not a vagrant. Elise," he added, pausing after his hastily spoken sketch, and speaking her name yearningly. They had passed be-

yond the sound of the buzz of voices, and the
music, idealized, floated to them through the cool
moonlit night. They stood still in the shadow of
a far-reaching elm.

Mrs. Redmond looked up at the passionate appeal of his voice.

"You did not come, you did not write," she
said unsteadily. "I feared my letter was a mistake."

"Your letter a mistake? Oh, what do you
mean? It lies against my heart, and will while I
live. I had nothing to forgive you. You had
much to forgive me. Those words of yours
changed this work-a-day world into an Eden.
They held a magic fire, inspiring, transforming.
They gave me strength to stay away, when staying
away tested more power of endurance than I
thought I possessed. They gave me permission to
guess — to guess. O Elise," his voice dropped
lower, and its intensity thrilled her to the heart of
her being, "if I have guessed wrong, I have had a
season of happiness which must be the solace of
all my after-life."

In the deep silence that followed, he saw how
pale she had become in the moonlight. Her wrap,
half fallen away, disclosed the star, rising, falling,
sending forth its countless coruscations of passionate color. Her beauty filled him with a strength
of feeling that was painful.

"You are always fearless," he added, in the
same low tone. "If you never felt as I hoped,

say so. If you imagined for a time you did, but afterward found it was not so, do not hesitate, — tell me. You are my queen in any case, always, for all time. Tell me, am I living in a fool's paradise, or is it heaven ? "

She drifted nearer him in her misty gown, and looked into his face with a tender smile that set every pulse in his body beating as he took her yielding form in his arms.

He pressed her close, close to his heart, and their lips met.

" Now that you have come, it is heaven," she breathed.

CHAPTER XXXII.

THANKSGIVING.

THE snow lay softly brilliant over every rise and fall of ground at Beech Knoll, and weighed down the branches of the pines with a sparkling burden. The river flowed darkly between dazzling banks. It was Thanksgiving Day, and a dinner party was expected at the old home as a parting festivity; for next month Mrs. Redmond would be married, and go with her artist husband to a foreign city, where he could carry out some of the dreams of his boyhood. Elise had had several earnest talks with Chester before she finally succeeded in convincing him that his proud independence was in this case misplaced; but he at last agreed that there should be no more talk between them of thine and mine, and he came to believe, as Elise earnestly averred, that had her father lived, his well-known love for his adopted son would have triumphed over the temporary fit of anger in which he cast him off.

The dinner party to-day was to consist of Terriss Chester, Mr. Terriss, who, from the day he was able to be moved, had been a member of Roxana's family, Phyllis, and Tony, beside the two hostesses.

Mr. Bellows senior would also have been of the number, had not business interests compelled him to eat his Thanksgiving dinner in Chicago. Mrs. Redmond had, as Phyllis phrased it, attended to him. Through the month of October she had taken apartments at the Vendome, and Phyllis had been her guest. Thanks to her tact, and the genuine charm of the young girl whose cause she espoused, she succeeded in her undertaking more quickly than she had dared to hope · and when Phyllis was retired from that brief dream of dinner and theatre parties, and cozy social evenings, she felt no surer of Tony than she did of his dignified sire.

Roxana had rarely in her life missed a Thanksgiving service in the church, but to-day she was obliged to omit it, being much hurried to get her work done at home in time to be on hand at Beech Knoll for the numerous duties she had set her heart upon performing there. Mrs. Redmond's servants liked Roxana. There was never any danger of her making trouble among them, and of course Mrs. Redmond had wished to include her in the invitation.

Mrs. Sherritt had scarcely yet grown accustomed to the astonishing news that was brought home from Deep Lake. She was wont to shake her head over her work, and sigh, and hope it would all be for the best; but when Tony had been at the house a few times, she smiled in secret more often than she sighed. She adjusted herself quite easily and with great satisfaction to the other match, and was fond of recounting to Mr. Terriss his cousin's excited behavior on the day he first saw Mrs. Redmond on the street.

"If ever I saw a man knocked all of a heap," she repeated, again and again, "Mr. Chester was that man."

The minister extracted a large amount of quiet amusement from Roxana in these days. He could see the stirring effect upon her of this new atmosphere of love-making. Mrs. Sherritt resurrected a song from the depths of her memory, which seemed to comprise her sentiments upon the subject of matrimony; and her singing being of the stentorian order, Mr. Terriss was often entertained by it as he sat, reading his paper, while Roxana, in the next room, laid down the law to slow music. Thus she sang, with much emphasis : —

> "She was not took out of his head, Sir,
>   To reign like a tyrant o'er *man*,
>   She was not took out of his feet, Sir,
>   By man to be trampled up*on*.

> "But she was took out of his side, Sir,
>   Man's faithful companion to *be*,
>   And now that they both are united,
>   The man 's at the top o' the tree."

Roxana usually gave the last line rather faintly. Mr. Terriss could but feel that just there the song did not truthfully express her opinion.

She was flying about the dining-room at Beech Knoll, lending an efficient helping hand, when sleighbells announced the arrival of the party from church. There was a great snapping fire of logs in the parlor to welcome them, and Tony's roses had made all the air sweet. As the sextette came in, glowing from the cold, even Rebecca's cheeks had a pink tinge. One could see now that the minister's illness had turned his hair very gray, but otherwise he looked natural, and his kind eyes were full of serene content to-day. They all drew near the cheery fire, and Tony took Phyllis's hands to warm them. Chester's face and form seemed all to have expanded in the last three months. He looked a fit mate for Elise as she stood there, radiant in her enveloping furs. Rebecca thought so as she regarded them, and when they had all doffed their outside wraps and were waiting the summons to dinner, she found him near her, and met the cordial look his eyes always held when they rested on her.

"The prince did finally come who won the lady," she said quietly, smiling at the memory of that long-ago talk.

"How wonderful it is!" he returned, simply and earnestly. "I am not yet accustomed to it. I sometimes wonder if I shall ever be."

Mr. Terriss, standing beside Rebecca, was included in the closing words.

"You will become used to it," he said, "because happiness is intended to be our normal state. We adjust ourselves to it with comparative quickness for that reason. Human beings are a good deal like suspended harmonies, craving to find the home key. Some are resolved into concord in this life, some later. I am very glad for you, Terriss."

The men shook hands, and Terriss, with the two serene, kind faces before him, suddenly had a novel thought, born of affection for them both.

It seemed to him a significant coincidence that Elise should advance at that moment, having received her maid's announcement that dinner was served.

"Mr. Terriss, will you take Rebecca?" she said.

"I will," responded the minister.

www.ingramcontent.com/pod-product-compliance
Lightning Source LLC
Chambersburg PA
CBHW021343110726
47900CB00005B/1589